Original Sins

Also by Erin Young

The Fields

Original Sins

ERIN YOUNG

FLATIRON
BOOKS
NEW YORK

ORIGINAL SINS. Copyright © 2024 by Erin Young. All rights reserved. Printed in the United States of America. For information, address Flatiron Books, 120 Broadway, New York, NY 10271.

www.flatironbooks.com

Designed by Gabriel Guma

The Library of Congress Cataloging-in-Publication Data

Names: Young, Erin, 1975– author.
Title: Original sins / Erin Young.
Description: First edition. | New York : Flatiron Books, 2024. | Series: Riley Fisher ; vol. 2
Identifiers: LCCN 2023025610 | ISBN 9781250799425 (hardcover) |
    ISBN 9781250799449 (ebook)
Subjects: LCSH: Women detectives—Fiction. | Serial murderers—Fiction. |
    Serial murder investigation—Fiction. | LCGFT: Detective and mystery fiction. |
    Thrillers (Fiction) | Novels.
Classification: LCC PS3625.O97 O75 2024 | DDC 813/.6—dc23/eng/20230605
LC record available at https://lccn.loc.gov/2023025610

Our books may be purchased in bulk for promotional, educational, or business use. Please contact your local bookseller or the Macmillan Corporate and Premium Sales Department at 1-800-221-7945, extension 5442, or by email at MacmillanSpecialMarkets@macmillan.com.

First Edition: 2024

10 9 8 7 6 5 4 3 2 1

To Rupert, thank you for everything.
We'll always have two cherry-berry colas and a cheeky chops.

1

The city was sullen in the last of the light. The clouds—rolling in on a raw wind that whipped the waters of the Des Moines River into peaks—had swallowed the gold dome of the capitol and were engulfing the tops of the skyscrapers downtown. Here and there lights still glowed, winking through the murk.

Hayley Abbot wrapped her arms around herself as she waited by her car, frowning at the sky. The weather forecaster had said it wouldn't snow today, but she could feel the threat of it in the air that sliced through her thermals and tore tears from her eyes.

A black pickup streaked with dirt pulled into the lot. The vehicle jolted through puddles, ice splintering beneath snow chains. A man climbed out. He looked over at her standing there alone, shivering in her windbreaker.

Hayley pulled her cell phone from her pocket. No messages. She'd tugged off a glove with her teeth and was scrolling through her contacts, fingers clumsy with cold, when she heard a shout behind her. Something slammed into her back, knocking the phone from her hand. She stumbled against the door of her car as something thrust intrusively between her legs.

"Banjo! Goddamn!"

Hayley straightened to find an Irish setter bounding around her. She pushed the dog's eager nose away.

The man from the pickup came over, hood held up against the wind. "Banjo, *get here!*"

Hayley bent to pick up her fallen glove, reeling from the dog's tongue as it curled toward her face. Meaty breath moistened her cheek. She snatched her phone from a puddle. The dog jumped up as she stood, planting muddy paws on her leggings.

The man grabbed the animal's collar. "Sorry, sweetheart," he said, glancing sideways at her.

He should be on a leash, she wanted to say. "No problem," she said instead.

As the man hauled Banjo toward the dog park, Hayley brushed the mud from her thighs. Her phone rang and she exhaled as she saw the name. "Tara! Where are you?"

"Hayley, don't hate me. My sitter's gone and canceled on me again."

"What? You're not coming?"

"I can't!" A child was screaming in the background. "Look, I'll speak to you tomorrow, OK? I'm sorry!"

The call cut off.

Hayley swore at the screen. Turning, she scanned the riverside path that curved out of sight beneath an overpass. A man was sprinting along it alone. He was overtaken by a couple of cyclists racing past in RAGBRAI jerseys. There were a few people in the dog park, swaddled in winter coats. Banjo was streaking circles around a lumbering pit bull. In the distance, cars streamed along the Grand Avenue and Locust Street bridges, headlights tracing through the gloom.

Scenes from the recent press conferences flashed in her mind. The cops grim-faced on the evening news.

Be vigilant.

But she'd left work early, driven all the way across town. It wasn't late—the darkness just storm.

Stuffing her phone into her pocket with a curse for Tara's useless babysitter, Hayley left the parking lot and set off at a jog along the path, skirting icy puddles that looked like cracked glass. Her muscles were stiff, but she quickened her pace as she entered the dank shadows beneath the interstate bridge, filled with the muffled thunder of trucks.

The squat concrete piers of the overpass were swirled with manic loops of graffiti—MAGA shouted scarlet among faded scrawls. There was a poster from the recent presidential campaign, peeling in the damp. On it, the president-elect's mouth had been sprayed with a wide black slash. A mask or a muzzle.

Emerging into the dim daylight, Hayley headed for the pale arch of the Iowa Women of Achievement Bridge. Built in honor of female civil rights leaders, scientists, and war veterans, it pinched the east and west sides of Des Moines together like a delicate brooch. The wind picked up, unsettling the river.

She ran faster, past the Wells Fargo Arena, fronted with a billboard for the Iowa Wolves. HOWL ALL SEASON LONG! The air filled with a freezing mist of drizzle. She tugged her pink beanie over her ears, nodding to the few joggers and walkers she passed who'd braved the wild evening. Her annoyance at being stood up by Tara dropped away, along with other worries and frustrations of the day: her mom's frantic call about her dad, who might need his operation sooner than expected, her boss's demand she work this weekend. Yards became miles.

Down by Principal Park, where the Des Moines and Raccoon Rivers converged, the trail continued, snaking toward a wooded area. A group of young men were loitering on a patch of snow-mottled wasteland. A couple of them straddled bikes. The rest hunched together, hoods up, cigarettes smoldering between clenched fingers. Heads turned to Hayley as she approached. An inaudible comment from one was followed by laughter from the others.

She slowed, sweat stinging her eyes. The trail beyond the youths ran on, empty, to a dark line of trees hissing in the wind. She and Tara would normally continue for another few miles. But it really was getting dark now and she was tired. At least, that's what she told herself as she turned and ran back the way she'd come. She heard more laughter behind her, felt the familiar prickle in her spine.

She had started running a year ago, after all the shit that went down with Bret Childs. It had helped with the stress, pounding out her anger beneath her feet, each mile a challenge she could overcome. But, in time, she discovered her new hobby came with its own issues. Sometimes, men would whistle from their cars or shout obscene things. Tara usually flipped them off, but Hayley had been wary ever since a man once followed her in his pickup on a lonely stretch of road, never speaking, just the low shudder of his engine over her running footsteps.

Once back alongside the main roads, puddled by streetlights, she shrugged off her unease and focused on the return stretch, pushing her legs into a sprint, lungs burning. The rain turned to sleet. The thought of a hot shower and a guilt-free glass of wine glowed in her mind. Under the bridges, back past the arena, its bank of windows reflecting the glowering sky. She could see the lights of the parking lot, her car a distant smudge of blue in the frozen rain. The overpass was coming up, a slab of shadow widening to receive her.

It came from the left—sharp and sudden—a flash of movement in the darkness of the pass. Something slammed into her stomach. Hayley doubled over and dropped to her knees, all the wind knocked out of her. She fell forward on her hands, ice and grit spiking through her gloves. She tried to drag in a breath, but pain had squeezed her lungs into an airless knot. Frantic thoughts scatter-gunned. Her nostrils flared, filling with a briny whiff of urine and river mud. Something loomed over her. *Someone.*

"*Please!*" The word wheezed out of her.

She caught a glitter of eyes in the shadows of a hood. There was darkness where a face should be. No, not darkness—a mask—some sort of symbol on it, red and sinuous, distorted by the curves of nose and jaw. There was something long and slender brandished in the figure's fists. She was struck by an image of her father on a baseball field in soft summer light, calling her to pitch the ball.

As the bat swung toward her, Hayley's cry was lost in the heedless roar of traffic on the interstate above.

2

The northeastern suburbs scrolled slowly across the cab's grime-smeared window. Riley Fisher watched the streets thread past, eyes fixing on scenes that lingered in the stop-start of morning traffic. Children dashing across an intersection, book bags bouncing on their backs. The dark opening of a body shop, spit of sparks within. The bare scar of a railroad yard crowded with rusting tank cars, power lines drooping overhead. Everywhere, sidewalks were banked with dirty heaps of snow, the last fall four days ago, and more to come.

On the cab's radio, a Christian rock ballad faded into a commercial for a free prayer app. "Hold salvation in the palm of your hand!"

The driver reached out and twisted the dial. The cab filled with the strident voice of a morning news anchor. "Coming up, after the weather, we bring you more on that breaking story of the young woman believed to be the latest victim. Hayley Abbot remains in critical condition at MercyOne. Her parents, keeping vigil at her bedside, have demanded answers from the police. The same question is surely on all our minds—how many more must fall prey to this monster before he is caught? Now, Chuck, with the forecast . . ."

Another twist and the voice was replaced by Johnny Cash's deep-down drawl.

In the window, the timber-fronted houses and railroad crossings of the suburbs jumbled into fast-food joints and motels. Beyond, in gaps between the buildings, Riley caught glimpses of the capitol, its dome a dull yellow in the winter light. The imposing structure—political and judicial heart of Iowa for nearly one hundred and fifty years—glowered over modern-day Des Moines, from the taprooms and boutiques of the East Village to the glass and steel high-rises of downtown.

It was twenty-six years since Riley had left this city and moved with her family to Cedar Falls. At the sight of the towering blocks of the Financial Center and the Plaza Building, memories stirred and whispered. Dinner with her parents at some fancy top-floor restaurant, her father entertaining clients; she and her brother, Ethan, pressing their noses to the glass over the plunging view. Walking hand in hand with her mom through the hazy humidity of the botanical gardens. A school trip to the State Historical Museum, tracing the changing city from the Sac and Fox Nation to the first European settlers and its beginnings as a railroad hub and powerhouse of coal mining. Through the expansion years when skyscrapers rose from the riverbanks and Des Moines shook itself from the smoke and dust of industry, transformed into a center for giants of finance and insurance.

Those memories belonged to another her. Another life. Before Hunter and that night at the state fair that shattered her childhood. Before those lost months in California, salt breeze and surging ocean. Before the car wreck that killed her parents, and Ethan's downward spiral. Long before Iowa's disgraced former governor, Bill Hamilton, her father's old boss, was caught at the heart of a national scandal. A scandal that almost cost Riley her career and, very nearly, her life.

As the cab swung into a line of traffic, she had a last clear view of the capitol. The puckered scar in her shoulder twinged as she turned to look. The surgeon who'd removed the bullet had proclaimed she was fully healed, but even now, two years later, it ached whenever she was tense.

"That's where it happened." The driver's voice came muffled through his mask.

"I'm sorry?"

"The attack. That young woman." He nodded toward the window. They were on the interstate, crossing the river. "Down there. My wife has a friend at MercyOne. A nurse. Said she'd never seen injuries like it. Girl was beat to a pulp."

Riley glimpsed figures in the shadows of an underpass. The familiar yellow line of crime scene tape that always opened a pit in her stomach. A satellite van emblazoned with the logo of a local news station. A single latex glove snagged in a patch of weeds, limp blue fingers waving up.

"The cops should set a curfew," said the driver, putting his foot on the gas. "No good just telling women to be vigilant when some crazy son of a bitch is on the loose. Out alone, down there? She was asking for trouble." He glanced at Riley in the mirror, waiting for her to agree. When she returned her gaze to the window, he sniffed and turned up the radio.

Fifteen minutes later, they were in West Des Moines—Des Moines's well-heeled neighbor. An out-of-date magazine Riley had found in her apartment informed her it had been voted one of the top one hundred hippest places to live in America. There were golf courses, a country club, and smart corporate hotels; a weekly farmers market, and a state park that cast a dark green web along the banks of the Raccoon River. It felt a long way from Black Hawk County—from cornfields and small-town manners, back roads and endless skies.

Following the GPS, the driver entered a labyrinthine business park, where the broad, tree-lined streets all looked the same. Offices of Realtors and insurers rose from snow-stippled lawns. It was early, but many of the parking lots were already full. Every look-alike corner had some sort of eatery. A Red Lobster and a Panda Express, an Irish tavern called Molly Malone's, an Italian deli called Gio's. You could feast your way around the world without ever leaving Iowa.

"This is it," said the driver, pulling into the entrance of one precinct, bordered by two fountains. "So, what is it you do here?" He peered up at the faceless brown building, with its tinted wraparound windows that showed only reflections of the outside world—ashen sky, bare trees, lifeless flag.

Riley said the first thing that came to mind. "I'm not sure."

It was also the truest thing.

After the cab's stuffy interior, the air was a shock. The mercury had plunged below freezing a week ago and showed no sign of slowing its descent. Meteorologists reckoned this winter could break records of previous years when it hit forty below, turning water in toilets to ice, freezing people's clothes and hair, and killing thirteen across the Midwest.

The cab pulled away, leaving Riley alone. She straightened the jacket of her new gray suit, which felt stiff and formal—a far cry from her old uniform of polo shirts and cargo pants. As she made her way toward the entrance, her black leather ankle boots crunched in rock salt. Maddie had helped her pick them out in T.J. Maxx a week ago, in the whirlwind of her departure. Afterward, Riley had taken her niece to Wendy's. Their last meal together.

Maddie had been unusually talkative, gabbling through mouthfuls of fries about coming to stay with her over Thanksgiving; how they could go ice-skating and to the Christmas markets. Riley had nodded silently through the conversation. Maddie had been so upset on learning of her move to Des Moines that, in a fit of guilt, Riley had painted a glittering picture of all the fun they could have in the city, without—until that moment—any thought of the practicalities.

New boots, new suit. New job. New life.

The only old thing about her was the long, black wool coat that had belonged to her mother. She'd come across it in a closet while packing. The inside pocket contained a one-cent coin, dated the year her mom died. Riley had left it in there.

She paused before the front doors, greeted by her reflection. Her mind swarmed with the events that had brought her here—from the phone call two years ago, standing in her backyard, Logan at her side, looking quizzical as she turned away, Elijah Klein's voice on the line. All those months of doubt and indecision, Klein's letter of recommendation sitting on her desk, greeting her each morning with the same question.

At last, the decision. Followed by the punishing interviews, the forms and tests. The confines of the lie-detector room: blood pressure cuff squeezing her arm, metal plates clamped on her fingers. The conversation she'd had to have with her family—Ethan stony and silent, Maddie in tears, Aunt Rose putting on a brave face.

Then, just when she thought she was ready, she'd faced some of the toughest months of her life, where all the questions that had dogged her from the start had been ground down—through relentless weeks of training and study, each day a wheel of exertion and exhaustion—to a single one.

What the hell are you doing here?

As she reached for the door and her reflection reached for her, Riley felt a lurch inside like vertigo.

Hot air billowed as she entered. There were plants and chairs along one wall, an elevator, and a set of stairs marching up. Most of the space was taken up by a long desk. Two receptionists wearing headsets sat behind plastic screens. A security guard observed Riley as she walked to the desk, gun on display at his hip. A phone shrilled.

Behind her, the door opened again, the frigid draft teasing her hair. A young man in old-fashioned thick-rimmed glasses and an olive green trench coat struggled through, Starbucks cup in one hand, a laptop and a black file squeezed under his arm. Before she could help, he stumbled in, cursing as he slopped coffee on the floor. He wiped ineffectively at the spill with a polished brogue.

"How can I assist you?"

Riley turned back at the receptionist's question. "I'm here to see Connie Meadows."

"Riley Fisher?" The voice came from behind. The young man in glasses approached. He went to offer his hand, then laughed apologetically as he held out his coffee cup. "Noah Case." He spoke over Riley's shoulder to the receptionist. "I can take her down." He nodded Riley toward the elevator. "Some weather we're having, Henry?"

"Colder than a well digger's feet," agreed the security guard.

Noah Case called the elevator, outside which were signs with the names and logos of the various businesses that occupied the building. Riley didn't see the one she was looking for. She noticed the file the man was clutching was in fact a slim bag with a lock on the zipper. Up close, he was younger than she'd first thought and the glasses she'd taken for old-fashioned were Tom Ford. A paisley-print silk scarf was ruched at his neck. He looked nothing like most of the men she'd worked with over the years—all buzz cuts, mirrored shades, and gun-toting attitude. Even in her new suit, Riley felt dowdy and awkward in comparison, like she was playing dress-up for a role she hadn't fully understood.

"After you," said Noah, gesturing with his cup as the doors opened. Once they were in, he pressed a button with his knuckle and the elevator slid smoothly down. "Oh, and you can take that off here. Meadows hates them. Says they're a license for criminals and a hindrance for law enforcement. How can you read a face if you can't see it?"

Riley hesitated, then peeled off her mask and stuffed it in the pocket of her mother's coat.

"What a year, huh?" Noah breathed, shaking his head.

The question was too big to answer and there was no time as the elevator doors opened.

Noah smiled brightly. "Welcome to the dungeon."

Riley stepped out into a short corridor with a door at the end. On the door was a seal—a blue circle adorned with thirteen gold stars. Scales for justice, laurel leaves for honor, red and white stripes for courage and valor, and a scroll with the motto FIDELITY, BRAVERY, INTEGRITY. As she got closer, the words that circumscribed the seal became clearer.

DEPARTMENT OF JUSTICE
FEDERAL BUREAU OF INVESTIGATION

3

The two men and the woman passed through the police barricade, ignoring the camera crew and calls from reporters. Dog walkers peered down from the grassy bank above the closed-off path. A couple had cell phones out. Traffic juddered across the interstate bridge, drivers slowing to rubberneck as they caught sight of the array of police vehicles on the riverside. Squad cars, unmarked SUVs, and the DCI Crime Scene Unit van.

Fogg pulled on a pair of gloves as he approached the underpass with his two colleagues, who were dressed in full protective suits. Fogg's eyes fixed on the figure trudging through the mud to meet them. The gold badge on Mike Whitfield's black cap marked his rank in Des Moines PD. He'd moved up a rung on the ladder since Fogg had been at the department. The sky was the color of milk and the sergeant's face was wan in the curdled light. His jawline was a shade darker with nightshift shadow.

"Morning, Fogg."

"Morning, Mike."

They nodded to one another in that new, awkward way, handshakes now problematic.

Whitfield lifted the caution tape. He tilted his head toward the reporters. "Been on the news all goddamn morning. They're claiming it's another before we've even worked the scene."

Fogg ducked under the yellow line with a grunt of effort. His younger colleagues followed, agile despite the bulky equipment cases they carried. "Is the officer here?"

"Yup." Whitfield motioned to the underpass, where two cops guarded a barrier.

There was no white tent at least. No body. Not yet. Fogg knew the young woman's injuries from the doctor he'd spoken to in the dawn hours at MercyOne—that it was still touch and go.

He's escalating.

"Your girls back for Thanksgiving?" Whitfield asked.

"Sherri's here. Keira's back from grad school next week."

"She's doing law, isn't she?" Whitfield smiled when Fogg nodded. "My boys are back tomorrow. My wife's been cooking up a storm." He led them beneath the bridge. Scraps of trash left by the paramedics drifted in the weeds. "Sure gonna be good to have them home."

"Sure is," echoed Fogg, scanning the squalid shadows. Graffiti and broken glass. Footprints in the dirt. Muddy scuff of wheels from a gurney. Heavy boom of traffic overhead, shuddering through the concrete.

Whitfield called to the cops at the barrier. One of them came over. His eyes went from Fogg to the two crime scene technicians, who'd set down their equipment cases. The woman crouched and pulled out a camera. There were dark spatters on the path ahead. As she took a test photograph, the flash lit them up in shocks of red.

"Officer Emery here was first on scene," Whitfield told Fogg.

Fogg nodded to the young man, who looked like he'd walked right out of training. "I'm Detective Julius Verne, from the Division of Criminal Investigation. My colleagues here are from the crime lab. While they work, perhaps you could walk me through what happened?"

Whitfield's radio crackled, a voice breaking through the static. He nodded to Fogg as he answered, moving back out into the cold morning light.

Fogg gestured Emery down to the waterside, away from the intrusive flash of the camera. The shallow bank was treacherous with ice, and his knees protested at the shift in weight. Everything seemed a little bit harder these days—putting on shoes, emptying the trash, climbing out of his car. His body, which had always been taut on his tall frame, was slowing and softening. Marcia had taken to playfully tweaking the doughy fold around his waist. It was done with a teasing grin and love in her eyes, but somewhere in Fogg's mind it had set a clock ticking. The mirror each morning, razor blade scraping away more white than black. Words like *retirement, pension, downsizing* nudging their way into thoughts and conversations.

"What time did you get the call?"

Emery pulled a notebook from his pocket and flipped it open. Fogg caught a glimpse of neatly joined-up writing. Conscientious. Eager. *Rookie.*

"I was on patrol downtown. Arrived just after the paramedics." Emery glanced at his pad. "Five fifteen. The um . . . the victim was being tended to."

"Was she conscious?"

"Barely." The young man's eyes drifted to the spot where blood stained the path. "She was . . ." He trailed off, shaking his head.

Fogg recalled the doctor's description of Hayley Abbot's injuries. Multisystem trauma. Broken nose, indirect orbital floor fracture, internal bruising, craniocerebral injury. "I was told a dog walker found her?"

"Yeah. Well, his dog."

"What's his name?"

"Banjo."

Fogg smiled slightly. "The owner?"

"Oh. Right." Emery flicked through his pad, blushing. "Bob Slater. Said he'd seen her about an hour earlier, in the parking lot." The officer pointed beyond the police barrier, back the way Fogg had come. "Her car's still there."

"Did Mr. Slater see anyone else in the area?"

Emery reeled off a list—dog owners Slater knew by name, others he knew by sight. Random joggers and cyclists. "It's a well-used area."

Fogg nodded. That meant he might actually have some witnesses to this one. It would also mean a lot of interviews and legwork. He thought of Marcia's excitement about Thanksgiving. First time in a while they'd had both their daughters back. Thought of the conversation he would have to have.

His wife had always understood there were three of them in the relationship. That the job was an insatiable mistress. But something about this past year—the world turned upside down—had made her less amenable to the long hours and unexpected late shifts. Maybe it wasn't even the pandemic. Maybe it was just this investigation.

Fogg knew she could see how it was eating him, however much he tried to hide it from her. He'd seen other detectives, over the years, pushed into a hole of horror by some monster that lurked out of reach. Part of them still trapped down there, even after they retired. Haunted by the victims they hadn't been able to save, shattered lives in their rearview like wrecks on a highway. He'd been determined he wouldn't be like them. Assured himself he was good at his job, good at compartmentalizing. But these past months—his boss's breath hot on his neck and the feverish media coverage—this investigation had been compelling him, inch by inch, toward that dark edge.

"Was the victim able to tell you anything?"

"She indicated her attacker took something from her. She kept touching her head, so I think it might have been a hat. Weird thing is, she still had her cell phone on her. Worth at least a few hundred dollars. But the psycho takes a hat?"

Trophy.

"You think it's the same guy?" asked Emery, in Fogg's silence. "The one who attacked those other women?"

"It's too early to say."

Emery was back to looking at his notebook. "Oh, yeah, one of the paramedics told me she was saying something when they first arrived. He wasn't sure, but he thought it sounded like—*my sorrows?*"

Fogg felt the chill go right through him. "Thy sorrows," he murmured.

"Hey, Fogg!"

They both looked around as the female technician called out. She was standing a little way up the bank, where mud rose in a wave of black to meet the bridge. Her camera was slack in her hands. She was staring at one of the piers. Fogg made his way to her, Emery following.

Behind the pier, where the concrete was scrawled with old graffiti, a symbol had been sprayed in red. It was fresh, still tacky, paint bleeding down the wall. It looked like the letter *S*. But Fogg had seen it enough times—in old photographs—to know it was meant to be a serpent.

His mind flooded with images. A bloody nightdress. A knife-nick in bone. A red fray of rope. Women lying in hospital beds and on mortuary slabs. And, always, that sinuous, blood-bright swerve on the walls of deserted parking lots and back alleys. A driveway. A bedroom.

A lot of cops in this city had retired since those days, a youthful parade marching in to take their places, but Fogg remembered. Back then, he'd been fresh out of the Iowa Law Enforcement Academy, years before he'd risen through the ranks of Des Moines PD to run homicide, before he met Marcia, then joined the DCI, felt the age in his bones. Over the past months of this investigation, those echoes had begun calling down the years, faint but familiar, each new scene of a woman's torment itching fingers up his spine.

He'd not been certain—not enough to push his chief to reveal his growing suspicions to the media or the public. But, now, as he stared at that serpentine sweep of red, there could be no denying it.

He had returned.

4

Riley sat in front of the desk, the chair creaking intrusively. Connie Meadow's windowless office was oppressively hot. The dry air smelled of furniture polish and burned coffee. Riley draped her coat over the chair's arm and placed her purse on the floor, where it sagged at her feet.

Her new boss was a slim, erect woman in her early fifties, dressed in black slacks and a crisp white shirt rolled to the elbows. Her short-cropped hair was threaded with gray. The skin was starting to crease at the corners of her eyes—a bracing winter blue.

Meadows laced her hands on her desk, which gleamed under the glare of the overhead lights. Its surface was as neat and uncluttered as the rest of the room. Just a laptop, a white mug with the FBI seal on it, and a single closed file. "So, what brings you to us?"

Riley faltered at the question. She felt for a moment like a schoolkid who'd wandered into the principal's office by mistake. Her eyes went to the closed file, which she suspected might be hers. If it was, it would contain her FD-302: the form that began every FBI investigation—including the one begun on her, when she sent in her application.

Meadows would know she'd gone to elementary here in Des Moines. Would know about her father, Michael Fisher, the eminent lawyer; and her mother, Jenny, the legal secretary, who'd given up that job to become a mom, then caregiver for Michael's ailing mother in Cedar Falls. She would know Riley had missed her last year of school there and the reason why.

Riley had spent most of her adult life hiding that part of her past—her rape by her brother's best friend, Hunter, that night at the state fair. A night that detonated a toxic bomb of shame and guilt and rage in the heart of her family. Her running away from home, hitchhiking west to California. The girl she'd become on that wild shore. Lost, until her grandfather found her, all those miles and months later. But she'd been unable to hide from any of it in the bureau's interview room. The lie detector measuring every skipped heartbeat, every bead of sweat.

Meadows would know she returned to Cedar Falls to finish high school before majoring in criminology at the University of Northern Iowa. Accepted into the Iowa Law Enforcement Academy. Straightened out and buttoned up. She would know about the deaths of Riley's parents just after she was sworn in. Her grandfather's slide from the world—the dementia that carried him to the old folks' home, then slowly ate his mind. Her brother's broken marriage and arrest for possession, which had left his troubled daughter, more often than not, in Riley's care.

Meadows had access to the testimonies of her friends and colleagues, her financial records, her test scores at Quantico, and her instructors' reports. The woman would know her, in some ways, more intimately than her own family did. *So what brings you to us?* That question was a trick. What Meadows wanted to know, she guessed, was why she'd chosen this obscure resident agency, buried in a basement, to be her first choice of posting. Not a vast field office in some dazzling city, darkened by the seething morass of human crime. White-collar and cyber. Terrorism and homicide. A chance to shine.

Riley thought of her fellow recruits at Quantico in those final weeks—the oldest still several years younger than her—listing their top choices. New York. Chicago. Miami. "I wanted to be close to my family, ma'am."

Half truth, half lie.

"In Black Hawk County?"

"That's right."

Meadows's expression was inscrutable, but her eyes flicked to the closed file, adding weight to Riley's suspicion. "You were twelve years at the sheriff's office?"

"Thirteen, ma'am. I worked Patrol for most of those, but I was head of Investigations for two."

"What got you into law enforcement?"

"My grandfather used to be the sheriff there. He encouraged me." *Saved me.*

Recent memories flickered: bright, painful sparks. Her roommate at Quantico calling her in from the training ground. Sweat cooling on her cheeks, smell of gunpowder on her fingers as she pressed the receiver to her ear. Aunt Rose's voice soft on the line. *He's gone, Riley. Joe's gone.*

The virus had swept like fire through the old folks' home. Joe Fisher hadn't stood a chance. One of millions. A drop in an ocean of tears. Her leave approved: the long drive home to a subdued funeral under weeping fall skies, the cornfields cut down to bristles. The truth—that her grandfather had been gone in all the ways that mattered for years already—didn't lessen the sorrow. When Riley graduated from the academy, weeks later, and she'd opened that envelope to see her first choice of posting listed, she'd returned to his graveside to tell him.

"What do you know about our resident agency?"

Riley reeled off the facts. That it was a small outfit, one of eight satellite offices spread across Iowa and Nebraska, all reporting to the FBI field office in Omaha. That the Des Moines agency covered thirty-five of Iowa's ninety-nine counties, from Winnebago and Hancock in the north to Appanoose and Decatur in the south. And that Meadows was resident agent in charge, reporting to the special agent in charge—the SAC—in the field office.

When she first learned about the organizational structure of the FBI, Riley had imagined all the field offices and resident agencies spread out across North America, and beyond, like the cogs and gears of some giant clock, moving beneath the face of the bureau in Washington, turning over information and chiming out threats.

She'd realized in her lessons since that, just like regular law enforcement, it wasn't as precise as all that. Sometimes, those chimes came too late. Sometimes, they never came at all. Chatter unnoticed. Signals missed. Thunder out of a blue sky.

Meadows nodded at her summary. "There are six of us here, including you. Myself, Agents Peter Altman, Stan Parks, Noah Case, and Audrey, our secretary. Covering such a wide area, you need to rely on developing good relations with state and local police. I require my agents to be proactive and efficient. To think for themselves. You'll likely be on your own a great deal. This won't be like the sheriff's office. I'm not a helicopter boss, hovering over your every move and decision. But I do expect results." She paused, her blue eyes implacable. "Cops and deputies usually come to the bureau from a big, messy family of partners and teams. Those of us at resident agencies are more like only children, capable and comfortable in our own company. It's why I normally only accept experienced agents."

Riley had known this when she made her choices from the list of departments with openings. Rookie agents learned best in a large field office with more guidance on hand. Dettman, one of her instructors at Quantico, had snorted derisively when he'd read over her shoulder and seen Des Moines at the top. *You're pissing in the wind with that one, Fisher.*

She hesitated, then asked Meadows the question she'd been wondering for weeks. "Can I ask why you accepted me, ma'am?"

Meadows's lip twitched, a tic of a smile. "It seems you have friends in high places here."

Riley thought she meant Elijah Klein—the special agent from the Behavioral Analysis Unit, who'd recommended her to the bureau. The man she'd worked with in Black Hawk County when she helped expose the truth behind a series of bizarre and brutal murders: a trail of blood and secrets that led her through cornfields and abandoned farms to a horrifying conspiracy. But no. Meadows had put the emphasis on *here*. There was only one person she could mean.

Jess Cook—the newly elected governor, who had risen to power on the scandalous fall of her predecessor, Bill Hamilton.

Riley shifted in her seat. How much influence did Meadows think she had with Cook? True, it was her investigation that had helped secure the woman's win for office, but she'd had no communication with the governor since the election two years ago.

She had the uneasy sense that she'd stepped out onto some precarious pedestal. She'd fought hard for this position in the bureau—had upended her whole life for it. She wanted her own grit and determination to have won her this role. Not some flimsy political connection over which she had no control.

The room's blank white walls pressed in, the lengthening silence racked and loaded.

At last, Meadows sat back and opened a drawer beside her. "To start with, you'll be taking over the case files of Agent Roach. He served notice two months ago."

Riley caught a bite in her voice. Disappointment? No—more like contempt.

"Audrey has your laptop and gun." Meadows pulled a black billfold wallet from the drawer and placed it on the desk. It was open to show an ID card with Riley's name and photograph on one side. On the other side was a gold badge crowned by a bald eagle and embossed with Justice holding up torch and scales, her eyes bound and blind. Meadows kept one finger on it when Riley reached for it. "The role has a two-year probationary period, Agent Fisher."

They'd been told the statistics as soon as they arrived at Quantico. Only six hundred per year make it to the academy, out of twelve thousand applicants who even qualify. Of those six hundred, up to twenty percent won't make it through training.

At each step, from the interviews where her life had been laid out before her like so much shabby junk at a yard sale, to those first days in Virginia where she'd dragged herself through the mud and rain, fighting to keep up with her younger classmates, Riley had felt like she shouldn't be here.

It was true what she'd told Meadows: that she'd chosen the agency because she wanted to be close to her family, Maddie doing better in school, but still struggling at home, Ethan just out of probation, stumbling through one dead-end job after another. What she hadn't said was that she wanted them to be close to *her*. Two hours to home—to her old house and her old job. Two hours to the graves of her parents and grandfather. To all the parts of her, packed down and rooted in that black soil.

The only time in her life, other than the academy, that she'd left the state—spread her wings west—she'd flown straight into trouble. She had picked Des Moines to be her safety net. But now that net seemed weak, insubstantial.

What if she couldn't hack it? Could she really go home? Back to her crumbling house and her brother's troubles? And her place in the sheriff's office? Her old partner, Logan Wood, was head of Investigations now. There was no job for her there.

She had no choice but to make it here.

Riley took the badge, the gold hard and cool beneath her fingers. What had felt like vertigo now felt like falling.

5

A bove the capitol, the sky was a bright and bitter blue. The
morning sun turned the sandstone walls to honey and dazzled on
the dome. Crows made harsh conversation in the branches of trees.

Governor Jess Cook made her way up the capitol's steps, passing the
statue that depicted a pioneer and his son being guided to their new
home by a Native American, whose bronze feather caught the sun's
shimmer in its barbs. As a senator she'd walked past this statue for years
without thought, hurrying to meetings and senate sessions, but several
conversations she'd had with protestors over the last few months had
altered her view of it. Was the Native seated at the feet of the white
men really a willing guide, or had he been persuaded by the ax in the
pioneer's hand and the rifle in the boy's?

"Someone's eager."

Jess glanced at Rebecca Page, walking in step beside her, briefcase in
one hand, coffee in the other. She followed her chief of staff's gaze to see
a reporter she recognized from the *Des Moines Register* hovering near
the entrance, stamping his feet in an effort to stay warm.

Jess fixed a composed smile on her face as the reporter spotted them.
He had his phone out ready to record before they'd even reached him.

"Governor Cook, can I get your thoughts on the latest victim of
what now looks to be a serial attacker? Do you have anything to say to
Hayley Abbot's parents?"

"I was appalled when I heard the news. This was a horrific and cowardly attack. Hayley and her family are in my prayers."

The reporter was nodding encouragingly even as he jumped to the next question. "What do you think of the DCI's handling of the investigation?"

"They have my faith that they are doing everything they can to apprehend the suspect." Jess felt Rebecca shift at her side. "If you'll excuse me."

The reporter followed as they set off toward the building's entrance. "Officers are now advising women not to go out alone at night, but some have suggested they order a formal curfew until the perpetrator is caught. What do you think of that?"

"I'll leave law enforcement matters to the experts."

"But would *you* support a curfew, Governor?"

Jess Cook paused. The reporter's phone was outstretched, his face expectant. "I don't think women should be punished for going about their business. Besides which, they're in as much danger in their homes as they are outdoors—more so—as we've seen with the shocking rise in domestic abuse this past year."

"Ma'am," murmured Rebecca, her eyes flicking meaningfully toward the doors.

"Curfews won't address the threats and challenges women continue to face in their daily lives," Jess continued. "For that we need investment, support, and education. We should start by giving women a fair chance in the workplace. Secure employment and better pay."

The reporter was nodding more vigorously. "You're talking about your proposed legislation to tackle Iowa's gender pay gap?"

"That would be a start, yes. We have one of the largest imbalances in the country. In terms of equal pay, our state is in the bottom fifth. That needs to change." Jess turned to go.

"I've heard you don't have the votes!"

She turned back, unable to keep the surprise from her face. "Heard from whom?"

The reporter smiled. "A source. Who reckons your bill won't get past the second reading in the senate." His phone was poised.

"Ma'am," said Rebecca more forcefully.

"Excuse me." Jess headed in through the doors, arrows of sunlight lancing in behind her. "Damn it." She yanked off her scarf, the sudden warmth of the interior deepening the flush that had colored her cheeks. "Who do you think he got that from?"

Rebecca glanced back. "I don't know. But—" Her nose wrinkled as she seemed to weigh something up.

"What?"

"It's not a problem. I'll have Mindy contact the *Register*, arrange a proper interview with you. Get some remarks prepared."

"Why?"

Rebecca met her gaze. "That line about women being in more danger in their own homes?"

"It's true."

"It's just that—with the restrictions you implemented—well, your opponents could point out that you put them there." Rebecca shook her head quickly at the governor's faltering expression. "We'll get ahead of it. Force our own angle. Talk about how the burden of care in homes and communities this year has fallen heaviest on women. How it's clear our society still views child care and housework primarily as a woman's responsibility, even alongside a career. Why we need to close the gap and encourage women into higher-paid roles traditionally dominated by men. Education. Investment. Support."

Jess drew a fortifying breath as they ascended the marble staircase to the first floor, passing beneath the grand vault of the dome that soared above them. The area was busy with clerks hastening between offices and a small group on a guided tour. The tours had only just started up again after the incident six months earlier. There was a state trooper close by, keeping a watchful eye. "OK. What's on the schedule?"

"You've got the crisis in social care meeting first thing and then—"

"Good morning, Governor."

Jess turned to see Ted Pierce. The senate minority leader was crossing to the staircase that led to his third-floor office, shadowed by a flock of aides, plucked straight out of private schools. Pierce liked them young and pliable. A fresh-faced man in a pin-striped suit carried his briefcase; a petite blond woman in a pencil skirt clutched his coat.

"Good morning, Ted." Jess heard the crispness in her tone and forced a smile to soften it. Partly because she didn't want to give Pierce—a powerful voice in the opposition and an old friend of Bill Hamilton— any more reason, other than the natural political fault lines between them, to go against her, but mostly because she didn't like him seeing how much he got under her skin.

"Important vote coming up next week?"

Seeing Pierce's thin-lipped smile, Jess knew whose camp the reporter's source had come from.

"I'm looking forward to it," she responded with false brightness.

His smile slipped. "And businesses? I wonder if they're looking forward to it, given the year they've already had? Many have been hit hard. Is it really the time to force them to expend further?"

"Community, Ted, not corporations. That's the platform I was elected on."

"Indeed. I suppose you'll just have to hope the *community* doesn't knock you off that platform at the midterms. Well, I have a busy day."

Jess watched him sweep up the stairs, shadowed by his staff. "Contact everyone in our camp," she told Rebecca. "Have them reach out, make sure no one's wavering on the vote."

She strode down the corridor, past the cabinets that showcased her achievements during her first year in office. There were press clippings and photographs of her with young farmers at the state fair, speaking at a conference for crop diversification, commending state initiatives to protect native habitats and improve soil health. Although she was proud of what she and her colleagues had achieved, the display gave her a twinge of frustration. This year they'd been just firefighting. She had wanted to do so much more. It was why this bill was so important to her. If she could use the pandemic—the inequalities exposed by it—to help change legislation, create real improvement in people's lives, then the sacrifices would have more meaning.

Outside her office, a brighter rectangle of marble marked the spot where the cabinet of dolls had stood, filled with porcelain replicas of all the First Ladies of Iowa. They'd offered to create a First Gentleman, which had greatly amused Mark, but Jess insisted the display be moved elsewhere. The rows of identical women in their dusty inaugural gowns, with their blank eyes and dead expressions, creeped her out. It reminded her of that awful expression her mother used to say: *Behind every successful man there's a good woman.*

Ted Pierce, of course, had been one of the loudest voices of protest during its removal, arguing that this was part of the capitol's history and mustn't be erased, but she'd stood her ground. It had been a stupid hill to die on really, but it was struggle enough being Iowa's first female governor. She didn't need reminding of her historic, and expected, place each morning.

As Rebecca headed on in through the opulent four-room suite to the governor's room, Jess paused at the desk of her secretary, who was picking through a pile of mail. "Morning, Sylvia."

"Good morning, ma'am."

"Anything I need to see?" Jess asked, eyes on the pile.

"Nothing that can't wait. More importantly, how was Ella's celebration?"

Jess smiled. "She made a very fine pumpkin." She took her cell from the pocket of her suit jacket, scrolled for a picture, then handed it over.

Sylvia popped on her glasses. "Oh, she's just as sweet as sugar."

Jess's smile faded as she took back the phone. She'd held her breath beside her husband at the school's Thanksgiving celebration as they'd watched their eight-year-old daughter waddle up the steps of the stage in the costume—all chicken wire, orange felt, and Krazy Glue—that Mark had made for her. It had been wonderful to see Ella back with her friends and teachers after the months alone. But it had hurt her heart to hear her daughter proclaim that the thing she was most thankful for this year was her daddy.

That night, in the mansion's oversize bed, Mark had drawn her into the warm crook of his arm when she'd confessed to feeling jealous. "Look at what you've achieved, in extraordinary circumstances. But you're not superhuman, Jess. You have to be governor first. The role demands it. We always knew that."

"I don't want to let Ella down. Or you."

"You couldn't," he'd promised, kissing her head.

Leaving Sylvia to the mail, Jess went through to her office, where Rebecca was already leafing through a stack of files.

Javier Morales, her office manager, was perched on the edge of his desk, on the phone. "Lieutenant governor," he mouthed, cupping his hand over the receiver. He pointed to the phone and raised an eyebrow in question.

"Put him through," Jess said, hanging up her coat and crossing to her desk, personalized with photographs of Mark and Ella. There was an envelope sitting there. A plain white one, unmarked. She opened it, guessing it was something she'd missed yesterday.

Inside were a letter and a photograph.

"Lieutenant governor on line one," Javier told her, nodding to the phone flashing on her desk.

Jess didn't respond. The photograph fell from her hands and slipped across the floor.

Rebecca bent and picked it up. She stared at it for a second, then looked at the governor's pale face, her eyes still transfixed by the letter. "Call security," she told Javier. "Now!"

6

Riley found her way through the maze of streets to the agency—her first day without a wrong turn. This morning, the building's tinted windows were deep reflective pools, filled with sunlight.

There was one space free in the lot by the front doors. She steered the white Chevy Caprice she'd inherited from Agent Roach into it. Her BuRide, Noah Case had called it when he'd handed her the keys two days ago.

The young agent had chuckled when she'd looked blankly at him. "You know—bureau-issued? BuRide. BuGun. *Goddamn BuReaucracy.*"

She'd laughed to cover her embarrassment. She had so much to learn.

Killing the engine, Riley finished the two-shot espresso she'd grabbed on the drive over, steeling herself for another day picking her way through her unfamiliar caseload.

She'd stayed up late last night to try to get ahead, determined to show Connie Meadows she deserved to be here on merit. She had spent hours going through the stack of Roach's files, squinting in the sallow light of her apartment's kitchen to read the former agent's writing. Suspected insurance fraud. Possible tax evasion by a local chain of sports bars. Counterfeit goods being sold from a warehouse in Madison County.

Threads to unspool. Trails to follow. Step by step, just like every other investigation she'd undertaken.

The focus of the work had eased some of the doubts that had crowded in on her first day. She knew how to do this: had been doing it for years in Black Hawk County, first as a rookie, then a deputy, then as sergeant and head of Investigations. But the cautionary voice that reminded her she'd swapped her position at the top in the sheriff's office to one here at the bottom was hard to silence.

While she'd read, the clouds that had blanketed the city since her arrival had drifted south, leaving clear skies, under which the temperature plummeted. When she traipsed into the bedroom in the early hours, the bed still marooned in a sea of cardboard boxes, she found it so cold her breath fogged the air. On closer inspection, she discovered the window, which opened onto a rusted fire escape, had warped in its frame and wouldn't fully shut. Another defect to add to the list—the showerhead that trickled pathetically, the damp that bubbled on the walls of the communal stairwell.

After firing off an email to the landlord, she pulled on her old college sweatshirt—*Go Panthers!*—and climbed under the blankets. But with the arctic air and the rumble of freight on the railroad, she'd barely slept.

Knocking back the espresso's dregs, Riley opened the glove compartment to stash her shades. As she did so, a rolled-up piece of paper slipped out. Retrieving it from the footwell, she unfurled it. She'd seen enough of Agent Roach's handwriting by now to recognize it.

Tomorrow never comes.

"Cheerful," she murmured.

She went to screw the note up, then paused and stowed it back inside. It felt wrong to throw the man's words away just as she was stepping into his shoes. Bad luck. She wondered what had made Roach hand in his notice, knowing what it took to get here.

As she closed the compartment, her cell rang. Her spirits lifted at the name on the screen. "Hey, sweetheart."

"Hey."

Riley smiled. Maddie's voice was a sweet slice of home. "How are you? All set for the holidays?"

"We have to make Christmas cards today. Our teacher is so clearly out of original ideas."

"Well, your favorite aunt would sure like one."

"My *only* aunt. Scrounger! Drop it!"

Riley caught a muffled woof in the background. "You're at your dad's?" She could see it in her mind: the pop star posters on Maddie's bedroom walls, the narrow bed she herself had slept in as a girl, with a quilt made by her grandmother. The corridor stretching away beyond, floral wallpaper yellowed by sun, lined with the Grant Wood paintings her mother had loved. Scrounger lumbering in on arthritic legs, tail dutifully wagging.

"He's eating my sock. Scrounger! Come here!"

There was another woof, followed by a wet snuffling on the line that gave Riley a stab of homesickness tinged with guilt. It wasn't just her own future she was gambling with by coming here, starting over again. Maddie, Ethan, Aunt Rose—they all relied on her. Without her salary they'd never be able to afford to keep the Fisher family home. Two years of a probationary period suddenly felt like a real long sentence of uncertainty.

Scrounger's snuffling faded and Maddie returned. "You know he farts, like all the time?"

Riley laughed. "He's just letting you know he's happy. His little love puffs."

"Ewww!"

"What did you do last night?"

"Rose and Lori came over with Ben. I watched a movie. Dad drank too much and fell asleep."

Riley pressed her lips together, imagining what sort of movie Ethan had let her watch. No doubt something inappropriate. One of his zombie flicks. Guts and guns. Before she could say anything, Maddie continued.

"I saw Logan yesterday."

Riley sat up straighter. "You did?"

"I went to Callie's after school with Aiden. He was there."

Aiden? A new name in the crowded field that seemed to be her niece's social circle. "Does this Aiden go to your school?" Riley braced for the answer. Two years ago, her niece had struck up a relationship with a much older boy. It had given Riley sleepless nights and forced her to have *the talk* with Maddie, knowing Ethan would just stumble through it after too many beers. The young man seemed to have been a good influence on Maddie, who'd started to settle down in school after a rough few years, but Riley had been quietly relieved when he'd gone back to family in Memphis.

She wondered if her brother would ever step up to the plate as a parent, or whether she would always be expected to play mom, however many miles away she was. And then, more uneasily, wondered if it was her own fault for stepping in too much. She heard her mom's voice.

Riley, sweetheart, I know you always need to be in control of a situation. But, sometimes, you just got to let people make their own mistakes. How else will they learn?

Maddie's answer brought her back. "He's a senior."

Riley closed her eyes. "Is he your boyfriend?"

"Er, *no.* Aiden's gay."

From Maddie's tone, Riley could see the eye roll—as if this should be obvious.

"He asked about you."

"Aiden?"

Maddie snorted. "Logan!"

"He did?" Riley felt a flush creep into her cheeks and was glad no one could see her.

She thought of the last time she'd seen Logan Wood, two weeks before she left for Des Moines.

It was late October, the corn fallen to the combines, the earth on her grandfather's grave still fresh. They had gone for a drink in Cedar Falls, the bar strung with cobwebs for Halloween; had chuckled their

way through shared memories at the Black Hawk County Sheriff's Office, skirting that one major investigation, where they'd lost a good colleague and barely escaped with their own lives.

After last call, they had sat together outside, the fall chill seeping in
as Logan waited for his sister to pick him up. Both of them had been
light-headed with beer, their words and laughter gone.

Seeing his sister's car approaching, Riley, suddenly awkward, had
stuck out her hand. "I guess this is goodbye?"

Logan had looked at her hand like he didn't know what to do with
it. When she dropped it, he'd stepped in tentatively and folded her into
his arms, tightening his grip when she returned the hug, her chin coming to rest on his broad shoulder. Down Main Street, the lights had
blinked red, offering them a few extra moments in which Riley had
stayed there, enveloped by Logan's warmth, a flutter of something inside. Something that surprised, and scared her.

"How is he?"

"OK."

Riley could sense Maddie's shrug. What were an adult's affairs to a
sixteen-year-old?

"What's your apartment like? When can I come see it?"

"Soon," Riley said after a pause, thinking of the damp walls and the
stacks of boxes.

"But for Thanksgiving, right? You promised we'd go skating."

Before Riley could answer, there was a rap at the window. A man
was looming there, looking down at her. He was dark-haired and stocky
with bloodshot eyes. His cheeks were pocked with old acne scars and
his nose had a slight sideways tilt, suggesting it had been broken more
than once. He was speaking. She opened the window a crack. "Sorry?"

"I said, you're in my space." As the man gestured, Riley saw a black
Chevy Tahoe idling behind her, the driver's door open. "Maddie, sweetheart, I've got to go. I'll call you tonight, OK? Love you." Stowing her
phone, she returned her attention to the man. "I wasn't told spaces were
allocated." She caught a glint of gold from a badge on his belt. "I'm Ri—"

"I always park here."

"I didn't know."

"Well, now you do."

As the man straightened, Riley closed the window. "OK, *asshole*." Turning to put the car in reverse, she saw the man had glanced back. She realized, by his expression, that he'd read her lips.

She was late into the office, the only free space a block away. Slush had soaked into her cheap boots, numbing her toes. Audrey, the agency's secretary, was on the phone. A whip-thin older woman, her skin, hair, and clothes all shades of ash, she exuded a steely, formidable manner that made Connie Meadows seem sunny by comparison. Audrey continued talking as Riley passed her desk, but tapped the register with a pen. Riley paused to sign in, careful not to disturb the glittering menagerie of crystal animals arrayed beside the woman's computer. A porcupine with bloodred spikes, a dolphin suspended on a tsunami of sapphire, an owl with onyx eyes.

After dumping her coat over the back of the chair in her box of an office, she went to the sparse kitchen and made herself another coffee. Reminding herself to bring a mug from home, she picked one from the jumble in the cupboard, hoping it wasn't someone's favorite. It was printed with an overly enthusiastic HAVE A GREAT DAY!

There was no sign of Noah Case. Other than Audrey, she'd barely seen another soul these past few days. Those who worked here seemed to follow Hoover's old rule to the letter—only ten percent of an agent's time was to be spent in the office. The rest you were out investigating.

She felt a pang as she thought of the sheriff's office—voices and laughter, phones ringing in the bullpen. She thought of Logan wandering in with some organic smoothie, hair damp from the gym showers, wagging his finger and grinning as she tried to hide her bacon burger. Maddie's voice sounded in her mind.

He asked about you.

"Agent Fisher?" Audrey appeared in the doorway. "Meadows wants to see you."

Coffee in hand, Riley went to her boss's office. On entering, she saw a man sitting in front of the desk. It was the jerk with the Tahoe.

"This is our new recruit, Riley Fisher," Meadows said, motioning Riley to the other chair. "Fisher, this is Special Agent Peter Altman."

"We've met," said Altman, eyes on Riley as she sat.

"I've had a call from State Patrol at the capitol," Meadows informed her. "There's been a threat made against the governor. She gets them all the time, of course. Mostly it's the usual cranks and crazies, but this one sounds credible. After the attack, I'm not taking any chances."

As Meadows locked eyes with Altman, Riley saw his jaw pulse. She felt a shift in the atmosphere.

The attack, coming shortly after restrictions lifted, had dominated the news at the time. A man named Karl Madden—already flagged for extremist views—had booked a place on a guided tour at the capitol. Partway through, he'd drawn a knife, shouting that he'd come to execute Jess Cook for crimes against the state. Madden had made it all the way to the governor's office, injuring a state trooper, before being apprehended.

"I want you to head over there together."

"Ma'am," Altman began, sitting forward, clearly about to protest.

"Take a look," Meadows cut across him. "See what we're dealing with." She switched her attention to Riley. "Speak to Governor Cook. Make sure she knows we're at her disposal."

Riley felt the unease from that first day creep back in. *Friends in high places.* She downed her coffee to cover her discomfort and saw the woman's eyes narrow.

"That's all," Meadows finished, her tone icy.

Altman pushed himself out of the chair in one fluid movement, nimble despite his bulk. "Nice mug," he murmured, as Riley followed him out.

She frowned at it as she headed down the corridor in Altman's wake. HAVE A GREAT DAY! As she turned it in her hand, she realized there was something else printed on the mug's underside. It was an image of a hand. The middle finger was raised.

7

To step into the governor's office was to step back in time. A time of law and order, firm handshakes, and gentlemen's agreements over a haze of cigar smoke and whiskey fumes. Old-world opulence breathed from every embellished corner—wood paneling, gilt carvings, cascades of light from chandeliers.

As Riley waited in the reception area with Peter Altman, the two of them having shown their badges to the state troopers guarding the suite, she imagined her father walking these rooms. For all the years he'd worked in this building, Michael Fisher had kept his work and his home life distinctly separate. As a kid, she'd felt aggrieved by that—jealous of this place that took him from his family. But, after everything that had happened, she wondered if her father had been protecting them. Had he known, back then, what sort of man Bill Hamilton was?

She thought of Hamilton's hand closing on her shoulder at her parents' funeral. The same shoulder now scarred by the bullet his man had fired into her—narrowly missing nerves that would have seen her out on disability. Thought of the trace of doubt she'd felt about the car wreck that killed her parents, rising like a warning drift of smoke. She'd stomped that doubt out after reading the accident report. Just another hit-and-run on the highway—winter dark and black ice. But standing here now, in Hamilton's old domain, a little ember flared.

Altman kept his eyes on the door the secretary had disappeared through. He'd slung his windbreaker over his arm and, beneath his suit jacket, Riley could make out the bulge of his gun—a .357 Smith & Wesson. For her own bureau-issued weapon she'd opted for a Glock 19, its weight reassuringly familiar alongside her new badge. She had the switchblade Logan had presented at her going-away party, tucked into an ankle holster, and she wore the gold star necklace her grandfather had given her. Each, in its own way, protection.

Altman had barely spoken two words since they'd left Meadows's office, except to say he would drive and to let him lead the interview with the governor. He was clearly antagonized by her presence on the assignment. Riley had worked with men like him before: overbearing, dismissive. But it was too soon to know if it was plain old sexism, or something else that had riled Altman. She had tried to make conversation, testing where she might forge a connection, knowing full well she needed allies not enemies here, but Altman had merely grunted in response to her questions, neither asking her about herself, nor volunteering anything.

The door opened and the secretary reappeared. "The governor will see you now."

Altman entered first, scanning the room and its three occupants. A young man with a sharp-boned face and black hair pulled back in a ponytail, a willowy woman in round glasses. And an older woman with short sandy hair and a furrowed brow.

Altman approached Jess Cook. "Governor."

"Agent Altman."

Riley caught some tension between them, hinted at in look and tone. Then, Jess Cook's gaze alighted on her and that tension evaporated.

"Riley." The governor's smile was open, genuine. "I was so pleased to hear you'd joined the agency. You'll be an asset."

Riley sensed Altman stiffen at her side, evidently irked by the warm reception. "It's good to see you again, ma'am. Although not under the circumstances."

Jess Cook's smile slipped. "Indeed." She gestured to the willowy woman. "This is Rebecca Page, my chief of staff. And Javier Morales, my office manager." She crossed to her desk, which was cluttered with framed family photographs.

There were three sealed bags, labeled by Iowa State Patrol. Altman reached for one as he sat in a wing-back chair in front of the governor's desk. "This is it, ma'am?"

Cook nodded tightly.

Inside was a letter, words written in block capitals in thick black ink. Riley had to lean in to read as Altman studied it.

YOU TOOK A PLACE THAT WASN'T YOURS
RETURN HOME AND CARE FOR YOUR FAMILY
THIS IS YOUR CURSE
THE PRICE YOU MUST PAY
OR THEY WILL PAY IT FOR YOU

Altman put it back on the desk and took a second bag. Inside this one was a photograph. Riley noticed Cook flinch as he picked it up.

A grainy image showed a vehicle outside what looked like a school building—kids' drawings of rainbows in the windows. Two figures stood by the car's open rear door. One was a man, with a flop of light brown hair and an easy smile. The other was a cherub-cheeked girl in a costume—a pumpkin with a little stalk hat. The man was holding the girl's hand. A third figure could just be seen, climbing from the passenger seat. The governor.

"My daughter, Ella," said Jess. Her voice was strained, emotion breaking through her composure. "And my husband, Mark. Two nights ago. We were attending her school's Thanksgiving celebrations."

"Looks like it was taken from a distance," remarked Altman. "Does the school have surveillance?"

"I'm not sure." The governor's cheeks colored and she looked down at her hands. "Mark usually takes Ella. Drops her off, picks her up. He'll know more. They're at the mansion. My security knows about this." She waved faintly at the sealed bags. "But I want to be the one to tell my family."

"I'll check with the school. Who might have known you would be there that night?"

"My daughter's school has been well documented in the press. We've had issues in recent months—reporters trying to bait my husband into talking to them at the gates. And to find the scheduled events you'd only have to look online."

Altman picked up the third bag, which contained an envelope. He inspected it, turning it over. "No postmark."

"No. My secretary is confident it never passed her desk. That means it must have been left here for me." The governor's voice thickened. "Some point between six o'clock yesterday evening and eight thirty this morning, someone came in and placed it on my desk."

"Why would they do that?" asked Javier, looking at Altman. "Why not send it? Why risk being caught?"

"It depends on the perpetrator's motive. The sort of message they want to send with this threat."

Riley knew what Altman didn't say—that the message was pretty clear.

I can get to you.

By Jess Cook's pinched expression, she guessed the governor had thought the same.

"Who has access to these rooms?"

"My staff. The lieutenant governor. Cleaning and maintenance. State troopers. Members of the house and senate. Even the public can come and go when I'm not here. The suite is part of the tour." She shook her head. "Security has been tightened since the attack, yes. But we don't want to barricade ourselves in. Or shut people out."

"Is there CCTV in the building?" Riley asked.

It was Altman who responded. "No."

"Legislators aren't all that keen about being spied on." Jess exhaled. "We've had meetings about it. But we all thought this was hallowed ground. I don't think many of us noticed how deep the cracks in our state—our country's—foundations had grown."

Altman set down the envelope. "Do you have any idea who might have left this for you? Any suspicions? Maybe you've had other odd messages—aborted phone calls, that sort of thing?"

"I get a lot of threats."

"It's unimaginable."

Riley looked around as Rebecca spoke.

The governor's chief of staff was watching them from behind her desk. "Threats of rape and torture. Mutilation. Execution."

"They're just keyboard warriors, Becca," Javier murmured. "Pathetic guys who still live in their mom's basement. Trolls. No way they'd say any of it to a person's face. Let alone act on it."

"You don't know that," Rebecca said, tensing. "Karl Madden acted on it. Got all the way here with a knife."

"I pass all of it on to my security," Jess cut in. "There has certainly been more abuse in recent months. People are scared. Angry about the restrictions." Her eyes went to the photograph of her daughter and husband getting out of the car, smiling, oblivious. "But this is—different."

"I'll speak to State Patrol," Altman told her. "Go over any threatening correspondence you've had since you took office. See if there are similarities."

"This doesn't seem like someone angry about the restrictions," Riley ventured, rereading the letter. The writing appeared old-fashioned, calligraphic affectations here and there. Distinctive curls and flicks at the ends of some of the letters. " 'You took a place that wasn't yours'? 'Return home and care for your family'?" She ignored Altman as he turned to stare at her. She had let him open the interview as he'd insisted, but she was damned if she'd keep quiet throughout. Meadows had sent her here for a reason and, much as it discomfited her, if her connection to Cook had secured her this posting she would sure as hell use it to her advantage. No one got ahead in law enforcement by hanging back. "Can you think of anyone who might resent your position as governor?"

Jess Cook gave a humorless laugh. "That's a long list. Bill Hamilton still has supporters here in the capitol. People who believe he was framed. Those who think I masterminded the plot against him, supported by terrorists. Well, you know all that," she said, glancing at Riley.

Riley nodded.

"Obviously, I have my political opponents, but it's not just Hamilton. It's the corporations. I've made enemies in boardrooms with my policies—fines for polluters and the sustainable measures we've introduced across the state. Some companies have seen their profits hit."

There was a knock at the door. The governor's secretary appeared. "Excuse me, ma'am. Security has been informed of a sighting of a possible suspect." Her gaze went to Riley and Altman. "An officer is outside."

"Show him in, Sylvia," said Jess, her tone lifting in anticipation.

After a moment, a state trooper entered. He removed his cap, nodding to the governor, then to Altman and Riley. "Ma'am, I've spoken with a janitor who saw a man leaving your office yesterday evening. The janitor was finishing their shift. Said it was around seven thirty."

"What man?" Jess asked quickly.

"The janitor didn't recognize him. But we have a description." The trooper glanced at the pad he held. "White. Over average height. Medium to heavy build. Wearing a hat and coat, both dark."

"Any idea who that could be?" Altman asked.

The governor looked at Rebecca and Javier. "Sound familiar?"

Javier scrunched up his nose. "Could be half the building."

Rebecca was already at her laptop, scanning the screen as she punched the keys. "There were no appointments scheduled after six and no public tours," she said, looking up. "Unless they were cleaning or maintenance, they shouldn't have been in here."

"Did the janitor see which direction this man went?" Altman interjected.

The trooper nodded. "Yes—and we may have gotten lucky. He left by the back entrance. We had a spate of thefts from cars last year," he explained at Altman's frown. "We installed a surveillance system in the parking lot. It's likely we'll have him on camera. I was about to go through the footage."

Altman stood, his eyes on the governor. "Ma'am, I'd like to take a look at that."

The governor nodded. "Agent Altman." She waited until he turned back. "I'm used to threats against me."

She let the words hang there and Riley felt that tension again, bristling in the silence.

"But this . . . ?" Jess Cook's eyes returned to the photograph.

Altman nodded. "It has my full attention."

Riley grabbed for her coat as Altman left with the trooper. She paused, seeing the fear and doubt in Jess Cook's face, wanting to offer reassurance. But Altman was already out the door. "Excuse me, ma'am."

"Agent Fisher?"

Riley looked around to see Rebecca had followed her out. "Yes?"

"Take this seriously." The chief of staff's gaze was on Altman, striding down the corridor beside the state trooper, boots clacking on the marble.

"We will."

Rebecca's eyes flicked to her. "I mean, more than last time."

Before Riley could respond, the young woman slipped back into the office.

8

----

egan Thomas shuffled the spread of magazines on the table into a stack. She straightened up the chair where her patients sat, thumped the cushion out of its slump, and plucked a rogue figurine from the carpet. It was a ghost—cartoon style, arms outstretched under a billow of white. A leftover from one of her niece's Halloween hauls.

She put it back in the box beside the chair. The box was full of toys and models, purchased or found over the years. They were useful aids for her patients when they were struggling to articulate their feelings. Representations of who they perceived themselves to be in that moment. The princess. The robot. The superhero. The witch. It was always telling when they chose one.

It was her Friday afternoon client, Alice, who had picked the ghost. It had worried Megan. There was a time, a few weeks ago, when she thought Alice was starting to engage with her suggestion that she was strong enough to leave her husband. The husband who ruled every aspect of her life, from the food she could eat to the clothes she could wear. The husband who made her sleep in another room when she was menstruating and called her ugly when she cried. The husband who once compelled her to pour scalding water over her own arm after she dared challenge his authority.

Weeks ago, Alice had picked the witch and accepted the literature on domestic abuse Megan had given her. The ghost indicated she was slipping away, back into invisibility and impotence.

Megan turned off the light and shut the door on her work for the weekend.

She was heading to the kitchen when she heard it. The hallway behind her ended at the door to the garage. Something was scratching at the door. She had closed the garage when her last client left, but it had been open most of the day. Her house backed onto Easter Lake Park, an old strip mine that had been turned into a nature area, with swampy creeks and a lake. The sprawl of trees grew right up against her yard and, now and then, things would creep and crawl into her property. Muskrats and raccoons, groundhogs and snakes.

She made her way to the door to listen, but the scratching had stopped. Unlocking it cautiously, she felt for the switch. The fluorescents stuttered on, flooding the place in white light. The front half of the garage, where her clients parked, was empty, the concrete stained with oil. She scanned the junk that took up the back half: boxes of files, some of her ex-husband's clothes, dusty camping gear, and broken gym equipment. The place was silent, except for the low hum of the lights, but there could be any kind of critter hiding among the jumble.

Megan crossed to the button that raised the garage door. She'd leave it open for the night, let whatever it was make its way out by itself. Call pest control tomorrow if necessary. She was reaching for the button when something moved behind her. Twisting, she saw a figure rising—a man dressed in dark clothing, the hood of his coat pulled up. A mask concealed the lower half of his face. There was something printed on it, red coiled on black. Her mind registered these things in an instant before she froze on the gun he held. The dark eye of the barrel stared back.

"Move, and I'll shoot you in the face." His voice was low behind the mask. His eyes glittered above it.

Her heart was a wild galloping thing. She thought of bolting, but her feet had rooted her to the concrete. Her thoughts raced. When had

he come in? This afternoon before her last client left? How long had he
been in here, crouched in the dark?

He put a hand in the pocket of his coat, pulled something out. Megan flinched as he tossed it to her. As it landed at her feet, she saw it was
some sort of white material, tied off at one end. It had a crude symbol
painted on it, red like the sinuous one on his mask, only this was a circle
with a short line flicking up from the top.

"Put it over your head."

When she hesitated, he racked back the slide of the gun. A jarring
metal threat.

Megan put it on, her hands trembling. The makeshift hood drooped
to her shoulders. It smelled bad. Mildew and rust. She could see the
world as little points of light through the material. She sensed him
come toward her. She cringed back, but he grabbed her shoulder. He
was wearing gloves. Worn leather on her skin, fingers digging into her
collarbone. He smelled of mud and frozen earth. He turned her toward
the door to the house, left open behind her. The gun pressed against her
spine, its menace cold through her T-shirt, forcing her forward.

As she entered the hallway and he marched her past her therapy
room, her mind teemed with thoughts of her clients. All those women
who'd sat opposite her over the years. The high-flying executives and
overworked doctors, the workaholics and the power moms. All those
manicured exteriors that hid secret gardens of pain: briars of trauma,
shadows of abuse.

God, she had become one of them.

Be the robot. Just get through this.

"Where's your bedroom?" When she quailed, he repeated it. "Where
do you sleep, bitch?"

A sob hiccupped from her. As his fingers tightened on her shoulder,
she pointed to the stairs.

"Go."

She climbed in a daze, her bare feet clammy on each carpeted step.
Her legs felt like water, like they weren't even attached to her body. She
couldn't see much through the hood, but she knew the way. The door
to her bedroom was ajar.

"You got clothes in here?"

She couldn't understand what he wanted, but she nodded, compliant.

On the way in, her hip bumped against her vanity. She heard something fall and guessed it was the photograph of her mother. An image of her mom's warm smile seared her. She always saw her for coffee on Sundays. What would she think when she didn't show? Her mom was alone in the world. What would happen if . . .

Don't think. Be the robot. Robots don't feel.

He was steering her toward the closet. "Choose something nice for me."

Oh God.

"N . . . nice . . . ?"

"Something pretty." He plucked disdainfully at her baggy T-shirt.

She opened the closet doors, thoughts jumping between what she should pick and whether there was anything she could use as a weapon. A wire hanger? The tapered heel of a stiletto? He had stepped back, but she could sense the gun still trained on her.

Her ex-husband was an occasional hunter. She'd gone with him a few times, camping in Allamakee County near the Yellow River. That last time he'd shot a whitetail deer—badly. A gutshot that had buckled it for a moment before it bolted. They'd found it three hours later, collapsed by a creek bed, a hole in its side, blood leaking black like tar. Megan remembered the look in the creature's eyes, unable to move even as the humans approached, snorting in agony, its body shuddering. She didn't want to die like that.

Her fingers scrabbled over clothes, hangers rattling. She grasped at a long flowery dress she'd worn to a cocktail party last Christmas.

"Shorter." He sounded impatient.

She left the dress and pulled out a skirt she hadn't worn in years. Black. Tight. Above the knee.

"Yeah," he said, his voice gruff with satisfaction. "Put it on."

Her fingers were trembling so badly she could hardly unbutton her jeans. She felt him watching her. Fear raised gooseflesh on her skin as she stepped into the skirt. She felt weirdly embarrassed that she hadn't shaved her legs, then he was commanding her to pick a top to go with it. Low-cut. Form-fitting. Next, a pair of high heels, rarely worn, that pinched her toes.

When she was stood there, dressed as he wanted, her jeans and T-shirt piled on the floor, he compelled her back down the stairs to the kitchen. He shoved her toward the sink. She stumbled in the heels, just catching herself from falling. She heard something clink as he moved in behind her. Felt the cold grip of metal around her wrist. Handcuffs, she realized, as they clicked shut. She was breathing hard, her adrenaline spiking. "Please." Her voice was a dry whisper. "I'll do what you want. Don't hurt me."

He forced her down slightly, so he could slide the other cuff through the handle of the dishwasher beneath the sink. She could feel him behind her, the pressure of him, his own breathing more labored now. He was getting off on this. The hood had sagged at the front and she could see his feet below her. He wore big work boots, scuffed with wear.

All of a sudden, he moved away, leaving her alone. Her nerves twitched as she heard noises behind her. Footsteps. The scrape of a chair. A low chuckle.

What was he planning?

"I have money. My wedding ring is upstairs. Take it."

"Close your eyes."

She obeyed and the hood was tugged off. Megan felt the air cool the sweat on her cheeks. She could no longer smell that damp odor.

"Keep them closed," he ordered, tapping her skull cruelly with the barrel of the gun.

She jerked away as something hard and waxy was pressed against her lips.

"Bite!" he commanded.

She bit down tentatively. A burst of cool sweetness told her it was an apple. He must have taken it from the fruit bowl on the table. The red symbol on the hood jumped into her mind. A circle with that little line at the top. Apple and stalk?

"Hold it there. Eyes closed."

He moved back. Behind her eyelids, Megan sensed the bright snap of a flash. He was taking photographs of her, chained at the kitchen sink in her short skirt and flimsy top, an apple in her mouth like she was a pig on a spit at a backyard grill. Her skin crawled with humiliation. She didn't want to be the robot anymore. She wanted to be the ghost. Fade away like Alice.

His footsteps approached, those big boots heavy on the tiled floor. "And the Lord said, I will greatly multiply thy sorrows."

9

Riley stepped out of the shower and quickly toweled herself dry, her skin tingling. The apartment refused to get warm, even though she'd turned the thermostat up as high as it would go and wedged a blanket in the gap in the bedroom window. She'd not heard back from the landlord about fixing it.

As she stepped into a pair of jogging pants and pulled on her college sweatshirt, she thought of California and that dingy room she'd ended up in all those years ago. A girl alone and vulnerable, with a man holding the keys—all the power in his hands. Now she was a woman with combat training and a gun. If the landlord didn't get back to her soon, she'd go down to his office, flip her badge to light a fire under his ass.

She could easily afford something better, even on her starting salary. One of those new homes down by the river, white marble counters and skyline views—several income brackets from this grimy outer crust of the city, with its cracked streets and railroad dust. But the Fisher family house in Cedar Falls was in serious need of upkeep. Ethan's paycheck from the gas station barely covered the utilities and there was Maddie's college fund to think of. How much time would she spend here anyway? It wasn't like she'd be having friends over for dinner parties.

What about Maddie?

Her niece had called that morning, left a message asking again when she could visit. Riley had been busy working, but that wasn't why she hadn't called Maddie back. There was a tug-of-war inside her. It wasn't just the crappy apartment, or even the fact she wanted to secure her footing in the job before she started taking days off with her niece.

When she'd driven from Cedar Falls, her belongings strapped in the back of her grandfather's rusted pickup, she had glanced in the rearview to see her family watching from the porch. Maddie with her arms folded tight around her thin frame, Aunt Rose's hand on her shoulder. Ethan gripping Scrounger's collar to stop him chasing after her. Something painful had tightened in her at that last sight of them, before the road turned and they were swallowed by trees. But, by the time she was on the highway, the tears had dried to salt on her cheeks and that grip had eased—become a lightness she now understood had been relief.

All her adult life, she had cared for her family. Had nursed her grandfather until he'd gotten too sick, then gone to see him each week in the old folks' home. Had coaxed and bullied her brother through his problems; been the arbiter between him and his ex-wife, and caregiver for Maddie. Had babysat for Aunt Rose and Lori when they needed a break. She was even the one who'd visited the graves of her parents, plucking weeds and clearing litter. She was their fulcrum. To step out of that position of support was terrifying in so many ways. But, perhaps, with no tethers—in the terror of free fall—she might finally find out who she was.

And what she could be.

In the kitchen, two rows of old-fashioned pine cupboards faced each other across a peeling faux-wood floor. There was a round table in the middle beneath a low-hanging light. She had, at least, started to unpack, putting plates in the kitchen cupboards and clothes in the closet. She'd set out some of the photographs she'd brought with her. Maddie in the backyard, caught in a rare grin, the creek in full summer behind her. Scrounger curled asleep on the porch chair. Aunt Rose and Lori, Benjamin toddling between them. And Grandpa Joe in his sheriff's uniform, gold star polished, eyes still clear—years before the fog clouded them, turned them watery and confused.

A copy of the *Des Moines Register* from two days ago lay on the table, beside one of Roach's case files that Riley had spent the day on. The paper's front page was dominated by the recent attack. The victim, Hayley Abbot, had been through two surgeries and was still in the ICU. There was a photograph of her. Shoulder-length honey blond hair framed a soft-featured face lit by a sunny smile. Another picture showed the riverside path where she'd been assaulted, the shadows of the underpass brooding behind. People had started laying flowers on the path, with prayers and good wishes. One note shouted a bold but unrealistic *Never Again!*

There was a smaller section beneath, covering Governor Cook's visit to a garment factory where she'd spoken about women in the workforce and how more needed to be done to safeguard jobs the pandemic had rendered even more insecure—especially those in manufacturing and food production, where conditions had worsened and women's pay still lagged behind men's.

There was nothing on the letter that had been left for the governor, threatening her family, although from what her chief of staff had said, it seemed Jess Cook got so many abusive messages that one more was hardly front-page news.

Riley hadn't seen Peter Altman since he'd dropped her at the agency three days ago, after their meeting with Cook at the capitol. They had indeed gotten lucky, as the state trooper had hoped. The parking lot surveillance camera caught a man fitting the janitor's description leaving by the building's back entrance. He'd had his hood up and there was no clear image of his face, but the camera picked him up getting into a car, from which they'd been able to take a partial plate. Riley had no idea how the investigation was now progressing.

Her eyes lingered on the picture of Cook at the factory, surrounded by women. The governor was smiling for the camera, but her eyes looked tired. Riley had tried to reason with Altman's dismissal of her help. That first day, Connie Meadows had said her agents worked mostly alone. Of course, she couldn't expect to waltz in and be in charge. But she had been sent to that meeting with the governor. She wanted to make a good impression on Meadows, her boss's reminder of the probation period, more warning than fact, growing in the fertile ground of her own self-doubt.

She also wanted to know what Rebecca Page had meant by asking her to take the threat seriously.

More than last time.

Did that mean Altman had worked on the Karl Madden case? Was that where the tension between the agency and the governor's office had come from? She'd intended to ask Noah Case what history there was, but she hadn't seen him yet.

She went to her refrigerator, which was stacked with meals for one. As she was scanning her options, music began to thump through the walls. The tenant down the hall liked it loud. She'd glimpsed him once the other evening, a hulk of a man in cargo pants and a wifebeater, faded tattoos spidering around his biceps.

Picking a random meal, unsure what she wanted, Riley put it in the microwave. At the ping, she took the tray and set it on the table, wincing at the release of steam as she peeled back the plastic. She slid the day's case file toward her. Suspected counterfeit goods, Madison County. She'd driven the forty minutes to Winterset that morning, remnants of snow lacing the stubbled fields, grain silos shining like steel drums in the morning light.

The sheriff, an older man with a military haircut and close-set eyes, had welcomed her enthusiastically, inviting her to breakfast at a local diner while they discussed the case. He'd talked more about himself than he had the investigation, chewing intently through a loose-meat sandwich and three sunny-side eggs.

Riley, aware that one of her key duties as a federal agent was to build a good rapport with local law enforcement, had nodded politely, all the while attempting to steer him back on topic, her gaze distracted by a dribble of yolk on his chin. He'd smeared it away with the back of his hand when they'd finished—the same hand he then extended to her, his card poised in his fingers like a magician doing a trick.

"That's my personal number there. You call me anytime now, Riley."

As he pulled out of the parking lot and honked his horn at her, she'd wondered if he had felt at ease enough to call Agent Roach by his first name.

She made some more notes on the file—details to look into, people to interview—then pushed it away, along with the half-eaten meal, already congealing at the edges. She thought of Logan at her going-away party, taking her phone and typing in some vegan recipes.

Promise me you won't eat like a college kid, Sarge.

Her neighbor's music stopped. The blast of a freight train's horn cut through the silence. The rumble of its passing trembled in the walls. When it had gone, the apartment's hush seemed deeper.

Taking her phone, Riley went into the living room and sat on the creased leather couch, flipping on the TV for some background noise. She flicked through channels before settling on the news. She looked at her phone, wondering if she should call Logan. Her hesitation made her irritated with herself. Why shouldn't she call him? They were friends and former colleagues. Their nieces went to school together, were close. There were a million things they could talk about. It didn't have to be weird. Brushing off the unexpected anxiety, she tapped on his number.

It went to voice mail, but she smiled to hear his voice.

"Hey, it's Riley." She paused. "Maddie said she saw you. That you'd asked about me?" She winced at how needy that sounded. "I've got those recipes you gave me. Haven't made them yet. Probably need to hit the local pet store for that rabbit food you eat. Anyway, call me when you get a chance. Just want to make sure you haven't completely screwed up my old department."

Exhaling, she checked the time. It was getting late, but she knew Maddie would still be up. Ethan wasn't good at keeping to a schedule. Riley scrolled for the number. If she wasn't intending to have her niece here for Thanksgiving, she needed to tell her, sooner rather than later.

On the TV a breaking-news logo flashed up. The camera switched to a live press conference. There was the chief of police in cap and gold braid, sitting at a table in front of a bank of microphones. Beside the chief was a man in a neat brown suit. Late fifties. Black hair frosted white and a sober expression. He was speaking.

"We now have cause to believe these recent attacks, including the violent assault on Hayley Abbot, were perpetrated by the same man. We also suspect they could be linked to a series of historic attacks in the Des Moines metropolitan area that started in the early nineties. That previous investigation surrounded an assailant who, over the course of a five-year period, is believed to have brutally attacked at least eighteen women—the youngest fifteen, the oldest sixty-eight."

The detective paused. His forehead was furrowed, his brown eyes weary.

Brutally attacked.

Riley could imagine the things he did not—could not—say to the eager press, the listening public. Her mind flared with memories from Black Hawk. Dead women found curled around their pain. Torn skin. Maggots inching. She felt herself drawn to the man's words, like someone calling her name.

Riley set down her phone and turned up the volume on the TV.

"There are indications this man holds certain religious convictions, which may prove key in our search for him."

"Detective Verne!" The camera panned to show a reporter straining forward, holding out a mic. "Are you talking about the Sin Eater?"

The detective paused. "That's the moniker the suspect was known by in the media, yes." He raised his voice over the flurry of clicks and flashes that followed. "We have a facial composite from the original case that I would like to direct your attention to." He turned to where a projector lit the wall. It blinked to life on an image. A pencil drawing of a man's face.

It was rough and irregular, parts pieced together from descriptions by different victims. The suspect looked relatively young—late twenties perhaps. He had shoulder-length straggly hair, a long face with a jutting brow, and a wide, flat mouth. The eyes were the most realistic part of the drawing. Deep-set and intense, they stared out of the screen.

That face set off a series of memories in Riley. Lining up with her mom and Ethan at a Red Cross station. Collecting bottled water in a shopping cart. Smell of sewage rising in the streets. Ninety-three. The year of the Great Flood—her family's last year in Des Moines. She remembered that face splashed across the headlines. Another girl claimed. And another. Sense of an evil stalking the city as the rivers burst their banks and the waters rose. *The Sin Eater.* A boogeyman whispered about at sleepovers. Only scarier. A monster that had even the grown-ups jittery and afraid.

"We believe our suspect has—or had—a tattoo on his right arm." As the detective spoke, another image appeared beside the face. It was a partial drawing of a snake with a cross hanging above it. "And he would often leave a mark at the scenes of his crimes, either on or near the victims." The face and the tattoo were replaced by the crude red symbol of a snake. It appeared to have been sprayed on concrete, over faded swirls of graffiti.

"Detective Verne!" came another voice. "Hayley Abbot's mom has accused the police of incompetence. If you now believe her daughter was attacked by a suspect who's been at large for three decades, do you have anything to say to her?"

The man in the suit appealed for quiet as more questions were fired at him. Riley, however, was fixed on the image projected on the wall behind him. The red serpent looked more like the letter *S*, with a bulbous head at its top and a whip at its end. There was something familiar about that symbol.

The message left for Governor Jess Cook. Those inked black letters with their old-fashioned affectations. Not calligraphy, perhaps.

But, maybe, little flicks of a tail.

10

"Yo, Kody."

Kody Lyle looked around to see Troy offering him the joint. He accepted and took a few shallow puffs. Smoke bloomed in his throat. He swallowed quickly, trying not to cough it back out, then passed it to Austin, who took it over his shoulder, his free hand still furiously working the controller's buttons. Austin's brother, Jace, was sitting on the floor beside him, hunched over the other. Explosions ripped across the TV screen that took up half the wall of Troy's bedroom, tearing soldiers into bloody ribbons.

"Take that, *cocksucker*!"

Kody took a swig of Coke to wash away the taste. He'd never liked weed. Didn't like the way it made his head swim, or the way it loosened his jaw and made him say stuff that made people laugh nervously. Besides, it ruined him for gaming. Dulled the dopamine hit of the kills.

Reagan slid off the windowsill where she'd been perched beside Alexa. "I'm bored," she complained, sinking down on the couch next to Troy.

Reagan had that blunt beauty of teenage girls, lips carved into a crimson pout, ice-blue eyes smoked with shadow. As she flicked her long hair over her shoulder, her perfume—soda sweet—filled Kody's senses like the pot. Made him feel dizzy and unsure.

"Fuck yeah!" shouted Jace, punching a fist into the air.

Austin swore as his soldier went down screaming.

There was a knock at the bedroom door. Troy snatched the spliff from Austin and handed it like a baton to Reagan, who hastened it to the window, waving out curls of smoke.

Troy opened the door to show a woman, framed in the crack. "Hey, Mom."

"Dinner will be ready at seven, sweetheart." She peered past him into the room. "Oh, hello, Kody. How's your mother?"

"OK."

"Still working at the Laundromat?"

Kody nodded, feeling heat prickle his skin as he heard Reagan and Alexa giggle.

"I'll have to stop by and see her sometime." Her polite smile told him she wouldn't. She frowned, sniffing the air. "Troy, have you been smoking?"

"No, Mom. Reagan brought some incense."

Reagan smiled sweetly as Troy's mom spotted her and Alexa.

"Well, it certainly smells better in here than it usually does. Troy, I want you to give the girls a lift home today, OK? It was just on the news. They're saying this madman who assaulted that girl is some serial attacker. I don't want them out there alone."

"Sure, Mom." Troy closed the door on his mother with a roll of his eyes. He looked over at Reagan. "You better make it up to me."

"Don't you want to protect us?" she challenged.

"Nah. Let the fucker have you for a few hours. Gimme some peace."

Austin and Jace sniggered. Kody felt a spasm of pleasure at Reagan's wounded expression.

"It's a joke!" Troy went to take her hand, but she snatched it away. In response, Troy picked her up and slung her over his shoulder, biceps bulging.

Reagan smacked his back hard. "Let me go, you jerk!"

Troy threw her down on the couch and pinned her there, grinning as she struggled. A dark wave of her hair slipped across Kody's knees.

Troy's grin faded, his expression sobering. "That son of a bitch ever came near you I'd rip his balls off."

"You better," she murmured. When he released his grip on her wrists, Reagan grabbed a fistful of Troy's hair and pulled him down, arching herself against him and kissing him hard on the mouth.

Kody looked away when she saw him watching.

Reagan gave a sly smile as she sat up, twirling the silver necklace with the horseshoe pendant that Troy had bought her—two months' worth of his considerable allowance—between her fingers. She slung an arm around Troy's shoulders, fixed her arctic eyes on Kody. "How'd you get your nickname?"

"Reagan," Troy warned.

"What nickname?" Alexa wanted to know, eager as she sensed some mischief.

"Maggot," said Reagan, with relish. "Troy told me they all called him Maggot."

Kody heard that name echo back to him from schoolyards and corridors. Slam of lockers and rapid-fire laughter. As the boys around him at high school had grown taller and filled out, soft features hardening into chiseled adolescence, he'd stayed the same size he had in junior high. Small, thin, and pale, no matter how much he worked out, trailing Troy and the other jocks to the gym.

Years back, before he left them, his father told him his mom smoked and drank all through her pregnancy. *It stunted your growth, kid. The bitch stunted your growth.*

Kody stood and grabbed his coat. "I gotta go."

"Wait, bro. I'll give you a ride."

Kody shook his head. "I'll see you soon." As he slipped out of the room, he heard Reagan's staged whisper.

"Bet I know how he got it."

Just before he closed the door, he caught a flash of pink lace. Reagan had unzipped her fly and was wiggling her little finger through the gap. Laughter stung his ears.

Downstairs, by the front door, the walls were busy with professional photographs of Troy and his mom, dad, and siblings. Kody pulled on his sneakers, laces knotted where they'd snapped, the off-brand labels faded with wear. He paused as he straightened, staring at the white-toothed family grinning at him from one of the framed pictures. He stuck a finger up one nostril, hooked out a booger and smeared it across Troy's mom's smiling, made-up face.

Outside, it was growing dark and had started to snow. Kody hunched his shoulders as flakes eddied around him, sneaking their way inside the collar of his thin coat. The wind sent swirls of them dancing down the street. In the nearby park the swings moved to and fro in the gusts, like they were occupied by ghost children. He had a memory of him and Troy playing there, pretend guns couched in their hands as they shot at each other.

Everything was different now. Reagan had shifted whatever equilibrium still existed between him and Troy, knocking his best—and only—friend further off orbit. Next year, Troy would leave for college and he'd be stuck here, alone.

Last month, he'd been let go from his job, working the shoe counter at the Big Pitch Bowl and Arcade. It was only a part-time gig—the pay was shit and the shoes stank—but it kept him in games and candy. He'd been idly looking for work, but many businesses had laid off staff this year or closed down altogether. Kody was already tired of the search. Even getting up in the mornings was hard. What was the point?

As he walked, the tall houses with their pointed gables and expansive porches gradually decreased in size. By the time he crossed the railroad tracks, the neighborhood had changed completely. Landscaped lawns became cluttered yards. Pruned hedges became chain-link fences that held back snarling dogs. Shiny SUVs became dirty pickups. The houses were mostly single-story, with rotting windows, weathered timber, and limp flags. The settling snow at least hid the worst of the weeds and the junk. Kody imagined it falling in his mind, covering the insults, cooling the sting of the taunts.

He turned the corner of his street and stopped dead. There, parked outside his house, was a black Dodge pickup. His mood sank into his shoes. For a moment, he thought about carrying on, past his house. Just keep on walking. But it was dark and cold, and he had nowhere else to go.

The pickup's cargo bed was covered in a tarp, under which things bulged. On the back, beside a decal of an eagle carrying the American flag in its talons, were several stickers. MY OTHER CAR HAS EIGHTEEN WHEELS. DON'T MESS WITH THIS CRAZY MOTHER-TRUCKER.

Kody braced as he entered the house. A big pair of scuffed work boots lay just inside the door. An old bomber jacket, the leather rubbed bald at the elbows, hung from a hook. In the kitchen, Dean Martin was singing on the radio. Kody made his way toward his room. The smell of food made his stomach tighten. He could hear his mom's voice, higher and faster than normal. The voice she adopted whenever he was here.

And there *he* was—sitting at the kitchen table in that faded red plaid shirt, sleeves rolled up to show hairy, muscled arms. He was digging a fork into a plate heaped with food.

Harlan Judd.

It was a while since Kody had seen him. Harlan had drifted in and out of their lives for the past few years like a bad smell. Sometimes lingering for months at a time before hitting the road again on some long-distance job. He had his own apartment somewhere in the city, but neither Kody nor his mom had ever been invited to it.

As Kody watched Harlan shovel food into his mouth, his mom appeared. She was still in her work uniform. She fluttered around the large man like a nervous bird, setting down a bottle of beer and a napkin decorated with holly.

"What the fuck's this?" Harlan grunted, picking up the napkin.

"They were on sale at Hy-Vee."

"You got the Queen of England coming?"

"I just thought they were pretty, you know? Festive?"

Kody hated that voice she used around him. The way she framed everything as a question Harlan would determine the answer to.

"Waste of fucking money, Shelley." Harlan paused, his fork halfway to his mouth, as he saw Kody in the hallway. "Well, look what the cat dragged in."

"Oh, hi, honey," said Shelley, bobbing into view. "You hungry? I'll fix you a plate."

"No."

Kody ducked into his room and closed the door. He kicked off his sneakers and went to the desk by his bed. Crushed Mountain Dew cans and candy wrappers littered it. A few plates fuzzed with mold lurked on the windowsill and under the bed. He could still hear his mom's phony voice and Harlan's gruff tones until he switched on the console and drowned them both out.

His mood changed almost at once. Gone were Reagan's sly laughter and Troy's indifference. Gone were his hunger and his anger at his mom, letting Harlan back into their house after the last time.

His system wasn't anything like Troy's—the screen was a quarter of the size and the console was an older model that glitched—but he could still lose himself in the game. Here, his world was full of sunshine and palm trees. He had guns and fast cars, and hot girls with fuck-me eyes and titties that strained their bikinis. He was alive.

Kody was deep in the game, on a side mission to bring down a rival gang, when he saw a shadow on the wall and realized Harlan was in his room. He'd been so engrossed he hadn't heard the man enter.

The fucker was lounging by the half-open door, bottle of beer in his hand, watching him play. Kody paused the game and turned. "What?"

Harlan cocked his head. "What've I told you 'bout respecting your mother? If she's fixed you food, you eat it."

Kody bit back what he wanted to say. Harlan was the last man he'd take that advice from. Respect his mom? The shithead had smacked her head off the kitchen door for burning his dinner when he was last here. He turned back to the screen and resumed play.

Harlan was across the room in three strides. He hauled Kody out of the chair and slammed him against the wall. The man was in his fifties, but he was more than twice Kody's size and was able to pin him there one-handed, the bottle still gripped in his fist, now frothing at the lip. Kody twisted his head away as Harlan leaned in, his breath rank with overboiled beans and beer. The man's eyes were like twin pools of black ice. Glassy and treacherous.

"Respecting me is way more important." Harlan forced his thick forearm against Kody's throat.

Kody choked at the pressure crushing his windpipe. Beyond, through his open door, he saw his mom standing there. Shelley had one hand pressed to her lips. But, as he locked eyes with her, she melted away, disappearing back into the kitchen. He began to retch and cough.

"You get me?" Harlan repeated, right in his face.

"Yes!"

"Say what?"

"Yes, sir!"

Harlan released him and he sank down the wall. "Looks like you've not minded your manners since I've been gone. That'll change," Harlan murmured, pointing the beer at him then raising it to his lips. "That'll change."

Kody touched his neck as he watched the man drink. The coiled snake tattoo on Harlan's forearm seemed to shift with the movement.

11

The black Tahoe dominated the space outside the front doors, ice melting under the treads of its wheels. It had started snowing last night, but hadn't settled. The clouds hung heavy this morning, threatening another fall. The air, trapped beneath, smelled polluted. Diesel fumes and factory emissions, wet mud and river stink.

As she passed the vehicle, Riley glanced inside. She wondered how Peter Altman had secured his premium parking spot. Longest-serving agent? Meadows's favorite? There were two coffee cups in the holders, lids askew, scum around the rims. Something was lying on the back seat. A child's stuffed bear. By its matted fur it looked as though it had been well loved.

She had taken Altman for a lone wolf rather than a family man. She'd known a lot of them in the sheriff's department—bachelors and divorcés—worn down by caseloads and paperwork. Too many hours on the road and in drab motel rooms; too many beers alone after a shift.

Inside the building, she slid her phone from her pocket. No new messages. She felt a prickle of disappointment, but forced it away as the elevator doors opened. She'd called Logan only last night. Besides, she didn't have time for distractions today.

Down in the basement, she signed in at Audrey's desk, then went straight to Altman's office. The door was closed, but she could hear his gruff voice. Knocking, she entered.

Altman swiveled in his chair with a frown. He was on the phone, notepad open on his desk. "Got it." He scribbled something down. "I'll be there shortly." He put down the receiver and stood, the chair scooting back. "Something you need?"

"Did State sign over the letter that was left for the governor?"

"Yup," Altman answered, grabbing his windbreaker and shrugging it on. "It's gone to the bureau's lab."

"Do you have a copy?"

"Why?"

She bit back her irritation. Was everything a fight with this man? "I might have something for you."

After a moment, he dug reluctantly into the pocket of his jeans for his cell. He typed in his code, keeping it from view, then turned the screen toward her. Riley stepped closer to look at the photograph of the letter that was displayed. She could smell coffee and something stale and vegetal on Altman's breath.

After last night's news report had ended, that spark of connection she'd felt between the snake symbol sprayed on the wall and the odd quirks in the letter left for Jess Cook had started to fade. But now, looking at the letter, she felt that thrill again. There were only six of them contained within the threatening message, but each *S* had a bulbous head and an unmistakable curl at the end.

She pulled that morning's edition of the *Des Moines Register* from her purse. "Look."

The front page had been given entirely to the press conference. The man in the brown suit who'd led it had been named as Julius Verne, a detective in the state's Division of Criminal Investigation.

There was the facial composite from the original investigation in the nineties and the partial sketch of the snake and cross tattoo beneath a bold black headline.

THE SIN EATER STRIKES—AGAIN!
THE SHOCKING RETURN OF IOWA'S MOST WANTED

Riley opened it on the double-page spread that went back over the historic assaults. There was a map of the attacks, most of them dotted across the city, a few beyond its limits. Each was marked by a photograph of the victim.

The eighteen women had dated hairstyles and clothing, but their smiles and eyes were timeless. Each photograph had been taken before the attack, given to police or press by family and friends—a holiday snapshot, a professional portrait, a school photograph. Each spoke of a story cut short. Three of the women had been killed by the Sin Eater, but the wounds sustained in body and mind by the fifteen who survived would have altered the landscape of all their lives. Riley knew the poisonous roots that could grow in that broken ground.

Below the map was a photograph of the snake symbol, sprayed in scarlet. She held it out to Altman. "See?" She nodded to his phone's screen, which still displayed the letter left for Cook.

His frown deepened. "See what?"

"Each *S* in the message. They're the same as this." Riley pointed to the sprayed symbol in the newspaper. "I thought it was just a particular style of the handwriting. But they could be markers. A signature of sorts?"

Altman was shaking his head, but his eyes, switching between the images, had slanted in study. "Could be coincidence."

"The state's first female governor gets a letter telling her to return to her place in the home and threatening her family at the same time as a prolific attacker of women is believed to have reappeared? The police say there's a religious element to the attacks. Look at the wording of the letter. *Your curse?*"

Altman was quiet now, inspecting the images. He went to speak, then stopped, his eyes casting over Riley's shoulder. He straightened. "Ma'am."

Riley turned to see Connie Meadows in the doorway, FBI mug gripped in one hand. "Morning, ma'am," she echoed.

Meadows nodded, but her attention remained on Altman. "How's the Cook case going? Anything more on this potential suspect?"

"I just got a lead on the car we believe the suspect left the capitol in," Altman told her, pocketing his cell. "A vehicle matching the one in the surveillance footage has been found by Des Moines PD. It was reported stolen six days ago. One day before the letter was left. They're still conducting their investigation. I'm on my way there now."

"Good. Make sure you keep State in the loop on this."

"I spoke to the chief this morning, ma'am. They've increased security for the governor and her family. Put a watch on her daughter's school."

"Keep me informed."

As Meadows turned to go and Altman made for the door, Riley realized he wasn't going to share her theory. She didn't want to make enemies here, but neither would she let a possible lead slip away without proper investigation. "Ma'am, we were just discussing another possibility."

Meadows looked back. "Yes?"

Ignoring Altman's glare, Riley told her boss her suspicions.

When she'd finished, Meadows turned to Altman. "Contact Julius Verne at DCI headquarters. See what he thinks. And keep Fisher with you on this for now."

The burned-out vehicle squatted on a patch of scrubby wasteground between Dean Lake and the Union Pacific rail yard, near a boxcar graveyard. It had started snowing as Riley and Altman left the precinct—Altman calling the DCI on the way, leaving a message with a secretary—and, by the time they arrived at the scene, the car looked like a blackened pudding surrounded by a dusting of powdered sugar.

A Des Moines PD cruiser and a black van were parked on a patch of gravel near the rail tracks. Two uniformed cops stood by the squad car, noses nipped red by the snow, which was settling on their caps. A third figure was moving around the vehicle, dressed in protective overalls. As they got out of the Tahoe, one of the cops gave a half salute to Altman before taking Riley in with a sideways glance.

Altman's boots planted big black patches in the white ground as he crossed to them.

"How's it going, Altman? Haven't seen you at Boone's in a while."

"For warm beer and stale chips? No thanks. Besides, that joint's always lousy with cops."

"You're just scared we'll bust your ass at pool again," said the other officer. "Can't handle the competition."

Riley stood in the intimacy of their banter, feeling like a third wheel. It didn't look like Altman was going to introduce her. An intentional slight, she guessed, to show his displeasure at the fact she was back on the case.

Altman took out his notepad. "What've we got?"

"Car was taken off the street six nights ago, from a suburb in Urbandale. Husband reckons the wife left the keys in it after the school run."

Altman gave a grunt. "Address?"

Leaving them to it, Riley headed to where the crime scene technician was inspecting the abandoned car. The vehicle—an older model Ford Taurus—was blistered black. Ash coated the earth around it, turning the settling snow gray. Although the fire had burned itself out, Riley could smell a trace of it in the frigid air. A caustic perfume of melted rubber and scorched metal.

"Hi," she called to the technician, who was crouched by the driver's side, carefully cutting away a charred piece of seat. She flashed her badge. "Riley Fisher, FBI."

The man didn't offer his name, but gave her a half smile before returning to his task. His goggles were misting with his breath.

"Gasoline?" she ventured.

"I won't know for sure until I get into the lab." He sniffed, his nose running in the cold. "So, you guys think it was involved in another crime?" He dropped the sample he'd taken into a glass jar.

Riley looked around for Altman. He was still chatting with the cops. "It might have been used by a suspect we want to question over a threat to Governor Cook."

The technician blew through his cheeks. "Politics, man." He screwed on the jar's lid. "Whole world's going to hell."

Riley felt the snow seeping into her boots. Altman had finished up with the cops and was heading over. Halfway across, his cell rang. As he took it from his pocket and looked at the screen, she saw his expression change. He turned on his heel as he answered, striding away. There was the rumble of a freight train approaching. She caught Altman's voice, rising above it.

"I'm not playing these fucking games anymore, Travis. You'll get me that meeting!"

The train loomed beyond the bare splay of trees that bordered the nearby lake, the clattering shriek of its wheels obscuring the rest of Altman's words. Crows took to the sky in a ragged black cloud.

"Got something here."

Riley turned back as the technician shouted over the clamor. Taking a camera from his equipment case, he crouched to take photographs.

She went closer, careful not to disturb the scene. The technician dug a gloved hand down the side of the driver's seat. "What is it?"

He rose and came over, meeting her beyond the circle of scorched earth, his protected feet making soft indents in the snow. He was holding up a key ring. A plastic disc dangled from a short chain. There was no key attached. Half the plastic was melted. "Could belong to the car's owners? Could be something from your suspect?" The technician shrugged as if to say the mystery wasn't his to solve.

On the undamaged half of the disc were looping yellow letters in an outdated script.

The O

There were ghost shapes of other letters beneath the charring, but Riley couldn't make them out. "I can't read it."

"Gotta say, I'm amazed it survived at all," said the technician, slipping the key ring into an evidence bag. "Whoever burned this vehicle was pretty determined to destroy it."

Riley followed his gaze to the warped remains of the car, slowly disappearing under the snow. Beyond, the last of the tank cars showed its rusted back to her and the train rattled on.

"What've you got?"

She turned to see Altman beside her. His phone had disappeared, but that blaze of anger she'd glimpsed remained branded in the hard lines of his face.

12

Riley stood at the window, looking out. The sun flared in her eyes through the gaps in the blinds. The headquarters of the Department of Public Safety was situated across from the capitol building, affording her an impressive view of its grand façade.

The DPS was the largest law enforcement agency in Iowa and various divisions came under its umbrella, from State Patrol and the state lab, to the fire marshal and narcotics enforcement. It dealt with everything from missing persons and criminal records, to forensics, cybercrime, and gambling regulations. In her years at the sheriff's office, she'd had dealings with the department, but mostly just calls to the lab to check on test results. This morning, when Altman told her they had a meeting with Julius Verne of the Division of Criminal Investigation, she'd had a surreptitious check of the division's website to familiarize herself with it.

The DCI was responsible for running complex criminal investigations across the state's ninety-nine counties, in collaboration with local and federal law enforcement. *If you have a passion for solving crimes—* read a job advertisement on the site—*consider a career with Iowa's very own "detective bureau."*

The promise of the place sounded more exciting than it looked, Riley thought, turning to the DCI's incident room, into which she and

Altman had been ushered. The drab walls were pocked and marked where things had been tacked or taped to them over the years. Two large boards took up one end. The only real color in the room was concentrated there, in two separate clusters of photographs, sketches, and maps. The air smelled of old carpet and marker pens.

The door opened and the young woman who'd shown them in reappeared with two mugs. She had neat blond hair and a tentative smile. She wore a plaid skirt and a high-necked cashmere sweater that Riley thought looked rather dated and demure for her age, but then, Noah Case dressed like an old English professor, so perhaps this was the height of fashion for twentysomethings.

"Thanks," Altman said, not looking up from his phone as the young woman set a cup carefully beside him. Sunlight threw tracks of light across the desk he'd seated himself at, making himself at home.

"Detective Verne shouldn't be long," she assured, handing Riley the other. Her eyes went to the wall of photographs before darting away. With a bob of her head, she left.

Riley cradled the coffee as she returned to her study of the boards. She could understand why the young woman afforded them only a fleeting glance. They were tough to look at, even for a seasoned investigator.

The first cluster of photographs surrounded a map of Des Moines and the outer suburbs. Taped above it was a timeline.

1990–1996

Riley had seen some of these pictures in yesterday's paper. The portraits and snapshots of eighteen women. What she hadn't seen was the aftermath: the popular schoolgirl and the retired nurse, the bright college student and the loving mother of three—turned victim. Bruises blooming black, eyes swollen shut, fractured jaws and broken bones, ligature marks and stitched-up stab wounds.

Most had been taken in hospitals—ID bands and patterned gowns visible. But in three the bodies had been photographed where they'd been found. One victim was slumped facedown on a bed, her night-dress bunched up to her back, the sheets around her stained brown with blood. Another was sprawled on a pile of sodden cardboard boxes behind a Dumpster, one scuffed high heel twisting away from her foot, her hair clotted with dark matter where a section of her skull had been bashed in. A third was half submerged in water, her bloated limbs tangled in tree roots.

Each of the eighteen pictures had a name above it—*Bobbi Kinzel, Abigail Dunbar, Nicky Johnson, Maria Perez*—along with a date and a time. A July evening. A November morning. A January midnight. One brutal moment. Each photograph was stuck with a pin that was connected by colored thread to another pin on the map, showing the location where the victim had been attacked. A web of pain that covered the city.

Among them were photographs and sketches of crime scenes. Several had close-ups of the snake symbol that had been the highlight of the press conference: daubed above a bed in what looked like blood, painted on a brick wall, scratched in mud. There was also a photograph of a partial boot tread in soil, a ruler beside it to show scale.

The second cluster of images displayed the victims of the recent attacks. Eleven in total. Most had question marks above them, with the exception of the now-familiar face of Hayley Abbot and another woman, with curly red hair and inquisitive eyes. *Megan Thomas*. Riley moved closer to study a photograph of a kitchen, where the snake symbol had bled lines down a tiled wall. There were spatters and smears of blood around a basin and an apple on the floor, a bite gouged out of it.

At the end of the two boards, pinned alone, was the facial composite of the suspect that had been shown on the news. The man the papers called the Sin Eater. Those deep-set eyes stared at her out of his jigsaw of a face, stitched together from disparate memories.

Riley imagined the gleam of them in the shadows of an alley, foot-steps quickening on a lonely path, the creak of a window sliding open. The shock each woman would have felt, flaring into terror. As she stepped back to survey all their smiling faces, horribly juxtaposed with

what had been done to their bodies, she could feel their helplessness as
a tightening in her own chest, their suffering as a catch in her breath.

"Fogg."

She turned at Altman's voice to see a man had entered the room,
carrying a file. She recognized him from the press conference. The detective wasn't wearing the brown suit today, just a pair of gray slacks
and a crumpled blue shirt. Salt-and-pepper stubble crusted his chin.
His badge was clipped to his belt beside his holster, where the rosewood
grip of a Colt protruded.

Altman had half risen, but the man gestured him to stay seated with
an easy wave of his hand. As his attention shifted to Riley, Altman
made the introductions. "This is Riley Fisher. Our rookie," he added.
"Riley, this is Fo—Julius Verne."

"Fogg is just fine," said the detective. He laid the file on one of the
desks and perched on the edge. "Sorry to keep you. As you can imagine, we're pretty slammed here." His gaze went to the photographs, his
brown eyes watery in the light slanting through the blinds. He looked
like a man who'd spent a long time staring at these images.

"How's the hunt going?" Altman asked.

"Phones have been ringing off the hook since the conference. Got
the team following leads. No breakthroughs yet."

The young woman returned, carrying another mug.

"Here you go, sir."

"Thanks, Jenna."

When she left, Fogg took a cautious sip, then set it down with a
wince. "If I could sneak past her, I'd make my own," he said in a con-
spiratorial murmur. "It's a bit embarrassing to have to tell your assistant
you don't like their coffee after four months of drinking it." He cleared
his throat, opened the file, and pulled out a copy of the message left for
Governor Cook. Each letter *S* had been circled in red.

Riley guessed Altman had mailed it to him yesterday after they'd
returned from the stolen car. The charred key ring the technician had
found beside the driver's seat had been signed over to the FBI and sent
to the lab at Quantico for analysis, in the hope they might be able to decipher the rest of the writing. This morning, on the drive over, Altman

had told her he'd sent a picture of the key ring to the family who owned the stolen vehicle. None of them recognized it.

"What do you think?" Altman asked Fogg, straight to business. "Could that be from your suspect?"

Fogg set the copy on the desk. "I'm not going to rule anything out. These letters . . . ?" He glanced at the message. "I agree, they look enough like his signature mark to merit investigation."

"But?" said Altman, tilting his head at Fogg's tone.

"It would certainly be a new approach for my suspect. He's never been political before."

"We've never had a female governor before," Riley said.

Both men looked around at her. She held their gazes. She might be the rookie, as Altman had so gracelessly noted, but she was still a special agent with the FBI. She had rank and power here.

Fogg, at least, offered a smile. "Can't argue with that." He looked back at Altman. "What about the Madden case? Could there be any connection there?"

Altman shifted. "Karl Madden was indicted by a grand jury last month. He's in federal prison, awaiting trial."

Riley thought of Rebecca Page's request outside Cook's office.

Take this seriously. More than last time.

"Any other suspects in view?" Fogg asked. "Someone specifically targeting the governor?"

"She's had a lot of abusive correspondence since she took office," answered Altman. "State has given me access. We're going through it for possible matches."

Riley had spent much of last night sifting through the stack Altman had dumped on her. It was, as Rebecca had intimated, horrific. Emails calling Jess Cook a bitch and a whore. Letters that wished she would get cancer and die. Messages describing in detail the ways in which they would torture her, burn off her breasts, and rape her with pieces of furniture.

The worst were anonymous, but some people had boldly signed their names. Many were from men, but there were a surprising number from women, who seemed equally appalled at having a female in charge. The technician at the burned-out car had said the world was going to hell. Wading through this torrent, Riley had the feeling they were already there.

"State police have tracked and arrested several of the worst offenders in recent months," Altman was telling Fogg. "Many of the others are probably just bored kids or the usual trolls."

Riley thought of Javier Morales from the governor's office saying much the same. Nothing to be afraid of. Ignore them. Sticks and stones. She looked at the broken bodies of the women on the wall.

"You said a man was seen leaving the governor's office? Did you get much of a description?"

"White. Over average height, medium to heavy build." Altman shook his head. "The car is our best lead, to be honest. That and the key ring we found."

"Our suspect has never warned a victim before, that we know of," Fogg said after a pause. "He doesn't threaten. He attacks. However, he definitely stalked many, if not all of these women, which could perhaps fit with the surveillance on the governor and her family." Fogg returned his attention to the boards. "He knew routes home from work and school. Knew what time shifts ended and that a husband worked away on certain nights. Knew she lived alone and didn't lock her windows."

Riley felt the chill of these words. Someone able to exercise both patience and planning before the savagery of his attacks. "Is it possible Cook's election could have been a trigger?" She pointed to the cluster of photographs where Hayley Abbot smiled her bright, unknowing smile. "The recent attacks all occurred after Cook became governor."

"It is possible." Fogg's careful tone gave little away.

"Any theories as to why he might have stopped back in the nineties?" Altman wanted to know. "Prison?"

"I'd say that's top of my list," Fogg replied. "Or a job or relationship took him out of the state. Either one of which could have ended recently and caused him to return, possibly to family or property. Any of those things could have been a stressor."

"Why does the media call him the Sin Eater?" Riley asked.

Fogg exhaled. "That damn name." He crossed to the boards and pointed to the picture of a college student from the early nineties. "Abigail Dunbar. The attacker pulled a sack over her head and beat her with a hammer. As she lay bleeding, he told her he would feed on her sins. Abigail's boyfriend gave an interview where he revealed this. Some hack coined the moniker and it stuck. Sin eating was an old religious practice in Britain. People would place a piece of bread on the recently deceased and pay a sin eater to consume it. It was believed, by this process, he would take on the sins of the dead. It has nothing to do with what's happening here," Fogg added. "But I'm sure the son of a bitch loves it."

Riley nodded. By calling him this the media countenanced the suspect's possible view that he was somehow doing God's work. They legitimized his crimes. Glorified him even. "You mentioned his religious convictions in the press conference?"

"Early on he started quoting from Genesis during his attacks. He seems obsessed with the story of Adam and Eve. The latest victim, Megan Thomas, was forced to bite into an apple before he brutalized her. This was a particularly vicious assault, even for him." Fogg tapped the board next to the photograph of the redheaded woman. "She's a therapist. Specializes in treating abused women. Works from home. Our suspect almost certainly kept some kind of watch on her. We're going through her list of patients and canvassing the neighborhood. I've been told the press has just gotten the details. It'll be everywhere by tonight."

Riley could hear the drag in his voice. That restless fatigue that comes from working a tough case. Too many victims and no end in sight. The pressure building. Reporters sniffing for a big scoop and demands from superiors. She knew that burden.

"He attacked her at home," Altman mused, still focused on Megan Thomas. "Is that unusual?"

"Very," said Fogg, glancing at him. "The only other time he entered a victim's property, back in ninety-four, he left a partial print." He pointed to the photograph of the boot tread. "And hair. Animal, not human. The original investigators believed he could be a hunter, given this and the weapons he favored. The stab wounds in some of the early victims were thought to have come from a hunting knife. He takes trophies too. Nothing materially valuable—a hairband, a sock, a bangle."

"What about the question marks you've got there?"

Fogg followed Riley's gaze to the other group of photographs around Hayley and Megan. "The first of the recent incidents we now suspect involved him occurred in February last year." He pointed to a picture of a young girl with plaits and a gap-toothed smile. "Beth Muir. A man passes her on the street, pulls her hair so hard he takes some out by the roots, tells her he can smell the sin on her. The girl told police he had a snake on his arm. It was logged as an isolated incident." Fogg moved on. "A few months later, Kelly-Anne Sawyer is attacked on her way home from work. He puts a plastic bag over her head and punches her repeatedly in the stomach. She was four months pregnant. She said her assailant had a large knife and wore a black mask with a red snake on it. Next, a sex worker, Colleen Traeger, is jumped at the end of a shift. He sexually assaults her, then beats her with a club. He daubs the image of an apple on her body with her blood, then photographs her before fleeing the scene. An old colleague of mine at Des Moines PD read the report on Traeger and recognized similarities with the original case. That's when I was brought in. Going through the state database, I found others I thought could be connected."

"And you're certain it's the same man as before?" Altman wanted to know. "Your suspect would be midfifties by now, perhaps older if that original composite is accurate."

"He could have taught someone," Riley offered, thinking of cases she'd studied at the academy. Infamous stalkers, rapists, and serial killers, and those who worshiped them. "Inspired them."

Altman kept his eyes on Fogg. "What about a copycat? The Sin Eater case was all over the press in the nineties."

"It's something I considered. Until Hayley." Fogg's eyes went to the smiling face that had made the front pages. "I said the suspect would quote from Genesis. One thing the original investigators kept from the public was a line he would say. *I will greatly multiply thy sorrows.* It's what God says to Eve after she's eaten the apple. In the Bible it's sorrow, but my guess is the suspect is referring to his multiple attacks or perhaps the wounds he inflicts. When the paramedics arrived, Hayley was saying what they thought sounded like *my sorrows*. I spoke to Megan Thomas before she went into surgery. She was able to confirm her attacker said this to her. That was never in the press. This, along with the snake signature—which he's started leaving again—makes me as certain as I can be that it's him. And that he's escalating. His final three victims in the nineties, before he went to ground, were murdered."

Riley had a recollection of Sunday morning services with her grandmother, cozied up on a pew, lulled by the droning voice of the priest. When her grandmother became too ill to leave the house, Riley stopped going to church too. She'd only ever been back for weddings and funerals. But the memory sparked an old knowledge. "It was her curse," she murmured. "After Eve ate the apple, God cursed her with the pain of childbirth and submission to Adam." She gestured to the letter. "This is your curse"?

Fogg was nodding, but it was a moment before he spoke. "This case is still open for a reason. The suspect is extremely good at what he does. He is strong, patient, tenacious, and cunning. He's evaded capture for three decades. My predecessors followed a lot of false trails in their search for him. They made mistakes. Overlooked leads. Dismissed witnesses whose testimony could have proved invaluable." Fogg's tone was measured, but his expression betrayed his frustration. "Let's just say I've inherited all that, at a point where the division's funding has come under increased constraints and where policing is subject to far greater levels of scrutiny. As I said, I think your letter merits investigation. There could be a connection. But let's not kid ourselves about what we're walking into. As you've seen, my case has just had gasoline poured all over it by the press. We add a threat to the governor's family . . . ?"

"The whole thing goes up," Altman finished.

Riley looked between the two men: one hostile and evasive, the other cautious and beleaguered; then her eyes returned to the women on the boards. Too many to take in at one glance.

A wall of sorrows.

13

Riley paced the empty room after the men had left. Altman had stepped outside to call Meadows. Fogg had been summoned by a colleague. They'd been gone almost an hour, leaving her alone in the incident room, with nothing but the women pinned to the boards for company.

Frustration simmered inside her, rising with every tick of the clock on the wall. She recalled how it had felt when her sheriff brought in the FBI back in Black Hawk—her investigation taken away from her, her position undermined; the humiliation that came with the feeling she wasn't good enough to solve the case alone. Elijah Klein had been at pains to let her know he wasn't there to step on her toes, but the power that had walked with him into her office—held up in that gold badge—had been unmistakable. So why didn't she feel something of that herself, here and now? The answer seemed obvious.

She thought of Altman introducing her as the rookie, then talking over her. Thought of the sheriff in Winterset, who'd called her by her first name and barely let her speak two words. Thought of some of her colleagues in Black Hawk—the laughter in the locker room that stalled when she entered, the murmured remarks, the sidelong glances. On entering this male world of authority, power, and violence, she'd still had to play the game. Speak up, but not too much. Do well, but not too well. Know your place.

YOU TOOK A PLACE THAT WASN'T YOURS

Riley paused by the boards. The sun had shifted around through the afternoon and the images were now cast in shadow. Her eyes went to the college student, Abigail Dunbar, whose attack had christened the Sin Eater. In one picture, Abigail was sitting in front of a birthday cake: nineties curls crispy with product, a broad grin, and eyes lit with candle flames. In another, wounds were dark brands on skin pale with trauma. She was only a few years older than Maddie.

Riley imagined the call coming in—from a hospital or police department. A call she herself had often had to make. Smiles slipping, knees weakening, a world crashing down. Two years ago, in the middle of her fraught investigation, Maddie had vanished without a trace. Riley remembered Ethan's voice on the line, frantic in a way she'd never heard. The clutch in her chest. The cold flood of fear. It made her think of her parents, that summer morning in Okoboji, all those years ago. Her mom opening the door of the bedroom in the vacation home, her surprise at finding it empty. Her voice calling in the yard, out across the still surface of the lake, not knowing her daughter was already gone, on a highway heading west, dust clouds rising beneath the truck's wheels.

As her eyes traveled across the horrors in the photographs—the woman in the water, on the bloody bed, behind the Dumpster—Riley knew how lucky she had been. One wrong turn on the way home. One missed ride or last-minute change of plan. One choice made in a lifetime of infinitesimal choices that had led them to where he waited.

The room felt suffocating. The musty air. The ticking clock.

Turning from the images, she headed out.

Fogg's assistant, Jenna, was tapping away at a keyboard. The young woman's desk was neatly ordered with pots of pens and stacks of files. She looked up at Riley with a wary smile. "More coffee?"

"No, thank you. I'm—" Riley turned as a door opened at her back.

Altman appeared, looking pensive. "Where's Fogg?"

Jenna stood. "He was on the phone. I'll see if he's free."

As the young woman hurried off, Riley turned to Altman. "What did Meadows say?"

Before Altman could answer, Fogg returned with Jenna. "Sorry to keep you. I've been on with MercyOne. Hayley Abbot is out of ICU. She's talking."

"Can I have a word?" Altman said, gesturing Fogg to the incident room.

Riley watched the two men disappear inside. Altman closed the door behind him, shutting her out. She stood there alone, the clatter of Jenna's manicured fingers loud on the keys. Pressing down her anger, she took out her phone. Still nothing from Logan, but there was a text from Maddie.

SO EXCITED!!!

It was followed by emojis of ice skates and snowmen. Riley's heart sank. She was thinking how to respond when Altman reappeared.

"We're done."

Riley followed him out, down the stairs into the parking lot. She matched his pace to the Tahoe, the chill galvanizing her. She kept her eyes on the agent, waiting for an explanation as to what was happening, but when Altman remained silent, her frustration spilled over. "OK, what's your problem?" she demanded, climbing in beside him.

Altman's brow knotted. "What?"

"You've got an issue with women? Is that it?"

He looked surprised, then indignant. "No."

"Then why are you sidelining me?"

"I'm not used to babysitting, that's all." He paused, a clenched expression on his face, then started the engine.

"I'm not some hick from the cornfields. I've got experience."

"You're on it, OK," Altman said, finally meeting her gaze.

She shook her head, exasperated. "On what?"

"Our priority remains the threat to the governor and her family, but Meadows is open to the possibility of a link with Fogg's investigation. The marks in the letter could just be coincidence, as I said. But she feels the wording of the threat and the timing—the Sin Eater's attacks starting up again after Cook's election—could point to a connection. She wants us to establish a task force with the DCI. Share leads and pool resources. She wants you on it."

Riley felt a fizzy mix of triumph and nerves. Two high-profile, high-stakes investigations. A chance to fly. Or to fall.

"I suggested to Fogg that you go with him tomorrow to interview Hayley Abbot," Altman continued. "You'll meet him at MercyOne. I'll go to the capitol and speak to the governor's security about this. In the meantime, keep going through Cook's correspondence, see if anything stands out—any possible links to the Sin Eater case."

Riley nodded, but remained quiet. Was Altman trying to get her out of the way by partnering her with Fogg? Did that matter? She'd spent enough time today looking at the photographs of the Sin Eater's victims to have every horrifying detail seared into her brain. She wanted on this task force. On this case. On the hunt.

"I'll drop you at the agency," Altman said, pulling out of the lot.

It was late afternoon and the traffic was building. "Drop me at my place," Riley told him. "It's closer. I can catch a cab tomorrow."

Altman turned on the radio, letting music fill the silence as Riley gestured him through the city past the fast-food joints of the strip mall, neon harsh in the subdued light.

As he pulled up outside the squat building by the railroad, with the cracks in the walls and the rusted fire escape that climbed to her window, she saw his look, caught between surprise and question. She got out and reached into the back seat to retrieve her purse. The stuffed bear she'd seen yesterday had gone.

"Riley."

Altman had wound down his window. She saw him hesitate and wondered for a moment if he was going to apologize.

"I'm happy for you to work with Fogg. A woman will look good on his investigation."

She bristled. Look good—not *be* good?

"But the threat against the governor and her family is my case," continued Altman. "I work alone. Always have."

"Meadows brought me into the agency because Cook knows me. She wanted me on this."

"And now you're on one of the biggest investigations in the state," Altman countered. "I'd make the most of that if I were you. Don't go picking fights when you've no need to. Trust me, Riley, you don't want me as an enemy."

She watched him drive off, engine gunning as he picked up speed.

14

Harlan stabbed out his cigarette and sat back with a grunt, feet propped on the coffee table. His empty beer bottles stood around the overflowing ashtray like soldiers at a dead campfire. The lingering smoke hung in a spectral cloud, shifting in the light from the TV.

Kody felt it scouring his throat. He noticed his mom, dwarfed on the couch beside Harlan, surreptitiously fan her hand in front of her face. She'd quit smoking a few years ago and now hated the smell of it. But she never said anything about it to Harlan.

Harlan sniffed and picked up the remote. He flicked irritably through the channels, complaining whenever he clicked on something he disapproved of. "Fucking cooking shows? Waste of goddamn time." He gestured at Shelley with the remote. "Like they're gonna get you making some fancy French shit? You'd burn water." He laughed and shook his head.

Kody put his plate on the table. The remains of the meal looked like something scraped from the bottom of a Dumpster. It hadn't tasted much better.

"You want some more, sweetheart?" asked his mom, leaning over to look worriedly at his plate. "You barely ate a bite."

"I'm good."

Kody felt his phone vibrate. He pulled it from his pocket. There was a text from Troy, talking about a new game he was playing.

Fucking sick, man!
You gotta see this.

Kody grinned. He could sit here bored and hungry, steeping in Harlan Judd's smell of smoke and beer farts—or he could head to Troy's. There, he'd be warm, Troy's mom would bring snacks and soda, and he could lose himself for hours in a new world. Kody jumped on it like an escape hatch.

He sent a reply, telling his friend he'd be right over. He was rising to leave when his phone went again. Another message from Troy.

Sorry, bro. Can't tonight.
Reagan's here.

Troy ended it with a winking emoji that made Kody's flesh burn. *"Bitch."*

"What did you say?" Harlan growled, looking around at him.

"Nothing," said Kody, sinking back in the chair and gripping the arms until his knuckles whitened. He realized Harlan was still staring at him. "Nothing, sir," he muttered.

Harlan flicked to another channel and landed on the news. An anchor was speaking. There was a breaking news logo on the screen behind her.

"We can now confirm there has been another attack on a woman in the metropolitan area. Four days ago, Megan Thomas—a renowned therapist from Des Moines—was assaulted in her home, close to Easter Lake Park. Sources in the police say they believe the attack was perpetrated by the same suspect who assaulted Hayley Abbot. The suspect known as the Sin Eater."

A picture of Megan Thomas flashed up. She had curly red hair and blue eyes, creased with a smile.

Shelley sat forward, fingertips pressed to her chin. "My God. Another one? I hope they catch this monster."

"Cops here couldn't catch a fucking cold," muttered Harlan, but he stayed staring at the screen, the remote poised in his grip.

"The DCI has a tip line open," continued the anchor. "The number is showing at the bottom of the screen. And—" She paused, as if listening to someone in her ear. "Yes—we have a composite of the suspect. This is from the investigation in the nineties, so he will be older now. But we also have a picture of a tattoo he is believed to . . ."

Harlan changed the channel. The cheers from a hockey game filled the room, brash and discordant after the anchor's gravity.

"Harlan, honey, I was watching that," Shelley protested.

Harlan glanced sideways at her and she shut her mouth. She stood and stooped to take the plates from the table.

"Get me another beer, would you?" Harlan called as she headed for the kitchen. "You got some of that dessert I like?"

"Of course, Harlan."

He smiled and drained the last of his beer. "Good girl."

Kody slipped out, leaving Harlan staring at the game. As he was closing the door to his room, he heard the cheers vanish, replaced by the news anchor's solemn tones. He peered back over his shoulder. Harlan was hunched forward on the couch, arms on his knees, face white in the light from the TV.

His mom appeared in the kitchen doorway. "You want some dessert, sweetheart?"

Kody shook his head and entered his room, closing the door behind him. Sitting at his desk, he grabbed his headphones and turned the console on. He paused for a moment, listening to the sounds of the TV coming muted through the door. Then, he placed the headphones over his ears and drowned out the world.

15

Riley hated hospitals. The stark, clinical decor interspersed with jarring attempts at homeliness: a picture of a lake above a plastic row of seats bolted to the floor, a potted plant on a reception desk, its leaves wilting. The pervasive odors of chemicals and indignity.

As she walked in through the front doors, the smell took her straight back to the old folks' home. The reminder of that place was shot through with guilt. She was the one who'd put her grandfather in there. She hadn't even been around to hold his hand as he died.

Fogg was already there, waiting in reception, coat folded over his arm. The detective was wearing the brown suit again today. A gold pen and a notepad poked from the breast pocket. With his mask on, she couldn't read his expression to know how he felt about her presence here. She wondered if Altman had put pressure on Fogg—made her his problem. Or was it another case of optics over talent? Meadows wanted her because of her connection to Cook. Had Fogg wanted her just because she was a woman? Someone to help soothe the victims. A sympathetic face for the media. A soft touch.

"So—*Fog*?" Riley ventured as she watched the numbers count down above the elevator doors.

He glanced at her. "Fogg, as in Phileas."

"Oh. Of course. *Verne*."

"My father's great-great-grandfather brought the name over from France." Fogg's eyes crinkled at her flicker of surprise. "My mother's family was from Haiti." The elevator opened and they entered. "My chief back in homicide once remarked that if there were eighty ways around a case I'd find them all and, well, Fogg just stuck."

"You were tenacious?"

"I guess that's a nice way of saying a *goddamn drain on the department's budget*."

The creases around his eyes deepened and she found herself smiling too.

The elevator bounced to a stop and the doors slid apart. As Riley got out, her phone pinged. She looked at it expectantly, then sighed when she saw a message from her landlord, saying he'd send someone to look at the broken window after the holiday.

Last night's text to Maddie sat below it, read but still unanswered. Back at her apartment, buried under the hateful mountain of abuse sent to the governor, she'd messaged Maddie to say she wouldn't be able to have her for Thanksgiving—that she'd been put on a critical case, but would make it up to her at Christmas.

"Something wrong?" Fogg asked, as she slid the phone back into her pocket.

"My niece. She's pissed at me."

"How old?"

"Sixteen."

"Ah." Fogg nodded sagely. "That might take a while then."

"Daughters?"

"Two. Both thankfully a long way out of that phase."

They made their way down the corridor, passing nurses in plastic aprons and visors.

As they approached the ward they'd been directed to, Riley braced for the inevitable wash of memories. When she'd finally signed the bureau's application there had been a hospital room in her mind. Part of her had glimpsed the road ahead, leading straight and true as an Iowa highway from sergeant to retirement. Her and Ethan rotting away in the old house, Maddie gone to college, visiting less and less. Then on to a room like her grandfather's, her mind collapsing in on itself, her body at the mercy of others' kindness or cruelty. Her signature on that piece of paper had felt like a reprieve.

Entering behind Fogg, Riley saw this room was nothing like what she'd been expecting. Yes, there was the metal cot, the machines, and the clinical furniture. But the rest of the place was a riot of color. Balloons scrawled with GET WELL SOON! clustered in a bright bobbing crowd by the window. Every available surface was covered in flowers, cards, and candy. She felt like she was at a fair.

A man and a woman rose from their places at the side of the bed.

Fogg greeted them at a respectful distance, a nod in place of a handshake. "Mr. and Mrs. Abbot? I'm Detective Julius Verne. We spoke on the phone."

"We know who you are," said the woman. "We watched you on TV."

Hayley Abbot's mother was short and slight, but she had a frenetic energy about her—a fierce charge in her eyes and posture.

Mr. Abbot was a tall, stoop-shouldered man who returned Fogg's nod in silence.

"And this must be Hayley," said Fogg, his smile showing in his eyes as he focused on the figure in the bed, hooked up by wires and tubes to the machines beside her. An IV bag sagged above her.

Hayley's mother moved aside reluctantly, allowing him to take one of the chairs. Fogg draped his coat over the back and sat. Crossing his legs, he took out his pad and pen.

Hayley Abbot watched him out of her one good eye, which fluttered briefly to Riley, standing behind him. Her other eye was covered with padded gauze. There were stitches at her temple and one side of her mouth: black caterpillars that crawled across her skin. Purple bruises sullied her nose and jaw. More were visible on her body, dark clouds of them disappearing beneath the collar of her gown. A section of her skull had been shaved and bandaged.

"Well, I can honestly say I've never seen so many flowers," Fogg remarked.

Hayley tried for a smile, but it was more of a twitch. Her blue eye remained flat and dull.

"I'm not going to keep you long," Fogg assured. "But I wondered if you felt up to talking about what happened?"

The attempt at a smile vanished, but she gave a small nod.

"That's great, Hayley." Fogg depressed the top of his pen. "You were out jogging, is that right?"

Hayley nodded again, but her gaze faltered and drifted to her mother, who scooted over and sat in the chair next to her, grasping her daughter's hand.

Fogg kept his attention on Hayley. "My wife's been on at me to start," he confessed. "But between you and me it's a bit late to be chasing my youth."

"It's hard at first." Hayley's voice was whispery. "But you get better the more you do it."

"You got the bug, huh?"

"Yeah. I enjoy it."

A cloud passed across her face, but before it had time to settle, Fogg spoke again. "Your mom told me you go with your friend Tara?"

"Sometimes. More recently. With the news and everything."

Fogg nodded. "But not that day?"

"No. She called last minute. Her sitter canceled. I shouldn't have gone." Hayley looked at her mother. Her eye glistened. "I'm sorry, Mom."

"You've nothing to be sorry about," her mother said fiercely. She narrowed her eyes at Fogg. "It's the police who should be apologizing. They should've caught this monster."

"I remember running to Principal Park," Hayley murmured, her gaze on the ceiling tiles. "I was almost back at the parking lot. I could see my car. Then—" She swallowed. "He was standing over me."

"Did you get a look at his face?"

She tilted her head side to side. "He was wearing a mask. Black. It had something red on it. The letter S I think? He had a baseball bat." She inhaled. "He hit me and I fell. He took my hat."

"Your hat?"

"A pink beanie."

Fogg nodded as he wrote.

"He put something over my head. Some kind of white hood. It smelled. It was hard to breathe."

Riley watched the young woman's fingers creep out from the blanket to clutch the side of the bed. She realized her own hands had tightened into fists. She flexed them, drew a breath.

"Smelled?" prompted Fogg.

"Like mold. Like it had been lying somewhere damp." She shuddered.

"It's OK, baby," her mother said, smoothing her hair. She leveled Fogg with a stare. "She needs her rest."

"Mom . . ."

"It's been on the news all morning," Mrs. Abbot continued, gesturing at the TV angled in the corner of the room, on mute. "Another woman almost killed. In her own home!"

Riley saw a copy of today's *Des Moines Register* on the nightstand by the bed. The vicious attack on the therapist, Megan Thomas, had made the front page.

"How many more will he hurt before you *do* something? I've been speaking to the families of his other victims. We want to know what you're doing to catch him. Why is it taking so long, goddamn it? Why aren't you telling us anything?"

"Mrs. Abbot," Riley said softly. "Why don't you take a break? You must both be exhausted." Holding the woman's gaze, she drew it to Mr. Abbot, stooped at the end of their daughter's bed, his head in his hand. "Go get yourselves some coffee. By the time you're back, we'll be done."

The woman looked as though she was about to refuse, but then Hayley glanced at her. "Please, Mom. You need to eat."

Something seemed to loosen inside Mrs. Abbot, the fight leaving her. Kissing her daughter's forehead, careful to avoid the stitches, she allowed her husband to steer her out.

"I feel so bad," Hayley whispered when the door closed. "I've never seen them so upset."

Riley experienced the memory as a twist in her gut. Her father sitting opposite her, his face clenched, demanding to know what Hunter had done to her. The shameful sense that what had happened was all her fault—cemented by her father's fury.

How often, as a woman, to be a victim also made you culpable.

Should have fought back. Should have reported it at the time.

"They've been crowdfunding." Hayley waved a weak hand, making the IV bag shift. "Insurance won't cover all this. My dad needs an operation. I don't know what they'll do."

"I'm going to put your parents in touch with an advocate," Fogg told her. "They can try and help you seek restitution from the victim compensation program."

Hayley wasn't listening. "I shouldn't have gone," she repeated in a whisper.

Shouldn't have walked that route. Shouldn't have worn that dress.

Had you been drinking, Riley? Tell me!

"It's not your fault." Riley's voice came out sharper than she intended. As Hayley focused on her, she thought she saw a flare of recognition in the young woman's face.

"Did your attacker say anything to you?" Fogg asked, not seeming to notice the moment passing between them.

"He said something weird. Something like—the Lord would multiply my sorrows? And I think he took photographs of me." Hayley's mouth trembled. "There were flashes. Like from a camera."

"Can you describe his voice to me? Did he sound young? Or old? Did he have an accent?"

"I—I don't know. It all happened so fast. And with his mask and the noise from the road . . . ?"

"That's OK, Hayley," Fogg said, nodding as he continued to write.

Riley watched Hayley's mouth open then close. Her brow was creased, her eyes distant. Riley saw something else in them now—some scared and timid question. "You can tell us anything, Hayley," she said, quietly, carefully. Not forcing her. Knowing, deep in her own body, how this kind of interrogation could feel. She sensed Fogg looking at her, but, unlike Altman, he seemed content to let her take the lead. "Even if you're not sure about something."

Hayley pressed her lips together, as if holding in her words. She exhaled them quickly. "What if it wasn't him? The Sin Eater?"

"You mean, what if you were attacked by someone else?" Riley glanced at Fogg, who was sitting up straighter, pen poised.

Hayley sucked nervously at her dry lips.

"Is there someone you think would want to hurt you, Hayley?" Riley pressed gently. "Someone on your mind?"

"I could be wrong. I'm sure I'm wrong."

"That's for us to worry about, Hayley," Fogg interjected.

Hayley closed her eyes, then opened them again. "I work at a Realtor's now. But before that I was a secretary at an auto sales and restoration place over in Capitol East. Mustang John's?"

"I know the one," Fogg said. "Off Maury? American muscle cars?"

She nodded. "There was a guy there. Bret Childs. He worked in repairs. He started leaving notes on my desk, saying how he liked my hair, or the perfume I was wearing." She gave a small shrug. "I tried to laugh it off. But it got worse. He would buy me things—a coffee, candy. I didn't want to hurt his feelings or make things weird at work, so I just accepted them. But when he bought me a necklace with my name on it, I knew I had to stop it. I gave it back. Told him I was flattered, but not interested. I was nice about it." She looked for support in Riley, who nodded. "After that he changed. He would say things to the other men and they'd laugh at me. He put porn in my desk drawers." Her skin reddened. "Hard-core. Horrible."

"Did he ever touch you?" Fogg asked. "Ever threaten you?"

"No. But I know he followed me home from work, because he started posting notes under my door. Said he knew a guy I'd dated. Said he'd bought"—she spoke haltingly—"photographs. Said he was going to send them to my parents." Hayley looked fearfully at the door. "I've never told them."

"Did you report it to anyone?"

"I told Tara. She said I should punch Bret in the balls, then tell my boss."

"Did you? Tell your boss?"

"Mr. Jessip said he'd talk to him. But I know he didn't take it seriously. Boys will be boys, right?" She shook her head. "Bret just carried on. In the end, I left. That was a year ago."

"Have you seen Bret since?"

"I haven't seen him. But—and I know how paranoid this sounds—I sometimes think he's still watching me." She let out a long exhalation. "I just thought—what if it was him?"

"OK, Hayley. Thank you. You might recall more as you recover. I'm going to leave my details with your parents. You can call me anytime, day or night."

The door opened and her parents returned.

After finishing up with the Abbots, Fogg led the way back down the corridor. "His photographing of victims has cropped up a few times in the recent cases," he said, underlining something in his notebook. "It's not something he used to do in the past, that we know of. But, then, with changes in technology, he wouldn't have to run the risk of getting them printed now."

"What about the hood?" Riley asked as they reached the elevator. "Did the cop not find it at the scene?"

"The suspect always takes any tools or weapons he uses away with him. He's meticulous about not leaving evidence. That was good work, by the way," Fogg said, sliding his notebook into his pocket. "Getting her to open up like that."

Riley felt a rush of satisfaction at the compliment. For the first time since she'd arrived in the city, she felt her feet had landed on solid ground. "What next?"

Fogg called the elevator. "We pay this Bret Childs a visit."

16

Mustang John's occupied a large plot of land between a salvage yard and a Git N Go. A weathered billboard outside showed a photograph of a man, with a crooked grin and a greaser haircut. There was a speech bubble popping from his mouth.

Let us rebuild your American Dream!

Riley walked with Fogg across the potholed street, where garbage skittered in the breeze. Despite the cold, she was glad for the fresh air after the hospital.

The photographs she'd studied in the incident room were shocking, but to witness Hayley's suffering firsthand was an experience that went much deeper. She'd been drawn to this case since the press conference, but she felt it in a different way now, the horror of it working in under her skin.

The sun was a ghost behind the clouds. Pale light glinted on the chrome trims and polished grilles of the line of cars at the front of the lot. Old Mustangs restored to gleaming glory, Chevrolet Camaros and Dodge Chargers.

A man approached as they entered, greeting them with a salesman's smile. "Welcome to Mustang John's. I'm Larry. How you guys doing today?" He looked between Fogg and Riley, clearly sizing them up for a pitch, a question in his eyes as he took them in—older Black man in a good suit, younger white woman in a coat that had seen better days.

"Can't complain," said Fogg, scanning the place.

Beyond the rows of cars was a glass-fronted showroom, plastered in sale stickers. Beside it was a large corrugated structure, from which came the forceful throb of rap music.

"So, what can I interest you in?" Larry's widening smile showed off his bleached teeth. He reeked of cheap cologne. "Weekend warriors? Track beasts? Or one of our classics, lovingly restored?" He motioned to the Mustangs. "Feel like Steve McQueen."

"Bret Childs working today?" Fogg inquired, his eyes coming to rest on Larry.

The man frowned. "Why? You want something detailed?"

"You could say that," Fogg said, showing his DCI badge.

"Er. Sure thing." Larry led them toward the corrugated structure, glancing uneasily over his shoulder.

The body shop was lit by strip lighting, which flickered intermittently. The music was louder here, the rapper's voice riding the heavy beat. Inside the cavernous space, cars were suspended on hydraulics over pits. The place smelled of engine oil.

"Hey, Bret," Larry called, disappearing behind a gray Mustang, which had its hood propped open. "Some people here to see you."

"Oh, yeah?" came a lazy drawl. "Who?"

Larry's voice dipped to a hiss. *"Five-oh!"*

The music cut off abruptly.

A moment later, a stocky man appeared from behind the car. His pallid face contrasted sharply with his short dark hair and the goatee that bristled at his chin. He looked to be in his midtwenties, with muscled arms that strained the long sleeves of his overalls. "What's up?"

"I'll leave you guys to it," Larry said, sidling away.

"Hi, Bret," Fogg said affably, holding out his badge. "Detective Julius Verne, DCI. Got a few questions for you."

"Yeah?" responded Bret, with a jut of his chin.

"Can I ask where you were ten days ago? Late afternoon?"

"Why?"

"Do you know a young woman named Hayley Abbot?"

"Hayley?" Bret cocked his head. "Yeah. Worked in the showroom a while back. Sweet little ass on her." His eyes went to Riley. The corner of his mouth twisted.

She felt a spike of disgust.

"I'm guessing you've seen the news?" Fogg said, seemingly unruffled.

"Don't watch it. All fake." Bret dug his hands in the pockets of his overalls, leveled Fogg with a stare.

"Ah, well, let me enlighten you. Ten days ago, Hayley was brutally attacked."

"No shit?"

"Yup. No shit, Bret. Some asshole beat her face with a baseball bat."

Riley was surprised by the shift in Fogg's demeanor. The detective was speaking calmly, still wore that placid smile even. But something had changed. Like a knife, switched from its flat surface to its razor edge.

"Sucks for her. But I don't know why you're talking to me. Haven't seen her in over a year. Never spoke to her much."

"That's not what we heard, Bret. Love notes? A necklace?"

Bret blew through his teeth. "I might've given the girl some compliments. That ain't a crime." He flashed Fogg a swift grin, showing a tight row of teeth. "Right, bro?"

"No," said Riley. "But stalking and harassment are."

"Stalking?" Bret kept his eyes on Fogg. "Like I said, I hardly spoke to her."

"You didn't put porn in her desk drawer?"

"Nah."

"Any idea how that might have ended up in there?"

"It's an auto shop, man." Bret gestured at the wall above a workbench, where a calendar hung. Miss November was straddling a motorcycle, wearing nothing but stilettos and a red thong. "There's porn in everyone's desk." He sighed. "Look, she was a cute girl. But too—you know—*sensitive*."

Riley thought of Black Hawk. The locker-room banter and snide comments had faded, for the most part, when she made sergeant, but she knew that view of her by some male colleagues as weaker—less capable, more emotional—had simply been swept under the carpet with her promotion. It was still there, beneath all those *yes, ma'ams*.

"Say, isn't there some psycho attacking women?"

"So, you do watch the news?"

"Shouldn't you be out looking for him? I know my rights. This is police harassment."

"Where were you ten days ago, Bret?" Fogg repeated.

Bret strode to the workbench. His bravado was back. He picked up a datebook, licked a grease-black thumb, and flicked through it. "I was here. Working."

"What time did you finish?" Riley asked.

"About seven." Bret met her gaze. "You can check with my boss."

Riley thought she saw that smirk again at the corner of his mouth. It was gone before she could be sure, but it set her nerves jangling.

"Is your boss here?" Fogg asked.

"Mr. Jessip's home with his family." Bret's attention was back on Fogg. "You know it's Thanksgiving tomorrow, bro?"

"Bret, we're about as far apart from brothers as you can get," Fogg said with a cool smile, writing in his notebook. "What's Mr. Jessip's address?"

Bret jerked his head toward the showroom. "Larry'll give it to you."

As she walked back across the lot with Fogg, Riley felt the anger, bubbling up through the interview, boil over. She had been that girl once—at the mercy of a man like Bret, who thought he could do whatever he wanted without consequence, because that's what he'd been taught. *Boys will be boys.* She halted, hand slipping to her badge. She wasn't that girl anymore.

"What is it?" said Fogg, glancing back as she stopped.

Riley patted her pocket. "I think I dropped my wallet. I'll meet you at the car," she added, turning toward the body shop before Fogg could challenge her.

As Riley entered, she saw Bret Childs at the workbench, his back to her. He had his cell pressed to his ear and was knocking his knuckles impatiently on the wood. He must have sensed her, because he froze. Twisting around, he set the phone down quickly.

She was gratified to see a wariness in his eyes, that swagger gone. "Let's cut the crap, Bret. We both know you harassed Hayley. Hounded her out of a job." Riley held up a finger as he opened his mouth. "We both know you're a creep, with some sort of toxic fragility when it comes to women."

Bret's face flushed. He took a step toward her. Riley moved her hand calmly to her hip, beside her Glock. His eyes followed the movement and he stayed rooted where he was. The heat in his face remained, livid but impotent. Her eyes went to the cell lying on the workbench, the screen now dark. "Who were you calling?"

"No one." This jumped straight out of his mouth. He seemed to swallow it back. "A customer."

There was the sound of voices. Riley looked around to see two men in overalls approaching. They glanced curiously at her and Bret. She could see Fogg in the car, watching, waiting. "Bret, I want you to know that if you ever go anywhere near Hayley Abbot, I'll do everything in my power to make you wish you hadn't." Riley made sure he could see her hand, resting between her gun and her badge. "You understand?" She held his gaze until he nodded, silent and sullen.

"Find what you were looking for?" inquired Fogg as Riley climbed into the passenger seat.

She exhaled the tension that had built up like a charge inside her. "I think he's hiding something."

"I agree."

"You do?"

"I think he's hiding what Hayley accused him of. Harassment. Look, the guy might be a lowlife. But I don't believe he's our suspect. He wasn't even born when the attacks first began." Fogg paused. "Riley, this isn't the time for us to be accused of intimidation, even by a man like Childs."

She looked around at his warning tone, felt that new sense of solid ground slip beneath her feet. "I know. I'm sorry."

"OK." Fogg turned the key in the ignition. "We'll check out the son of a bitch's alibi."

17

The house on Beaver Avenue was a long single-story dwelling, with wooden shutters on either side of the windows, painted yellow. A two-car garage attached to the house was open to show a black Pontiac Firebird, the iconic gold bird splayed across the hood. The recent snow had melted, just a few patches left in the front yard.

There were lights on in the house. As Fogg parked his unmarked Buick in the shadow of a white oak, the roots of which had cracked the asphalt, Riley saw the twitch of a curtain.

Fogg was reaching for his coat when his cell rang. It connected to the car's system, flashing up on the screen. *Marcia.* He answered, cradling his phone to his ear. "Hey, I'm just—" He nodded. "I know." Another few nods. "I'll be there soon. Love you." Ending the call, he climbed out. "We'll make this our last stop today," he told Riley over the hood. "If I don't get home this evening the turkey isn't the only thing that'll be stuffed."

The oak's fallen leaves had formed a withered red carpet that shifted around them as they headed up the driveway. The afternoon sun had slipped below the houses. The air was sharpened by woodsmoke. Three pumpkins nestled by the front door, to which a wreath of maple leaves had been pinned. Fogg rang the bell, which played a tinny version of the theme song from *Bullitt*.

After a moment, a woman answered. She was wearing an apron patterned with cranberries. Her cheeks were heavily rouged and big gold hoops hung from her ears. Her smile faded as she looked between Riley and Fogg, her face drawing in. She edged in front of the door. "Can I help you?"

Fogg showed his ID. "Is Mr. Jessip home, ma'am?"

"He is," the woman said hesitantly. She looked nervously over her shoulder. "We're expecting people for dinner."

"We have a few questions about one of his employees. I promise we'll be out of your hair in no time."

She let them in reluctantly.

The foyer had polished wood floors and two little girls were skating about in their socks. "To your room, now," said the woman sharply, shooing them down the hall.

Riley could smell roasting meat. It made her think of home, as it used to be. Her mom in the kitchen, peeling potatoes for the Thanksgiving dinner. Her father in rare form, home for the holiday, pouring wine and arguing with her grandfather about politics. Her and Ethan squirting whipped cream for the pumpkin pie into their mouths when none of the adults were looking.

Thanksgiving wasn't the same after her parents' deaths. The dining room empty. The crystal glasses and china platters gathering dust. Most years, after her grandfather had gone into the home, it had been just her and Ethan, perched at the kitchen counter, sharing takeout in silence, until one of them gave up and retreated to their room. Often, she would take a shift in Patrol rather than suffer the awkwardness.

The woman led them to a door off the entrance hall, which had a plaque on it.

MAN CAVE—ENTER AT YOUR OWN RISK.

"I'll go get my husband. You can wait for him in here."

The room had a desk with a chair behind it and a leather couch opposite. There were shelves lined with books and models of classic cars. On the walls, framed photographs jostled for space. Many showed

Mr. Jessip—recognizable from the auto shop billboard—at car shows and drag races. One was of him leaning against the Pontiac Firebird. In another, he was younger, sporting a mullet and seated around a table with a group of men in a grand room with gold-papered walls. In the background was stage with a banner over it: RELEASE THE BEAST!

Beside this photograph was a page cut from a newspaper, in a gold frame. Mr. Jessip stood on the auto shop's lot in front of his employees. The headline above read "Mustang John—Speeding Ahead of the Competition." Riley stepped closer to study it. There was Bret Childs, arms folded, unsmiling.

The door opened and a man entered. John Jessip still looked like the photograph on the billboard, only ten years older and twenty pounds heavier. His hair, which had thinned and receded, was greased back, showing off his forehead, shiny with sweat. He wore a sweatshirt with the Mustang horse galloping across his chest.

"Hey there. How can I help?"

"Good evening, Mr. Jessip," Fogg said. "Sorry to bother you at this hour."

"It's Mustang John now," the man cut in. "My customers were calling me that for years. Made sense to change it officially." He gestured them to the couch. "This about Hayley? It shook me up some when I saw her on the news."

"I'm afraid it is." Fogg sat awkwardly beside Riley, the couch too low and his legs too long.

"Can't imagine what her folks are going through. Got daughters myself."

"When did you last see Hayley?"

Mustang John sat behind his desk. "Must be coming up on a year since she worked for me."

"How was her relationship with Bret Childs?"

"Bret? What's he got to do with this?"

"Was there anything between him and Hayley when she worked for you? Anything romantic? Or inappropriate?"

"I guess you could say he had the hots for her," Mustang John admitted. "A few of the guys did. She was a pretty girl."

"Did she ever complain to you about him? His behavior?"

Mustang John sighed. "She did. But I've had young women like Hayley work for me before."

"Like what?" Riley asked.

"I told her, when she first started in the showroom, a bit of flirting with our customers never hurt. An attractive female wandering around can be a bonus. Gets a man's blood fired up, you know?" His attention was back on Fogg. "But she started showing up in these short, *short* things." He whistled. "Didn't leave much to the imagination. Bret would follow her around like a puppy."

"Would you say he harassed her?" Riley pressed.

"No," Mustang John responded firmly. "He might've asked her on a date once or twice. Sent her flowers. But after a while, he realized she just liked the attention. He went out and got himself a real girlfriend. Happiest I've seen him."

"And Hayley?"

"To be honest, I think she was jealous. She wasn't the center of his world anymore. She made some pretty serious allegations against him. The kind that can ruin a young man's career. I did my due diligence," Mustang John added. "I spoke to Bret's colleagues, asked around. They all said she was making it up. I asked her for evidence, but she never produced any. After that she left. Didn't even give her notice." He leaned forward, arms on the desk. "I'm sorry about what happened to her, but honestly I thought she might end up in trouble. She was the sort to court it. The sort who cries wolf a few too many times, then complains when she gets bit."

Riley thought of Hayley's face, the bruises and stitches. Even when the physical signs of the attack faded, the damage would remain, beaten deep into her. She would never be the same.

"OK," Fogg was saying, "we need to check Bret's whereabouts ten days ago. He claims he was working."

"Ten days? You can't think Bret had anything to do with her being attacked?" When Fogg didn't answer, Mustang John opened one of the desk drawers and pulled out a datebook. He flicked through it, then nodded. "Yup. He was pulling a late shift at the shop. Didn't finish until seven."

"You saw him personally?"

"Sure did." The man paused. "Bret can be a dumbass. And he sometimes thinks with the wrong head, like most men his age. But he's a good kid at heart. Wouldn't hurt anyone."

"All right, sir. Thank you for your time."

As they walked back down the driveway, Fogg was the first to speak. "I think we've gone as far as we can down this road." He shook his head at Riley's taut expression. "Let's say Bret did all the things Hayley accused him of and that Jessip turned a blind eye. Other than possible sexual harassment charges and maybe constructive dismissal we have no real evidence of any other crime here." He opened the Buick's door. "We'll regroup after tomorrow. Start fresh."

Riley lingered for a moment, eyes on the house. Down the street, lights had winked on in many of the windows. She could hear festive music coming from somewhere. She climbed into the car, rubbing at her stiff neck muscles, feeling the knot of scar tissue under her fingers.

Fogg waited until she was looking at him. "Look, I'm glad to have you guys on board. The DCI budget is straining at the seams. We've got the usual backlogs at the state lab and rapid access to Quantico will be a real help. A fresh pair of eyes is always welcome, and Altman told me you have experience with complex cases."

Riley was surprised Altman had sold her as a virtue, then guessed he'd most likely just been trying to palm her off on Fogg. Get her out of his way.

"But I've been working this investigation for a long time, Riley. There's a lot of pressure here. That means we need to chip away slowly, carefully, or risk the whole thing coming down on our heads in court. If we're going to make this task force work, I need you to understand that."

She felt, again, the precariousness of her place, caught between Meadows and Jess Cook, Altman and Fogg: all their different positions and expectations. She wasn't at the top of the ladder anymore. There were people and politics way above her. One wrong step and the fall could kill her career. "I hear you."

Fogg nodded, seemingly satisfied. He started the car, his voice lightening as he spoke. "Seeing family tomorrow?"

"Yes," she lied.

"Glad to hear it. My wife gets frustrated by the job sometimes, but she keeps me sane. Lord knows we need good people around us in this line of work."

As Fogg drove through the darkening streets, Riley slipped her phone from her mother's coat. There was a text from Aunt Rose, with a selfie of her and Lori, snuggled with Benjamin at the Waterloo Thanksgiving parade.

Happy holidays from us.

Nothing from Maddie. Nothing from Logan.

She thought of her cold apartment. Unpacked boxes around the bed and a stack of meals for one in the refrigerator.

18

Riley pulled on the black dress, having to contort herself to do up the zipper at the back. As she stood in front of the bathroom mirror, smoothing it down, she saw a stain on the shoulder. She'd last worn the dress that final weekend at the academy.

She and her fellow recruits had gone into Quantico for one last drink before they scattered across the country to their new postings. The younger ones had chosen some neon nightmare overlooking the Potomac, with a permanent happy hour. Fresh from her grandfather's funeral, Riley hadn't been in the mood to celebrate and she'd ended up at the bar, talking to a guy there on government business. A couple of beers in, they'd started on the bourbons and, in a haze of alcohol and unwanted emotions, she'd agreed to the invitation to his motel.

The next morning, in a cab back to the base, window down, air full of the green scent of sap, she'd not even felt regretful. It had been so long since she'd been kissed or touched. Skin to skin. No questions. No strings.

She faltered, staring at her reflection, then reached across the bathroom counter for her phone. She tapped on voice mail.

You have one saved message.

"Hey, Sarge." Logan's voice filled the silence. Easy. Familiar. "Just wanted to wish you happy Thanksgiving."

There was muffled conversation and laughter in the background. Riley could imagine him at home with his family, relaxed in T-shirt and jeans; his sister, Carol, pouring the wine; his niece and nephew vying for his attention.

"Got your message. Sorry I didn't call back sooner. Too busy sorting out your old department. Jeez, the mess!" He paused. "Seriously, it's been crazy here with the holiday. But I wanted to ask if you're—?"

Carol's voice called out. "Logan! Dad says the nut roast is burning!"

"Ah, shit." Logan sighed on the line. "Gotta go. I'll call you soon, OK."

End of message. Press one to delete. Two to save.

Riley's finger hovered over the screen. She pressed two again.

It was three days since Thanksgiving, and she hadn't heard back from Logan. She'd wanted to call—find out what it was he was going to ask her, the question of which had been itching at her. But work had kept her busy and, besides, she didn't want to seem overly keen.

Message saved. You have no new messages.

She had spoken to Ethan over the holiday, hoping to talk to Maddie. Her brother had sounded tired. "She's at her mother's."

"She's not answering my calls."

"She's just pissed she couldn't come visit you. You shouldn't have promised her, Ri."

Riley had clamped down the urge to snap back. Ethan's own broken promises would fill a goddamn book. "Just tell her I love her, OK? That I'll make it up to her."

"Sure," he'd said on a long exhale.

Finishing the call, Riley had been left wondering if her brother was tired—or stoned. Had Ethan fallen back into bad habits without her there to keep an eye on him? She'd thought about calling Aunt Rose, asking her to check in on him, but had stopped herself. She had to cut the cord sometime. Focus on her own life. As much for them as for herself.

She inched on a pair of pantyhose, then squeezed her feet into some peep-toe pumps. There was nowhere to hide the switchblade Logan had given her, but a snug shoulder holster under her black suit jacket concealed her Glock. She rubbed at the stain on the dress until it faded a little. It would have to do. She had nothing else suitable for a black-tie event and no time to get anything. Meadows had given her the assignment that morning, telling her Jess Cook was speaking at a charity gala in the skywalk downtown and she was to go along and—in Meadows's words—babysit. Cook's family would be attending the event and Meadows wanted an FBI presence there, alongside troopers from Iowa State Patrol. Riley wondered how Altman might react, given his insistence the governor was his territory, but Meadows had made it clear that whatever leads they might pursue in connection with the Sin Eater investigation, she wanted their primary focus to remain on the threat to Cook and her family. She was simply following orders.

She was glad for the chance to fly solo this evening, rather than tiptoeing her way around Altman and Fogg in their respective—and guarded—domains. A chance to show Meadows she was willing and able to take on any assignment, even if it was just babysitting.

A ping of her cell told her the Uber was here. Outside, in the corridor, music vibrated in the walls, coming through the door of the reclusive tenant down the hall. She headed downstairs, damp creeping up the corners, the smell of it permeating the place. The evening air stung her skin as she exited the apartment block, tiptoeing in her pumps along the pathway shoveled through the snow. It had fallen last night in a storm that brought down power lines in several counties. The wind had dropped off, leaving the snow banked high, powdery and sparkling under streetlights.

On the drive through the city, Riley caught two sightings of the Sin Eater, staring down from roadside billboards between advertisements for Coke and health-care plans. Meadows had spoken to the field office in Omaha, which had secured the task force use of the FBI's National Digital Billboard Initiative. There had been some concern about the value of the nearly thirty-year-old facial composite, but with the recent attacks all being perpetrated by a masked suspect, who often blinded his victims with bags or hoods, there was little else to go on. If Fogg's speculation that the Sin Eater could have returned to the area due to some connection was correct, the hope was that someone might still recognize that face.

Fogg had spoken to the latest victim, Megan Thomas, the day after Thanksgiving. The details of her ordeal had been chilling—the way her attacker had humiliated her, making her dress up for him before brutalizing her. He'd forced her to put a hood over her head that she thought had been painted with the symbol of an apple. Megan had corroborated Hayley's account of the hood smelling damp. She also confirmed he'd taken photographs of her.

In their meeting yesterday, Fogg reiterated his fears over the suspect's escalation. From fleeting violence on the street, to surveillance of his victims and calculated and prolonged attacks.

He's getting more confident.

They'd also gotten the results back from the bureau's lab on the letter and photograph left for the governor—no prints, other than those of Jess Cook and her staff. Chemical testing had shown a standard ink pen had been used and the paper for the letter and photograph were both common brands. A forensic document examiner had looked at each *S* in the letter and compared it to the snake symbols left by the Sin Eater at crime scenes over the years, but concluded that any match of writing style was impossible, due to the nature of the different materials and surfaces used.

The key ring found in the burned-out vehicle used by the man seen leaving the capitol remained at Quantico, awaiting results. They'd continued to trawl through the governor's correspondence, but had found no obvious links to the Sin Eater.

After crossing the river, the oil-black water slick with lights, the cab dropped Riley on Grand Avenue at the entrance she'd been directed to for the skywalk—a series of elevated walkways that connected fifty-five buildings downtown, stretching over four miles. A red carpet lolled like a tongue from the open doorway. Attendees in tuxedos and gowns were filing through, past reporters snapping pictures at a step and repeat, covered with the names of sponsors. The glacial air held a pungent, animal taint. This affluent area of the city, with its high-rise offices and hotels, was close to several meat processing and rendering plants, reminding modern inhabitants of their city's agricultural heritage.

Showing her ID to security, Riley followed the line of people up a staircase to a glass walkway. Music and conversation drifted from deeper in. Masked waiters held trays of drinks and canapés. She declined their offerings as she headed along the system of sky bridges, streams of cars flowing through the streets below.

The walkways opened into the vast, vaulted space of a former mall, recently abandoned—an empty heart at a confluence of deserted arteries. A band was playing at one end on a makeshift stage, in front of a row of shuttered shops, where signs saying EVERYTHING MUST GO! still hung.

There were cloth-covered tables around which men and women clustered, chatting and bidding on items for the charity auction. Among them were senators, members of the city council, and players for the Iowa Wolves. High above, the glass ceiling was slabbed white with snow, like icing on a cake. All around, state troopers maintained a visible presence, guarding dormant escalators and gloomy corridors.

It didn't take long for Riley to spot Jess Cook. The governor was smiling for a reporter's camera in the midst of a group of women. She was wearing a dark green dress, simple but elegant. Rebecca Page, the governor's chief of staff, and her office manager, Javier Morales, were with her. Seeing Riley, Rebecca leaned in and spoke to Cook.

Excusing themselves, the two women came over.

"Riley, thank you for coming," said Jess. "I told Connie Meadows it wasn't necessary. As you can see, we're well protected." The governor looked to the level above, where cops surveyed the throng. "I hope I haven't ruined your evening."

"It's no trouble, ma'am."

"Please, call me Jess." The governor gestured to an area away from the music.

Riley followed and the three women sat together at an empty table.

"We've been told the agency has formed a task force with the DCI on the Sin Eater case," said Rebecca. "That you're working on it?"

"That's right."

"I remember those attacks in the nineties," murmured Jess. "That man haunted Des Moines back then." She scanned the crowd, then fixed on a man dancing in front of the band, with a girl in a blue dress. "I feel guilty, worrying so much about my own family."

Riley recognized the man and girl from the grainy photograph—Jess's husband, Mark, and their daughter, Ella. The ones the suspect had promised would pay the price, if she didn't give up her place as governor.

"We have all this protection, while most women in this city remain vulnerable." Jess met Riley's gaze. "How do you deal with it? Knowing he could strike at any time? Knowing you can't protect them from that?" She faltered, shook her head. "I'm sorry, I don't mean that you *can't*."

"It's OK," Riley assured. "It is tough, especially in violent cases." She paused, thinking of her anger after seeing Hayley in the hospital bed. Bret's smirk and Mustang John's implication that Hayley was somehow to blame for what had been done to her. She'd forced that anger down after Fogg's warning, but it remained, a hard lump inside. "You have to step back and separate yourself. Work the problem. Sometimes, pray for a bit of luck. Police work is ninety percent perspiration, ten percent inspiration, my grandfather would say."

"Sounds like politics."

A shadow loomed over them. Riley shifted instinctively, hand to her side.

"Good evening, Governor." A man with slicked-back hair, tall and slim as a pencil in his tuxedo, was looking down at them. He held two glasses of champagne. He offered one to Jess, ignoring Riley and Rebecca. "I haven't had a chance to congratulate you."

Jess accepted the glass and placed it on the table. "Thank you, Ted."

Riley heard the terseness in her tone. The governor's face had lost any vulnerability, her expression now cool.

"You flexed some muscles for that reading. I was impressed." The man looked around as a petite blond woman moved up beside him and murmured something. He gave Jess a thin smile. "We'll see what happens in round three."

"If you don't mind, Senator," said Rebecca coolly. "We're in a meeting."

The man's smile wavered, his eyes growing flinty, but he turned and left them to it.

Jess watched him go. Absently, she picked up the champagne, then changed her mind and set it down. "I'm pretty sure he came this evening just to ruffle my feathers. Maybe catch a few photo ops," she added darkly to Rebecca, as the man paused to have his picture taken, his arm sliding snakelike around the blonde's waist. Jess met Riley's questioning gaze. "Ted Pierce, senate minority leader. He was one of Bill Hamilton's staunchest supporters."

Riley looked anew at the man. He had joined a large group at a table across from them. They were laughing at something he was saying.

"I sometimes wonder if he genuinely hates all my policies, or whether he just stands against me in some show of loyalty to Hamilton."

"What was he congratulating you on?"

"A bill I've been trying to pass." Jess hesitated. "It's something we wanted to discuss with you, in fact. I was planning to talk to Connie Meadows, but when she insisted on sending you tonight, I thought this would be the better opportunity. I've been wondering about it since Agent Altman came to discuss the possible link between my letter and the attacks."

"Wondering what?" asked Riley, her attention fully back on the governor.

It was Rebecca who answered. "In all states there's a gap between men and women when it comes to pay, but Iowa is one of the worst. Women here earn an average of seventy-seven cents on the dollar compared to men. It's even greater for women of color. The pandemic will have only widened that gap. Despite federal and state law, it's still possible for employers to suppress wages, especially in sectors dominated by women."

"My opponents argue this is down to choices made by women," interjected Jess. "To have families alongside careers and to seek out lower-paid professions like teaching, nursing, and clerical work."

Rebecca was nodding fervently, her eyes on Riley. "But even when women enter higher-paid sectors—as financial managers, or surgeons—they still receive less than their male counterparts."

"What would the bill do?" Riley asked.

"New legislation could compel employers to keep proper track of any wage gaps. We want to make certain there are no reprisals for employees who discuss earnings with colleagues and that job candidates aren't required to give their salary history. If a woman earned less than her male counterparts in a previous role, an employer can use that to justify paying her less in a new job—even for the same role as a man—getting around the Equal Pay Act. Forcing women to reveal their wage history perpetuates this discrepancy."

Riley looked from Rebecca to Jess. "And you think there could be some connection between this bill and the threat made against you?"

"I've had fierce opposition in the senate." Jess looked over at Ted Pierce, making the rounds at another table. "To ensure equality, employers can't drive down men's salaries, but must increase women's to the same level. Some companies would struggle, admittedly. The bill scraped past its second reading and has gone back to committee for amendments. But we still have one more vote in the chamber before we can hope to enshrine it in law." She returned her attention to Riley. "I don't want to create trouble where there is none or accuse anyone without evidence. But when Agent Altman said the bureau had established the task force with the DCI to investigate the possibility the Sin Eater could be targeting me and my family, I started wondering if maybe . . . ?" She trailed off, shaking her head.

"You can tell me," Riley encouraged.

"Well—what if someone wanted me to think that?"

"To what end?"

"Throw me off my game? Scare me? Keep me preoccupied with a serious investigation in the middle of a political fight?"

Riley thought this through. The wording of the letter, speaking of Cook's place, could be the work of a violent misogynist with a religious obsession, or a political opponent opposed to female equality. She thought of the suspect seen leaving the governor's office. The photographs taken outside Ella's school. Thought of those curled snakes in the message. "You received the letter before the DCI held the press conference where the snake symbol was shown."

"The Sin Eater used that in the past. I remember it in the news."

"But if whoever left it wanted you to think you'd been targeted by the Sin Eater, it would have to be someone who knew the police already suspected he had returned."

Jess exhaled, pushed a hand through her short hair. "I guess. Yes. I just couldn't bear the thought—if this was some hoax—that another woman might get hurt while you were all busy protecting me and my family."

"Have you had public meetings about your bill?"

"Several," answered Rebecca. "We've discussed it in the media too."

"OK, then if we stick with the theory the Sin Eater did leave that message, he could have easily learned about the bill. Clearly, a hatred of women compels him in his attacks. It's entirely possible this would be something that would rile him."

"So, it's back to sleepless nights," Jess murmured.

Riley followed the governor's gaze to her daughter, spinning careless circles to the music. She thought of Maddie and how she would feel if this predator had glanced in her direction. Thought of Hayley and Megan, Beth Muir and Abigail Dunbar—of what had happened to all those women when his gaze had become fixed. "I'll do everything in my power to catch him. You have my word."

Jess reached out and placed a grateful hand over Riley's.

Javier Morales approached. "Governor, I'm sorry to interrupt. It's time for your speech."

Jess rose, smoothing down her dress. "You'll keep me informed?"

"Of course," Riley said, standing. As Rebecca moved to follow the governor, Riley caught her. "Can I ask you something?"

Rebecca hesitated, glancing after her boss.

Riley pressed on. "What you said at the capitol? About us taking this seriously?"

"Yes?"

"It seemed there was something more?"

Rebecca nodded after a pause. "Word is, your office was given information on Karl Madden. Someone close to Madden knew he was planning the attack at the capitol. They contacted Des Moines PD days before Madden booked a place on the tour. An officer called your agency, left an urgent message. The agency never followed up." Rebecca turned as Javier gestured her toward the stage, where the band had finished playing. "I'm sorry, I've got to go."

"Do you know who the officer left the message for?" Riley called.

Rebecca looked around. An arch of her eyebrow confirmed what Riley suspected.

Altman.

P eter Altman pushed open the door of the Last Chance Saloon. Dead leaves stirred around his feet, whispering in with him to scuttle across the bare boards. The joint, all scarred wooden beams and stained tables, was dimly lit with red lights and smelled of stale beer and fried ham balls. There was a pool table, its cloth spattered with something, near a popcorn machine with dusty glass sides and a jukebox. Garth Brooks was singing "The Thunder Rolls."

Four men sat at one end of the bar and a skinny middle-aged woman huddled alone in a booth, empty glasses and peanut shells littering the table in front of her. She looked at Altman with unfocused eyes and a broken smile as he headed for the bar.

The barman sauntered to meet him. "Front row seat or booth?"

"Booth," said Altman, digging in his pocket for his wallet. "I'll take a Bud."

"Wanna cap?" the barman asked, tipping his head toward a row of baseball hats with the bar's name on them. "On special after Thanksgiving?"

"I'm good."

Altman handed over the cash, then retreated to the booth at the far end, near the pool table. A couple of the men glanced sideways at him before returning to their conversation. He slid in, placed the beer down, and checked his phone. There was a voice mail from Connie Meadows, demanding an update. She had been riding him for months now, looking over his shoulder, breathing down his neck. *No more mistakes, Altman.* His jaw tightened as he put the phone away.

Ten minutes later, the door opened. An icy breeze rushed in with two figures. A man and a boy. The boy wore a parka, several sizes too big, and a ratty-looking deerstalker. The man had the hood of his coat up, his hands stuffed in his pockets. He scanned the bar as he entered, checking every shadowed corner. He locked eyes with Altman last.

"Over twenty-ones only," called the bartender.

As Altman watched, the man strolled up to the bar. There was a brief exchange, at the end of which, the bartender nodded tensely and returned to wiping glasses with an old beer towel. Gesturing the boy toward the pool table, the man went to Altman's booth and slipped in opposite.

"You brought your kid?" Altman said, eyes on the boy, who'd grabbed the white ball and was shooting it up and down the table.

"My turn to have him." The man met Altman's gaze. "Could've just called you up. Saved us both a trip."

Altman ignored this. He wouldn't give Sawyer his shoe size, let alone his number. "Travis said you've got it."

"Ain't touched your beer." Sawyer pushed his hood back to show the shaved sides of his head, spiraled with black tribal-style tattoos. His mouth curled up when Altman narrowed his eyes. "Yeah, I got it." He tapped the table. "If you have."

Altman reached into his inside pocket, slowly, Sawyer watching him intently. He pulled out an envelope and placed it between them.

Keeping his eyes on Altman, Sawyer opened it. His gaze flicked down to check the contents, then he made it disappear in the folds of his coat. There was a loud bang as the white ball shot off the end of the table, making the men at the bar grumble.

"Hey," called one. "This ain't a playground."

Sawyer looked around at them. "Ain't no old folks' home neither, but you're sitting here, Grandpa."

The bartender stopped polishing the glass and the men turned in their chairs. The one who'd spoken looked as if he was going to retort, but one of his companions placed a hand on his arm. After a few beats, everyone eased back to what they'd been doing. The atmosphere had changed though. Garth Brooks's yearning voice gave a false sense of comfort.

Altman leaned forward. "Your turn."

Sawyer sniffed, then placed a crumpled piece of paper on the stained wood between them. "Heard you got yourself saddled with a new partner."

"She's a rookie from Butt-Fuck County. No one to worry about."

"No? That's what you said about the last one."

"I dealt with Roach, didn't I. Anyway, she isn't my goddamn partner."

"OK, OK." Sawyer grinned and held up his hands. "Don't get your panties in a bunch." His smile faded. "We got a good thing going now. You and me. Better not let some bitch fuck it up."

"There is no you and me. We're even."

Sawyer smiled coolly. "Sure, boss."

Altman snatched the crumpled piece of paper from the table. "Take your kid home, Sawyer." He exited the booth, leaving his beer untouched and the old men mumbling in the corner.

19

Riley sat alone at the table, scanning the couples shuf-
fling around the dance floor. The speeches were over, the
charity auction had ended, and the crowd was starting to thin out. She
felt redundant, given the number of state troopers still here, but Meadows had sent her to show the governor the agency took her security
seriously, so she would wait until Jess Cook had left before making her
own exit.

The band was playing a slow song and the governor was dancing in
front of the stage with her husband. She looked rather stiff and embarrassed as the press circled, taking photographs, but as her husband
murmured something in her ear, her face relaxed into laughter and she
gripped his hand tighter.

As the band finished to loud applause and plunged into a lively number, Jess beckoned to her daughter, who raced out onto the floor. Taking her father's hand, Ella spun around. Cameras flashed appreciatively.

Watching them, Riley found herself marveling at the governor's ca-
pacities. Jess Cook was a woman in a man's world, but she'd managed
to have it all—the highest position in the state, and what appeared to
be a loving family. Not only that, but she was fighting, undaunted, for
the rights of other women, even as she herself was being targeted. On
the heels of Riley's admiration came a twinge of envy.

She was thirty-seven. Most women she knew of her age had a family, many were at the top of their careers, yet here she was just starting out again. Did she even want kids? A husband? She had always told herself the demands and rewards of police work were enough for her. Besides which, she'd pretty much raised Maddie as her own. But what if those were excuses? A way of not facing what she didn't have? It wasn't too late. Aunt Rose and Lori had Benjamin when they were older. It was still possible. If she wanted it.

But that was the thing. She had spent so much of her adult life tending to the needs and wishes of others—her family, her colleagues, victims—she had no real idea what it was she wanted for herself. That void had yawned even wider since she'd arrived in the city, no familiar routine to keep her occupied: making sure Maddie had done her homework, picking Ethan up from the gas station after a shift, stopping by for coffee with Aunt Rose. There were empty spaces in her life now, spaces she'd never really had the time—or the inclination—to notice before. They filled her with disquiet. Made her long for distraction.

Unsettled, Riley wandered over to the makeshift bar. Wistfully eyeing the bottles of beer, she asked for a water. As a flush-faced couple moved away, gripping flutes of champagne, Riley saw Ted Pierce standing at the other end of the bar. The senate minority leader was talking to a young man, handsome in a slick sort of way, slim of build and dressed in an immaculate suit. Pierce appeared riled up about something, his hands gesturing as he spoke, but the young man looked calm, listening and nodding occasionally.

Riley edged closer, but she couldn't hear what Pierce was saying over the music. She thought back over what the governor had said about the possibility of the threat being some kind of political hoax, meant to distract her. The timing still seemed unlikely, with the letter arriving before the press conference at which Fogg had announced the Sin Eater's return, but the DCI headquarters was right across from the capitol. State police would move constantly between the two buildings and she knew law enforcement could be as leaky as a sieve. It wasn't impossible that someone could have let the news slip before the press conference. If

Ted Pierce was one of Bill Hamilton's biggest supporters, even after the scandal, was it such a stretch to imagine him targeting the governor in such a way? He certainly seemed to take pleasure in taunting her about the bill.

Riley knew she would have to discuss this with Altman if there was even a small chance they were going down the wrong track looking into a connection with the Sin Eater—a connection she'd been the one to make. But Rebecca's confirmation that Altman was the one who had missed the warning about Karl Madden, and the agent's aggressiveness in insisting the governor was his domain, left her troubled by the prospect of confiding in him. She had walked into a web, sticky with doubt and uncertainty. Noah Case seemed her best bet to help her untangle it.

She'd made up her mind to seek Noah out first thing tomorrow and was turning back to her table when shouts rose from the dance floor.

Someone screamed, the shrill sound cutting above the music.

Riley dashed forward, pushing past people, going for her gun. She wasn't used to the high heels or the short dress and, halfway across the space, her foot skidded in a puddle of spilled drink. She went down hard.

Between the legs of the crowd, she glimpsed two state troopers wrestling with an older man. He'd torn open his tuxedo to reveal a T-shirt, big red letters shouting across it:

TRAITOR!

"You killed my business, governor!" he yelled hoarsely as he was manhandled by the cops. "What do you say to that? What do you say to my family? We lost everything after you locked us down!"

The band had stuttered into silence, but as she scrabbled to her feet, Riley saw Javier Morales motioning frantically for them to start up again. The officers dragged the man away.

Jess was standing with her family, her hand on Ella's shoulder. Rebecca was out in front of them, gesturing to the crowd for calm. The press was making hay, snapping pictures of the man being hauled out, his shouts still echoing. Jess was trying to smile, but Riley could see the fear in her eyes, her fingers gripping her daughter, pulling Ella in close.

Her own heart was still pounding from the unexpected rush of adrenaline.

"You play for State or something?"

Riley turned to see the young man in the suit who'd been talking with Ted Pierce. "Sorry?"

"Looked like you were planning on taking that guy out at the knees!" The man grinned, a boyish dimple appearing in his smooth cheek.

Glancing down, Riley saw she'd ripped her pantyhose. "Damn it." As she bent forward, her jacket fell open, offering the man a peep at her gun.

"Police?"

"FBI." She pulled her jacket closed, then followed his amused gaze to her pumps. She gave a brief smile. "Yeah. Not exactly regulation." She turned at a flurry of flashes to see the governor heading out with Mark and Ella, surrounded by a huddle of state troopers and shadowed by the press. The band was playing again, but the remaining crowd was too excited to dance and were gathering in groups to gossip about the commotion.

"Well, I'll let you get back to it," said the man.

"I saw you talking to Ted Pierce?"

"Oh?" said the man, frowning as he turned back.

"Can I ask how well you know the minority leader?"

"Pretty well. I'm a senator." The lines in the young man's brow had deepened in question.

"It seems he's not on the best of terms with the governor?"

The man laughed, the frown lines disappearing. "That's putting it mildly. But I daresay that's no different from many political rivals." He cocked his head. "I'm guessing you're investigating the threat, then?"

"You know about it?"

"Everyone in the capitol knows about it. It's all anyone's been talking about."

"Any idea who might want to hurt the governor? Threaten her family?"

His gaze went to the doors the man had been dragged through. "You mean other than the protestors?" He didn't wait for her to answer. "Ted Pierce is a fierce critic of the governor, he'll be the first to admit that, but I cannot imagine he would want to see her hurt."

Riley reached into her pocket. She pulled her card from her wallet. "Senator, if you see or hear anything at the capitol, anything that strikes you as unusual in regard to the governor—beyond the usual political angst—can I ask you to give me a call?"

He paused, then accepted her card. "Of course." He read it, squinting in the dim dance floor light. "Special Agent Riley Fisher." He offered his free hand. "Nate Davenport."

As Riley shook it, she caught a whiff of his cologne. Cedar and spice. She found herself looking at him a beat longer than she should.

Nate smiled. "I think your phone's ringing."

"Oh." Riley pulled out her cell to see Fogg's number. "I'm sorry, I need to get this." As she moved through the crowd, she could feel the senator's gaze following her. "Fogg?" She pressed a hand to her ear, trying to hear him over the music. "Hang on." She hastened up a set of steps, making for one of the passages out of the mall. A state trooper stepped in, blocking her path, but moved aside when she showed him her badge. "I'm here, Fogg. Go ahead."

"We just got a potential hit on the tip line. Possible former victim. She saw the composite on the billboards. Thinks it could be the same man who attacked her."

"One of the victims in the nineties?"

"No. Later. Eight years after the last reported attack. She went to the police at the time, but they didn't connect it to the original case. I'm going to see her tomorrow. Free to join me?"

"Of course."

"Her name's Sydney Williams. I'll text you the address."

Riley was making her way back toward the party, eyes on the cell's screen, when a woman emerged from a shadowy intersection and collided with her, making her drop her phone.

"Oh my gosh! I'm so sorry!" The woman bent, awkward in a long red evening gown. She picked up the phone and handed it to Riley. "I'm such a klutz."

"It's no problem." Riley saw the woman had been crying. Black streaks of mascara had tracked down her cheeks, carving lines through a thick layer of foundation. There was a darker smudge just visible around her eye. The tell of an old bruise. "Are you OK?"

The woman gave a shrill laugh. "Oh, I'm just fine. Gotta take the bitter with the sweet sometimes, right?" She sounded drunk. "I'm sorry about your phone. I hope it isn't broken."

Riley looked down to see a hairline crack across the screen. She glanced up, but the woman was already hastening off. Her cell pinged as the text from Fogg came through.

Riley retraced her steps along the skywalk, her reflection walking beside her in the glass.

Beyond, in the grid of streets, a billboard flickered to life in the dark and the face of the Sin Eater appeared.

20

Kody eased open the top drawer of his mom's dresser, which squeaked in protest. He tensed, tilting his head to listen. His mom was in the kitchen. He could hear the clatter of plates. Harlan was asleep in the living room.

He picked through the drawer, nose wrinkling as he undertook the task of rifling among his mom's drab gray panties and bras. They smelled of Juicy Fruit. A couple of packets nestled among beige ribbons of pantyhose, looped like intestines. He came across the velvet box that once contained a silver charm bracelet from an upmarket jeweler's downtown. His mom had bought it as a gift to herself with her first paycheck from the Laundromat, added more charms to it over the years—a cross, a horseshoe for luck, a plump silver heart. She'd lost it a year ago and had been distraught.

Kody remembered her scouring the house in vain, one cheek swollen where Harlan had slammed her against the kitchen door. The bracelet was gone, but she had kept the box. It gave him a stab of pity that vanished as his fingers found what he was looking for.

The Jif label was peeling where the jar's lid had been screwed and unscrewed over the years. Even as he opened it, Kody knew it was empty. This was an unpleasant surprise. His mom kept her savings in here. Every so often, he would steal a few bucks—buy a game from the thrift store—and she'd never notice. There had been at least three hundred dollars here when he'd last looked.

He stowed the jar, slid a stick of gum from a packet, and folded it into his mouth. He was heading out, feeling cheated and unsettled, when his foot bumped against something under the bed. Harlan's carryall.

Kody paused. He could hear his mom putting the plates away while the TV continued to blare commercials from the living room. He gritted the gum between his teeth, thinking of Harlan pinning him against the wall, the man's arm against his throat. It still hurt to swallow.

Crouching, he unzipped the bag and dug around, hunting for Harlan's wallet. He'd spent the last of his meager allowance and he desperately wanted this new game Troy hadn't stopped texting him about. There was a stale smell in the carryall. Unwashed clothes and cigarette smoke. His heart thumped harder the deeper he dove among the man's belongings. He was half excited, half nervous—like coming across a bonus weapons pack, but with the possibility it was a trap.

He seized on a plastic bag and pulled it free. It was one of those large Ziploc bags, puffy with trapped air. There were things inside—scraps of material—but no cash that he could see. He was about to shove it back in when his gaze focused on the contents. There was a piece of white material. It was spattered with a dried, reddish brown substance. He turned the baggie over in his hands. There was also a fold of black material, something red and sinuous painted on it. He thought of Harlan's tattoo—the coiled snake that spiraled around his thick forearm. Thought of the breaking news he'd seen a minute of the other night before Harlan changed the channel.

Something tapped at the back of Kody's mind, like a fingernail scraping against a window. Slowly, he unzipped the bag. A sour smell rose up. Old pennies.

"What the fuck are you doing?"

Kody dropped the bag. He straightened, heart in his mouth. Harlan was in the doorway, his bulk filling the frame. The light from the TV across the hall flickered on the side of his face.

Game over.

"I was—"

Harlan entered the room, mule-kicking the door closed behind him. "You were what?" He stalked to Kody, face tightening as he saw the open carryall. "Going through my stuff?" Harlan stopped as he saw the Ziploc bag lying open on the floor. "Oh, you stupid son of a bitch."

Those last words were no less threatening for being murmured, but there was something different in Harlan's tone. Something wary, maybe even scared. Harlan looked at Kody and Kody looked back, the little tap-tap at the back of his mind now a terrifying, insistent knocking.

21

Riley and Fogg followed Sydney Williams down the narrow hall, into a small, sun-filled kitchen. Through the windows, the little garden out back was a pristine square of snow. No footprints marked it. Water dripped from the peeling branches of a paper birch, the fresh fall already melting. The temperature had risen ten degrees overnight, bringing a surprise sense of spring. Riley was hot in her wool coat.

"Can I get you some coffee?"

"Thank you, Miss Williams," said Fogg.

"Sydney's just fine," said the woman, gesturing them to sit at a table. She busied herself pulling out mugs, her back to them.

Riley sat, wincing at the tenderness of the bruise on her hip where she'd fallen last night. The morning paper had run with the story of the protestor at the gala. Jess Cook's face had been plastered all over, caught in a moment of fear, eyes wide, mouth parted. Riley imagined she would hate how vulnerable she looked. How it undermined her.

She hadn't spoken to Altman or Fogg about the governor's suggestion the threat could be some kind of cruel hoax from within the senate. She wanted to understand the politics at play in her own department first. She'd checked in with Audrey and the secretary had told her Noah Case was due into the office that afternoon.

Riley looked around while Sydney made coffee. The room was

immaculate. Not a thing out of place. There was a row of plants on the windowsill in the full flush of green life. She thought of the ones she'd bought to try to brighten up her apartment, the leaves already curling brown at the edges.

Sydney set the mugs on the table, then stepped back. "Sugar? Cream?" Her tone was bright, but brittle.

"Black's good for me." Fogg smiled. "I'm sweet enough after Thanksgiving."

Sydney paused, one hand gripping the back of a chair as if she wasn't sure what to do now.

"I'll take some cream," offered Riley.

The woman took a breath and nodded. This time, when she returned with the cream, she sat.

"It must have taken courage to call," Fogg said after the silence had steeped a little while. "I want you to know we appreciate it."

Sydney wrapped her hands around the mug. Her brown hair formed a soft nimbus around her face, shot through with whorls of gold. Her eyes were fixed on the table, arms tight against her body. Riley noticed the skin around her fingernails was raw from being picked at.

"I've not been able to sleep since I saw those billboards. That face." Sydney's voice was husky. She cleared her throat. "I wondered before— when I saw the attacks on the news. But I guess I didn't want to know. The thought he's been out there? Sixteen years?" She shuddered, as if her body was trying to shake the thought away. "I'd hoped he was dead."

Riley felt a familiar knot pull tight inside. It had always been easier to imagine Hunter—her own attacker, from years ago—in the ground. Justice by death when there had been no other punishment, no consequence for his crime—knowing only she would live the life sentence.

After the FBI interviews, where she'd been forced to relive that night and the aftermath, she had spent some time sitting among the painful pieces of it all, wondering if her new career might offer access to answers. To finally seek Hunter out and know the truth—whether he was dead or alive, in prison or a position of power. But in the end, she'd packed it all up and stuffed it back inside, not wanting to walk into her future with the mess of her past dragging at her heels.

"Perhaps you could start at the beginning?" Fogg suggested. "Talk us through what happened that night? Take as long as you need."

When she began to speak, Sydney kept her eyes on the table. "I was working at a club over in Capitol Heights, off the interstate. It's been gone for years. Torn down and turned into apartments."

"What was it called?" Fogg had taken out his notepad, but kept his attention on Sydney.

"The Little Prairie Girl, steakhouse and strip club." Sydney glanced at them quickly, defensively. "I worked behind the bar. I was at college with one of the girls there. She said I could make good tips. The owner tried to get me on the stage. Said I'd make an *exotic* addition." She shrugged tightly. "But I only ever served drinks."

Fogg nodded, waiting for her to continue.

"I usually caught the night bus home, but that evening we'd had issues with some frat boys acting up, breaking glasses. I stayed late to clean and I missed it. My apartment was three miles away, but it was summer, so I walked. Maybe that was stupid. I know the cops thought so. Hell, my own family thought so." She looked up. "But what do people think when they tell women not to walk home alone? That we all have cash for cabs? Alternative means? We're not all so privileged."

"Do you remember the route you took?"

As Sydney listed the names of streets and landmarks, her voice lost some of its serrated edge. Fogg wrote it all down.

"I'd turned off the main streets, close to the railroad. Kind of an industrial area. It was about one in the morning." She drew a steadying breath. "I heard his footsteps first. He was walking behind me, head down, hands in his pockets. He had shoulder-length hair. Untidy. He wore a thin jacket. Dark in color. Maybe green? I got nervous. Walked faster. He picked up his pace too. I looked around and he was staring straight at me."

"You got a look at his face?"

"There weren't many streetlights and he was shadowed by the wall of a building, but I saw enough to know he meant me harm. Those eyes." She inhaled again. "I began to run, but he came after me. I shouted for help. He caught my arm. I struggled, but he threw me against the wall like I was—nothing. He slammed my head against it. I guess I lost consciousness." Sydney pushed back her tight brown curls to show a puckered indent at her temple. She let her hair fall in place to cover it. "When I came to, he was on top of me. I couldn't move. He had a knife in his hand. He was cutting into me." She stood, the chair scraping on the floor, peeled her sweater up above her navel.

Riley and Fogg stared at the jagged swerves of a snake carved into the soft skin of her stomach. A twisted tattoo of scar tissue.

Sydney sat, her eyes distant, trapped in that moment. "He said he was punishing me for my sins. I must have passed out again. When I woke, he was gone."

"Did he take anything from you that you recall?"

She looked at Fogg, surprised. "Yes." Her brow furrowed. "I had this little pocketbook. My aunt brought it back from Nigeria. All these blues and golds and pinks. There was maybe three dollars in it. When I woke up, it was gone. I managed to retrace my steps to a diner that was open, near a truck stop off the interstate. They called the paramedics. The cops came to interview me the next day. I told them what had happened. And what I thought."

"What you thought?"

"I remembered the Sin Eater attacks. I was only twelve, thirteen. But it was everywhere back then. That face was burned into the city— into us."

Riley remembered. They were around the same age. Had a teenage Sydney whispered with her girlfriends about the monster, as she had?

"I thought it was him." Sydney picked at a bit of torn skin around a fingernail. "But they said it was probably a customer who'd followed me from the club—wanting more. I told them I only served drinks. They didn't listen. They interviewed everyone who'd been at the Little Prairie Girl that night. I lost my job. The owner didn't like the heat. I wouldn't have returned anyway. When I was discharged from the hospital, I moved back in with my folks. It took months for me to even leave the house. I still sometimes—" She pressed her lips together, looked through the window.

Riley followed her gaze to the garden, where the snow was unmarked by footprints.

A crow was sitting in the branches of the birch. *One for sorrow.*

"After a while, the cops stopped calling with updates. They told me the chances of catching my attacker were small. Case closed." Sydney sat back, pushing her untouched coffee away. "Not a priority, I guess. Not a pretty white girl, who makes the front pages. Candlelit vigils and press conferences with the top brass." She leveled Fogg with a critical look, then turned to the window again, her eyes filling with sunlight. "I don't want to be that person," she murmured. "I don't want to have anything other than pity for another woman who's been through this. But it's hard not to feel there's injustice piled on injustice here."

"I can understand why you feel that."

Riley looked at Fogg. His tone was calm, professional, but there was a ripple of emotion beneath it. Did he feel guilt for how her case had been handled back then? Or was he perhaps thinking of his own daughters? How they might have been treated? Might still be?

"I can't change the past, Sydney. But I can tell you that it matters—your experience. It matters very much to me. To us," Fogg added, glancing at Riley, who nodded. "When you called the tip line you said you'd remembered something from that night?"

"It was maybe a year later. I was making dinner one evening and I cut myself. Not badly. But when I saw the blood, I had this—flash. An image of him sitting on top of me, that knife in his hand. I remembered there was something on his jacket. Here." She touched the left side of her chest. "Some kind of logo." Sydney rose and went to the counter. She returned with a pad and pencil. She sketched something, then tore off the page and slid it across the table. It was two squares, positioned diagonally, with a line zigzagging between them. "These were white," she said, pointing at the squares. Her finger moved to the sinuous line. "I think this was blue."

Fogg took the paper and slipped it into his notepad. "Did you report it to your case officers?" He guessed the answer before she gave it. "It's OK."

"I just couldn't." Sydney's voice was weary. "I'm sure some would say that makes me irresponsible or a coward. But I'd started to move on, rebuild my life. To be honest, part of me was relieved they hadn't caught him. That I didn't have to face him in court. Go through it all again. Not be heard. Or believed. All your words torn apart for the jury. Like it's you who's on trial."

Riley thought of her parents, shushing it all away—what Hunter had done. Her father, the lawyer, who'd seen too many women broken by the system. She understood their need to protect her, but it had taken away her choice. Her role in that crime would forever be passive. The silent victim. She thought of her badge. Justice holding up those scales, her eyes bound. Thought of the cops dismissing Sydney's account of her experience—a young Black woman who worked at a strip club.

Could justice ever really be blind in a biased world?

Fogg finished up the interview by clarifying details and asking more questions. Sydney didn't recall her attacker taking any photographs and there was no hood that she remembered, but those missing moments caused by her head injury made it impossible for her to be certain. Fogg showed her the sketch of the tattoo—the snake and the cross above it— but the jacket's sleeves had covered the attacker's arms throughout her ordeal. Fogg had nodded, unsurprised by the lack of a lead there. Following the press conference, the DCI had received a lot of calls about the partial tattoo, but with snakes and crosses being popular choices, it seemed it would be a needle in a haystack.

When they were done, Sydney showed them out. She looked spent. Fogg stayed for a few moments, speaking with her at the door before joining Riley on the street where they'd parked their vehicles.

He rubbed at his jaw. "Every time I think I've plugged a hole in this case, another one opens up. If this was our suspect, it means he was still attacking during the period we thought he was dormant. It changes how I was looking at this." He slapped his palm on the hood of the Buick. "Damn it."

"But it might mean something else too," Riley ventured. Fogg looked at her. "There could be other victims out there?"

22

Leaving Fogg to head to the DCI headquarters to look into the logo Sydney Williams had drawn, Riley sped across the city to the resident agency. She wanted to catch Noah Case and ask him the questions that had been bubbling in her mind about Peter Altman.

The young man emerged from his office, shrugging his trench coat on over a well-fitted black suit, every inch the sharp special agent. He looked how she wished she felt: confident and at ease in this place where everyone seemed to fiercely guard whatever square of authority they'd been given. Audrey with her desk of crystal animals, tapping the register each morning, unsmiling. Altman's defensiveness. Meadows's hard-nosed directives.

Noah turned as she called to him. "Oh, hi. All settled in?"

"Yes, thanks. I was wondering if you're free for a drink?"

Noah looked surprised, almost startled. "Well, I don't drink, to be honest, Riley."

She realized, by his expression, that he thought she was asking him on some kind of date. "I just had a couple of questions about an old case," she clarified quickly. "Thought you might be able to help?"

"Right," Noah said, relaxing. "Molly Malone's does a decent coffee."

They rode the elevator out of the basement. Clouds were gathering, turning the bright afternoon to somber dusk. Noah led the way down the block to the tavern, which stood on a corner between a funeral parlor and a life insurance broker. He opened the door for her, then followed her in.

The place was quiet, the working day not yet done. Riley had driven past on a Friday evening when the windows were fogged with a jostle of suited bodies from the surrounding office blocks. There were stools set along the dark wood counter, the walls were painted green, and signs advertised Guinness and Jameson's.

Noah smiled at the woman behind the bar. "I'll take a coffee."

"Same," said Riley. "On me," she added, getting out her wallet.

They chose a table in the corner. Noah took a moment to carefully fold his coat and remove his silk scarf. She noted, again, his expensive taste and old-fashioned dress sense. It made her wonder where he came from.

Back at the academy, not only were her classmates much younger, many had come from real privilege: straight out of elite law schools, or fresh from a stint in Daddy's accounting firm. The only people she'd found a vague connection with were a former soldier and an ex-firefighter, the three of them the only grit in a class of polished gems.

She wondered if Noah looked down his nose at her like some of them had—like she was too old and too country to be starting out in the FBI. But as he sat opposite her, his smile was open and genuine, inviting her to talk.

"What can you tell me about Karl Madden?" she asked, cradling her coffee for warmth. "What do you know about his attempted attack on the governor?"

"He made the attempt. He failed. Case pretty much closed. Madden's in federal prison. What more do you need to know?"

Noah asked the question lightly, but Riley sensed a shift in his tone—a wariness creeping in. "I heard someone knew about Madden's plan. That there was a call made to Des Moines PD, but when the cops contacted our agency, they never heard back. I heard it was Peter Altman who missed the warning."

Noah pressed his lips together. "Riley, I don't know how things worked at your sheriff's office, but we try to avoid bad-mouthing our colleagues here."

"This isn't me bad-mouthing him. You must know I've been paired with Altman on the task force with the DCI? I just need to know I can trust him to get the big calls right. He's not exactly Mr. Chatty."

Noah gave a half smile. "Well, that's for sure." He relaxed a little. "Altman has always kept to himself. But we all do here. Meadows expects us to keep our heads down, achieve our targets. She believes office relationships should be purely professional—that things get messy when agents become too personal."

Riley thought back to Black Hawk. Even with all the politics and sexism, there had still been moments of levity. Games at Christmas and cakes for birthdays, beers at Duke's when they'd solved a case. She tried to imagine Meadows wearing some silly Santa hat, coldly reading out pop quiz questions to a stone-faced Altman. "The trouble is Meadows assigned us both to this investigation and Altman has made it clear he's not happy about this."

An understatement, given his last words outside her apartment.

You don't want me as an enemy.

Noah seemed about to say something, then reached for his coffee instead.

"I left a top position to become a rookie here." Riley waited until he met her gaze. "I've got family who rely on me, Noah. I need to know where I stand."

Noah put his coffee down. "About six months ago, Altman got paired with Agent Roach on a case. There was some issue between them." The young man shook his head at her questioning frown. "I don't know the details. Neither of them talked about it and I didn't want to get involved. But I had the impression Roach was getting in Altman's way somehow, stepping on his toes."

"What happened?"

"All I know is Roach ended up quitting. He wasn't due for retirement for at least five years. It was unexpected to say the least. Meadows was pissed." He took another sip of coffee. "I'd advise you to keep your head down, Riley. Don't rock the boat. Follow orders and you'll get along fine."

Noah's tone was briskly professional, but she caught something else in his expression. It was there only briefly, but she thought the young man looked lonely.

"And if Meadows orders me to do something that might piss Altman off? Do you think I can talk to her candidly about it?"

Noah's face told her what she'd guessed. "I'd try to keep complaints to yourself. Work around the problem. One thing I can tell you is Connie Meadows will go to bat for Altman every time."

"Why? After the issue with Madden? I've seen the tension it's caused with the governor's office."

"He's the most accomplished agent in our department. That one case aside, the man gets results."

Because he's good? Riley wondered, or because he cuts corners and screws over colleagues?

She had fought for a place on this investigation. It was her hunch that had led to the creation of the task force with the DCI. But if anything went wrong, she'd be first out the door. Her position as a probationary agent was precarious enough without Altman undermining her for whatever reason. Professional jealousy. Incompetence. Or something else?

Noah set down his cup and glanced at his watch. "I'm sorry, Riley. I have to go."

Outside, sleet salted the air.

As they made their way back down the block, through the parking lot, Riley thought of the stuffed bear she'd seen in Altman's BuRide. "Does Altman have kids?"

Noah half laughed. "Altman? Happy bachelor."

Before she could ask anything else, Riley saw someone over by her car. A tall, broad-shouldered man, dressed in a dark coat and hat. He was leaning over the windshield. It looked like he was trying to wedge something under the wipers. "Hey!"

The figure turned, something gripped in his fist. Riley felt a stab of fear until the man's face arranged itself into familiar lines and angles. She let out a breath.

"Hey, boss," called Logan Wood, smiling sheepishly.

As she approached, she saw the thing in Logan's hand was a piece of broccoli. He'd wrapped it with a red ribbon.

He followed her gaze and held it up. "Brought you some rabbit food."

"Logan? What the hell are you doing here?"

"The receptionist said you'd be back shortly. I saw your purse in the car." He nodded to the Chevy. "I was going to leave a note."

"I mean *here*. In Des Moines?"

"I had an appointment scheduled in the city. I was going to tell you at Thanksgiving but then the meeting got called forward, so I thought I'd surprise you." His smile wavered as he glanced at Noah.

"This is Noah," she told him. "One of my colleagues at the bureau."

Noah inclined his head to Logan, then turned to Riley. "I've got to go."

"OK. Thank you for the advice," she added.

"No problem, Riley. Anytime."

At his tone, Riley realized he meant it. She doubted the young man had been out with any of his colleagues before.

She waited until Noah had gone to his car, collar turned up against the sleet, then looked back at Logan.

"Sorry, boss," he said. "I should've called."

She felt a smile tug at the corners of her mouth. "You know you can stop calling me that?"

"Old habits die hard."

Her gaze went to the broccoli, bent where he'd tried to stuff it under the wipers. She began to laugh, all the tension of the past weeks flooding out. "I thought you were holding a gun, you idiot. I could have shot you!" She shook her head at his arched eyebrow. "Things have been a bit crazy."

"Not in Kansas anymore?"

"That about sums it up."

"Are you free for dinner this evening?"

"Yes." Riley cringed, thinking of her apartment. "But—can we go out?"

Logan held up the mangled broccoli. "I was kinda hoping you'd say that."

23

Riley leaned close to the mirror, smoothing on lipstick. Pressing her lips together, she reached for her perfume—a gift from Ethan and Maddie two Christmases ago that she rarely used. She faltered, catching sight of herself: short black dress and pumps, hair loose around her shoulders, cherry lips. Same clothes she'd worn to the gala. Same clothes she'd worn that last night in Quantico.

What was she thinking? Logan didn't know her like this.

This was another her, from another time. Nameless bars and faceless men. Dust in the wind and the wild, briny bite of ocean. Knock back shots and never care. The way she would put herself together on those nights, only to tear herself apart.

A ping from her cell informed her the cab was outside.

Kicking off the pumps, she shimmied out of the dress, tossing it on the bed among the small heap of clothes she'd already picked out and discarded. She pulled on black jeans, a navy turtleneck, and her ankle boots, rubbed off the lipstick with a wipe, and knotted up her hair. Last she put on the gold star necklace from her grandfather, reclaimed from the soil where Hunter had held her down. The chain of the necklace was new, untarnished, but the star was marked with hairline scratches, always visible in certain lights.

As her cell pinged again, Riley crossed to the closet in the hall. At the base, bolted to the floorboards, was the lockbox she'd brought from Cedar Falls with the rest of her belongings, strapped in the bed of her grandfather's rusted Dodge pickup, which she'd parked down the block and hadn't used since. Keying in the code, she stowed her gun inside. She would normally bear arms even off duty. But she didn't want to be an agent tonight.

Closing the safe, she headed out, feeling strangely light and free.

The restaurant Logan had booked was only ten minutes away, but with the wardrobe indecision she was running late. As the cab pulled up at the place—a modern, glass-fronted affair—Riley slid out. She paused on the sidewalk, the air stinging her cheeks. Through the large window she could see Logan. He was sitting at a table in a corner, the light of his phone shining on his face. In this city of ice and shadows, he looked like a door open into the warm light of home.

She entered feeling a heady mix of emotions. Nerves battled with excitement. Logan glanced up from his phone. He grinned as he saw her. He was wearing a white shirt and dark blue jeans. He looked fresh and fit. Clearly, he'd managed to keep up his routine of the gym, protein shakes, and vitamins as sergeant.

"Sorry," she said, as he rose to greet her. "Traffic."

"No problem," he said affably. "Gave me time to catch up on some work. Jeez, the bureaucracy. Here—have a promotion—and a fuck-ton of paperwork."

They stood in front of one another, uncertain. Did they hug? Kiss? Shake hands?

A masked waiter came to take Riley's coat, breaking the moment. She sat and Logan followed suit. There were other couples at tables nearby, faces bathed in the soft radiance from globe lights suspended above. Festoons formed a delicate constellation behind a bar, all whites and golds to match the aesthetic. To Riley, it looked like a place for people other than her.

"I've heard it's great here," Logan enthused, sliding one of the menus toward her. "All kinds of plant-based stuff. But don't worry, they've got dead animals too."

"You always did have such a lovely way with words."

He grinned. "Drink?"

She glanced at his beer, half drunk. Hearing the bartender shaking a cocktail, she realized she wanted something stronger. "I'll take a martini, please," she said as the waiter reappeared.

Logan arched an eyebrow. "Serious." He ordered another beer. "So, *Agent* Fisher. How are you? Missing our little sheriff's office? Is it all car chases and shoot-outs?" Logan's smile faltered, his gaze darting to her shoulder. He pushed a hand through his hair. "Shit, I didn't mean—" He shook his head.

They'd never really talked about it. That day in Black Hawk—the day of fire and bullets. By the time she was out of surgery, the FBI had taken control of their investigation and they were back to drunk drivers and burglaries.

Her mind flung her into the passenger seat of that car—Logan shouting, pressing his torn T-shirt into her shoulder, her blood quickly soaking it. Flames blooming beyond the windshield. Her vision slipping.

"How are things back home?" she asked, steering the conversation away, relieved as the drink was placed in front of her. She took a sip, the vodka pouring like cold fire down her throat. "Jackson Cole giving you any trouble?"

Logan's nose wrinkled. "Nothing worth losing sleep over."

They fell into an easy enough back-and-forth, talking about the sheriff's office and Logan's new role as head of Investigations, then on to his family and hers. He ordered some sort of vegetable dish with herb-flavored foams that he insisted she try, betting—correctly—that she'd not cooked any of the recipes he'd given her. She ordered the steak and another martini, the first already glazing her mind with a calm she hadn't felt since she'd arrived in the city.

Partway through ordering dessert, the lights extinguished. Streetlights guttered out down the block. The other diners paused their conversations, looking around.

"Power cut," said the waiter. "Been going on and off since the storm."

"Looks like it's ice cream then." Logan looked at Riley's empty glass. "Or a drink?"

"One more," she said, already knowing she'd regret it in the morning and was past caring.

The waiter returned with their drinks and a candle. The flame danced shadows across Logan's face. He sat forward, hand curled around his beer, not drinking. "OK, we've talked about everything, except all this." He waved a hand, agitating the candle. "Your whole new life. How are you, Riley? Really? You seem—I don't know? Not yourself?"

The vodka had thawed her mind, softening the brittle edges. She felt marooned at the table, surrounded by darkness, anchored only by the candlelight and Logan's searching eyes. "I think I fucked up," she murmured, meeting his gaze. "Coming here. I think I've made the biggest mistake."

"Tell me."

And so she did. All of it, from the first day to now.

He stayed silent for a long moment after she'd finished, watching her take a deep drink. "So, you think your partner is shady?"

"There's nothing concrete. I mean, it's clear he messed up on the attempted attack against the governor, but that could have just been a mistake. He missed a phone call. It happens." She frowned, shaking her head. "But the way he's trying to steer this investigation? Keep me from it. Shut me out." Riley knew she was starting to sound garbled. She shouldn't have had that last drink. "I don't know. But Noah implied Roach quit because of Altman. Because of some case they were on together."

"Roach?"

"The guy whose place I took."

"I remember what it's like to be the rookie. Some cops are just dicks. You know that." Logan watched her toy with the olive in the bottom of her glass. "You really think you only got the job because of your association with the governor?"

"I know so. Meadows told me. That first day." Riley paused. "I came here to get away from politics and departmental bullshit." She let out a breath. "That's not true. I came here to get away from *all* of it. My grandfather. My brother. Cedar Falls. After—after everything that happened—I didn't want to stay. But am I just running away again?"

"Again?"

She looked up at him, remembering that Logan didn't know about her past, not all of it. Would he still respect her if he did? The girl she had been. The things she had done.

She could feel it burning beneath the exterior she had always shown him—shown the world. People saw her as cool and calm and dependable. They didn't know that inside her was a molten core of grief and rage, self-hatred and longing. A volcano beneath an ice sheet. She had let it all go once and it had destroyed her family. The thought of doing so again was terrifying. She pressed her lips together.

Logan continued into her silence. "OK, so what if you did get the posting because of that? Does it matter?"

"Yes—if I can't do the job. If I'm just a checkmark in a goddamn box."

Riley thought of Hayley, helpless in her hospital bed, tears in her eyes as she worried about how her parents would pay for her treatment. Thought of Sydney Williams in her home, trapped in the past, reliving that nightmare every time she undressed to see the scars that branded her. Thought of the fear in Jess Cook's face and Ella in that pumpkin costume, her small hand in her father's, smiling unaware as the camera clicked, capturing her from a distance.

"Logan, you should see what the bastard does to these women. What happened in Black Hawk was awful. But this?" She shook her head, her mind filling with images from the incident room. "The way he leaves them. Scars them. I want to catch this son of a bitch."

"Then work the case. Step by step. You know how to do this." Logan leaned forward, forcing her eyes up to meet his. "Klein would never have recommended you if he didn't genuinely believe you would be an asset to the bureau. Think about what it took to get here, Riley. The tests, the interviews, the training, for Christ's sake. You know how many don't make the grade. Stop thinking you're still some small-town deputy. I've seen what you're capable of. Our investigation?"

"You seem to forget—in *that* investigation—I almost got us both killed."

"Well, I'm not saying all your decisions were perfect." Logan half smiled. "But you fought your way into this position. Walked through fire to get here. Maybe you can't control the actions of the people you're working with, but you can control your own. Right?"

Riley thought of the Sin Eater. His face—haunting the news through her childhood—flickering now on billboards across the city. The mistakes made by the cops in the past. The victims ignored. Sydney and others. The arrogance of Bret Childs and the way Mustang John had poured scorn on Hayley's ordeal.

What had Meadows said that first day?

I require my agents to be proactive. To think for themselves.

"Right?" pressed Logan.

Riley met his gaze, felt a new determination settle inside her. "Right."

As the waiter brought the check, the lights blinked on. A few diners cheered.

Riley sat back, the spell broken. "God, I've talked your ear off."

"I'm always here, Riley. At the end of the line, or down the road. Besides," he added with a grin, pulling out his wallet, "you can't have your old job back."

At Riley's insistence they split the check, then got their coats.

Outside, Logan hailed a cab. "You coming home for Christmas?"

"I promised Maddie I would."

A cab pulled up, wheels churning through slush. "You take this one," he offered. "So, maybe we can catch up then?" Logan spoke lightly, but she could see the hope in his face.

"I would like that." Riley paused on the sidewalk. The martinis had made her bold. She stepped in and hugged him, standing on her toes to kiss his cheek.

He drew back, enough to look at her. She thought she saw a war in his eyes: hesitation versus impulse. The driver gave a toot of his horn.

Logan reached out and cupped her cheek with his hand. The faint brush of his thumb across her skin sent a charge right through her. "You know where I am."

Riley climbed into the cab.

She turned as it pulled away to see him standing there, watching her go.

24

Riley and Fogg drove out from Des Moines in Fogg's Buick, following trucks spraying fans of salt onto roads slick with ice. Fogg had done a search for the image Sydney Williams had sketched for them during yesterday's interview—recalled on the jacket of her attacker. It had led to a logistics company in Lone Creek, a township in the north of the state. The radio babbled news of delays and dangerous conditions, and it took them three slow hours to reach it. Fogg had turned the heat up high, and Riley's head throbbed from the three martinis she'd had last night.

Lone Creek was an unremarkable speck on the vast flat of the Iowa plains. Population 895. The township had one church, one gas station, a convenience store, a diner, and a motel. It was surrounded by snow-covered crop fields and girdled by a frozen creek. Grain elevators rose like giants across the fields, where red-tailed hawks circled.

Arriving at the company's warehouse, they were told the former owner, a Mr. Morrow, had sold the business some years earlier but still lived with his wife in town. Riley noted the old logo above the warehouse doors: two white boxes with a blue line—the creek she guessed—winding between them.

As they pulled up outside the address they'd been given, Riley felt her hangover subside at the rush of anticipation. Might their suspect live here? The house was a timber-fronted one-story, painted a disturbingly bright blue. It hunched low to the ground, its windows mean and narrow.

Pulling on her coat, she caught a whiff of Logan's cologne trapped in the wool. Last night, his words of encouragement had been a welcome shot of courage, but on the drive north her thoughts had returned to her talk with Noah and her growing unease that Peter Altman could pose a serious risk to her position.

Together, she and Fogg made their way up an uneven path to the front door. Fogg knocked. After a pause, there was a rush of noise. A German shepherd lunged at the door, barking furiously. Fogg startled off the stoop as the dog's teeth gnashed at the glass, steaming it up in hot, angry bursts.

Riley turned as the dog continued to bark. She scanned the empty street. Lone Creek held that eerie hush of rural settlements in winter, no through traffic, no kids playing. Drapes and shutters had already been closed against the day's dying light. The air held a steel bite.

"Let's check with the neighbors," Fogg suggested.

They'd reached the street when a silver pickup, spattered with dirt, pulled up. A woman was driving. She stared at them as she opened the door and jumped down into the slush of the sidewalk. She wore loose-fitting jeans, logger-style boots, and a tatty parka, the fur trim on the hood sticking up in stiff spikes with the cold. She had a ruddy complexion and long dark hair that was coarse and graying. A cigarette was couched in the corner of her downturned mouth.

"Help you?"

Fogg smiled and offered his badge.

Her gaze went first to the Colt, protruding from his holster; then she took his ID and studied it for a full minute, glancing between Fogg and his photograph, smoke puffing from her nostrils. "You look younger in this," she stated, handing it back.

"I felt it," Fogg admitted. "We're looking for Mr. Morrow."

"What's that motherfucker done now?"

"You know him?"

The woman tossed her cigarette down and ground it under her boot. "Son of a bitch was my husband." She brushed past them and headed up the path to the house, leaving a cloud of smoke in her wake.

"Was?" Fogg said, glancing at Riley with a raise of an eyebrow, then following.

"Quiet, Peaches!" the woman yelled through the door as the German shepherd howled. She glanced back as she dug her keys out of her pocket. "Cocksucker left me. Five months ago. Ran off with my bitch of a sister."

"What's your name, ma'am?"

"Eileen."

"Do you know where your husband is now, Eileen?"

"At the bottom of a lake—I hope." She paused, narrowing her eyes at Fogg. "Why do you want him?"

"We need to ask him about his company. The logistics business he sold?"

"If this is something to do with the IRS, you can keep me the hell out of it. The shithead cleaned out our bank account. Left me with nothing."

"It's not taxes," Fogg assured her. "We have some questions about a possible crime committed in Des Moines, sixteen years ago."

"What kind of crime?"

"A violent crime," Riley interjected. "Against a young woman. We believe the suspect may have been wearing a green jacket, with the logo of your husband's company on it."

Eileen locked eyes with Riley. After a moment, she nodded. "That's what his workers wore. Their uniform."

"What sort of work did they do?"

"Storage, packing, distribution." She shrugged tightly. "Logistics."

"Do you have a list of his former employees? Company records? Pay slips?"

"I burned everything after he left. All of it. His clothes. His papers. His shitty fucking vinyl collection. Had myself a grand ole bonfire in the backyard with a quart of bourbon and some gasoline."

Fogg took out a photocopy of the facial composite. "Do you recognize this man?"

Eileen studied it. "He's been on the news," she said, looking up at them. "That psycho down in Des Moines." She stared at it, her brow knitted. Finally, she shook her head. "I don't think so. But I never went to the warehouse much."

"Do you have a photograph of your husband?" Fogg asked carefully.

The woman hesitated, then exhaled. Reaching into the back pocket of her jeans, she took out her cell, unlocked it, then showed them the screen. It was a younger her in a wedding gown, her hair piled on her head, adorned with baby's breath. Her face shone with happiness. The man beside her, arm cradled protectively around her waist, was a few years older and already balding, with chubby cheeks and big grin. He looked nothing like the composite sketch, even allowing for any change in age. Fogg nodded, and Eileen put the phone away, her face soft with sadness.

"You've no way of getting in touch with your husband? Or your sister?"

Eileen's expression closed in again. "No one's heard from them. All I know, they could be on the goddamn moon." She turned to the door as the dog whined. "I gotta feed her." She paused on the stoop. "Try Richard Kitch. He might remember some of my husband's workers from that time." She jerked her head down the street, toward a row of larger houses in the shadow of the water tower that loomed over the town. LONE CREEK was written around its bowl in large red letters. "Kitch inherited the property from his parents in the eighties, after he got out of prison. Set up a halfway house for ex-cons to start a new life. Caused a lot of trouble at the time. People didn't want felons living down the street. Not near their kids. But then folk suddenly had all these young men desperate for work and happy to do it for cash. Cheap labor. My husband recruited a lot of his workers from Kitch's place over the years."

"What's the address?"

She nodded to the houses again. "Clear over there, by the tower. Closed down years back. But Kitch still lives there with his son. The old sign's hanging over the front door. FRESH START. You can't miss it."

The room at the Lone Creek Inn was stuck firmly in another decade. There were two queen beds with chintzy quilts and cushions, a bulky TV on a stand, a mini fridge, and a heater, its vents plugged with dust. The walls were decorated with dingy landscapes: sunsets in forests with dirt-dark skies, copper light seeping like blood through the trees.

They had found Richard Kitch's house without trouble, but although there had been a light on in one of the upstairs rooms, no one had answered, so they'd booked two rooms at the motel and planned to try again in the morning. As Riley set the room key on the nightstand, she wondered if Altman had heard back from the lab at Quantico on the key ring found in the burned-out car. She guessed he probably wouldn't bother to tell her if he had.

Kicking off her boots, she sat on the edge of one of the beds, which creaked loudly. She felt weary, all the anticipation of the day unrealized, only her hangover and her worries about her job and the investigation left to niggle at her brain.

Step by step, she reminded herself, thinking of Logan's calm advice.

Taking out her cell, she tried Maddie again. She was fully expecting to have to leave another voice mail, so it was a surprise when her niece answered on the final ring.

"Hi."

Riley held back a sigh at Maddie's flat tone, forced herself to sound bright. "Hey, sweetheart."

Silence.

"I've missed you. How's school? Did you make me that card?"

A noncommittal murmur.

Riley tugged at a loose thread on the quilt, where flesh-colored flowers bloomed and spread. She changed tack. "Guess where I am?"

"Where?" A spark of wary interest.

"The worst motel you could imagine."

"Really?" A pause. "Worse than *Psycho*?"

"Yup. Definitely not taking a shower here."

A brief laugh that vanished quickly. "Why are you in a motel?"

"This case I'm working on."

"The case you were working on over Thanksgiving?"

"Yes—that one. Maddie, I'm so sorry. I know I made you a promise. I shouldn't have. I've not been in the job that long and it's a complicated situation. And, to be honest, my apartment isn't much better than this motel. I want you to be comfortable." Riley thought of the Sin Eater on billboards across Des Moines. *And safe.*

"I can sleep on the couch." Maddie's voice sharpened, turned plaintive. "I just want to see you. You don't know what it's been like here."

"What do you mean?" Riley asked quickly. Then, slow and careful. "Has your dad been smoking again, honey?"

A long sigh. "It's not the same, is all. Just me and him. The house is so quiet. I don't have anyone to talk to."

Riley closed her eyes at the hurt in Maddie's voice. Guilt closed its fist in her chest. "You've got so many friends, sweetheart. And you'll be off to college soon. It won't always feel like this."

"Can't I come for one night? I can catch a bus. I looked up the route."

"Not yet, Maddie. I'm sorry. But I'm coming home for Christmas, OK? We can make proper plans then. I promise."

"That's what you said about Thanksgiving." Maddie's tone had hardened. "I gotta go."

"Maddie, wait—"

The line went dead. Riley swore. She was about to tap Maddie's number again, but stopped herself. She would give her time to cool off, call again tomorrow.

She brushed her finger across the fracture in the phone's screen, made when the drunk woman at the gala had knocked it from her hand in the skywalk. What was it the woman had said?

Gotta take the bitter with the sweet.

"Ain't that the truth," Riley murmured.

She looked up at a knock on the door.

25

Hungry?" asked Fogg, turning with a smile. He gestured to the bar across the motel's lot.

"Starving," Riley admitted.

Shutting the door on the dingy room and her guilt, she walked with Fogg past the Buick to the box of a building, which looked like a good gust of wind would blow it over. There was a row of motorcycles outside. A Budweiser sign flickered in the window.

Heading in, they halted at the threshold, taking in the interior. The bar had a Hawaiian-style grass canopy festooned with lights. The stools were rattan and there was bamboo detailing on the walls, painted in gaudy tropical shades. Ukulele music drifted from speakers. There was a young woman leaning against the bar, dressed in a Cyclones jersey. Six men sat on stools in front of her, drinking Pabst Blue Ribbon, watching a hockey game on a TV. A chalkboard had details for the forthcoming SATURDAY NIGHT LONE CREEK LUAU!

The men were all oversize, dressed in jeans and leathers. Long beards and graying hair in ponies. They turned as the cold rushed in. One, who had a handlebar mustache and an ear full of metal, looked from Fogg to Riley, then back to the TV.

"How can I help you guys?" asked the young woman, meeting them at the bar.

"You have a menu, ma'am?" Fogg asked.

"Sure." She dug a stained one from behind the bar and handed it over. "Ribs are good."

They took the menu to a table by the window. Beside a crate of condiments was a plastic napkin holder in the shape of a pineapple. After they'd ordered, Fogg turned to Riley, his face lit unsettling shades of neon by the sign above them. "We'll try Richard Kitch first thing, see if he recognizes our composite. I'm trying not to get my hopes up, but this halfway house could be something. Ex-cons? Our suspect could easily fit that bracket. That and the logistics company—access to a vehicle, for starters. Maybe the gaps between the attacks could be explained by the transient nature of his work?"

"If Kitch doesn't recognize him?"

"We'll ask around. People here will know each other's business for sure."

Riley nodded, thinking of Cedar Falls. It was a metropolis in comparison to Lone Creek, but there had still been elements of small-town rumor and association.

Fogg's nose wrinkled as he looked out of the window. "I don't think I could stand it."

Riley followed his gaze to the empty street, where a single light blinked from green to red—no traffic to direct. "Always been a city boy?"

"Louisiana born, but I was raised in Des Moines. Sure, it's got its faults, but it's where I did my training, got my first job. Met Marcia. It's where my girls went to school."

"Your daughters still live there?"

"Both at college now. But they came home for the holiday." Fogg took out his cell. He showed her the screen. "Just decorated the tree."

Riley leaned over to see two young women, early twenties.

"Sherri," Fogg said, pointing to the slightly older of the two. "And Keira." His finger shifted to the younger woman. Her head was tilted on her sister's shoulder. She was pulling a silly face and had a swirl of red tinsel wrapped around her neck.

There was a Christmas tree in the background, all baubles and lights. Riley could see part of a couch, scattered with cushions and a tasteful throw. There were pictures on the walls and books on shelves. Lamps cast the room in soft amber light. A proper home—cozy and lived in.

It made her think of Maddie in their old house. Rotten timbers and peeling paint. The empty rooms, no longer used, dust gathering on the china in the dining room, the yellowed curtains drifting. Ethan shut away in his room, wallowing in country music and bitterness, dwelling on his ex, his job. His dead-end life.

She thought about the nights she and Maddie used to spend together whenever her niece stayed over—Maddie perched at the kitchen counter, leg kicking idly, pen in her hand as she sighed over her homework. They would talk about each other's days—share the annoying or amusing— crack a root beer, order takeout. Sit together on the porch swing, Scrounger at their feet, as the sun slipped and the evening came alive with cicadas. Riley could understand the depth of Maddie's loneliness, stuck there alone in winter, nothing but a gassy old dog for company.

A reckless thought jumped into her mind. What if they just sold the place? Ethan could use his share to get a modern apartment with a nice room for Maddie, stand on his own two feet for a change. Maddie could stay until college, which they'd be able to afford. A new start for all of them. No maintenance. No unexpected bills. No pressure on her to hold it all together.

But then she thought of her grandfather and his father before him— all the sweat and tears poured into that house over the decades. The births, lives, and deaths. She knew her parents and grandparents would have wanted it passed on to Maddie and Benjamin. The connective tissue of the Fisher family, going back generations, was bound up in its walls. That house was the bones of them.

She nodded to the picture on Fogg's cell, managed a smile. "Got two beautiful girls there."

Fogg nodded appreciatively. "Thank the Lord they take after their mother." He looked at the screen, his own smile fading. "But now they're gone maybe it's time me and Marcia moved on too?"

Riley had seen this look in his eyes before, back in the DCI incident room when he was looking at the wall of victims. In them, she could see the dark roads this investigation had been walking him along. How his city had become a place of pain under his watch.

They sat back as their food arrived. Two plates piled with ribs in a sticky sauce, mashed potatoes on the side.

Fogg waited until the young woman retreated. "I've been thinking again about our victims."

Riley waited for him to continue.

Fogg dug his fork into the mound of potato. "Colleen Traeger was working on the streets. Beth Muir was a defenseless kid. Bobbi Kinzel was elderly and frail. Nicky Johnson lived alone and Sydney Williams was walking through a deserted area late at night."

Riley nodded as he listed them. "All easy prey."

"Right. But Hayley Abbot?" Fogg paused, the forkful of potato suspended. "She was alone, yes, but it was a busy area in daylight and she's a fit young woman. He incapacitated her quickly, but he took a big gamble. Same with Megan Thomas. Sneaking around her garage? He could have easily been spotted by a neighbor."

The door opened and two youths entered. They strolled to the bar and eased themselves onto stools. One took off his beanie, releasing a thatch of straw-colored hair. He scanned the room, ignoring the older men, then stared at Fogg for a long moment. He nudged his companion, who glanced around and grinned at something he said.

If Fogg noticed, he didn't show it.

"Could his MO have changed during the period he was dormant?" Riley wondered, looking back at him.

"In what sense?"

"Is he attacking a different type of woman now? You said the cops on the original investigation thought he might be a hunter." Riley's mind filled with memory—creeping through woods with her grandfather, the stock of her Winchester snug against her shoulder, squinting into the sights. "Maybe he wants more of a challenge?"

"Or perhaps his message has changed?" said Fogg, chewing thoughtfully. "In the nineties, maybe it was about sin? Maybe now, it's more about power? Two or three decades ago, the majority of women in this state could only really expect to go into nursing or teaching as professions. Now, my daughters are studying law and finance. Your agency is run by a woman. We have our first female governor. Things have changed."

Riley thought of the reaction to her promotion in Black Hawk and the torrent of abuse received by Jess Cook. Thought of the stats she'd learned at the academy.

One in five women in America will be raped in their lifetime. One in four experience severe physical violence by a partner, which will be witnessed by one in fifteen children. One in seven will be stalked.

Had things really changed? Or was it more like a snowfall that had covered a landscape? You might not see all the ruts and potholes so well, but they were still there underfoot, ready to trip you.

Fogg set down his fork, the furrows in his brow deepening. "But there's my problem, see. If our suspect did leave that message for the governor, it was another big risk. He's always been extremely careful about not leaving evidence, yet he left enough of a trail for you guys to track him to that car?" He shook his head. "I gotta say, since we spoke to Sydney, I've been struggling to connect those dots. Sydney's attack showed all his classic markers. As did Hayley and Megan's, even if they were riskier assaults. But the threat to Cook?"

Riley stayed silent for a long moment. She thought of Jess Cook's hand, reaching out to rest gratefully on hers at the gala. What if there was no connection to the Sin Eater, as Jess herself had wondered? Fogg, Altman, and Meadows had followed her willingly enough down this track, but what if she was leading them wrong? What if something happened to the governor or her family while they were here, hours from Des Moines?

She felt like a bridge, flexed out between two sides, with no idea of her footing. If either side shifted, she'd be the one to come crashing down. She might not trust Peter Altman, but she had to confide in someone.

As she spoke, telling Fogg about Jess Cook's theory and the political resistance to her controversial bill in the capitol, the detective listened intently.

When she'd finished, he took a napkin from the pineapple, wiped his mouth. "I wish you'd told me this sooner."

"I'm sorry. I should have."

"Why didn't you?" His brown eyes had hardened.

Riley hesitated. If she was being honest, part of her simply hadn't wanted to torpedo the task force, not without concrete reason. She wanted on Fogg's case—truly, deeply. The victims' stories were planted in her now. Seeds of trauma. They had grown into stalks that bristled with a need to find them justice. Instead, she told him the easier truth. "Honestly, I still thought it could be the Sin Eater, given the governor received the letter before the news of his return." She paused, then conceded, "But it *is* possible that information could have been leaked beforehand. And that someone could have used it to try to scare her."

"Any suspects in mind?" Fogg's eyebrows shot up when Riley answered. "You're serious?"

"I know," she said quickly. "But I saw how Ted Pierce interacted with the governor. Real passive-aggressive. It's not inconceivable he could have learned of the Sin Eater's return before your press conference. Pierce would have access to the governor's schedule. Would know . . ." She faltered, not wanting to talk herself off his investigation, or sound like a crazy person. But now she'd started, she wanted to share the scattered thoughts swirling through her mind these past days. "He would know there are no cameras in the capitol."

Fogg leaned forward, keeping his voice below the hum of the TV. "You're suggesting the senate minority leader threatened the governor? That he photographed her family? Stole a car in order to leave a message in her office? Then had at it with a can of gasoline?"

"I know it sounds—"

"And besides, you guys saw the footage from the parking lot surveillance. Altman said your suspect was medium to heavy build. Ted Pierce is built like a string bean."

"I'm not saying he would have done these things himself. He could have paid someone else to do it." At his expression, she felt herself flush and wished she hadn't said anything. She sat back, tense and awkward. She was about to tell him to forget it when a spasm in her shoulder shot her back to Black Hawk. "Hamilton," she said quietly, meeting Fogg's eyes. "We'd have all thought that was ridiculous. Before it wasn't."

This time, Fogg held her gaze. After a moment, he shook his head, but the incredulity had gone from his face. "All right. Like I said, I've been struggling to link the governor to the other victims myself. I agree we need to keep an open mind, but let's start off a little lower down the mountain, shall we? We know Cook was targeted by Karl Madden, a violent extremist. There was another protest against her restrictions at the gala. You've told me the sheer level of abuse she receives from all manner of folks."

"But you said yourself the snakes in the letter looked enough like the Sin Eater's signature to warrant investigation," Riley reminded him. "The threat talks about her curse, her place as a woman. We all saw the similarities in the Sin Eater's obsession with Eve. Unless those connections are coincidence, it would need to be someone who knew of his return before it was made public. And that wouldn't just be some guy on the street."

Fogg gave a small nod of concession. "There's a number of people that knew. My team at the DCI, cops over at Des Moines PD, others in law enforcement agencies I'd been dealing with." He rubbed at the worry lines that had collected at his brow. "I told you in our first meeting I'm already on thin ice with this investigation. I've got media all over this. I've got victims and families desperate for news. I can tell you now, Riley, we start openly pointing fingers at a man like Ted Pierce—even indirectly—this whole case gets blown to shit." He waited until he was sure she understood him. "Have you talked about any of this with Peter Altman or Connie Meadows?" Fogg nodded, relaxing a little when she shook her head. "OK. We'll start with Kitch tomorrow. See where that takes us. Then we'll—" He looked down as his cell rang.

Riley glimpsed the name: *Marcia*.

"Excuse me," Fogg said, swiping the phone from the table and heading outside.

Riley noticed the straw-haired youth at the bar watching him leave. She picked at her meal, but the sauce on the ribs had turned cold and congealed, and their strained conversation had spoiled her appetite.

Her eyes flicked to the window as Fogg appeared outside in the snow. She saw him speak, his breaths clouding the night air. After a few moments, he laughed, all his worry lines disappearing. Her eyes caught her own reflection in the glass, staring out, face pinched in thought.

Let's start off a little lower down the mountain.

There was one man she could see down there in those foothills, a man already shrouded in question. Might there be another—more treacherous—reason for Peter Altman to want her away from his side of the investigation? So much so he would threaten her? Altman, whose lack of action once before had led to the governor's life being put in danger?

The black Tahoe squatted in the shadows, between pools of street-light that cast a sour glow, turning the snow on the sidewalks a urine yellow.

Peter Altman rested his head back against the seat, the fans pumping out heat. The interior still smelled of the burrito he'd eaten three hours earlier, the foil crumpled on the dash. He'd gone through his flask of black coffee, but all it had given him was indigestion. His eyes kept closing.

Pushing his hands through his hair, he sat up straight, fixing his attention back on the house. Trees sprawled around it, the branches obscuring some of the windows, all of which were shuttered. Light glowed between the gaps. Earlier, when he'd lowered the window to wake himself with a blast of freezing night air, he'd heard music coming from the place.

This was the second day of his surveillance. In the five hours he'd been here tonight, he had seen only three people enter: two men carrying bulging plastic bags and a skinny woman pushing a stroller, who'd made him sit up for a minute. No one had left. On the dash, beside the foil, was the scrap of paper Sawyer had given him at the Last Chance Saloon, the house number and street scrawled in the man's untidy script.

Altman took out his phone as it vibrated in his pocket. *Missed call.*

Unknown number. It would join all the others in the folder from Connie Meadows, demanding an update from him. If he didn't report in soon the shit would hit the fan. He couldn't afford to make any more mistakes. Not now.

He tensed, seeing the door of the house crack open. A lone woman slipped out. She walked down the path cleared through the snow, unsteady on her feet. She wore a hat, blond curls frizzing beneath. The coat she wore swamped her thin frame. Altman sat forward, hands gripping the wheel.

He let her get a little farther along the deserted street. His hand was reaching for the door when the phone flashed again. *Caller unknown.* Cursing, he answered, keeping his eyes on the woman, who appeared briefly in a puddle of streetlight, then disappeared, swallowed by the shadows beyond. "Who is this?"

There was a long pause on the other end. "Hey, Altman."

Altman felt coffee rise bitter from his gullet. "How did you get my number?"

"The question you should be asking is—why did I go to the considerable trouble of getting it? We had a deal, you and me. I made good on my end."

"And I made good on mine," Altman said through clenched teeth, eyes on the woman, appearing in another pool of light. Some distance away now.

"It's a question of value though, isn't it? My intel was more valuable to you than yours was to me. Therefore, we ain't even. Not close."

"Fuck you, Sawyer," Altman growled, flinging the phone onto the passenger seat. He cast his eyes back to the street, scanning the darkness.

The young woman was gone.

Altman slammed his fist into the door. His shout filled the car.

26

The Buick sat low to the ground, its tires deflated—the rubber slashed open. Its windshield was blistered with ice. Across it, someone had scrawled a racial slur. The letters were starting to bleed in the sunlight.

Riley looked away, unsure of what to say, as Fogg continued to study it.

"Well, that's gone and pissed on my morning," he said after a long pause.

Fogg was walking around the vehicle, surveying the damage, when the street filled with the throaty growl of a motorbike. Riley saw a large man approaching, in shades and a leather jacket. She raised a hand to shield her eyes from the sun. It was one of the men from last night, with the handlebar mustache and an ear full of metal. Come to gloat over his handiwork?

The man pulled up in the motel lot and killed the bike's engine. "Heard you folks found yourselves in a spot of trouble. Lizzie texted me," he explained, nodding to the bar. "Kid who served you last night." He shook his head as he studied the car. "Gabriel Marsh. Caught him sniffing around out here when we left. Saw him off, but I guess the lunkhead came back."

Riley thought of the straw-haired youth who'd sat at the bar, shooting glances at Fogg. "How did he know it was ours?" she asked, her eyes on the vehicle.

"Easy guess," said the man, nodding to the back seat, where Fogg's DCI jacket lay. "I've got a pal with a tow," he added, taking out a phone. "Leland will get you to the nearest auto shop."

"That's OK. I've got roadside."

"You'll be waiting hours." The man held up his cell. "It's no trouble. Leland owes me."

"Well, if you're sure?" Fogg looked at Riley—their plans for the day shot.

"I'll go see Kitch," she offered.

Fogg handed her the composite. "Call me when you're done."

As she headed off on foot, folding the sketch into her pocket, Riley heard the man call to Fogg.

"Why don't you go see if Lizzie'll put a fresh pot of coffee on? I'll scrape this shit off."

She felt bad for thinking he'd done it.

The water tower rose ahead, looming over the rooftops of the town, as she retraced yesterday's steps through trails of slush. She passed a playground with a rusted slide and merry-go-round. Beside it was a cemetery. Life and death huddled close together. There were festive decorations in yards, strings of lights and wicker reindeer. She thought of her promise to Maddie—that she would come home for Christmas. Thought of the hope in Logan's face when he'd asked the same. Then she thought of her conversation with Fogg and her own suspicions, now coalescing around Peter Altman. This investigation was starting to feel like a riptide, pulling her out into deeper, darker water.

Richard Kitch's house was the last one on the street, by the water tower. It was larger than those around it—a redbrick Victorian. A peeling sign hung above the door. FRESH START. She rang the bell and waited. The door was opened by a middle-aged man in glasses. He had a book in one hand, finger keeping his place.

Riley showed her badge. "Sorry to disturb you, sir. I'm hoping to speak to Mr. Richard Kitch."

"My father. Can I ask why?"

"I've got a few questions about someone who might have stayed here, back when it was a halfway house."

"You'll be mining the depths of his memory there."

"I have a sketch that might help." Riley showed him the composite.

The man peered at it through his glasses, then recoiled with a frown. "That case in Des Moines? Jeez, you don't think he stayed here?"

"That's what I need to find out. He may have worked for Lone Creek Logistics at the time."

The man was still staring worriedly at the composite. "A few of our residents worked there." He glanced at her. "You've spoken to Eileen Morrow then?" There was a curious lift in his tone.

"She sent me here."

"What a year she's had." The man shook his head. "Come on in," he said, opening the door wider. "I'm Maynard. Maynard Kitch."

He set the book on a table in the gloomy foyer. Riley recognized the cover as one Maddie had read. Something about vampires and teenage girls.

Maynard looked sheepish as she spotted it. "I'd rather the FBI had caught me reading Shakespeare, or Proust. Or, better still, Conan Doyle."

Riley followed him up a sweeping staircase over the entrance hall, a well of shadows beneath. On the upper floor they passed many doors. The few that were open showed small rooms with narrow beds, desks, and chairs. There were crucifixes on the walls. The windows were filmed with dust, the air stale and chilly.

Maynard saw her looking. "This place was once full of people. Men coming and going. It's all quite different now."

"Why didn't your father keep it up?"

"As a halfway house?" Maynard shook his head. "That old devil, money. After the crash, a lot of our funding dried up. It's gotten worse in the years since. Round here, it's mostly farms and other agribusinesses, but many have been forced to sell to larger corporations—those that get government subsidies."

Riley knew this story.

"The kids who grow up here leave—those with brains, cash, or sense at least. Those who stay aren't always our brightest and best."

Riley—thinking of Gabriel Marsh and the word on Fogg's windshield—was inclined to agree.

"Companies sell up. Families move away. Businesses close down and the dollars go with them. We're left with the elderly, getting older." Maynard led her down the corridor. "I've heard of a few rural towns where federal investment is now all but a trickle, trialing ideas. Community-funded social projects that could entice more young people to stay, add value to the local economy. Real interesting stuff. But—this year? Well, folks are just clinging to what they've got left."

Maynard halted outside a door at the end of the corridor. He knocked, then entered.

Inside was a large room cast in dusk by the partially drawn drapes. An iron-framed bed was piled with blankets, dwarfing the old man who lay there asleep, snoring gently.

Maynard held out his hand for the sketch. Riley passed it over and waited in the doorway as he took it to the bed. He touched his father's shoulder. "Pop?"

Richard Kitch stirred. "Is it dinnertime?"

"Not yet. There's someone here to see you. She wants to know about one of our residents, back in the day. A man who might have stayed here." Maynard turned the bedside lamp on. "Worked for Mr. Morrow."

The old man shuffled his way up the bed, blinking as his son propped cushions behind him. Wisps of hair floated around his scalp. "Morrow?" he huffed. "That fucker?"

"Pop," chided Maynard, with an apologetic glance at Riley.

Richard Kitch followed his son's gaze to her, standing in the doorway. "Who's this?"

"She's investigating the attacks on those women, in Des Moines." Maynard handed his father the sketch. "Do you recognize him?"

The old man took the sketch and peered at it. He started to shake his head and Riley set herself for disappointment. Then, he paused and held it closer to the lamp, illuminating the jigsaw of a face. "It's a shit photograph," he murmured.

"It's a composite, Pop."

Richard Kitch looked up at Riley. "Attacking women?"

"Yes."

"Like I said, your photograph's a piece of crap. But it looks like a younger version of Raymond."

Riley straightened. "Raymond?"

"Stayed here for a time. Seventeen or so years back. Just got out of the joint. Got a gig driving for Morrow." The old man handed the photocopy back to his son. "He was older than this though."

"Do you know which prison he was in, sir?"

Richard chuckled at his son. "What lovely manners she has." His mirth faded. "I never asked them where they came from. Here, we were only interested in where they were going. Fresh start, right?" He paused. "Raymond was a little—different. Mostly kept to himself. But he had these episodes. Hallucinations and shit. Yelling at people who weren't there. Creeped some of the other guys out." The old man was back to staring at the composite. "I remember, he told me he was rich. Heir to some huge family fortune. But then he also said he'd once been shut up in Clermont. So, maybe that was all just delusion."

"Clermont?"

"Great big asylum, up in Winnebago County."

"Mental health institute, Pop." Maynard looked at Riley. "Clermont Manor. Just south of Scarville. Used to be a state-run hospital. I think it's mostly private now."

"When did you last see Raymond?"

"Late summer, about sixteen years ago. He'd been here about a year. Then, one day he just up and vanished."

Riley's heart quickened as she wrote this all down. The attack on Sydney Williams had been in the summer, sixteen years ago. Had he left here and found her?

She spent a while longer with them both, asking questions, until it was clear Richard Kitch had told her all he knew, or at least remembered.

The old man smiled broadly when she thanked him and called him sir again. "Hey, numbnuts," he barked, smacking his son's arm. "When you gonna find yourself a good woman?"

"Jeez, Pop."

"Ah, I know," said Kitch, sagely. "Still holding that candle for Eileen Morrow."

Downstairs, in the foyer, Riley gave her card to Maynard, told him to call if his father recalled anything else. She headed out, leaving him to raise a hand in farewell, his vampire book back in the other.

White clouds had rolled in on a brisk wind. Sunlight flashed in and out. Riley was halfway to the motel when she heard shouts coming from the playground.

There was a group of young men gathered around something on the ground, all jeering and jostling. Through the thicket of legs, she saw a thatch of straw-colored hair. *Gabriel Marsh.* Hearing a cry of pain, she went closer. Marsh was straddling a younger kid, pounding fists into his face.

"Hey!" She went shouting through the gate, into the playground. "Break it up!"

The five youths—not much more than boys really—backed away at her shout, but Marsh continued pummeling his victim, who was yelling, trying to hold his arms up to defend himself.

Riley ran to Marsh and grabbed him by his hood, hauling him off. As his tormentor staggered back, the younger boy scrabbled to his feet and ran, clutching his nose. The snow was flecked with his blood. Riley let go of Marsh's hood.

Marsh, panting, swung to face her. He was skinny, but tall for his age, standing over her. "What the fuck?"

"Think you're the big man? Beating up a kid?"

"Shithead had it coming."

"What about vandalizing people's cars?"

"Yeah?" Marsh wiped his nose with the back of his hand, his knuckles raw. "Prove I did anything."

One of the other youths, who'd backed off at Riley's intervention, stepped boldly in. "Fuck you!"

Marsh grinned. "Say, where's your boyfriend?" His eyes were cold.

Shadows of clouds stole across the playground, the sun disappearing. There were no sounds—no people around, no traffic. Riley sensed a change in the group. The way they moved in closer, like a pack. All eyes on her. Her instincts sharpened, her training kicking in.

De-escalate.

"Why were you fighting that kid?" She softened her voice, relaxed her stance. Almost immediately, she saw a change in a couple of the youths, who shifted to mirror her energy.

"Cuz he's a—"

Gabriel Marsh planted a hand on the chest of the one who had spoken, shutting him up immediately. "None of your business. What're you doing here anyway?" he asked, his tone sly. "Getting boned by your boyfriend for the weekend? Bit old, isn't he? Or can he still—you know?" He made a fist, raised his arm erect. "Get it up?"

"Do your parents live around here, Gabriel?"

A couple of the youths looked alarmed by her knowledge of his name.

Marsh didn't even blink. "Why don't you stick with your own kind?" He kept his eyes on her, then shrugged idly, hooking his thumbs in his pockets. "I'd do you, I guess. If I was desperate." He turned to his friends, gesturing at Riley. "You'd hate fuck her, right?"

A few of them grinned, looking at her.

Riley felt all the hairs on her arms and neck stand up. *Go.*

As she turned and walked away the youths laughed.

Gabriel Marsh didn't join in. He was following her. "Hey! I'm not done with you."

As she headed into the street, she saw a couple of the others glancing at one another, their bravado slipping.

"Gabe!" called one. "Let's go. I'm freezing my balls off!"

Marsh didn't listen. "Hey, bitch!"

A dam burst and she felt it. All of it.

Men old enough to be her father whistling at her from a construction site on her way to school. Feeling exposed, trying to tug down her skirt to cover her bare legs, her face flaming. *Give us a smile, baby!* Smiling because you were supposed to. *Sugar and spice, and all things nice.* Smiling just in case one got angry if you didn't.

She felt Hunter taking her hand, leading her into the dark, her head spinning with alcohol. The chain of her necklace snapping as she struggled against him. *Stay down, or I'll hurt you.* As if what he'd done wasn't hurt? His hand clamped on her mouth, the weight of him crushing her into the dirt.

Had you been drinking, Riley?

The rape whistle they'd given her in the welcome pack at college. The quiet words girls shared in dorms—which boys to trust, which ones to watch out for. The warnings on the backs of restroom doors never to leave your drink unattended. The numbers to call if you were a victim of sexual assault. The casual groping in bars. The way some turned when you said no. *Whore! Lesbo!*

Walking home alone at night, keys like blades between your fingers. Black Hawk County Sheriff's Office—a tampon left on her desk after she'd chewed out a male colleague in a briefing. The way she'd seen some of them deal with female victims and witnesses. *Calm down, sweetheart. No need to get hysterical.*

Hayley Abbot in that hospital bed. Her flat blue eye looking out on a world that would forever be changed. Sydney Williams still scared to go outside.

Like I was nothing.

Gabriel Marsh was calling to her. His voice was louder. His feet crunched in snow, coming up behind her. Riley felt her hand reaching to her hip.

She had her fingers on the Glock's grip when a door opened in the building beside her with the jingle of a bell and a woman in a brown apron stepped out.

27

"Here you go, honey."

Riley smiled faintly as the woman set a mug of coffee in front of her. Steam curled up to mist the window of the diner. Outside, the street was empty. Gabriel Marsh had gone, slinking off after the woman had yelled at him.

"Wanna tell me what that was about?" The woman sat down opposite, the cracked leather seat squeaking. Her brown apron creased into folds at her waist. She had fluffy fair hair, just starting to gray at her temples. Her nose was scattered with freckles over a faded tan and there were creases around her blue eyes. She wore a crystal pendant on a knotted leather thong. "Did Gabriel do something?" She shook her head. "That boy."

Riley set down the mug. She had almost drawn her weapon on a kid.

It had come like a flood, swamping her mind, making her forget her training. She had been so wrong, thinking she could box up the past by coming here, walk into a new future without it all dragging at her heels. How could it not when her past was her own damn shadow?

Maybe such vulnerability was OK in a county sheriff's office. But in the FBI, under the hard gaze of Connie Meadows? She felt that pitch of vertigo again—the dizzy realization that she couldn't return to her old life, even if she failed in this one.

The waitress was looking expectantly at her.

"It's fine. I'm fine."

"Clear as day you're not." The woman nodded to the kitchen. "Why don't I get Antonio to fix you some breakfast? He makes the best pancakes in town."

"The only pancakes in town," corrected a voice.

Riley turned to see a man in a stained white apron had appeared behind the counter. He smiled at her.

"Honestly, I'm good. But thank you." She needed to call Fogg, tell him what she'd learned—Raymond and Clermont Manor. *Get it together.*

The woman glanced through the heat-fogged window. "They're not all bad, those boys. Catch them on their own and they'd be *yes ma'am-ing* you and holding open the door. It's when they get together in a gang. That's when the trouble starts." She blew through her cheeks. "Gabriel Marsh is another story. He's one bad apple. Spoils the whole barrel."

"He was beating up a kid."

"Let me guess—little bitty boy, dark brown hair?" The woman sighed when Riley nodded. "That'll be Dean Alloway. Tough to be gay, growing up in a place like this. I'll speak to Gabriel's parents. And I'll check on Dean after my shift. His mom's a good soul, but she doesn't always know how to cope."

"Always getting involved, Patty," commented Antonio, behind the counter as he wiped a pie dish. But he said it kindly.

The woman—Patty—rolled her eyes, then smiled at Riley. "Well, I've known most of the folk here since we were kids."

"You've always lived here?"

"I went away a long time ago," Patty said after a pause. "Came back this year to look after my mom. Even got my old job back." She looked over at Antonio, but he'd disappeared into the kitchen. There was a clatter of dishes. "Here," she said, sliding out of the seat. "Let me get you a refill."

"You might be able to help me," Riley called, as Patty crossed to the counter and picked up a pot of coffee. "I'm looking for anyone who might recognize this man." She took the composite from her pocket, smoothed it out on the Formica. Patty was heading back, holding a coffeepot. "It's possible he stayed at Richard Kitch's halfway house sixteen years ago. Worked for Lone Creek Logistics."

Patty stared down at the creased face. "No," she said. "Sorry. I don't know him." She poured coffee into Riley's mug. Some sloshed onto the table, seeping into the edge of the paper. "Goddamn," she muttered. "Let me get you something to wipe that up with."

"It's fine," Riley called, but Patty was already hurrying into the kitchen, the door swinging closed behind her.

Riley was digging in her purse for a tissue when she saw her phone was flashing—she'd had it on silent since Kitch's. Her gut tightened as she saw the caller.

Connie Meadows.

"Ma'am?" she said, answering.

"Where are you?"

"Lone Creek." Riley glanced around at movement beside her, expecting to see Patty. Antonio smiled briefly as he leaned over and wiped up the spilled coffee, his eyes flicking to the sketch, which had turned brown and soggy at one edge. "I'm following a lead with Fo—Detective Verne."

"Have you been in contact with Agent Altman?"

Riley hesitated. What could she say but the truth? "I've not heard from him in a few days. He asked me to work with Fogg while he followed up lines of inquiry on the threat to the governor." She waited, but Meadows didn't speak. She ventured into her boss's silence. "Is something wrong?"

Meadows's voice returned, brisk as ever. "No. I'll try him again. But I want you back in the city as soon as possible, Fisher. As I made clear to Altman when I agreed to this task force, the governor remains the bureau's first priority. I don't want you distracted from that in any way, understood?"

"Yes, ma'am," murmured Riley.

From the coffee-stained paper, the dark puzzle of the Sin Eater's face stared up at her.

28

Clermont Manor appeared on the brow of the hill miles before they reached it, its rooftops and chimneys stark against the morning sky. A Victorian behemoth, brooding over scrubby fields.

Riley peered through the windshield at it as Fogg drove, the Buick's new wheels sure-footed on the icy road. It felt good to be gone from Lone Creek. She had filled Fogg in back at the motel, telling him what she'd learned from Richard Kitch, but leaving out the incident with Gabriel Marsh. Fogg had been quiet on the drive today and she wondered if he was still pissed at her for holding back her conversation with Jess Cook, or whether his thoughts lingered on the ugly message left by Marsh.

She checked her phone again. Nothing from Maddie, which was to be expected. No more from Meadows either, although her boss's curt reminder of her priorities had wedged in her mind, along with the impression Peter Altman was AWOL. If Clermont Manor didn't yield anything today, she would have to head back to the city, let Fogg continue on this trail alone.

She had lain awake last night, thoughts jumping agitatedly between her reaction to Marsh and her concerns around Altman. She'd wondered about talking to Fogg, asking him how well he knew the agent, but things were complicated enough. She had no evidence of any wrongdoing or corruption, just scattered dots of doubt without lines of reason or motivation to connect them. Besides, after Fogg had balked at the mere suggestion of Ted Pierce being in the frame, she knew if she now pointed a finger at a colleague on their own task force, the detective would probably start to question her faculties. She was starting to question them a little herself.

By the time dawn arrived, pale tendrils of light creeping around the motel's dusty curtains, Riley had made her decision. If she couldn't confront Meadows or Altman without endangering her position—or, worse, the governor herself—that left one person who might be persuaded to talk. An ex–special agent with, perhaps, a grudge to bear.

Entering the grounds, they passed a graveyard, headstones jutting like teeth from the earth. Beyond were outbuildings, including an old grain silo strangled in ivy. Riley, reading a brief history of the place, knew it once had a working farm attached. Now the grounds had been turned over to vegetable gardens. The plots were mostly bare, winter seeds sleeping under the soil. A scarecrow with a burlap face hung from a post.

Up close, the large building appeared less intimidating. One wing looked newer than the rest, the pale blocks of stone more pristine. There was a welcome sign—CLERMONT MANOR, INSTITUTE FOR MENTAL HEALTH—with images of smiling patients and staff. Parking in the busy lot, Riley and Fogg headed for reception. After showing their badges and asking to speak to the manager, they were led by an orderly along a maze of corridors.

The orderly, who wore a brightly patterned uniform and matching mask, treated it like a tour, pointing into various rooms. "Down there we have our award-winning drug and alcohol rehabilitation unit. It's not just counseling and drug management programs here. We have art classes and therapeutic writing." He gestured through a set of doors. "And there's our museum, showcasing the history of Clermont. The students who come here on day tours love that." He waggled his fingers. "Spooky photographs from the old wing for the criminally insane and rusty lobotomy equipment. Things are very different now though," he added swiftly.

At the far end of the top floor, they arrived at a door. The orderly knocked.

"Enter," came a voice.

The orderly ushered them in, leaving them to be greeted by a portly, middle-aged man with thinning auburn hair. He wore a tan suit. The wall behind him was decorated with framed commendations, going back years.

They introduced themselves.

"Henry Whyte," the man said in turn, gesturing to two chairs in front of his desk. "Reception said you were here to ask about a former patient?"

"A possible former patient," Riley said, sitting. "A man named Raymond. He would have been admitted here some time ago. At least seventeen or more years. Perhaps suffering from hallucinations and delusions. It's possible he had certain religious convictions and may have exhibited hostility toward women."

Henry Whyte shook his head. "That's going to be a problem."

"I'm sorry?"

"The fire. Six years ago. It destroyed part of a wing. Terrible tragedy. We lost two staff."

Riley thought of the newer blocks of stone on the building's façade.

Whyte continued. "All our records from more than a decade ago were stored there."

"How long have you worked here?" Fogg asked.

"Started as an orderly straight out of school. Worked my way up."

"Do you recognize this man?" Fogg placed the composite on the desk.

Whyte stared at the face. He shook his head, but his eyes lingered on the image. "No. I'm sorry."

"You've not seen it on the news?" Riley pressed.

"I don't get a lot of downtime in this job. Not enough to watch TV."

"Are there any other staff or patients we might speak to?"

"Who were here more than seventeen years ago?" Whyte smiled tightly. "I'm afraid I'm the only one mad enough to be here that long. Look, I have a meeting. I'm sorry I can't be of more help."

As Riley shook the man's outstretched hand, she felt sweat slick on his palm.

Out in the corridor, she glanced back as Whyte closed the door behind them. "Not much of a talker."

"We didn't give him a lot to go on," Fogg countered as they headed down the stairs. "Place like this would have had thousands in through its doors over that time frame. I'll call Jenna, get her to look into state records and—" He stopped when Riley halted, looking down the empty corridor toward the doors the orderly had pointed out earlier. "What?"

"Worth a shot?" she ventured, nodding to the sign painted on the glass.

CLERMONT MUSEUM

The museum was jumbled with things. Mannequins in old staff uniforms. Dusty glass cabinets showcasing medical tools, restraints, and other equipment. Photographs lined the walls, alongside paintings and poems by patients over the many decades the facility had been in use: stick figures and remarkable portraits in charcoal, unsettling hellscapes and serene watercolors.

Riley took one end of the room and Fogg the other, studying the photographs. Most were black and whites from years ago, nurses and doctors in starched uniforms, rows of metal beds in gloomy dormitories, padded cells and electroshock therapy rooms. Some showed patients working on the farm. Riley paused on a photograph of an elderly woman with a big, toothless smile, cradling a lamb.

"Well, I'll be damned."

She turned at Fogg's murmur. He was at the wall opposite. She crossed to join him, staring at a grainy color photograph of a large group outside in the gardens. They all had eighties hairstyles and clothing.

LABOR DAY PICNIC.

Riley followed Fogg's finger to a broad oak. Standing in dappled shade, away from the rest of the group, were two men. One was older, with a mustache, beard, and glasses. He had his arms crossed and looked as though he was in the middle of speaking, his gaze on the younger man, who was staring at something out of shot. The younger man was tall and slim, maybe early twenties, with straggly shoulder-length hair, a long face, and a wide, flat mouth. It was his eyes, though, that Riley was drawn to—that intense stare.

For the first time in days, she forgot all about Altman and Meadows, and her fears for her job. A shiver went through her. "It's him." She looked at the date. "Thirty-three years ago."

"Let's not get ahead of ourselves," Fogg cautioned. But she could hear his excitement too. He took a picture with his phone. "Looks like his friend there has a name tag." Fogg zoomed in on the screen with his fingers.

"Dr. Hale," said Riley, reading over his shoulder.

Henry Whyte stared out the window. He'd taken an Alka-Seltzer as soon as the agents had left, but his chest was still burning. He put a hand on his heart, feeling an irregular thump. He stiffened as he saw them appear below him in the parking lot. They had taken their time leaving.

The young woman was holding a piece of paper and talking animatedly to her partner. He watched them climb into a white Buick and drive off. He waited until the car had disappeared down the icy sweep of driveway before turning to his desk, his eyes going to the gold plaques on the wall behind.

Sitting heavily, he opened a drawer and rifled through until he found the old address book. He flipped through to the page. The ink was faded, but still legible. Picking up the phone, he cleared his throat and dialed. He sat up straighter when a man's voice answered.

"It's Whyte speaking, sir. Henry Whyte. The manager at Clermont Manor?" He swallowed thickly when the silence continued. "I was told to call—if anyone ever came asking about Raymond."

29

The bass from the club drummed the night like a heartbeat. Occasionally, figures spilled out through the black-painted doors past a doorman and, for a few moments, the beat thumped harder.

The pickup was parked in the far corner of the lot, away from the lights. The area lay under the flight path for the Des Moines International Airport and, every now and then, a plane would rise, engines roaring, to crest the darkness.

Kody, shivering in the truck's cab, followed their trajectory with envy. He'd never been on a plane, but he could imagine the places they might take him to—all the locations in his favorite games. Miami, Afghanistan, San Francisco. Sun, sand, and hot girls. Gangs and brothers-in-arms who'd never leave a man behind. The way he wished things still were with Troy. He ground his gum. It had lost its flavor hours ago, but it stopped his teeth from chattering and gave his mind something to focus on other than the man sitting beside him, tapping a thumb on the wheel, out of time to the beat from the club.

Harlan had come into his room earlier, asked him to take a ride. By his tone, Kody had known it was an order. They hadn't spoken since last night, when he'd found that Ziploc bag among Harlan's stuff. The uneasy silence between them had ended, but what came next Kody couldn't guess. He had no idea what Harlan was doing, parked here for the last hour. He was cold, needed a piss, and wanted nothing more than to go back to his room, forget all about this. But he didn't dare say so. There was a change in Harlan. The man was quiet and pensive, but his energy was that of a brewing storm. Kody was certain he didn't want to be in its path when that storm touched down.

"So, which one?"

Kody looked around sharply as Harlan spoke. "What?"

"There." Harlan nodded through the windshield to a group who'd just emerged from the club. Four men and two girls. College age. They were walking together through the lot. One of the girls stumbled and laughed, her breath puffing in clouds.

As Kody watched, the two girls exchanged kisses and hugs with the young men before heading, arm in arm, toward the road. The headlights of a truck cut white lines through the darkness. The men piled into a car and drove off, beeping at the girls, who waved.

The two of them huddled on the icy sidewalk, talking and sharing a cigarette.

After five minutes, a car pulled up and one of the girls gestured to the other, who shook her head and pointed down the road. They embraced, then the girl who'd gestured climbed in and blew a kiss to her friend. The other young woman began to walk away alone, weaving a bit on her feet, a few pale inches of her bare legs visible between the tops of her knee-high boots and the whisking hem of her coat.

"Her," murmured Harlan, a smile starting at the corners of his mouth.

Kody chewed his gum harder as Harlan turned the key and the pickup rumbled to life. He jigged his knee, his bladder aching. He didn't know what Harlan meant. *No.* He did know. That warning tapping at the back of his mind had stopped; the window had opened, and a new knowledge had crawled its way inside. He could still smell the sourness inside that Ziploc bag. Old pennies and dead things.

"Look at them like a lion would." Harlan's eyes were black pools, glinting in the shadows. The engine purred, low and deep. "Which one do you choose?"

Kody swallowed dryly. "Something weak?"

"Or alone," answered Harlan, turning his gaze back to the girl tee-tering along the dark road.

Kody's heart hammered as Harlan steered the truck out of the lot. They crawled along, headlights off, following the girl. He chewed furi-ously. "I need a piss. Can we stop?"

The older man ignored him, still following the girl. Eyes fixed for-ward.

"Harlan, please!"

Suddenly, the cab filled with a chiming ringtone. Harlan's cell, lying in the central console's tray, lit up. Kody saw a name on the screen.

Billy.

Harlan brought the truck to a halt by the curb. He grabbed for the phone. Answering, he listened for a moment, just nodding. Kody caught a voice on the other end, too faint to hear over the ticking of the engine.

"Shit," Harlan murmured. "OK. Got it."

Kody kept his eyes on the road. A cab drove past. He watched the girl raise her hand. Watched the cab pull up alongside her.

Get in. Get in.

"I'll sort it out." Another pause from Harlan. "Billy, man—I said I'll sort it out."

The girl had climbed into the cab. Kody watched it drive off, relief flooding through him. Harlan put his foot on the gas and set off again, hands tight on the wheel, face clenched in the shadows. He didn't even mention the vanished girl.

Kody was starting to relax, focused now on getting home, getting out of this whole fucked-up situation. FUBAR, Troy would call it. *Fucked up beyond all recognition.* Then, Harlan turned sharply down a rough road, the truck's wheels smashing through frozen puddles. Half-way down, he braked so hard, Kody swallowed his gum.

Harlan opened the glove compartment and pulled out a gun. He racked back the slide and pointed the weapon at Kody's face.

Kody cried out and threw up his hands. His mind filled with im-ages. Soldiers falling before his barrel, twisting and jerking as they were pumped full of lead, bursts of crimson from chests and skulls. His finger on the button. Harlan's finger on the trigger.

"You know some things now," Harlan said. "Things you ain't supposed to know."

"I won't tell anyone. No one!" Kody meant it.

Harlan watched him, those shark eyes unblinking. "Oh, I know you won't, kid. Cuz if you do, there are two bullets in this gun. One for you. One for your mom. I'll do her first, so you can watch."

Kody clenched his teeth to stop them chattering. "I promise."

After a long moment, Harlan lowered the gun. "I've got some things I need to do. Reckon you can help me. We're gonna need supplies." He nodded to the door. "Take that piss then."

Kody wrenched open the door and jumped down into a puddle. Freezing water burst up through the holes in his sneakers, but he only cared about unzipping his fly. He let go with a gasp, his piss steaming in the cold air. He could feel the gum stuck in the back of his throat.

He had a flash of memory—a teacher in junior high, catching him sticking a wad under his desk. She had told him to peel it off and swallow it. The other kids all laughing as he obeyed, red-faced, gulping down the cold, hard ball. Stacy Angel leaning over with those big blue eyes of hers, whispering that it would wrap itself around his heart and suffocate him.

30

Jess Cook squinted in the sunlight as she watched her daughter dashing about the mansion's lawns with her dog, Boo. The white terrier disappeared into a snowdrift, barking madly. Ella jumped in behind, shrieking as snow went over the tops of her rubber boots.

"Don't get cold feet, honey!"

"I'm OK, Mom!" Ella shouted back. She paused to wave at the two state troopers on patrol of the grounds. One waved back as she flopped down in the drift, kicking her arms and legs out as Boo jumped around her, snapping at flying snow.

"Here you go."

Jess looked around as Mark handed her a coffee. "Thanks, sweetheart." She cradled the mug in her hands, the warmth seeping through her gloves. It was bitter this morning. Enough to burn her lungs with every breath. She smiled as Mark wrapped his arms around her, then giggled as he kissed her cheek, his stubble tickling her neck. "This is nice," she murmured after a moment, closing her eyes and soaking it in: the feel of her husband's closeness, the happy shouts of their daughter, the trill of birdsong in the trees that bordered the mansion's grounds.

"It's good to have you home for a bit," Mark told her.

She heard him give a little intake of breath, a sign he wanted to say something further. She twisted slightly. "What is it?"

"Nothing."

"Mark."

"I can't stop thinking about the other night."

"At the gala?" Jess reached up, gave his hand a squeeze. "It's OK. Look, I understand it. The man had every right to be frustrated. Angry even. This year has been hard for everyone. Devastating for some."

"It's not so much him. It's the others out there. This—*monster.*"

"We don't know for certain that I'm being targeted by him. And, anyway, the FBI are on it."

Mark released his grip suddenly. "What about Madden? The FBI weren't on that, were they? How can you be so calm about all this?"

She looked around at their daughter, still playing with Boo. Ella was well out of earshot. Jess turned to her husband. His eyes were sharp with sunlight and concern. "What do you want me to do, Mark? Give up? Fall apart? That's what people like this want, you know."

"Can't you pull back a bit? At least do a few less town halls, until they've caught him?"

Her eyes narrowed. "So, the victim has to change their behavior to suit the aggressor?"

"Christ, Jess, this isn't some TV interview. This is me!"

"I just can't believe you'd ask me that!" Her voice had risen.

"You're not the only one he's threatened."

The two of them turned as Ella gave a whoop and landed in a fresh pile of snow.

Jess flinched as her phone rang. "I've got to get this," she murmured.

"It's OK." Mark took her coffee as she put the phone to her ear.

Rebecca's voice came on the line, her tone grim. "Ma'am, I'm afraid we've lost Senator Robuck. She's pulled her support for the bill."

"What?" Jess stalked away across the lawn, passing into the long shadow of the mansion's tower. "When did this happen? Have you spoken to her?"

"I was about to call her."

"Leave it with me. Jill and I might not always see eye to eye, but we go back a long way. Damn it!" Jess kicked at a lump of snow. "Pierce must have gotten to her." She looked around, hearing Boo barking furiously. The dog had disappeared among the trees that cloaked the mansion from the road beyond. Her daughter was ducking in and out of the bushes, calling the dog's name. "Ella!" she shouted. "Don't go too far!" As she saw Mark jog across the lawn toward their daughter, Jess turned her attention back to the phone. "Let me call Robuck. See if I can win her back. We need her support." Jess breathed out her frustration. "I want this bill passed."

Boo was still barking loudly. Something had clearly upset him. Ella had gone after him, vanishing into the thicket of trees. Jess turned to scan the undergrowth.

The air was torn apart by her daughter's rising scream.

31

Grandpa's stuff is all in here," said the young man.

Riley and Fogg watched as the garage door rattled up and the crowded interior became visible. Chairs and books were stacked in teetering towers, as if tossed up by a poltergeist. There was an old couch shoved against one wall, a bed frame strung with cobwebs, suits hanging in plastic covers, and piles and piles of boxes.

"I haven't managed to sort through it yet."

Fogg surveyed the chaos, drew a resigned breath. "Does Chick-fil-A deliver here?"

He and Riley started at one end of the jumble of belongings Dr. Hale had left to the world, dismissing furniture and personal items to work their way through the boxes.

Yesterday, following the details the receptionist at Clermont Manor had given for Dr. Hale—a retired psychiatrist tenured to the facility—they discovered he had died two years earlier. Hale's remaining family was a daughter, living abroad, and a grandson who'd inherited his property.

The air in the garage was freezing. The temperature had plunged overnight while they'd slept at a Holiday Inn off the interstate. Storm warnings had been issued, a polar vortex pushing down from Canada. The sky was a white veil, wreathed in dark ribbons of cloud.

"Thanks," said Riley as Hale's grandson reappeared with fresh coffees, then left them to it. "Anything?" she called to Fogg, who was hidden behind a stack of boxes.

"Nothing." Fogg stood with a groan, clutching his back. He perched on the edge of a dusty cabinet and continued flipping through a file before adding it to the growing pile of papers he'd discarded.

An hour later, Riley—cold and hungry—was wondering if they should give up, call Jenna at the DCI to take the search for Raymond into state records, when she opened up another box and saw scores of cassette tapes neatly arrayed in their plastic cases. Each was labeled with a name. *Anna. Christian. Pablo. Janice.*

Raymond.

"Here!"

Fogg came over. "Just need a cassette player."

"Thought your car would have one," she said with a quick grin.

"Ha, ha."

"You folks need anything?" Hale's grandson appeared again. "More coffee?"

"Do you have something to play this on?" Riley asked, holding up the tape.

"Wow." The young man's eyebrows raised. "Vintage! I can check my mom's old room."

Twenty minutes later, he returned with a pink boom box covered in stickers of big-haired eighties music stars. He left them to make more drinks.

Riley set the boom box on a cabinet and inserted the cassette. There was a loud hiss, followed by the harsh whine of feedback. She winced and turned the volume down. After a moment, a man began to speak, his voice muffled.

"Another breakthrough session with Raymond today. He talked at length about his family, always a painful subject for this young man. But I think he is, at last, starting to engage with reality. His recollections are clearer. I believe we're getting to the real memories, beyond the fantasies. He spoke about his younger brothers—about how their father pitted them against him. How they became instruments in his abuse. Raymond admitted he never felt he belonged in his family and found relief when his father sent him away to parochial school. His relief was short-lived, as the bullying continued in this environment. The other boys sensed his eccentricities and humiliated and tormented him. He found solace in his religious studies, but this is where, I now believe, his fantasies began to take a darker turn . . ."

The fuzz of noise on the tape increased and Hale's voice zoned in and out, becoming garbled.

"We can probably get this cleaned up in a lab," Fogg said, frowning as he fiddled with the volume.

"It sure has a lot to answer for."

Fogg glanced up at Riley's murmur. "What's that?"

"Religion."

"I think religion is an easy scapegoat in cases like this. People use it for their own ends. Use it to justify their actions, good or bad."

"You're a believer?"

He smiled. "Enough to go to church every Sunday."

"I haven't been in years," Riley admitted. "I used to love going with my grandmother. But I don't see how I can believe in a God who allows the sorts of things I've seen to happen. I'm amazed anyone in law enforcement can."

Fogg paused. "For me, religion isn't the same as faith. I have faith in a higher power, a higher purpose that gives even the most awful things meaning and resonance. I think I would find it more untenable to imagine those things happening in a vacuum. I have to believe there's purpose and hope. Chance for growth. Redemption."

The hiss on the tape dissipated and Dr. Hale's voice returned, more muffled than before.

". . . which led to his expulsion. Raymond left school early and was offered work in the family business, but the menial role, beneath his siblings, only increased his sense of isolation and feelings of inadequacy and jealousy. Raymond is less forthcoming about this period . . ." The tape crackled. "But I believe the key to the development of his more aggressive tendencies—his paranoia, his hostility toward the opposite sex—may lie here in . . ."

"Damn it," Riley muttered, as the tape cut out again.

Fogg was reaching for the buttons when Hale's voice returned, much clearer now.

". . . the lodge is the one place he seems to have found any serenity in life. He speaks calmly, lucidly, about days on the river and out in the woods. Fishing and hunting."

Riley and Fogg looked at each other.

"Coffees," called Hale's grandson, returning with two mugs gripped in one hand. He was carrying a box awkwardly under his other arm.

Fogg paused the tape.

"And I found this in Mom's room. Must have got mixed up with her stuff. More of Grandpa's files, I think."

Riley took the box from the young man and set it on the floor. Fogg grabbed a coffee, then started the tape again. Riley pulled the lid off the box as Dr. Hale continued to speak.

"The lodge may be an environment which could prove therapeutic, but I worry about the isolation. I have put Raymond on a new antipsychotic, which has fewer side effects, but he still needs supervision. Of course, many patients with this disorder can go on to lead healthy, balanced lives. But, in Raymond's case, without proper observation, I believe he will slip back into old behaviors. A danger to himself and, I fear, society."

Riley was half listening, half pulling papers from the box. They were drawings in all manner of styles, like the ones they'd seen displayed in the museum—some basic sketches, others astonishing works of art.

"His fantasies are indicative of . . ." The sound distorted. ". . . disturbing and violent, with specific religious motifs and . . ." More garbled words that made it sound like Hale was speaking underwater. "Of course, Jung would say that these archetypes offer us a clear . . ." The doctor's wry tone disappeared in a flurry of white noise.

Riley peeled another drawing from the pile inside the box, her protective gloves now smudged with charcoal. The paper beneath was a chaos of shapes and words scrawled in red and black. "My God."

Fogg crossed quickly to her as the tape hissed and crackled.

Together, they stared at the paper. It was covered in snakes, looping in and out of one another. Plunged into the coils of each serpent was a sword, tongues of fire licking around the blade. All around the margins were strings of words. The same sentence repeated, over and over.

Riley murmured it out loud. "*I am the son of Adam.*"

"Wait a minute," said Fogg, pulling out his phone. "Look." He crouched beside Riley, holding the phone alongside the drawing. On the screen was the partial sketch of the Sin Eater's tattoo: the snake with the cross hanging above it.

Riley saw what he'd seen. "It's not a cross," she said, hovering her finger over the paper and drawing a line in the air, from the blade's cross guard to the coils of the snake. "It's a sword."

On the tape, Dr. Hale's voice emerged from the static. "Together, we explore his fantasies in a safe space. Raymond speaks to me of building a church . . ." The tape cut out, whirring away to itself.

Riley's cell rang in the silence.

Meadows's voice came urgently on the line the moment Riley answered. "Are you still in Lone Creek?"

"No, ma'am. Winnebago County, I'm—"

"I need you back here now. Something's happened at the governor's mansion."

32

The figure hung from the broad branch of an oak, twisting in the wind. The noose around its neck creaked with every turn. It was a young girl in a white dress, hem fluttering around the crude stumps of her legs. Her hair, made of yellow ribbons stuck to her misshapen head, shivered in the gusts that whisked powdery snow from the drifts banked up around the trees. She had two pink circles for cheeks, two black ones for her eyes, and a wide red gash of a mouth, stretched in a scream. A mark was scrawled across her chest, over the lumps of wire and papier-mâché beneath the dress: a red snake with a bulbous head and a whip of a tail.

Riley, Fogg, and Altman stood a short distance back, staring up at the effigy, as the DCI crime scene technicians moved in the undergrowth, anonymous in their protective suits, hoods, and masks. A camera flashed in the surly late afternoon light.

The storm had tracked in behind Riley and Fogg as they'd driven south at speed, slate-dark clouds settling over the city.

"You've checked the security cameras?" Altman asked one of the troopers standing with them. The mansion's grounds were a hive of activity, state troopers combing through the trees. There were vans and squad cars, and the K-9 unit, dogs panting in the raw air.

The man nodded. "But as you can see there's a slope here. They don't cover this area. We'll check the neighborhood. Some of the houses on the street might have CCTV."

They all turned at the approach of another trooper. "The governor can see you now."

Altman looked at Riley. "You should take this one."

Riley met his gaze. Was this some unexpected show of trust? Or was he positioning her to take any flak? Altman's eyes were more bloodshot than usual. She could read nothing in them but tension and tiredness. He looked like he hadn't slept in days. She wanted to know where he'd been and what he'd been doing, but now wasn't the time to ask.

With its brown bricks and white eaves, the governor's mansion looked like an ornate gingerbread house. The state trooper led Riley inside, through a grand foyer and down a wide, wood-paneled corridor, where the stuffed heads of an elk and a caribou formed an arch of antlers. She was escorted into a large reception room, which smelled of childhood Christmases. There was a tree bedecked with lights. Garlands of winter greenery were draped across a mantle, framing a gold clock.

Jess Cook sat on the floor, crossed-legged, with her daughter, Ella. They were working on a puzzle. As the state trooper showed Riley in, a small white dog jumped up and scampered over.

Riley crouched to let the dog sniff her fingers. "So who's this?"

Ella looked to her mother for reassurance, then at Riley. "He's called Boo."

"That's a good name," Riley told the girl. She straightened with a smile.

Jess Cook rose, brushing a stray pine needle from her slacks. Her face was rigid. "Agent Fisher." She gestured Riley to a couch, then sat opposite, leaving her daughter by her feet, putting pieces in the puzzle. The dog returned to his place by the girl's side, head on his paws, eyes blinking up at Riley.

"Ella, my name's Riley. I just have a couple of questions for you and your mom. Are you OK with that?"

The girl kept her eyes on the puzzle, but nodded.

"That's great." Riley watched the girl place a piece into a space. "Can you tell me what time it was when you found the—the object in the tree?"

"The doll," murmured Ella. "The ugly doll."

"It was just after ten this morning," Jess answered.

Riley nodded. Around the time she and Fogg were listening to Dr. Hale's tape. "Did you see anyone nearby, Ella?" From what she'd noted of its positioning, the effigy was well concealed from both the street and the mansion, hidden in the trees, but she didn't know how far the girl might have ventured before she spotted it. "Someone on the street? Or in a car, perhaps?"

"I didn't see anyone. Boo found it. Not me." Ella stroked the dog's head. "He was barking. He didn't like it." She dropped her head, blond curls falling to hide her face. In the silence, the clock on the mantel-piece ticked loudly. Ella looked up suddenly, eyes darting to Riley. "Is it me? The doll?" She turned to her mom. "It looked like me."

"No," Jess cut in quickly. "No, sweetheart." She put her arms around her daughter, leaned in and kissed her cheek. "It's just some people play-ing a mean joke on Mommy."

Ella frowned at Riley. "Will you tell them to stop?"

Riley saw Jess's expression, caught somewhere between a plea and a challenge. Before she could answer, a man's voice called from the door-way.

"Are you almost done?"

Riley turned. She recognized the governor's husband, Mark. His face was strained, none of that relaxed warmth she'd seen at the gala while he was dancing with his wife. She felt bad to see the change, frus-trated she hadn't been able to do more to prevent it. On its heels, she felt a spike of anger. Altman had wanted the governor's case all to himself, had palmed her off on Fogg, but Riley knew full well Meadows would lay the blame for this at both their feet. She recalled Noah Case saying that their boss would always go to bat for Altman. Maybe just her feet then, she thought, threads of worry spooling around her anger.

Mark was dressed for outdoors and held a puffy pink coat. "I was thinking I would take Ella to my mother's?" He lifted the coat in suggestion.

"I think that would be a good idea," said Jess, rising. She looked at Riley, who nodded. "Sweetheart, Daddy's going to take you to Grandma's, OK?"

"Can Boo come?"

"Of course."

Jess stood, her arms folded tight, as she watched Ella head out, the little dog at her heels. The governor waited until the voices of her husband and daughter had faded down the hall, then turned to Riley. "She's right, isn't she? It's supposed to be her. That—*thing*."

There was no point denying it, but Riley dodged the question to ask one of her own. "You've spoken to your security? None of them saw it on their patrol?"

Jess shook her head. "We know it wasn't there yesterday, at least before five in the evening. There was maintenance work on the grounds. No one saw it then."

"So, it was put up between five yesterday and ten this morning," Riley repeated, writing in her notepad. "That gives us a good short window for checking any CCTV."

Jess looked to the door. "Maybe they shouldn't go to my mother-in-law's?"

"They'll have protection," Riley assured her.

"Should I get Ella out of the city? Out of school? She's missed so much already this year. What should I do?"

Riley felt the weight of the questions. Who should she answer? The state governor, the victim of an ominous threat, or the terrified mother? "You and your family have a lot of security here," she said carefully. "You have around-the-clock protection in the mansion and at your office, and security has been heightened at your daughter's school. I think you could discuss increased protection with your team. But I think it's premature to do anything drastic. Your daughter will be out of school soon anyway, for the holidays."

"I want this son of a bitch caught."

"I understand."

Jess turned on her. "How could you? You don't even have kids, do you?"

Riley felt the sting of that accusation. A wounded part of her wanted to say that was unfair—she'd brought up her brother's kid as her own. She didn't need to be a mother to feel pain or fear for a child. But she held her tongue.

Jess let out a breath. "I'm sorry. I shouldn't have said that. I'm . . ."

"It's OK."

"I'm just trying to do my job. Just trying to make people's lives better. How can he do this? Hurt these women? Threaten me? My child? Why?"

Riley heard Dr. Hale's voice on that tape.

A danger to himself and, I fear, society.

She was wondering how much to divulge to the governor when a state trooper appeared in the doorway.

"Agent Fisher, we've found something."

Outside, Riley headed back across the grounds to the team. The sky was an ugly gray-green. Snow was starting to fall. One of the DCI technicians was crouched by something on the ground, under the tree where the effigy hung. A marker flag had been stuck there. The technician was taking photographs.

"Footprint," Altman said gruffly as Riley joined them.

Fogg was on the phone. He hung up and came over. "Jenna's sending it now. The boot tread," he added, for Riley's benefit. "From Nicky Johnson's house in ninety-four."

"Looks like a sneaker," called the technician, taking another photograph. She crossed to them and showed them the camera's screen. "There's a partial mark on the tree trunk too. Appears the suspect climbed up to hang it."

Fogg looked at the image. He went to speak, then stopped as his phone pinged. He nodded at the screen. "The original print is almost twice the size." He showed Riley and Altman the photograph of the boot tread, left by the Sin Eater all those years ago, then gestured at the effigy. "This isn't our guy."

"A prank?" murmured Altman, frowning in thought. "Some political stunt?"

Riley saw Fogg's eyes flick to her. She felt some satisfaction at his rueful expression, but it vanished as she realized that she now had no choice but to tell Altman what they'd discussed in Lone Creek. Still, perhaps it was an opportunity? She watched the agent's face as she told him Cook's fear the threat could be a hoax.

Altman listened closely, but his thoughtful expression didn't change. He shook his head, now realizing the problem with the theory. "But we've not publicly released the fact we believe the Sin Eater could be targeting the governor's family." He gestured to the snake painted on the effigy. "A prankster wouldn't know to use that symbol."

"Well, if neither this nor the letter is the work of the Sin Eater, it would have to be someone who knew about the investigation," Fogg admitted. "Someone with intimate knowledge of his crimes." He looked at Riley, who'd gone quiet, her gaze on the small sneaker print beneath the fluttering marker flag. "What is it?"

Riley didn't answer. She was back in Lone Creek, the youths crowding around her in the playground, all eyes turning on her. Moving as a pack. Gabriel Marsh's footsteps crunching behind her in the snow. Patty's voice in her mind. *It's when they get together in a gang. That's when the trouble starts.*

"Riley?" Fogg stepped in, forcing her to focus.

"There is another possibility," she murmured, eyes on the footprint. "Something that might explain the change in his MO. The differences in the victims. Something that would account for his apparent recklessness in targeting the governor, but also his familiarity with the Sin Eater's methods." She kicked herself. She had made this suggestion in their first briefing in the DCI incident room, but Altman had spoken over her and she'd been too cautious to challenge him at the time. She turned to them. "What if there's more than one?"

33

Kody gripped the door handle as the pickup bounced along the rutted road. Harlan was hunched at the wheel, eyes forward, the wipers flipping back and forth. Snow was coming down fast, the trees along the river phantom shadows in the whitening world. Ahead, the road ended at a metal gate, buckled on its hinges. Kody made out the yellow sign. NO TRESPASSERS.

Harlan had brought him here on the promise of a reward for his help last night. The two of them had spent hours crouched in the chill of his mom's storm cellar, the smell of glue in the confined space making Kody light-headed, his gloved fingers sticking to all those yellow ribbons. Harlan silent beside him, shaping wire and twisting rope. It was five in the morning by the time they got home from the governor's mansion, where Kody had shinnied up the tree with the thing they'd made.

He'd been dead asleep when Harlan had come into his room, ordering him to get dressed. But here, on this lonely scrap of land on the edge of an industrial area, where the Des Moines River made a big, lazy loop around itself, didn't look like a place for any kind of reward.

Harlan pulled up at the gate and opened the cab's door. Kody flinched as snow and wind swirled in. He watched Harlan jog to the barrier. His eyes went to the glove compartment and he thought of the gun inside. As Harlan pushed the gate, which groaned open, drawing

a half circle through the snow, Kody leaned forward, reaching tentatively toward the compartment. He snapped back in his seat as Harlan
turned. The man climbed into the cab, shaking snow from his head. As
he drove on, it melted in lines down his face.

After a quarter of a mile of rough road, they came to an abandoned
lot surrounded by trees. There was a tumbledown building, the roof of
which had collapsed. Faded writing on the side read SITE OFFICE. In
its shadow stood a single trailer home, propped on blocks, lawn chairs,
propane canisters, and garbage strewn around it, half buried in snow.
There were four other vehicles on the lot: three pickups and an old
Jeep.

Light bled from around the trailer's faded curtains. The sharp edge
of Kody's fear was blunted by the sense of occupation. Surely Harlan
wouldn't kill him in front of other people? But his heart rattled like the
ack-ack of gunfire as Harlan brought the pickup to a halt.

They crossed to the trailer, Kody following in the tracks made by the
larger man's boots. The flimsy steps bowed beneath Harlan's weight. He
rapped on the door. It was opened by a grim-faced man with a coarse
beard. His muddy yellow eyes were big in their sockets. He had a gun
tucked in the waistband of his jeans, visible beneath the folds of his
flannel shirt.

"Dirch," said Harlan, with a curt nod.

The man looked over Harlan's shoulder, eyes pinching at the sight
of Kody. He stayed where he was, planted in front of the door, until a
smooth voice called from inside.

"You gonna let all that cold in, Dirch?"

The man stepped reluctantly aside.

Kody looked around as he entered. The trailer was old-fashioned
and grubby, but clearly lived in. There was a kitchen area with a grease-
speckled stove, plates piled high, a trash can overflowing on the peeling
linoleum. A countertop was littered with Chinese takeout cartons. The
walls were covered in flowery, sun-yellowed wallpaper, and there was a
ceiling fan with a light. From somewhere came the hum of a generator.

There was a fat man perched on a stool at the counter, a tire of flesh overhanging his jeans, a plate of half-eaten noodles beside him, stiff with cold. His waxy skin had an unhealthy sheen. Two younger men, midtwenties, lounged on a squashy-looking couch, booted feet propped on a low table strewn with plates and fortune cookies. The men were twins. They both had white-blond hair, buzz-cut to their scalps, and long, chiseled faces. Kody noticed that one looked slightly different—his features less well put together, as if whoever made them had gotten bored halfway through.

Dirch closed the trailer door and moved in behind, so close, Kody could smell the man's body odor, pungent beneath a whiff of cigarette smoke. Harlan was in front of him and, with the trailer's low ceiling and narrow walls, he felt trapped. Then, Harlan stepped aside and Kody saw a fifth man.

This man reclined in an armchair by an electric heater, the red glow from the bars lighting one side of his face. Beyond him, a folding door was open on a bedroom. There was a pump-action shotgun lying on top of the crumpled sheets. The man's skin was smooth and slightly tanned, a shadow of stubble around his jaw. Wavy light brown hair hung long and loose around his ears. His eyes, winter gray, were bright and deep. Ice glittering over dark depths. He was hard to age. There was a youthful energy in his face, but the silver in his hair and the creases around those eyes told a different story.

The man uncurled and sat forward, elbows on his knees, long fingers threaded. He wore black jeans, boots, and a denim shirt over a faded black T-shirt. His movements were languid, catlike. He was slim of build, no real meat to him at all, but while Harlan presented strength with his size, this man radiated it from within. That power was dazzling by comparison—made Harlan Judd seem like a low-watt bulb.

Taking something from his pocket, Harlan crossed to the man and handed it over. It was a bundle of dollars. Kody sucked in a breath as he recognized the hairband wrapped around the wad. It was the one his mom used to keep her stash together. The missing three hundred from the Jif jar. He choked back his surprise.

"Got some receipts too," said Harlan, passing over the slips from the stores he'd made Kody trawl around last night, buying cornstarch and newspapers, wire and glue.

"You got the stuff from different places?"

"Course, Billy. I ain't no fool."

Billy.

The man who had called, saving that girl outside the club from whatever it was Harlan intended.

Billy unwrapped the wad, discarding the hairband on the table among the fortune cookies. He counted out dollars, then gave some back to Harlan. Kody watched as his mom's money disappeared back into Harlan's pocket. The lion's share went into Billy's. Anger prickled through him.

"You did good. It'll keep the cops busy while we make our preparations."

"You asked him? 'Bout me taking the sword?" Harlan sounded cautious, but his voice was edged with anticipation. "After this and that shrink, I've proved myself, right?"

The fat man at the counter grunted appreciatively. "The apple was a nice touch. You sure fucked that bitch up good."

Billy glanced at the fat man, then back at Harlan. "He knows. Don't worry."

"At the next gathering then?"

Billy smiled, but didn't answer. Instead, he sat back, eyes flicking past Harlan. "So, this is Kody?"

When Harlan tilted his head at him, Kody stepped forward. He flushed, unable to meet Billy's stare, looked down at his wet sneakers instead, feeling like a bug under a magnifying glass.

"This is crazy," the man called Dirch cut into the silence. "Why'd you involve him?"

Harlan turned. "We need new blood, Dirch. The kid proved himself useful."

Kody realized something then. Harlan had brought him into this because he'd fucked up—letting him see that bag and what was inside it. Somehow, that, and the weird doll they'd made, all had something to do with these men. Billy was still studying him.

"But now? When we're . . . ?" Dirch trailed off. "How do we know he'll keep his trap shut?" He dug in his pocket, pulled out a squashed carton of cigarettes and stuck one in his mouth. He gestured at Kody, eyes on Harlan. "What the fuck d'you know about him, except the hole he came out of?" Dirch snapped the flame of a lighter at the cigarette. "Banging his old lady don't count for nothing."

"What have I told you about smoking that shit in here?" Billy's voice didn't rise, but the atmosphere in the trailer changed. The other men stilled, all eyes on him.

Dirch—with his ire and his gun—let the flame wink out. With a last look at Kody, he pushed his way out into the snow, the cigarette still in his mouth.

Billy turned his attention back to Kody. "My ex-wife, Darlene, used to smoke. Filthy habit."

"What would you expect from that dirty whore?" grunted the fat man at the counter.

"Amen, Cuddy," said the better-looking of the twins.

The tension dissipated.

Billy sat forward, rolling up the sleeves of his denim shirt. Kody stared at the tattoo that gradually revealed itself on the man's right forearm. It was similar to Harlan's, only far more elaborate. There was the same coiled red snake. But, on Billy's arm, the blade of a sword wreathed in flames plunged through its scales. Above the blade was a set of golden gates and beneath the serpent's coils were two trees. One was white, the other black, their branches entwined. Between them was an apple, like a heart at their center.

Billy picked a fortune cookie from the table. Unwrapping it, he snapped it in half, then tugged the slip of paper from the broken shell. As he read, a smile spread slow across his face. "We'll give him a shot," he told Harlan. He looked around the trailer. "In his name."

"In his name," the men echoed as one.

Billy looked at Kody, that smile still dancing in his eyes. "Wanna play a game, kid?"

34

Connie Meadows stayed standing when Riley and Altman sat. She planted her palms on the desk. "Well?"

Altman spoke first. "The governor and her family are secure, ma'am. State Patrol has maximized their presence at the mansion and at the capitol. They're installing a panic button at her daughter's school. State troopers are going door to door, looking for witnesses. I've organized for the effigy to be sent to the bureau's lab."

"And the governor's mood?" Meadows asked, her attention switching to Riley.

Riley was irritated by the reminder of her role here as pacifier, but didn't let it show. "She's understandably upset. But knows we're doing all we can."

At last, Meadows sat. "Lone Creek. Walk me through it."

Riley told her boss about the trail they'd followed: from the logo Sydney Williams recalled on the jacket of her attacker to the logistics company. She recounted Richard Kitch's memories of Raymond, who'd spent time in Clermont, and the tape and drawing they'd discovered at the home of the psychiatrist. "Ma'am, everything points in the direction of this man—Raymond. He appears to have suffered episodes of psychosis. He came from an abusive, possibly wealthy family. We believe he's done jail time. He owned, or had access to, a hunting lodge.

We know the original attacker favored a hunting knife. There was animal fur found at one of the scenes and he takes trophies from victims. Raymond went to a religious school, where he seems to have become obsessed with its teachings. Hale described him as danger to himself and society. I can say, from all the evidence, including the photograph we saw at Clermont, we're almost certain Raymond is the Sin Eater."

"Yet you've not been able to identify him?" Meadows observed coolly. "No last name. No address." She didn't wait for Riley to respond. "Where is this tape?"

Riley placed the lock-bag Audrey had issued her with on the desk. "I was going to send it to Quantico for fast-tracking. If we can get the sound cleaned up, we might be able to identify Raymond."

"I don't need to see it," Meadows said, waving a dismissive hand as Riley went to open it. "This drawing you found indicates the suspect's tattoo might be a sword and a snake, not a cross?"

"Yes." Riley recounted what she and Fogg had discussed yesterday on their way back to the city. "In Genesis, after Adam and Eve are driven from the garden, God sets a fiery sword at the gates of Eden to guard against their return. That's what we believe the drawings—and the tattoo—could be referencing. Raymond wrote *I am the son of Adam.*"

"I'll speak to the field office, see if they'll authorize an update on the billboards." Meadows didn't look pleased by the prospect.

Riley noticed the older woman's hands, clenched together on her desk, were paper dry. Perhaps from the cold, or maybe from all the hours she spent in this basement, stewing in her own stale air. She realized she'd never seen her boss outside these walls. Knew nothing of her personal life. There were no photographs in here, no sense of self beyond the job. She remembered Noah Case's words, that first day. *Welcome to the dungeon.*

"But now you believe there could be more than one?" Meadows continued. "That this Raymond has an accomplice?"

Riley glanced at Altman, who remained silent, hands resting on a closed file in his lap. His eyes were unreadable. She was surprised he'd let her have the floor so long. Giving her enough rope to hang herself, perhaps? "We have the difference in shoe sizes at two of the scenes. It might also help explain some of the discrepancies in the more recent attacks—the photographs he takes, which he wasn't known to do before. And the fact he seems to be going after riskier victims."

"Not a copycat?"

"Detective Verne thinks not, given his intimacy with the Sin Eater's methods." Riley paused. "Perhaps a younger family member?"

"That's a leap," said Meadows, but she didn't seem to be shutting this down.

"The print at the scene in ninety-four indicates a large man. The one at the governor's mansion is much smaller. Maybe Raymond had a family between the earlier attacks and now? Maybe there was some sort of stressor? A breakdown in a relationship?" Riley pressed on when Meadows gave a half nod. "Two family members working together isn't unheard of. We know abuse can be passed down. That it can be a cycle."

Altman gave an intake of breath and sat forward. "These are all neat theories, but the man we saw in the parking lot surveillance footage was large, much larger than whoever who made that print outside the mansion."

"So that could be Raymond," said Riley, glancing at him. "And Sneaker Print is his accomplice."

"But I thought part of your speculation was that it would be unlike a man as cautious and meticulous as we know the Sin Eater to be to let himself get caught on camera with a stolen car that he then leaves evidence in?"

"Maybe he's getting careless?" Riley shot back, but already she could see the frown creasing Meadows's brow. "Ma'am, I'd like to go back to Clermont Manor. I got the sense the manager might have known more. He seemed nervous."

"FBI agents turning up on your doorstep isn't usually grounds for relaxation," Meadows observed dryly.

"Lone Creek then. If we dig deeper, I think we'll find more people who remember Raymond from Fresh Start. If we can get a last name, we can—"

"I should stay in the city, ma'am," Altman interjected. "Whoever's targeting Governor Cook is most likely still here. Last night I got a lead on the key ring. The lab was able to decipher more of the writing."

Riley watched in taut silence as Altman opened the file in his lap. He set a piece of paper on Meadows's desk. It showed a close-up of the charred key ring the technician had pulled from the burned-out car, several more looping letters rendered faintly visible beneath the burned plastic.

The Old For

"I believe it's from the Old Fort Hotel, here in Des Moines," Altman told Meadows. "I was going to head over there now."

Meadows stared at him for a long moment. Finally, she spoke. "I want you in the city."

"Got it." Altman went to rise, clutching the paper.

"Both of you," Meadows cut in. Altman faltered, hand tightening on the file. Meadows kept her eyes on him, as if daring him to challenge her. He didn't. "Sign the tape over to Detective Verne," she added, nodding to Riley's lock-bag. "The state lab will deal with it."

"And the task force?" Riley asked, feeling everything sliding away from her, just as she'd started to get a grip on it. "Ma'am, if it is the Sin Eater or an accomplice of his targeting Cook and her family, I believe they are in real danger. We shouldn't lose sight of these suspects."

"And we won't. Verne is more than capable of following those leads. As I said, I don't mind you sharing information and resources, but let Verne concentrate on the other victims. Right now, I want both of you in the city, focused solely on the governor. This cannot be allowed to turn into a political storm." Her face tightened. "My superiors in the bureau have made that very clear."

They took the Tahoe to the Old Fort Hotel, driving through the blizzard that had descended upon the city yesterday evening. The sky had opened its ugly gray maw and spewed forth a white blast that had covered everything. It showed no signs of abating. The wipers sprang back and forth as Altman followed the GPS, snow banking higher at the edges of the windshield.

They sat in silence for several blocks, neither willing to break the ice.

Finally, when Riley could stand it no longer, she turned to him. "Meadows called me when I was in Lone Creek."

"Oh?" Altman kept his eyes on the road, squinting through the wipers' rapid dash.

"She gave the impression she hadn't heard from you in days. That she didn't know where you were."

They stopped at an intersection. A snowplow churned past, lights flashing. It was morning, but the storm had cast the city in murky twilight.

Altman glanced in the rearview. "I was going through the governor's correspondence. Checking you hadn't missed anything."

"I thought you might have kept yourself reachable." There was an impatient beep-beep of a horn. Riley realized Altman was still staring in the mirror. "Lights changed," she prompted.

He put his foot on the gas. His face looked strained.

"Given what went down with Madden?" Riley knew she was pushing him now. But she wanted to goad him. Get him to explode. Yell. Anything other than this unbearable tension.

"I had some family shit, OK?" he snapped, looking at her.

They slowed at another intersection.

Riley took this in. What had Noah said? No wife. No kids. She was about to press him further when she saw he was peering in the rearview again.

She looked in the side mirror. There were three vehicles back there. A pickup was directly behind them, three men in work overalls jammed into the cab. As they shunted forward, she saw a station wagon. There was a teenage girl in the passenger seat, face lit by a cell phone. Behind the station wagon was a pimped-up Toyota, white and shiny, with tinted windows. She couldn't see any passengers at this distance, through the swirling snow. Then, as the pickup edged out into another lane, she caught the shadow of a single figure in the driver's seat of the Toyota.

The lights changed.

This time, Altman gunned it, slamming his foot on the gas. Riley was knocked back in her seat. He turned suddenly down a narrow side street, flinging her into the door. Her shoulder spasmed painfully as she grabbed for the handle. The Tahoe's wheels skidded as he fought to keep control of the vehicle on the icy road.

Riley cursed, rubbing at her shoulder. "What the hell?"

"Sorry," he muttered, easing up on the gas as he reached the end of the street and moved out into a stream of traffic. "Wrong way."

Riley glanced at the GPS. It was rerouting. Not a wrong way. But a new one.

She went to challenge him, but Altman was back to looking in the rearview again. She'd seen plenty of emotions play out on the agent's face since her arrival—hostility, impatience, anger—but this was one she hadn't seen before.

Peter Altman looked scared.

35

"Haven't seen one of those in a long time." The manager of the Old Fort Hotel squinted at the paper, which showed the close-up of the burned key ring. "Where did you say you found it?"

"Inside a car, stolen by a suspect we want to question," Altman answered brusquely. "It's not something a recent guest would have been given then?"

"Oh no. We haven't used that font in at least a decade. Our whole branding has changed. We're much more in the family market these days, rather than corporate customers." The man handed the paper back to Altman. "We used to give those key rings out as part of a loyalty package to our top clients."

"Clients?"

"People who ran big seminars and events in our ballroom. Beauty pageants, preachers, psychics—that sort of thing. If I remember right, the package was a key ring, a pen, and a baseball cap, along with discount rates on rooms."

"You still have records of those clients?"

"I believe so." The manager motioned them to follow as he led them from reception, down a bright-lit corridor, to a set of double doors. "If you'd like to wait in here, I'll go look."

The manager pushed open the doors into a cavernous space. As he flipped on the lights, Riley saw round tables pushed into the corners and chairs stacked up along the walls. There was a stage, red curtains hanging. More drapes covered the windows.

"Haven't been able to use the ballroom much this year," he said resignedly. "Make yourselves comfortable. I'll be back with those records."

As he left, Riley looked around, frowning. She had a weird sense of recognition. The walls, covered in decorative wallpaper, shimmered dully in the harsh overhead lights. The beige carpet was colored in swirls of crimson. Maybe she'd come here with her parents when she was a kid? Her father was always out entertaining clients back then. "A decade or more seems a long time for someone to have kept the same key ring," she wondered out loud. "Unless maybe it had sentimental value?" She turned when Altman didn't answer.

He was leaning against the stage, focused on his phone.

She thought of his erratic behavior on the ride over. Her arm ached where she'd been slammed against the car door. What—or who—had scared him? And why was he so keen to stay in the city, when there were potential leads opening up elsewhere?

Between him and Meadows, she felt like a pawn shoved out on a board. A minor piece that could be sacrificed at any moment. Then, she thought of Hayley and Sydney, Megan and Abigail—and all the Sin Eater's victims. She had got in close, felt their trauma. She knew how it would ripple through them down the years. Flashbacks and aftershocks. She had felt, too, the thrill of closing in on their suspect, catching his scent on a trail gone cold.

As she watched Altman, his brow furrowed as he stared at his phone, Riley's frustration hardened into resolve. Whatever was going on, she wouldn't allow this man to screw up this case.

Riley shouldered open the door of her apartment, wincing at the bruise she could feel blooming there. She kicked the door closed, then headed into the kitchen and dumped the box file she was carrying on the table. The place was freezing. Still no word from the landlord on the damn window, but she didn't have time to deal with that now.

She took off her damp boots and cranked up the thermostat. Then she took the lock-bag from where it rested on top of the file—speckled with snow from the walk from her car. She crossed to the hall closet. Crouching by the safe, she typed in the code and pushed the bag in alongside boxes of ammo, her cuffs, and her switchblade.

She had called Fogg on her way home, intending to drop off the tape and drawing with him, as Meadows ordered, but Jenna informed her Fogg was out to dinner with his family. Riley would sign the evidence over first thing tomorrow. Explain everything then.

Grabbing a beer from the refrigerator, she opened the box file. Inside were the records the manager at the hotel had handed over—all those who'd been on the loyalty list and would have received the key ring. She'd taken one box, Altman the other. There were over one hundred names in her batch alone. Sitting on top was a torn slip of paper.

Taking a sip of beer, Riley took it out and sat. There was a number scribbled on the paper.

That afternoon, back at the agency, Audrey had shaken her head when Riley asked how she might contact Roach. "I can't give out a former agent's personal details."

"I need some information on one of his old cases."

Audrey had paused at the reasonable request. "All right. I'll call him for you tomorrow. See if he's happy to call you back."

Riley had gone along with it. Later, when Audrey was in the restroom, she'd hastened to the secretary's desk and checked the files on the shelves behind her. Audrey was meticulous and orderly, and it hadn't taken long for Riley to spot the personnel records.

Despite her haste to copy it down, Roach's number was legible. She checked the time. Not yet six. A decent hour to call.

As she dialed, her eyes drifted down the first page of names from the hotel.

Marcia Ackton
William Ames
Bart Bayard
Ed Carter

The ringing switched to an answering machine. A computerized voice told her to leave a message. She cut off before the beep. Would try again tomorrow.

Riley pushed the file away, at once too tired and too restless to make a start on the hotel records. She sat back, massaging the tight muscles in her shoulder. She thought of Meadows's warning words earlier—that this situation with the governor couldn't be allowed to escalate. If her boss was worried about the reaction of superiors in the bureau, then she should be too. *Shit rolls downhill.* But what could she do when she believed that in turning their attention to the city, they were leaving other, potentially vital leads dangling elsewhere? That first day, Meadows had told her she wouldn't be a helicopter boss, but Riley could feel her shadow hanging over the whole agency; the heavy thrum of her demands.

She took another swig of beer, looked back at her phone. She wanted, more than anything, to call Logan. To hear his voice. It was—what? Five days since she'd seen him? It seemed like weeks. All the intimacy of their dinner had leached from her. She felt only the emptiness that had dogged her since her arrival in Des Moines.

No, not emptiness. Loneliness.

Her thumb brushed across the crack on the phone's screen. His thumb on her cheek.

You know where I am.

She pulled back her hand. She didn't want him to think her weak, that she couldn't hack it here. His words of encouragement had meant the world to her—she didn't want him to stop seeing her as strong and capable.

Downing the beer, she crossed to the refrigerator. She had picked one of the meals stacked in their boxes and was putting it in the microwave when her cell rang.

It was Ethan.

"Hi," she said, at once alert. Her brother never normally called unless something was wrong.

"It's Maddie."

A sick rush of fear. "What's wrong? What's happened?"

"She's in one of her moods again. Every time you speak to her, I have to pick up the pieces."

Riley's fear ebbed, replaced by a flare of irritation. "What am I supposed to do? I can't have her here. I'm in the middle of a case. What did you expect would happen when I became an agent? You knew things would change."

"You're only a couple of hours away, Ri. Not on the goddamn moon. Can't you take her skating? You get days off, right?"

Riley caught the slur in her brother's voice, knew he'd been drinking. Her anger bit deeper. "Even if I did, I might want to spend them doing my own thing." Her mind chimed with Jess Cook's accusation. It still stung, but it was also the truth. "I'm not her mother, Ethan. She's not my daughter."

"Jesus, that's cold."

"Well, it's true. You know what else? You're her father and, for once, you're going to have to fucking act like it." Before he could respond, she quit the call and tossed the phone on the table.

She strode to the microwave, turned it on with a stab of her finger, then returned to the refrigerator and yanked it open, going for another beer.

Shit.

She hung her head, squeezed her eyes shut. She shouldn't have been so harsh. They were all adjusting. As she opened her eyes on the sad stack of meals for one, she was hit by a wave of emotion. She thought of Fogg, out to dinner with Marcia and his daughters—the way she'd seen his face light up when he was speaking to his wife. Thought of Jess, her husband's arm around her at the gala, how he'd drawn her into the comfort of his orbit, set her at ease.

You know where I am.

Could they really have something? Her and Logan? Different cities, different lives. Complicated by work and by family obligations. She cared for him as a person, respected him as a former colleague, and trusted him as a man she'd spent one crazy, blood-soaked summer with—a man who had saved her life. But she'd not had a relationship since college—nothing that lasted more than a night. *No strings.* She wasn't sure she was even capable of one.

As the man down the hall started up his nightly music and the heavy bass thumped through the walls, she felt it bubble up—all the longing, rage, and fear rising to clog her throat. She screamed it out into the cold belly of the refrigerator.

When the ragged sound had faded, left her hanging there breathless, the beers and boxes sat unmoved and the dull thud of music continued. The microwave pinged. She turned tiredly toward it, then paused as her cell rang again. She took it off the table without looking. "Ethan, look, I'm sorry. I don't want to fight, OK."

"Hello?" A male voice, but not her brother. "Is this Special Agent Fisher?"

"Speaking. Who is this?" She could hear noise in the background: soft jazz, the faint clink of glasses, a muffled hum of voices.

"Senator Davenport. Nate." A pause. "You gave me your card?"

Her mind filled in the memory—handsome face, cheek creasing as he smiled, smart suit, nice cologne. "Of course. How can I help, Senator?"

"I was wondering if I could help you. You asked me to keep an ear out at the capitol? Well, I might have something. Something that might help your investigation?"

She felt her tiredness drain, replaced by a swell of anticipation. "I'm listening."

"I'm in the middle of a meeting right now but should be finished in the next hour. Unless that's too late for you to meet?"

Riley looked over at the microwave. The glass was foggy, steam curling from the limp plastic tray. "Where are you?"

36

Kody huddled under the shelter in the empty playground, hands wedged in his pockets. He shifted on his feet, cold and nerves getting the better of him. From the eaves of the shelter, icicles bristled. It was still snowing, but gently now, like ash drifting from a dying fire. The storm was tracking south into Missouri, having laid a white shroud over Iowa.

From his position, Kody could see Troy's house. He peered around the edge of the shelter, across to the other side of the playground and the street beyond. Harlan's pickup was still there. In the shadow of the cab, he made out the smoldering eye of Harlan's cigarette. The man was watching him. He couldn't wimp out and go home, lie and say he'd done it.

He turned, hearing voices. The door to Troy's house had opened, light spilling. Kody watched Reagan step out. Troy stood framed in the doorway. Kody's throat constricted as he watched them kiss. Afterward, Reagan made her way down the path, where snow had been shoveled to either side. She pulled the hood of her coat up, trimmed with fake fur. Her boots were tufted with more of the same. Skintight jeans made her legs look lean and long.

Kody had known she was here when he'd called Troy earlier—heard her giggling in the background. Troy had laughed at something she'd said, his voice fading as if he'd forgotten Kody was even on the line. It was in that moment that he'd made up his mind, twin barbs of anger and jealousy spurring him on. Now, standing here, frozen to the bone, he was terrified by his decision. But Harlan was watching. And Harlan had a gun.

It wasn't just threat, though, that kept Kody's eyes on Reagan as she reached the sidewalk and set off along the quiet road, the grand houses twinkling with Christmas lights. Yesterday, when they were driving back from the trailer, he'd mustered enough courage to ask Harlan about his mom's money—handed over to Billy.

Harlan had chuckled at his timid complaint. "That's pocket change, kid. You do what Billy says, you'll see more money than you can dream of."

Kody thought that seemed highly unlikely. By the look of that trailer, Billy and his friends were even poorer than he was. But when he'd wondered this out loud, Harlan had laughed again and tapped his nose like he had some big old secret.

Now, Kody felt the tug of his fear warring with the pull of that promise. Reagan was passing the playground. He pressed himself into the shelter's shadows, but she didn't look his way. She was on her phone, her voice clear as a bell in the evening hush.

"Yeah, I'm just leaving his place now." Reagan laughed. "I know, right? Snap my fingers and he comes running."

Kody had no doubt she was talking about Troy. He guessed one of her girlfriends was on the other end of the line. Probably that dumb bitch, Alexa.

His fear loosened its grip. As Reagan moved away down the street, Kody pulled up the mask he'd taken from his mom's bag at Harlan's instruction, tugged his hood over his head, and walked out of the park where he and Troy had played as children.

Reagan, focused on her phone, didn't notice as he followed, stepping through the prints her boots had made. A breeze whisked the snow and blew strands of Reagan's hair from around the sides of her hood. Kody caught a whiff of her candy-sweet perfume. His heart was thudding, deep as a drum. He fixed on the thought of her sly voice, her peals of laughter. Thought of the way she'd tempted Troy away. Taken the only friend he'd ever had.

"I'll catch a cab. Yeah. See you there."

Reagan had her phone in front of her. The light from the screen cast a halo around her. It looked like she was texting. Maybe summoning a ride. He didn't have long. He quickened his pace. Out of the corner of his eye, he saw Harlan's pickup crawling along the street on the other side of the park. Reagan was nearing a crossroads. Beyond, headlights streaked through the darkness. Now or never.

Reagan stiffened as if sensing the danger. She looked up from her phone. She was turning toward him as he ran, closing the last yards between them. Her eyes widened when she saw him—a hooded figure in dark clothes and a mask—coming straight at her.

Kody barreled into her, knocking her off her feet. He went down on top of her, both of them plunging into the snow. The phone shot from her hand, disappearing under a parked car. She let out a high-pitched yell. They scuffled about, legs and arms flailing, making wild patterns all around them—a chaos of angels.

Kody was panting. As Reagan screamed again—a piercing mix of fury and terror—he heard a dog barking in one of the nearby houses and knew it might be moments before he was discovered. He had his instructions.

Struggling against the girl's surprising strength, he grabbed a fistful of her hair and shoved her face into the snow. With his free hand, he reached around her neck, gloved fingers clumsy, scrabbling for purchase. He felt a sharp twinge as she bit him, her teeth finding skin between his glove and his coat. The pain galvanized him. Grunting, he fought against her jerking limbs to straddle her, knees pressing down on her arms. Her face was still in the snow. She was starting to choke and cry now. He lifted her hair, saw the glint of silver. Grabbing it, he tugged. Hard. The chain snapped against her throat, the necklace coming free in his hand.

Kody pushed himself to his feet and ran, leaving Reagan sprawled in the snow, the barks of the dog and a woman's voice calling out in the night behind him.

Harlan picked him up a block later. Kody jumped in, slamming the truck's door. He yanked down his mask, sodden with snow and saliva. He was panting for breath.

"You get it?" Harlan said, joining the streams of traffic, cars plowing lines through the fresh fall.

Kody uncurled his clenched fist. Lying in the palm of his gloved hand was Reagan's horseshoe pendant—bought with Troy's allowance. He could smell her perfume all over him. He swallowed a plug of nausea. The skin of his wrist was bloody, stinging where her teeth had nipped him. "What now?" he breathed.

Harlan turned, his hard face lit by the flare of passing headlights. "Now, you're in."

37

The Five Acres Country Club nestled by the state park, close to the river in West Des Moines. Riley pulled up in the parking lot outside an impressive building fronted with columns. She could see floodlit tennis courts and expansive lawns blanketed in snow, the dark stretch of a fairway beyond. The lights of the city glittered across the skyline.

She headed across the lot, past Porsches and Escalades. Now the worst of the storm had passed, staff had been out shoveling snow and scattering salt. No inconveniences allowed here. She gave the senator's name at reception to a woman who looked her up and down with a tilt of her nose, then was directed down a plush-carpeted corridor.

A man was playing a grand piano in the corner of the bar. A few people sat about in groups—mostly businessmen by the looks of them. She wondered if her father had come here with Bill Hamilton, back in the day. There was a polished bar lined with high leather chairs. Two men in white shirts and black waistcoats were making drinks. Riley paused in the arched opening, scanning the place. A man stood and turned to her. Nate Davenport. He said something to the group he'd been sitting with, then came over.

"Agent Fisher, thank you for coming. I'm sorry if I sounded cryptic on the phone. I was in the middle of a crisis. Business as usual." He sighed. "Anyway, that's not important. Please." He motioned to the bar, away from the group.

She headed over at his direction, took one of the seats. He was still wearing that cologne, she noticed, as he sat beside her. He wore a different suit today. Mother-of-pearl cuff links glinted as he gestured to one of the bartenders.

"I'll take a beer, Matt."

"Certainly, sir. And for the lady?"

"I'm fine," she told him.

"I'm afraid you have to drink if you sit here," Nate said solemnly. "House rules." He smiled at her expression. "I'm kidding. I'm sure Matt can make a coffee?"

Matt flipped the top off a bottle of beer. "Of course."

Riley watched enviously as the young man poured beer into a crystal tumbler. The foam formed a snow-white layer on top. When Matt disappeared through a door behind the bar, she turned to the senator.

Nate spoke first. "Who's Ethan?"

"What?"

"You thought I was him? On the phone?" Nate's nose wrinkled. "Sorry, that's none of my business, is it."

"It's OK." She paused as the bartender returned with a coffee in a china cup and saucer. "Thank you." She took a sip, saw Nate still looking at her. "Family stuff."

"Ah." He nodded sympathetically. "If it ain't one thing, it's your mother, as my father used to say."

"Brother, in my case." She set the cup down. "So, what information do you have?"

"Right." Nate drank some beer. "I was talking yesterday with one of the janitors at the capitol. Just the shooting the breeze. But during the conversation he told me he'd heard that one of his colleagues saw someone leaving the governor's office, the night before she received the threat. A man. Didn't recognize him."

Riley felt all her expectation deflate. "We know this. State police spoke to the janitor in question at the time. Surveillance caught the man leaving. We're following it up."

Nate pushed a hand through his hair. "Well, there goes my career as a special agent." He met her gaze. "I'm sorry. I've wasted your time."

"You couldn't have known." She finished her coffee, offered him a polite smile. "Such is the job sometimes."

"At least let me buy you a proper drink. Matt here makes the best cocktails in the city."

Matt, polishing glasses, turned and smiled.

Nate's eyes caught hers. The little crease appeared in his cheek.

She thought of his gaze lingering on her, the night of the gala. She glanced at the senator's hand. No wedding ring. She found herself wondering if there might be another reason he had called her here.

Matt came over and placed a glass bowl in front of them, filled with olives—the big Italian ones she sometimes saw in the grocery store. The expensive sort she would never buy herself. She'd not eaten all day. Her stomach rumbled hopefully.

Nate seemed to notice. "They do food here as well. The burgers are out of this world." He placed a hand on his chest. "On me. Please. For dragging you all the way out here."

She hesitated, but the thought of returning to her cold apartment and another microwave meal sealed the deal. Nate ordered a club sandwich, while she opted for the burger. She knew she shouldn't drink, but the crystal glasses and bottles of top-shelf liquor were too tempting to resist.

"What business are you in?" she asked Nate, as Matt set about making her a martini. "You said you had some crisis?"

"Ice cream." He laughed at her surprise. "I know. Not very glamorous." He reached into the pocket of his suit, which was lined with blue silk. He took out a wallet, from which he pulled a card. The writing on it was embossed in gold script.

Nate Davenport
CEO Buckie's Dream

As she took it, Riley's mind seesawed, tilting her toward childhood. She was back in Cedar Falls, sitting on the porch, racing to lick the melting drips before they reached her fingers. Always arguing with Ethan about which flavor Buckie's their mom should get.

"Wow," she said, glancing up at him. "You own Buckie's Dream?"

Nate nodded. "Buckie Davenport was my grandfather."

"Brings back memories," she murmured, looking at the card again. She thought of how she'd been with Ethan on the phone earlier—made a promise to herself that she'd call him in the morning. *You won't believe who I had dinner with last night.*

"Yup," said Nate. "Not many kids in this state who haven't had us in their freezers." He shook his head and grinned. "Well, that came out a bit creepy, didn't it?"

She laughed and took a sip of the martini. It was, as promised, fantastic. The burger, when it arrived, was one of the best she'd ever eaten. Nate ordered another beer and talked about his work in the senate, helping other Iowa businesses through the pandemic. The struggles they had faced. She found her stress fading, the vodka and the gentle rise and fall of the piano soothing away the sharp edges of her day. She hadn't felt this relaxed since the dinner with Logan. But this was different—easier somehow. Less complicated.

"It's hard for people outside business to really understand how bad it's been this year," Nate was saying. "Just keeping your head above water is a challenge." His jovial manner had faded. Lines creased his brow. "People are just holding on to what they've got. Terrified of losing it."

Riley thought of Maynard Kitch, at the halfway house in Lone Creek, saying much the same.

At all once, she felt light-headed—the warmth of the room, the lull of the music, the pure alcohol hit of the martini. She reached for the jug of water Matt had set down. As she poured out a glass, some splashed over the rim, soaking into Nate's business card, sitting on the bar. "Damn it. Sorry."

"No worries. Hey, Matt, do you have a napkin over there?"

Riley set the jug down, her eyes fixing on the water spreading across the card. In her mind, she was back in the diner, the waitress, Patty, spilling coffee across the composite of the Sin Eater, the stain seeping slowly across the puzzle of his face. It had been Antonio, not Patty, who'd returned to clean it up. That had struck her at the time, but the call from Meadows had distracted her.

Eileen Morrow and Maynard Kitch both recognized the facial composite from the news. Most people would have seen it by now. But not Patty. The woman's reaction had been quick—almost immediate.

I don't know him.

"Is something wrong?"

"I'm sorry, I've got to go."

"Oh." Nate looked disappointed.

"Thank you for dinner," she said, grabbing her coat. "It really was a good burger."

He stood with her. An old-fashioned move. "I'm sorry I couldn't be of help."

Actually, you were.

She smiled, held out her hand. "Thank you, Senator."

Back in her apartment, all the warmth seemed to have faded, even though she'd left the heat on. Or perhaps it was just that the country club had felt so damn cozy. *How the other half lives.* Her breath fogging the air, she went into the bedroom and pulled on a sweater, then sat on the edge of the bed.

It didn't take long to find the number. It was almost nine and she was expecting to have to try again in the morning, so she was surprised when someone answered.

"Lone Creek Diner."

Riley recognized the voice. "Patty? My name's Riley Fisher. I met you three days ago. I showed you a drawing of a man?" There was silence on the other end. But the woman hadn't hung up.

"You're police, aren't you?" Patty's voice was a dry murmur.

"FBI."

There was a long pause, then a rapid exhalation. "I knew you would call. I just knew."

Riley sat up straighter. "Patty, did you recognize that man?"

More silence. "Is it really him? Is he really back?"

"I believe so."

"I'm not sure I can do this. I just want to forget it all."

"But you haven't, have you? It's always with you, isn't it?" Riley knew that martini had loosened her a little too much.

Another pause. Had she lost her?

Finally, Patty spoke. "I won't go to court. I'm no fool. I know how victims are treated in those places. I know how few men like him ever get what they deserve."

"We're only talking about a conversation. Just you and me. I want to catch him, Patty. I want to stop him hurting any more women. Thinking he can get away with it all this time. I want to show him he can't."

She did. God, she did.

"Not here. Not in Lone Creek. There's a pancake joint off Route 69. Mae's Flip 'n' Sit. I can get there tomorrow, late morning."

"I'll be there. Say eleven?"

As the line went dead, Riley let out a breath.

She went to put her phone on the nightstand when she realized the bedroom curtain was drifting as if in a breeze. She rose and parted it. The blanket she'd wedged in the gap had moved enough to allow in a chill stream of night air where the window didn't fully close. Had the landlord finally sent someone to look at it? She checked her phone. No messages and it was surely too late for repairs?

She looked out of the window, down the fire escape. Each tread was banked with snow. There were footprints all the way up and all the way back down. Fear tickled cold fingers across her neck.

Stowing her phone, she made her way across the bedroom. From the shelter of the doorframe, she checked the kitchen and living room. The overhead light was on, illuminating the box file and other papers on the table, all where she'd left them. The rooms were small, few places to hide. She listened intently. Hearing nothing except the bubbling of water in the pipes, she went quickly to the hall closet. Crouching, she keyed the code in the lockbox and pulled out her Glock.

With the gun racked and loaded, she checked the apartment thoroughly. Nothing seemed out of place. Nothing had been taken, that she could see. There were wet marks on the kitchen floor, but they could have been made by her own boots when she'd entered. She returned to the closet and flipped on the light. She went to close up the safe, then paused. The bottom edge of the lockbox was scratched in places and one of the boards beneath it was cracked. She stared at it, casting her mind back to when she had bolted it to the floor. Had the damage occurred then? She couldn't say.

She returned to the window and stared at the footprints on the fire escape.

Beyond, the streets stretched into darkness.

38

Riley sat in the old Dodge, the fans roaring out hot, musty air. Eighteen-wheelers thundered past on the highway. Across the snowy lot was a brown brick building. There was a sign on the joint's roof—a cartoon girl holding a stack of pancakes, red syrup dripping. MAE'S FLIP 'N' SIT.

The pickup's dash was pitted and sun-faded, the steering wheel shredded from years of handling. As Riley hung on her cell, listening to it ring, she imagined her grandfather humming along to Glenn Miller as he threaded that wheel through his hands, evening sun in his eyes as he made his way home, air gauzy with dust from the cornfields.

She stifled a yawn. She hadn't slept much after finding the footprints on the fire escape. She'd spoken to her neighbor, but the man—his gruff voice coming through the crack of his door—had heard nothing. She had asked around on the block, but no one had seen anyone suspicious. She'd told herself it could have been kids, messing about on the fire escape. That the blanket could have shifted over time on its own. That the scratches around the safe could have been made when she'd installed it. But her unease remained and, no longer willing to wait for the landlord, she'd called someone out first thing, at an eye-watering cost.

While the repairman set to work fitting a new lock on the window, his radio warned of another storm front moving in, due to reach northern Iowa that evening. Knowing she'd be driving straight into it, Riley had opted for the pickup—an old horse but a sturdy one—its wheels strung with snow chains. She'd stuck a shovel in the cargo bed, then tossed a flashlight, some water, and a blanket on the back seats, along with spare clothes and boots. She was going only two hours north, but the temperature was ticking steadily down, and she knew, very well, the dangers of Iowa roads in winter.

Her first stop that morning had been the DCI headquarters, but it was still early and Fogg hadn't been in. Not wanting to take the lock-bag with the tape from Dr. Hale on the road, Riley signed it over to Jenna to be sent directly to the state lab. She would call Fogg later, after she'd met Patty.

As far as Altman and Meadows knew, she was at home today, going through the list of clients from the Old Fort Hotel, checking if any of them lived in the area. She knew she was taking a big risk. If Patty's information was valid, she would have to admit she'd ignored her boss's order to stay in the city. But she would worry about that when it came to it. First things first.

"Hello?"

She sat up at the voice on the line. "Mr. Roach?"

"Who's this?" The man's tone was curt. Wary.

"Riley Fisher. I just joined the FBI resident agency in Des Moines."

"My replacement." Roach didn't wait for a response. "How did you get my number? What do you want?"

"Some advice, if possible?"

A long pause. "Go on."

There was no point tiptoeing around it. "Peter Altman. I—"

"What's that son of a bitch said about me?"

She was surprised by the question. "Honestly—nothing."

"Figures. Probably forgotten about me already. His old pal. Old partner." Roach's laugh was as dry as the crackle of dead twigs.

Riley thought he sounded drunk. It wasn't even noon.

"Altman's an asshole. Climbed his way up the ladder, elbowing off anyone who got in his way. He's in it for himself. Him and that woman."

"Meadows?" Riley recalled the contempt in her boss's tone when she'd spoken about Roach's departure.

"Get the job done, no matter how you do it. Throw their own mothers under a bus if it would advance their careers."

"Is that what they did to you?" Roach didn't answer, but she could hear his shallow breaths. "Noah Case implied Altman forced you out? Something to do with an investigation you were both assigned to?" There was silence. The phone hissed in Riley's ear. Reception had been patchy since the blizzard.

"Look, I'm done with that place. I've moved on. Best of luck to you."

"Tomorrow never comes?" The words jumped out before she could consider them. The line hummed again, but she knew he was still there. "Your words, Mr. Roach. I found them my first week on the job. Please. I just need to know if I'm in trouble here."

When he spoke again, Roach's voice had changed. He was quiet now, less hostile. "Altman went undercover a few years ago. Operation to bust a meth ring in the city. DEA was in on it. I heard a rumor he got sucked in. Never really made it back out."

"In what sense?"

"It was suggested he was taking kickbacks. But you know how cops talk. I didn't believe it myself. Until I started working with him."

Riley could feel the heavy thump of her heart. "What was your case?"

"Fraud. Not particularly unusual, but complex. Altman was against us working together from the start. Really up Meadows's butt about it. I thought he was just pissed about sharing a case. We all worked alone there, most of the time. But then he started acting strange. I'd catch him in a lie about where he was, or what he'd been doing. We got behind in our investigation. He missed a meeting with a key witness."

Riley thought of the phone call from Des Moines PD, warning about Karl Madden. So, Altman had been messing up everywhere?

"I knew he was using his BuRide for personal trips. I've known other agents do stuff like that. But he was really pushing the envelope, so I confronted him. Said I knew his head wasn't in the game. That he'd better get it on straight or I'd report him." A pause. "I'm not a snitch, but our work was being affected and I wasn't going to take the blame for his crap. You understand?"

She did.

"That job, man. Some of the stuff we have to deal with? The shit we see? I was—" A sharp inhalation. "Well, I'm not ashamed to say I was in therapy. Altman found out. Threatened to go to Meadows if I said anything about him. Said he'd tell her I couldn't hack it. That I was on antidepressants and hadn't disclosed it. Mutually assured destruction, right? Maybe I should have stuck it out, stood my ground, but life's too short. Tomorrow never comes?" His laugh was hollow. "That's what I was afraid of, if I stayed in that place."

"Is Altman dangerous?"

"I don't know. But if he's still involved with the gang he went undercover with?" Roach let the words hang there.

"Do you have anything that could help me find out?"

"Sawyer. Scott Sawyer."

39

The pancake joint was humid with steam from the coffee machines and smelled of bacon and maple syrup. Patty was in the far corner by the fogged-up window. She sat up straighter as Riley entered. Her freckled face was pale. Her eyes anxious. Riley took the seat opposite. As she sloughed off her coat, Patty's gaze darted to her utility belt, taking in her gun, badge, and cuffs.

"Thank you for meeting me."

Patty nodded tautly. "Antonio's covering for me. I can't be long."

Riley glanced around as a waitress appeared. "I'll take a coffee, thanks." Her mind was buzzing from the conversation with Roach, but she made herself focus on Patty.

Patty looked back at her when the waitress left. "How does this work?"

"For now, I just want to listen. To hear what you know about my suspect."

"Raymond." Patty seemed to force the name out. She took a breath after she'd said it. "Raymond Adamson."

Adamson? The snakes in the drawing, looping around those repeated words.

I am the son of Adam.

Riley took her notepad from her suit jacket, slowly, knowing one wrong move could make Patty scoot straight out of here. It was odd how the tables had turned. Only days earlier, Patty had been the one calming her.

"It took years for me to even say that name." Patty looked out of the window to the icy road and the rutted white fields beyond.

She began to speak, haltingly at first, then more surely, finding her voice.

She had been twenty-eight. She'd lived in Lone Creek all her life, knew everyone there—never really traveled beyond the township. Her world was small and as she grew, she felt the walls pressing in. The diner had offered a window: stories from people passing through, dreams of new places. But, after a while, as her girlfriends married the boys they'd grown up with and started families, she realized she wanted more. Like Lucy Jordan in the ballad.

Raymond had appeared out of nowhere, one early morning in fall, seventeen years ago, the bell ringing above the diner door as he entered. He was tall, with unkempt hair and intense eyes that seemed to dart everywhere at once, like he was looking for trouble and expecting to find it.

He ordered coffee, counting out change on the table with a long finger, the nail bitten short. She had tried her usual sunniness on him, but he'd shrunk from it, as if her smile hurt him. She found herself intrigued, wanting to know this stranger's story, but by the time she returned to his table, he'd gone, leaving an empty cup and a little pile of coins. He popped into her thoughts over the next few days, little chimes of curiosity, but after a few weeks, she'd forgotten all about him. Until she saw him coming out of Richard Kitch's halfway house.

The following day, he returned to the diner. He'd been wearing one of the green jackets from Lone Creek Logistics. Patty knew, given his lodgings, he was probably out of prison, but she'd not been deterred. In her experience, folk in trouble were mostly just down on their luck.

Over the next few months, he came in often. Gradually, he started talking, at first just mumbled replies to her comments about the news or the weather. But as the year turned, spring softening into summer, the corn growing tall, he started to ask her about herself. It had been a sweltering afternoon in July, the asphalt tacky under their shoes, when Raymond sat beside her on the diner's back stoop and told her his story.

He had grown up the eldest son in a wealthy family. His father had seen what he'd judged as a wickedness in him early on and subjected Raymond to regular beatings to drive the devil out. His mother would stand and watch, cowed in the face of her husband's authority. The addition of two more sons to the family only increased Raymond's torment. His younger brothers were smarter and stronger, and their father used them against him in his brutal campaign.

On the surface, they were the American Dream. They had built a successful business over generations, from dirt and grind to private schools and vacation homes. They were upstanding citizens of the local community, involved in church and charity. But for Raymond, beneath that polished façade lay a daily battlefield of taunts and violence that he fought to survive. He found solace in religious studies and in nature.

Some respite came when his father bought a hunting lodge in woods in Winneshiek County. There were plans to knock down the old cabin and build a summer home, but they never came to fruition, his father too invested in the business to devote any time to it. The family kept the lodge, however, using it occasionally during hunting season. Raymond would camp out there alone. It became his refuge from the world.

Leaving school early, he went to work for the family. There was an incident—here he'd grown tight-lipped—that saw him interred in Clermont Manor. When he was released, he found his younger brothers had taken over and he'd been disowned, cut out of the family and his inheritance. Raymond talked of this time as his wilderness years, stumbling from one job and one town to another, never settling. He slept rough, did some bad things, and ended up serving time in the Iowa State Penitentiary for first-degree burglary. In that cell, he found God and returned to the comfort of prayer.

On his release, he'd come to the Fresh Start halfway house for what he hoped would be a new chance at life. He'd not forgotten his family, even though they had forsaken him. In recent years, he had reconnected with one of his brothers and developed a relationship with his nephew, the boy spending time with him at the cabin, hunting and fishing.

Patty had been so caught up in Raymond's story, she'd been surprised, by the time he finished, to find the sun had dipped beyond the trees and the cicadas were singing. Flushed from the heat and by his trust in her, she'd been overcome by boldness and kissed him.

She'd not been sure what to call what they had after that. It wasn't dating in the way she'd ever known it, more like an intense friendship where attraction flitted in the air around them, but never settled. Moths around a flame. She never told anyone. It wasn't just the age gap: she twenty-eight, Raymond forty-four. She knew her folks would be worried—their daughter shacking up with an ex-felon, and a strange one at that. But she'd found herself touched by his hope of redemption and was determined to be a light in his life. When, in late August, he invited her to his family's hunting lodge, she'd seen no reason to say no.

The moment she arrived at the place, hemmed in by trees, the air thick with bugs, she knew she'd made a mistake. Sitting out behind the diner listening to his stories, sensing danger in some of his silences, she'd always felt safe. She'd been able to skate with him over those patches of darkness, never falling in. The things he said, the way he talked, switching so suddenly from light to shade, it was as though she'd been spun into blackness, but like a fairground ride—you screamed, but knew you were secure. Alone with him, deep in the woods, there was nothing holding her in.

The cabin was ramshackle. There was no electricity. No water. It didn't look like anyone had been there in years, the floors white with dust. She planned to stay one night, then think of an excuse for him to take her home first thing, realizing she wasn't ready for anything more. They'd eaten the snacks he'd picked up on the road and she curled up on one of the bunks to sleep.

She'd woken in the night needing the bathroom. Raymond's bunk was empty. Stubs of candles had melted in pools on the table. She searched through the place, hunting for toilet paper, looking through drawers and chests. She came across photographs of him and his family—his father in stern Sunday best, his diminutive mother, his brothers. There were later ones showing his nephew, the little boy proudly standing over a dead deer among the trees. Her need pressing, she'd moved on—and stumbled upon a nightmare.

At first, she thought it was junk: bits and pieces left or discarded by the family. There was a girl's pink sock, frilled with lace. A scarf. A scuffed high-heeled shoe. A driver's license belonging to a Hispanic woman. The dawning of her horror was slow, only rising when she'd seen that some of these things were stained with what could only be blood. She had known then, what some part of her had always known.

Here it was—the thing that lurked in Raymond's silences.

He had returned, a dead rabbit hanging in his fist, to find her packing her things, the drawers open, spilling his secrets.

He changed then.

Like a wild thing he'd been, ranting and raving. Stomping around the cabin, his boots making the boards quake and the dust quiver. He'd always been so meek, so timid, that she'd never really noticed how big he was. How strong. How capable of violence. He had flung the rabbit's limp body at the old timber wall and it had broken into blood.

He dragged her out onto the porch and down the old steps, splinters spiking her bare feet. He bound her to a tree, wrists and ankles, not heeding her pleas. He cursed her, spit striking her face. Told her she was just like the others. That she was a whore. The scourge of man. Born of Eve. One of a billion curses.

He had thrown back his head and roared, beat his head with his fists. When he stalked away into the trees, she thought he was going to fetch a weapon to kill her. Had closed her eyes and prayed.

Hours passed. When he didn't return, she began to struggle, pulling at the ropes that bound her. As dawn broke, she cried for help, but she'd seen the empty roads on the way to the cabin, the dense woods, riven by creeks and animal tracks.

She was out there for two nights before she managed to fight her way free. Weak with exhaustion and dehydration, blood dripping where the ropes had rubbed her skin raw, she made it to the road and flagged down a car.

Back home, she hid her wounds, told her parents she'd been staying with friends. She never told them. Never told anyone. She knew she should have, seeing what she'd seen. But she was scared and ashamed. It was her fault—she'd been attracted to his fire, seeking its light, but still knowing it might burn her. She had kissed him first. Gone willingly to his cabin. She knew how people in Lone Creek gossiped. How they would speak of her.

Raymond never returned to the halfway house. Patty went back to work at the diner, but every time the bell rang over the door she would flinch, thinking it was him. In the end, she left, went to stay with a friend in Texas, pushed it all to the back of her mind.

Until the world turned upside down and pulled her back to Lone Creek.

As Patty finished speaking, Riley felt the diner come back into focus around them. The chatter of waitresses and the hiss of coffee machines, the trucks roaring past outside. Her hand ached from writing. She had filled up pages. Patty looked exhausted, but lighter, as if relieved of a burden.

"Did you suspect who he was?" Riley asked, careful to keep any judgment from her tone.

"Did I think he was the Sin Eater?" Patty shook her head. "Not at the time. Not even when I found those things in the cabin. I mean, those attacks happened years before. I don't know. You think things like that happen to other people, not you. The brain does funny stuff. Pulls the wool over your own eyes. Sometimes, the truth can be too horrifying." She looked down at her hands. "Maybe I did, deep down. It all got stirred up again with the news. That face everywhere. Maybe I saw what I'd always seen."

"His family—do you know anything about them? Where they live?"

"No. Even though he was traumatized, he was still protective of them. He always skirted details when it came to them. I think he hoped they would take him back. I know the brother he reconnected with sent him money. Raymond told me he was using it to create something wonderful. Something that would change the way people thought of him."

That sounded ominous. "Do you know what?"

Patty shook her head.

Riley wrote these last details down. She thought of the nephew Patty had mentioned and the sneaker print in the snow at the governor's mansion. Had Raymond groomed his nephew to follow in his footsteps? Were they working together?

She finished writing, met Patty's gaze. "OK. Can you tell me where the cabin is?"

40

It took Riley almost three hours to reach Winneshiek County, heading east. Conditions were bad and forecast to get worse. She passed two jackknifed trucks, people huddled on the side of the highway, state troopers with red flares directing traffic. She thought of her parents, images of their wrecked car crowding her mind. The whole state was back on storm watch, the afternoon light fading fast.

The map Patty had drawn for her, on paper with the pancake joint's logo, lay on the passenger seat. The cabin was near Decorah, close to the Upper Iowa River. Riley had been to the area a couple of times as a kid, hunting with her grandfather. It was a landscape of hardwood forests and rivers, bluffs and prairie. In summer it was green and placid, a place for fishing and hiking. Now, it was another world. The trees were caked with snow, branches bowing under the weight, the creeks all frozen veins of white.

After three wrong turns, Riley found it. It was years since Patty had run out of this forest and flagged down that car, but there was the tumbledown barn she'd described, just after a bend in the road and a steel bridge. Then, to the left, a sharp turn onto an unpaved road.

The road grew increasingly narrow and overgrown, the trees hemming Riley in on both sides, the Dodge plunging through the snow. With the heavy fall, there was no way to tell if anyone had come this way recently. The road ended at a gate, rotten and half buried in a drift.

A sign said PRIVATE PROPERTY. Patty had told her the hunting lodge could only be reached on foot, about a mile in. As Riley turned the engine off, the world around her settled into silence.

She checked her phone. She had called Fogg immediately after meeting Patty. When he hadn't answered, she'd left him a voice mail, telling him where she was going, then called DCI headquarters to leave a message with Jenna. The signal was weak, just one bar. But it didn't look like Fogg had responded. That seemed strange, given the urgency of the situation.

Riley stared at the blank screen, wondering if something had happened back in the city. The thought was troubling. Meadows had expressly told her she wanted her in Des Moines. What would the woman do when she discovered she'd disobeyed that order? She wondered about getting ahead of it—fessing up before she got caught—but Roach's words stopped her. Right now, she didn't know who she could trust.

Logan's voice sounded in her mind.

You fought your way into this position. Walked through fire to get here.

She thought of Elijah Klein's letter recommending her to the bureau, and the choice she made to leave her family. Thought of those forms and tests; the hours spent pulling her soul open for the men behind that desk, feeling their judgment with every word, every spike of her heart. Those months struggling through the mud of the training ground, lying awake in her dorm, beyond the point of exhaustion. Getting yelled at by instructors and humiliated by teachers. Shot at. Kicked in the face. Pepper-sprayed in the eyes.

She hadn't gone through all that just to be some pawn in whatever game of politics Connie Meadows was playing, or whatever shit Peter Altman was into. And she hadn't come this far in the investigation to back down now. This was bigger than Meadows, bigger than the job. This was Abigail Dunbar and Colleen Traeger, Maria Perez and Sydney Williams, Megan Thomas, Hayley Abbot, and Patty.

All those women. All that pain.

Yes, she could check herself into the nearest motel—smooth things over with Meadows, then wait for Fogg or Altman, but if the coming storm was as bad as forecasters feared, her colleagues might not make it up from Des Moines. This road was only just passable now. Another big fall and it might be days before they could get back in. The afternoon was marching on, but there was enough light left to do some reconnaissance.

The decision made, Riley got out, sliding her cell into her pocket. Her boots sank in snow as she grabbed her backpack from the back seat, where the suit she'd worn to meet Patty lay folded. She had changed in the restroom of a gas station, putting on the spare clothes she'd brought from home after hearing the forecast that morning. Thermals and a fleece, waterproof pants, boots, a quilted jacket, mittens and hat. It was well below freezing, but not yet as cold as was threatened. Riley stuffed a balaclava in her pack just in case. Frostbite was a real danger in these conditions. Even twenty minutes on exposed skin could be critical. Buttoned up, armed with her Glock, she edged around the gap in the rotten gate and set off, a lone figure threading through a white world.

The path was overgrown and covered in snow, but still visible as a thin tunnel through the trees. The silence was absolute, just the sounds of her own boots crunching in powder. Snow pattered from branches as she brushed past.

The trees were knit close together. She checked the path behind. Her footsteps were clearly marked, a trail to take her back. She paused, hearing a muffled crump in the distance. Hunters? These forests were full of deer and turkey, coyotes, even bobcats. Her grandfather used to love it up here. Said his soul sang in these trees.

Sudden movement to her left had her jumping. She jerked around, going for her gun. She glimpsed the hind of a whitetail deer, springing away through the trees. Riley thought of her grandfather's grip on her shoulder as she narrowed her eyes into the sights. His voice calm in her ear. *Easy, Riley.* She placed a hand at her throat, where the gold star lay beneath the layers. Then, continued on.

She came across it suddenly, the trees stopping at the edge of a clearing. Squatting in the center, surrounded by snow, was a log cabin. Riley felt a mix of unease and excitement. Keeping to the trees, she scanned the area. The cabin looked old enough to be from pioneer times, although it appeared to have been added to over the years, with a porch that extended the front. The roof was smothered in snow, a chimney sticking up at a crooked angle. It looked like something out of a storybook, where no one good ever lived. She thought of Patty. Two nights alone out here, struggling to get free until the blood ran down her arms.

There were no lights, no smell of woodsmoke, no footprints in the snow that she could see. It looked deserted. It was entirely possible, after Patty uncovered his secret, that Raymond had never returned. He would have surely feared discovery? Besides which, if he was responsible for the recent attacks in Des Moines, it seemed unlikely this would be a useful base for him. There was another crack of gunfire in the distance. Riley checked her phone. The one bar was gone. A gust of wind shook a flurry of white from the trees.

Putting the phone away, Riley drew her gun and made her way across the open ground toward the cabin. The porch steps creaked beneath her boots. There was a rocking chair, stippled with lichen. There were two small windows on either side of the door, sun-yellowed curtains hanging. She knocked, alert for any sound within. Carefully, she tried the handle. The door opened into gloom.

The curtains swirled in the wind, dust drifting. The place smelled of ancient timber and empty years. There was a rustic table pitted with scars, five chairs around it and a bare bulb hanging above. There were shelves piled with chipped crockery and several chests of drawers. Two bunks lined the walls, covered with moldering blankets. There was a wood-burning stove surrounded by a circle of ash. The heads of deer were mounted on the walls, eyes glazed with dust.

Closing the door, Riley holstered her gun and headed to the drawers. After swapping her mittens for protective gloves, she checked each in turn. Cutlery. Candles turned nicotine-yellow with age. Old cans of soup and meat. One was full of rusty tools, twine, and frayed rope. Others were empty, sliding open with clouds of dust and the panicked skitter of spiders. All the anticipation she'd felt, after hearing Patty's story, was seeping from her like the last of the warmth she'd built up on the trek. Clearly, no one had lived here in a long time.

Deciding to return to the Dodge—come back with a forensic team and hope there might be some lingering evidence they could uncover—she closed the last drawer. There was a flicking sound, as if the drawer was caught on something. As Riley reached in, her fingers brushed something. She took hold and pulled until it came free.

It was a photograph, bent where it had been trapped at the back of the drawer. It was of a man on a stage, red curtains hanging behind him. There was a podium with a banner above it to one side, but the man stood at the front of the stage, one arm flung out, the other holding a mic to his lips, in the act of delivering some passionate speech. He was slim with brown hair. Maybe midthirties. His gray eyes glittered in the stage lights. There was writing on the banner, but only the bottom parts of the letters were visible. Riley had seen this place somewhere.

She peered closer in the gloom. Part of a wall was in the shot to the edge of the stage. It was decorated in shimmering gold paper. Recognition struck like a bell. She was certain this was the ballroom of the Old Fort Hotel. There was something else familiar too. Again—that prickle of déjà vu she'd felt when she had walked into the hotel. Had she been there before?

She took out an evidence bag and stowed the photograph. As she shrugged her pack back on and picked up her gun, her eyes alighted on the bare bulb above the table. Hadn't Patty said the place had no electricity?

Out in the woods the shadows had deepened and it was starting to snow. She knew she had to get back to her vehicle before the light fell, but curiosity spurred her on around the side of the cabin. She halted, spotting a quad bike parked behind the dwelling. There was a thin line threading away through trees on the other side of the cabin. Another trail led to this place.

Next to the quad bike was a pile of logs and a large metal box. She went over, brushed snow from the top. A generator. That meant someone must have returned here at some point after Patty's escape. Her wariness increasing, she scoured the tree line. Close by, partly obscured by trees, were two outbuildings. Near them was a mast. It looked like a small cell tower.

The first of the two outbuildings housed a filthy toilet. A rat scuttled into a corner as she opened the door. The second, which wasn't much more than a shed, was locked. There was a padlock and chain around the bolt. This seemed odd, given the cabin had been left open. The chain and lock didn't look particularly old, only lightly stained with rust. Moving quickly now, she returned to the cabin and hunted through the drawer of tools.

The bolt cutters were stiff. It was an effort to break the lock, and by the time she'd done so her fingers were tingling. Early warning sign of frostbite. The snow was falling steadily now, starting to cover her footsteps. Pulling the chain free, she opened the door. Inside were several old-fashioned trunks, layered with dust. Webs strung like lace from the rafters drifted in the wind now hissing through the trees.

She crouched by one of the trunks and opened it. It was stacked with old newspapers, copies of the *Des Moines Register* and others, going back decades, the paper brittle and yellow. She moved on to another. This was full of photographs, many of them black-and-whites. Some were loose, others taped in leather-bound albums. She picked through them, seeing images of people she guessed might be Raymond's family. A somber suited man standing outside a grand house. The same man outside the gates of what looked like a factory, with a line of workers in white coats and three young boys arranged in front of him. One boy, taller than the other two, stood awkward in the center. That long, thin face and those intense eyes were eerily familiar—the eyes of the boy who would grow up to become the Sin Eater.

There were bundles of torn-open envelopes addressed to Raymond, penned in a child's scrawl, with letters folded inside. There were scraps of paper covered in writings and drawings. It was far too much to go through in the time she had left before she was in real danger of exposure, but she skim-read a couple of loose pages. It was mostly weird ramblings about the natural order of things. Her eyes caught on one sheet. She pulled it free. It was similar to the one she and Fogg had found among Dr. Hale's belongings. Snakes and swords covered every inch.

Where the papers had been dislodged, she saw something poking up.

A baseball cap. She tugged it out. There was yellow writing looped across the front, same font as on the key ring they'd found in the burned-out car. THE OLD FORT HOTEL. Another rummage unearthed a matching pen. All part of the same loyalty package. Her heart thudded with excitement. This was it. The link between the Sin Eater and the threat that had been left for Jess Cook. The proof she needed.

The third trunk was full of objects. She scanned the jumble. A glove. A button of an old pop star. A key. A scarf. Then, she saw the brightly colored pocketbook.

My aunt brought it back from Nigeria. All these blues and golds and pinks.

The pocketbook belonged to Sydney Williams, taken from her that night when Raymond held her down and carved his mark into her skin. Here were all the things Patty had found in the cabin. All the trophies Raymond had taken from the women he'd attacked. His vile mementos.

Riley sat back on her heels. There were many more items here than attacks recorded. Her feelings of excitement and vindication faded as the horror settled in her. She pulled out her phone, took a few photographs to send to Fogg and Meadows. They would need forensics up here as soon as possible.

A missed call popped up on the screen, followed by a voice mail. It was Fogg. She pressed the phone to her ear in the hush of the shed.

"Riley, just got your message. Some complication here. There was a mix-up with the evidence you left this morning. Not to worry, we'll get it sorted. I'll explain when I see you. I'm on my way. Call me as soon as you get this and let me know where to meet you." A pause. "Wait for me, OK?"

Riley had returned the phone to her pocket and was shutting the lid of the trunk when she heard the sharp report of a breaking branch. She straightened and pressed herself against the wall by the door.

Snow was coming down fast. The trees were swaying. Her eyes darted, catching sight of something solid—moving between the trees. Too big and upright to be an animal.

The man was tall and broad, dressed in camo gear, his face swaddled in a scarf, hood pulled low. A rifle was slung across his back. Riley pulled the shed door closed, leaving just enough of a gap to watch as he entered the clearing. She stiffened as more men followed him out of the woods, along the second trail she'd spotted at the back of the cabin. Five of them dressed in similar gear, all armed, heads bowed into the snow.

One, at the back, was much smaller than the others. Just a skinny youth with chapped cheeks. Two of the men were pulling sleds laden with equipment. Were they the hunters she'd heard? Maybe they were looking to shelter from the storm? As the sleds came into view, Riley realized that the equipment piled up in them wasn't hunting gear, but cans of gasoline. A worm of fear uncurled inside her. The snow had started to obscure her footprints, but they were still visible, leading straight to her hiding place.

She realized there would be a brief moment where the men would disappear around the side of the cabin. She had only a tiny window. As they vanished, the sleds dragging lines behind them, she darted from the shed and plunged into the trees. Her footprints would leave a trail, so all she could hope to do was put enough distance between her and them as possible.

She glanced over her shoulder as she ran, breathing hard. The cabin had almost disappeared from view. Suddenly, her foot struck something. She flew forward, landing with a winded grunt in the snow. She pushed herself up on her hands, her clothes caked white. She thought it was a branch that had tripped her, but there, rising out of the snow, was a wooden cross. Snow had settled over a raised mound in front of it. About six feet long.

She heard a shout at her back.

Scrabbling to her feet, she dashed away through the forest as the storm blew in.

41

The Happy Turtle water park had closed down more than a decade ago, after a child drowned in the wave pool. It stood alone on the city limits, condemned and abandoned, its crumbling buildings and dilapidated rides illuminated only intermittently by the headlights of trucks roaring along an overpass.

Kody had come here as a kid with Troy's family: summers of burned noses and Popsicles, racing Troy up the steps to be the first down the tubes. It all seemed very different now as he walked toward it along an overgrown road, the beam of Harlan's flashlight lighting up signs covered with graffiti. His feet tramped in snow pitted with prints. Many people had passed this way recently.

Ahead was a gate, a sign hanging lopsided.

DANGER.
KEEP OUT!

There was a stocky man guarding it, dressed in camouflage. He had a hunting rifle in his hands and wore a mask. It was black, daubed with the symbol of a red tree. Harlan spoke to him in low tones, then the man opened the gate to let them pass. Kody felt the man's eyes trailing him. He wiped at his cold, running nose. His fingers still reeked of gasoline.

Yesterday afternoon, Harlan had entered his room, told him they were needed on some urgent mission for Billy. Kody, still reeling from his encounter with Reagan, had been too nervous to ask where they were going—merely sat in silence in the pickup, watching the sky darken as Harlan sped north.

Just outside Decorah, they'd met up with four other men, then headed into the forest. At a cabin deep in the woods, Kody had taken the can of gasoline Harlan thrust at him and did as he was ordered. But if he was scared yesterday, tonight he was terrified.

Once through the gate, Harlan paused to pull on a mask. It was the same as the one Kody had found among Harlan's belongings, painted with a red snake. Had that been only eight days ago? It felt like another life. Before he met Billy and the men at the trailer. Before he pushed Reagan down in the snow. Harlan had told him to bring the necklace he'd pulled from her neck. It sat curled in the pocket of Kody's jeans, the horseshoe poking his groin as he walked.

Troy had called that morning to tell him some psycho had attacked Reagan and stolen his gift. Kody had listened in panicked silence, expecting Troy to say he knew it was him—that Kody was a sick fuck and he was going to the cops. But when Troy broke down, he realized his friend had no clue. They all thought it was just a robbery. Reagan hadn't even called the police yet.

Kody managed to stutter a few words of comfort, but inside he'd been buzzing, like he'd sucked too hard on one of Austin's spliffs. Troy had always been the strong one. Kody had never beaten him at anything: sports, exams, girls, or games. To hear his friend so weakened—to know he was the cause—had been weirdly intoxicating.

"Keep up," Harlan grunted.

Kody hastened to obey. Somewhere in the darkness ahead, he could hear men's voices. Through the trees, he saw sparks drifting like fireflies, smelled woodsmoke.

Past a building, the walls of which were crawling with ivy, they passed through a set of broken turnstiles guarded by another armed man. Their feet crunched in glass from shattered windows. Kody, disoriented by the dark and the undergrowth, took a moment to realize the structures that loomed in the night sky, curling around one another like snakes, were the tubes he'd rushed down, shrieking, as a kid. One had collapsed, the slide hanging in midair, a tangle of metal beneath. Icicles glistened in Harlan's flashlight.

The voices grew clearer as they approached the old wave pool. It opened ahead, a dark void at the heart of the park. The shallow end, surrounded by fake rocks, was covered with snow. From there, it yawned down into a pit, where the grilles that once covered the machinery were bared like black teeth. Two bonfires had been lit at the bottom of the empty pool, throwing light across the walls. Snow had banked in a frozen wave on one side. The other was littered with leaves and trash. The whole place stank of damp rot.

As he walked behind Harlan, jittery and unsure, Kody counted at least forty men standing around the fires. All were swaddled in winter clothes, some in hunting gear. Many of them were armed with handguns, rifles, and knives. One man had a samurai sword in a scabbard across his back. All wore masks, each painted with a red symbol. In the firelight Kody saw many snakes, a few swords, and one or two trees. They reminded him of characters in one of his platform games, although most of these men didn't look like they'd be capable of jumping any rooftops.

Harlan led the way down to join them. Kody followed on the slippery slope, grabbing the rocks for purchase, then a rusty ladder. Harlan headed to one of the fires, flames surging from an oil drum. Several of the men paused their conversations to nod to him. Kody could see only their eyes, many of which turned to study him. He bent his head, shifting from side to side, wanting to get closer to the fire but not daring to.

After some time, the beam of a powerful flashlight swept across the pool. Another joined it. The men hushed, turning to stare up at the deep end wall that rose sheer before them. Kody saw a procession of masked figures approaching. Two, at the front, held the flashlights. They lit the way for a third man, slim of build, dressed in a long duster coat. He, too, wore a mask. It was adorned with a symbol Kody had not seen on any of the others—five yellow vertical lines. Bars, like on a gate? He thought of the tattoo he'd seen on Billy's arm in the trailer: the snake and sword, with the two trees and the golden gate. By the way this man walked, slow and calm, like he had all the time and no cares in the world, Kody felt certain it must be him.

Behind, four more followed. They were hauling something between them. Kody realized it was a tree—not a real one, but something like the dummy girl he'd helped Harlan make, out of wire and cornstarch and newspaper. It was painted black and bound with tape in places, looking like it had been handled a lot. As the men brought it to the edge of the pool, Kody saw ropes attached to its trunk. The slim man stood aside, hands clasped behind his back, watching as they took hold of the ropes and lowered the tree until it touched down in the snow. They secured it to two ladders on either side, so it stood erect at the bottom of the empty pool, as though planted.

As the firelight shifted across it, Kody saw there were many things tied to the tree's branches. He stood on his toes to see, but the crowd had pushed in front of him, blocking his view.

The slim man took center stage. He stood on the pool's edge, scanning those below. Kody felt sure his gaze lingered on him and his cheeks grew warm at the attention.

"Welcome, brothers."

As the man spoke, Kody was left with no doubt it was Billy.

"We come together in his name."

"In his name," murmured all the men.

"We come to celebrate our triumphs. To advance our cause." Billy spread his hands to the fires. "Together, we march toward the light. One mind. One spirit. One sword."

"Amen," came a few calls.

"We are the Sons of Adam. We draw out the poison wherever we find it. We crush the serpent and restore order to the world." His voice strengthened. "Who here has made a stand?"

Kody saw hands going up.

Billy climbed down the ladder into the deep end, nimble on the rusted rungs. The men with him followed, one by one. Billy and the others gathered in front of the black tree, between the fires. Kody craned his head. He saw a large man in a hunting jacket and baseball cap called forward to scattered cheers from the others.

The man turned and addressed the crowd. His voice, through the mask, was shaky. "So, I found my ex. The one who cheated on me. Tracked that whore down."

A couple of the men clapped. One whooped.

The man's voice strengthened at the encouragement. "She was in Illinois, living with that son of a bitch. I found where she works. Some shithole bar. I mean, what the fuck? She had it good with me." He beat his chest. "Never had to work a fucking day. I gave her everything!" His gaze went to Billy.

Billy nodded for him to continue.

"I waited for her. Sat in the parking lot for five hours. Damn near froze my dick off."

A few of the men laughed.

"But my time came. And I taught her the lesson she needed to learn."

"Show me," said Billy.

The man took a phone from his pocket. He showed Billy the screen. As the men hushed, Kody heard a faint sound coming from it. It was a woman, screaming. Her screams went on for some time, the men all quiet and listening, the only other sounds the crackle of wood bursting in the fire. When the woman fell silent, the man took back the phone.

Billy reached out and gripped his shoulder. "You are a true Son of Adam."

The man hung his head and nodded. When he looked up, his eyes were grateful and bright.

Billy gestured to one of those with him, who stepped forward and handed the large man something. "This is how we restore balance—how we bring order to the world. One battle at a time."

As the large man raised his fist, Kody saw he'd been given a wad of cash.

"And what do you bring as a token of your commitment?" Billy asked.

The man reached into the pocket of his hunting jacket and pulled out a flimsy scrap of black material. "The panties the bitch pissed herself in!"

There was a roar of approval from the crowd. Stuffing the dollars in his pocket, the man went up to the strange tree. Reaching for a wire branch, he tied the panties on, where they hung like a wilted leaf.

After this, several more men were called up.

Each spoke of a woman in their lives who had cheated on them, abandoned them, belittled, or rejected them. Wives, girlfriends, stepdaughters, mothers, colleagues. All the men had meted out some form of retribution. Some were violent, others more subtle. One man had served his nagging wife undercooked chicken to make her sick. Another had planted drugs in the desk of his demanding boss and got her fired. All were confirmed to Billy by photos or videos. Each man was given a fistful of cash, seemingly based on the severity of their punishment. Each had a token that they tied or taped to the tree.

Kody now understood Billy's question, back in the trailer.

Wanna play a game, kid?

It all seemed so weird, until he thought of his own games, where each level brought more risk, but more reward. Then, it made a strange kind of sense. *More rewards*—just like Harlan promised. Kody's heart skipped as he thought of the horseshoe pendant in his pocket. Did this mean . . . ?

"And we have among us a new recruit. A new soldier for our war."

The crowd parted and Kody saw Billy holding out a hand to him. He walked nervously through the snow, between their armed ranks. The wire branches of the tree rising behind Billy made him look like some horned god.

"Tell us," Billy said. "What battle have you fought?"

Kody's heart jackhammered as he saw the attention of every man was now on him. Harlan was among them, arms folded. He felt like he was back in school. Standing flame-faced at the front of the class at show-and-tell. Girls whispering, boys sniggering, as he mumbled some nonsense about his favorite game. He couldn't speak. He blinked, eyes smarting with smoke from the fires.

Then, Billy placed a hand on his shoulder and those cool gray eyes looked right into him. "Tell me."

Kody swallowed. "There's this—girl."

"Yes?" Billy encouraged.

"Reagan. She's with my best friend, Troy."

"Is she a whore, Kody? Is she a bitch?"

Kody thought of Reagan. The way she'd swayed so brazenly into Troy's world, snatching his attention, his time. The way she kissed Troy, like she owned him. The way Troy looked at her, like he was under some spell. Her little finger poking through her jeans as Alexa shrieked with laughter. *Maggot.* "She's a whore *and* a bitch." He didn't stammer now.

Some of the men applauded.

"Did you teach her a lesson? Did you put her back in her place? Beneath Troy? Beneath you?"

Kody sucked at his lip, uncertain how to respond. "I . . . ?"

"Who did God make first? Man or woman?"

It had been years since Kody had been to church, but he remembered the basics. "Man. Adam."

"That's right. And second?"

"Eve."

Billy shook his head emphatically. "No, Kody. And the Lord God said, 'It is not good that the man should be alone.' And he formed every beast of the field and every fowl of the air. Only then, after this, did God take one of Adam's ribs and out of it—out of man—made woman. She came *after* the beasts. Do you see?"

Kody nodded, but he wasn't sure if he did.

"What happened next, Kody?"

"Eve ate the apple?"

"Yes. God told the man that he could eat of any tree in Eden, except the tree of the knowledge of good and evil. If he did, he would die. But along came woman, weak and willing, and she was tempted by the serpent to eat the fruit of this tree. Worse, she beguiled the man to eat of it." Billy turned his gaze to the rapt crowd. Standing before them in the empty pool in his duster coat and mask, he looked like a priest at the strangest pulpit. "When God saw what they'd done, he cursed them. He cursed the man to a life of hard labor—a life that would end in death. And to the woman, he said, 'I will greatly multiply thy sorrow and thy conception; in sorrow thou shalt bring forth children; and thy desire shall be to thy husband, and he shall rule over thee.'" Billy looked at Kody. "God cast Adam and Eve out of the garden. He set a sword to guard the gates of Eden, lest they return and eat from the tree of life, and gain immortality. Woman is the cause of this original sin. She is the reason for our pain and suffering. The reason we toil and sweat, sicken and die. But does she still suffer for this crime? Suffer as God intended?"

"No!" came fierce replies.

"No," agreed Billy. "For decades now, women have wormed their way out of the curse God laid upon them. They sleep around. Choose not to marry, or bear children. They divorce us. Take everything we've worked work for. Our homes. Our kids. Our dignity."

There were shouts of agreement.

Billy scanned them. "Many of you here have suffered. As have I. My ex-wife, Darlene, took me for a fool, as you all know. I learned my lesson hard. But I sure taught her one, brothers!"

Many of the men laughed, like they knew the punchline to some private joke.

"How many wives truly obey their husbands? How many talk back, or refuse their wifely duties? Feminism is a cancer that has seeped through every vein in our society. Women take our jobs. Our places. Our roles. We cannot allow this. Do you see, Kody? It goes against *God*."

Kody had never thought about this—any of it. He'd never been interested in religion. Never believed in anything. But he couldn't deny that everything Billy had said made sense. He nodded, surer now.

"As the Bible commands, I suffer not a woman to teach," Billy continued, turning to the crowd. "Nor to usurp authority over the man, but to be in silence. For Adam was formed *first*, then Eve." He moved his attention back to Kody. "Would Reagan be the sort of girl to marry your friend? Bear his children and be ruled by him, as she should as a daughter of Eve, bound by the curse of woman's original sin?"

"No," said Kody, certain of that. "She wouldn't."

"And did you punish her? Did you put her in her place?"

Kody felt something like electricity go through him. "Yeah. I did. She made fun of me. Called me maggot. So, I pushed her down, shoved her face in the snow."

The men cheered.

Kody grinned so wide his cheeks hurt. He noticed Billy look over at Harlan, who gave a nod. He guessed the man was confirming what he'd done. His witness.

"She called you maggot?" Billy tightened his grip on Kody's shoulder. "Then be the maggot in the apple that chokes her."

"I took this from her." Kody pulled the necklace from his pocket.

Billy motioned to the tree. "Show your commitment. Show you are one of us."

Kody walked up to the tree. He had to stand on his toes to thread the pendant through one of the wire branches. Now, up close, he saw that all manner of things adorned it. Items of clothing, a prize ribbon, a doll, what looked like a limp lock of hair. There were other pieces of jewelry too. One piece, in particular, caught his eye. A silver charm bracelet.

Recognition froze him to the spot. Horseshoe. Plump heart. Cross. The bracelet was his mom's. The one she'd lost right around the time Harlan was last in the city. The time he smacked her head off the kitchen door.

He jumped at Billy's hand closing on his shoulder again. The man was holding something out to him. Kody took it, seeing it was a folded bill. One hundred dollars. He felt momentarily exhilarated, until he remembered the pendant was worth more than that.

"There's more where that came from, son," Billy assured, as if reading his thoughts. He turned to the watching men. "In his name!"

Kody barely heard their answering calls.

No one had ever called him son.

42

Riley's clothes still smelled of smoke. Its bitter tang permeated the office. She was exhausted and finding it increasingly hard to concentrate on Connie Meadows's relentless questioning.

"There was nothing left? Nothing at all?"

"No, ma'am. The cabin, the outbuildings. All of it was destroyed. The DCI forensic team will comb through the wreckage, see if they can salvage anything. State troopers are helping them secure the area. They tracked the route our six suspects came in on. There was evidence of two vehicles at the head of the second trail."

By the time Riley and Fogg had left the burned-out cabin, still smoldering two days later, state troopers had been directing in diggers that would plow paths through the fresh fall, allowing the forensics team access. The possible gravesite she had stumbled upon had been marked for examination. Riley guessed Patty might not be the only woman Raymond had lured there. With the number of trophies in that trunk, she feared there could be more. Cadaver dogs would be brought in.

"So, this is all you have?" Meadows stared at the evidence bag on her desk. Inside was the photograph Riley had found in the drawer—the man on the stage of the Old Fort Hotel's ballroom.

This wasn't entirely it. Riley had the pictures she'd taken of the trunk of trophies and she had Patty's account of her experience with

Raymond Adamson. But the letters and the photographs she had found, they were all gone, consumed by fire. She had to agree with her boss's assessment.

"What, exactly, was the issue with the tape you signed over to the DCI?"

"It seems it got mixed up with another batch of evidence. Got sent to the wrong lab."

"What the hell is Verne's team playing at?" Meadows's tone was acid.

Riley said nothing. She had been pissed when Fogg told her this two nights ago, meeting her at the motel in Decorah she'd checked into after fleeing the forest. He'd been at pains to tell her how upset Jenna was by the mistake. The lab the tape was now on its way to had been contacted, and it would only be a matter of time before it was retrieved and redirected. But the delay—involving one of their only concrete pieces of evidence—was a frustration none of them needed.

Fogg's team was going through all the databases they had access to in the hunt for Raymond Adamson. His name had been flagged with the Iowa State Penitentiary, where Patty said he'd done time for burglary, and they were looking into the cabin to determine ownership, hoping to track down his family. Jenna was also looking into recorded name changes, given it seemed likely Raymond had changed his to suit his religious obsession.

"The key ring found in the car," said Meadows, her attention back on the photograph. "You think this is the same hotel?"

"I'm sure of it. The baseball cap I found at the cabin was part of the same package. It's possible Raymond stole the car. Used it to get to the capitol, where he left the message for Governor Cook."

Meadows's eyes remained narrowed in question. "He burned the car to cover his tracks, but dropped the key ring in the process. Doesn't that seem particularly careless?"

"Yes," Riley accepted. She'd thought the same. "But I wonder if he wanted us to know it was him? The snakes in the letter to Cook and her family, and the one on the effigy at the mansion—that's always been his signature. It's not unusual for serial attackers to want to be recognized for their work. To take the credit."

"So, who is this man?" asked Meadows, tapping a finger on the photograph.

"There's clearly some link between him and Raymond. This picture. The loyalty package. We've got around two hundred names on the list of clients from the hotel who would have received one. If we can match a name to that face?"

"What about the men at the cabin? You believe they're working with Raymond?"

Riley went back over the thoughts running through her mind since she'd seen the men walking out of the trees, dragging the sleds stacked with gasoline. She recalled Patty's talk of a nephew Raymond had a relationship with and the brother who sent him money. Money Raymond had some grand plan for. "It's possible. We know whoever hung the effigy was most likely not the same person who delivered the message to the governor. Alternatively, Raymond could have simply paid these men to burn the cabin down, somehow knowing we were getting close to him? They could have been following orders, not even knowing the reason why. Perhaps the same group even put up the effigy?" she added, thinking of the skinny youth she'd seen trailing the men and the sneaker print at the mansion. "Either way, they must have had contact with Raymond. We need to find them."

"Could this waitress, Patty, have tipped Adamson off? Warned him about your plan to travel there? You said she had an intimate relationship with him."

Riley had to agree this could be the case, but her instincts told her no. Before she could answer, there was a knock at the door.

Noah Case appeared, clutching a laptop and looking troubled. "Ma'am, there's something you should see." He set the laptop on her desk and opened it.

Riley shifted so she could see the screen.

It was a paused video, two figures in the frame. One was Hayley Abbot. The other was her mom. They were sitting together on a couch. Hayley's face was still sullied by bruises, but the bandages were gone.

"It's just been on the news," Noah told them, pressing play.

"And how are you, Hayley?" came the voice of a female interviewer. "Are you recovering?"

Hayley opened her mouth, but her mother spoke first.

"She barely sleeps. Barely eats. I don't believe she will recover—that any of us will—until this monster is caught."

"Have you had any word from the police about the investigation? Are they any closer to naming, or apprehending a suspect?"

"We've heard nothing for weeks." Mrs. Abbot's eyes were fierce. "If they've not caught him by now, I doubt they ever will. He'll terrorize the women of this city and they'll let him, just like they did all those years ago."

"So, you do not believe the claims that detectives are doing all they can to apprehend the suspect?"

Riley knew what was coming; could feel it sliding toward them, an out of control thing like a truck on an icy highway.

"No." Mrs. Abbot paused. "I think they're covering." She looked straight at the camera. "Covering for one of their own."

The screen switched to show a female reporter standing in the snow by the underpass where Hayley had been attacked. "It has now been confirmed that Governor Cook's husband, Mark, and their daughter, Ella, have also been the subjects of a disturbing threat made by the Sin Eater, who managed to gain access to the capitol and the mansion. It is not difficult to understand the Abbot family's frustrations. How can the police and the FBI keep the women of our city safe, if they cannot even protect our highest official?"

The video cut away to show scenes of a vigil for Hayley Abbot and interviews with local residents, scared and angered by the attacks and the lack of progress.

"If the cops won't find him, we should," said one man.

"I wouldn't be surprised if it was one of them," a woman added, nodding emphatically. "They think they're above the law. We should stop paying their salaries."

Meadows struck the pause button. "I need to call the field office," she murmured. "Before Washington gets wind of this." She glanced at

Riley and Noah as she pulled the phone toward her. "You're dismissed. And Agent Fisher," she added, as Riley stood. "I'll decide what to do with you when this is contained."

Riley hadn't expected Meadows to have forgotten she'd disobeyed her order, but the threat still sank like a stone inside her.

Back in her office, she called Fogg. It went straight to voice mail. She guessed he, too, would be dealing with the fallout from the Abbot interview. A lit match in a puddle of gasoline.

She sat forward in her chair, elbows on the desk, head in her hands. Her exhausted mind raced in different directions. Hayley and her mom. Meadows's wrath. Patty. Could the waitress have tipped Raymond off? Warned him she was headed to the cabin? It didn't make sense—why then tell her any of it? But who else had known? Fogg. Riley sat back in her chair. And Peter Altman.

Fogg said he had called Altman when he was leaving Des Moines, left a message telling him everything. Neither of them had heard from the agent since.

She thought of Altman's behavior since her arrival—the threats, the disappearances. Thought of the footprints in the snow outside her apartment window and Roach's warning. Mrs. Abbot turning to the camera.

Covering for one of their own.

Riley opened her laptop and pulled out her phone. She saw Ethan had called twice. He hadn't left a message, but she didn't have time for her brother's problems right now. She tapped on notes. She had typed in the name as soon as she'd gotten off the call with Roach.

Scott Sawyer.

Entering her password, she accessed the NCIC database. It didn't take long to get a match. Scott Sawyer had had a long and varied career. *Theft. Possession. Kidnapping of a minor. Possession with intent to supply. Aggravated assault.* There were several mug shots going back years. The latest showed a hard-faced man with a shaved head, his scalp covered with tribal-style tattoos. She copied down his last known address.

As she left her office, pulling the door closed, the scar in her shoulder spasmed. She'd been lucky at the cabin. The pain was a reminder of what could happen when luck ran out. She paused, looking down the corridor to Meadows's office. Even without what Noah and Roach had told her, she had enough experience with her boss to know this wasn't something she could take to her. Meadows dealt in absolutes and targets. She had neither right now.

Riley turned to Noah's office. The agent's light was still on.

43

The snow on the abandoned lot was carved with ruts from trucks and pocked with footprints. The lone trailer home, propped on its bricks, stood in the center of a storm of activity.

In the shadow of the ruined site office, a metal hulk stood gleaming. Harlan Judd's eighteen-wheeler. The men were taking equipment from the cargo beds and trunks of pickups and Jeeps, loading it in the back of the semi. Bulletproof vests, helmets, and weapons. Knives, pump-action shotguns, and semiautomatic rifles. A pick'n'mix of ugly death.

In the trailer, Billy stood at the kitchen counter, giving orders to men as they came and went, conferring with others. A map of Des Moines was spread out on the counter's grimy surface, next to the plan of a school. Red crosses had been scored on both.

Kody perched alone on the couch, watching the comings and goings. He recognized many of the men from the ceremony. Dirch was here, cigarette stuck behind his ear, and Cuddy, the fat man, whose family, he'd since learned, owned the old water park. There were the white-haired twins, both of whom were ex-military, dressed in camouflage.

Last night, when the ceremony was over, they'd all removed their masks and stood around the fires, talking and laughing. A camping table had been erected and some of the men put out beers and snacks. For the most part, Kody had stood alone, listening to snatches of conversation

about declining birth rates and that the reason young men were turning to crime was that there were no male role models; now so many of
the heroes in films and TV were women.

Billy had moved through the crowd, pausing to speak to each man
in turn. They treated him like a rock star, or one of those evangelist
preachers Kody's mom sometimes watched on TV, their faces lighting
up whenever he clasped their shoulder. He shared stories and gave advice. And he spoke often about his ex-wife, Darlene, who seemed to be
an object of deep hatred among the group.

Kody had watched many of the men hand cash to Billy, including
those who'd just been rewarded, digging in their pockets to pull out
some of their winnings. Harlan explained that in order to play the
game and be part of the group, you had to pay a regular fee.

"For the bigger targets there's a chance of winning big. Seriously
big," Harlan had added, eyes hungry in the firelight.

Kody had thought of the charm bracelet hanging in the weird tree.
He'd wanted to challenge Harlan—ask the man if it really was his
mom's. But before he'd been able to pluck up the courage, Harlan had
gone off in a huddle with Billy, Dirch, Cuddy, and the twins. Kody
overheard something about a special operation.

Now, sitting on the trailer's couch, feeling invisible, he stuck his hand
in his pocket and pulled out the one-hundred-dollar bill he'd won, un-
folding it so the light shone through. He didn't want to give it up. He
could buy any game he wanted with this. But, then, if what Harlan said
was true, maybe he could win enough to buy a new console? Even a big-
screen TV. One like Troy's.

He was struck by a memory of his dad. When he was very young,
his father sometimes took him to a dog racing track where they had slot
machines. Kody would perch on his father's knee, watching as he fed
the machine with quarters, sometimes for hours. Kody had never seen
his dad so happy as when a line of matching symbols whirled together
and the machine jingled and buzzed, spitting out coins. His father always seemed to leave with less than he'd come with, but somehow that
never bothered him.

Stuffing the note back in his pocket, Kody winced at the pain in his arm. Carefully, he peeled up his sleeve to look at the serpent coiled around his pale forearm. The tattoo, covered with Saran wrap, was still dappled with blood, red and sore at the edges. He hoped the man he'd been led to after the ceremony, with the crooked grin and the wireless tattoo gun, had sterilized his equipment. He didn't want to have to get his mom to call a doctor.

Harlan had been done after him, getting the addition of a flaming blade that plunged through the snake. He was given a new mask too, one with a sword, along with a fistful of cash. Kody had felt aggrieved, wondering if Harlan was getting all the credit for the dummy girl and the cabin, but there'd been talk about a shrink who'd been targeted for punishment—and it seemed Harlan's reward was for that.

Kody had been handed a mask with a red snake, along with a white hood—same as the one he'd found in Harlan's bag. There was an apple painted on it. It smelled moldy and damp, like the park. He was told to destroy it after use and that he would then be given another. Harlan had glanced sideways at him, both of them knowing he'd fucked up by leaving it in his bag to be discovered.

The twins finished speaking with Billy and headed out, barking orders at those loitering near the vehicles, passing around cigarettes and hip flasks. There was a mix of excitement and nerves among the group, which lent the night a feverish atmosphere.

Kody straightened as Billy's gaze fell on him.

Billy came over, Dirch glancing after him. He sat on the low table in front of Kody. "You have questions?"

Kody didn't want to say the wrong thing, so he just nodded. He was caught in the man's gaze, so close he could smell Billy's sweat. It felt somewhere between held and trapped.

"I was hoping to have more time to train you, as I have the others. To talk more about our purpose. Our plans. But things are moving fast. We must be agile. Adaptive."

"The cabin?" Kody hadn't been told much, but he'd gleaned there were things at that place that mustn't be found. The others were concerned when they'd seen the prints in the snow and the broken lock on the shed. The twins had lifted their rifles and fanned out through the trees, while Harlan had shoved the can of gasoline at him.

"It belongs to our founder. The man who inspired all of this—all of us. We were warned the cops were getting too close. Our timetable had to change."

"Timetable?"

Billy smiled. "Can I rely on you, Kody?"

"Yes." Kody meant it, but he felt worried, unsure of what was being asked of him. The men outside looked like they were gearing up for war. He'd only ever shot things on a screen.

"Good." Billy leaned back and reached into his jeans. He pulled out a bundle of cash. All one-hundred-dollar bills. "When we've completed our mission, our founder has promised us a fortune."

"A fortune?" Kody kicked himself, realizing he was just repeating everything Billy was saying. But the man made him so nervous—so eager to please—he could barely get his words out.

"A jackpot," said Billy, a glint in his eyes. "But I want you to have a token of his appreciation so far." He handed over five of the notes. Kody took hold of them, but Billy didn't let go. "You're a Son of Adam now. Don't forget that."

Kody knew there was another meaning beneath this camaraderie. He didn't just belong. He was liable. Rewards and blame, for whatever came next. It was as clear an admission that things were about to shift toward something else as the weapons being loaded into Harlan's eighteen-wheeler. This wasn't beating up ex-girlfriends or punishing nagging wives. This was something altogether bigger.

But, with this knowledge came a swelling sense of pride. He'd never been chosen for anything. Always the last to be picked at sports or in lessons, ignored by classmates and teachers alike. Suddenly, he didn't care what it was he would be expected to do. Sitting there, consumed by Billy's gaze, Kody realized he would do anything the man asked of him.

Billy smiled, let him take the notes.

"We're set."

They both looked around at the voice to see Harlan had appeared in the trailer's door. His brow furrowed seeing them together, his eyes full of questions and suspicion.

Billy rose smoothly and crossed to the counter.

Kody stuffed the notes in his pocket, not liking the way Harlan was staring at him.

Billy looked from Cuddy and Dirch to Harlan. "You all have your assignments."

"In his name," said Cuddy and Dirch.

"In his name," echoed Harlan, still looking at Kody.

Harlan was silent on the drive home in the pickup. The eighteen-wheeler remained at the lot, loaded with weapons and gear.

The house was dark, Shelley working a double shift at the Laundromat.

Harlan let Kody get in through the front door and kick off his muddy shoes before he spoke. "Hand it over."

Kody turned, halfway through taking off his coat. "What?"

"What Billy gave you."

Kody shrugged his coat on and backed away. "No." His hand went protectively to his pocket. "He gave it to me."

"Well I got sweet fuck all. I drove us to the cabin. My truck. My gas. Tell me, how is that fair?"

Kody just shook his head.

"Ain't even got a fucking answer, have you?" Harlan followed down the dim hallway as Kody retreated backward. "Hand it over!"

"It's mine. Billy gave it to me!"

"I got you into this. If not for me, you wouldn't have a single fucking cent."

Kody thought of the bloody hood under his mom's bed. He wanted to tell Harlan if he didn't want him involved it was his own fault for being so careless. He didn't, but as his gaze flicked to his mom's bedroom, he knew—by the man's narrowing eyes—that Harlan had read his mind.

He dodged into his room, but before he could shut the door, Harlan shouldered his way in. The door slammed into Kody, knocking him off his feet. He landed with a grunt on the floor, scattering cans of Coke and candy wrappers.

Harlan dropped on Kody like a rock, knee digging into his chest as he rooted in the pocket of his jeans. Kody struggled, all of Harlan's weight driving into him. His ribs felt like they might crack. He gasped, pushing feebly at the big man's knee.

Harlan found the crumpled notes and pulled them out—the five hundred Billy had just given Kody and the one hundred from the ceremony. He rose, stuffing them in his own pocket. He paused, looking down on Kody, eyes full of contempt. "In future, do as you're told. Fucking *maggot*." He swung his boot into Kody's side.

Kody yelped and squirmed away, but Harlan had him trapped. He kicked him again, then reached down and hauled him up by his collar. He drew back a fist and punched him in the face. Kody felt the snap as something broke. Pain exploded through his nose. Blood poured down the back of his throat. He hung in Harlan's grip, gagging, until the man let him go and he crumpled to the floor.

He lay there, curled in a ball, blood and snot and tears streaming. Harlan walked past him to his desk. Kody heard something being yanked out. He tried to raise his head to see what was happening, but there was no need. Harlan dropped the console on the floor next to him. Kody shouted as Harlan's boot came down on the slim box. Again. And again.

When it was done, Harlan left. Kody heard the refrigerator being opened, the crack and hiss of a beer bottle cap. He lay there, unmoving, staring at the remains of his console, his pockets empty, pain throbbing through him, his blood trickling onto the carpet.

He thought of Troy and his friend's growing indifference. Thought of his dad, who'd gone years ago, leaving a space that had always been occupied by men like Harlan. He thought of the three hundred Harlan had taken from his mom's stash to pay his dues to Billy, and her charm bracelet hanging in that black tree. He remembered that day, his mom making Harlan dinner, all the while trying to smile through the bruises on her stupid face.

Then he thought of Billy.

Billy who had looked into his eyes without judgment or scorn, who had clasped his shoulder and welcomed him, chosen him to be part of something.

Billy who had called him son.

44

So, who's this guy you need to interview?" Noah asked, looking out at the neighborhood as Riley drove. It was a rough part of the city—low rent, high crime. "What's the case?"

Riley sucked at her lip. They were almost at the address. She was going to have to tell Noah something more. As she turned down the street, a vehicle came roaring toward her, powerful headlights blinding her. She had to swerve to avoid it, knocking over a garbage can.

"Whoa!" exclaimed Noah. "Came out of nowhere!"

Riley didn't answer. Her eyes were in the rearview. In the mirror she could see the gleaming hulk of a white Toyota speeding away. "Hold on," she said, forcing the Chevy into a quick reverse, then spinning it around at the intersection, wheels slipping.

Noah grabbed the handle. "Jesus!"

Riley put her foot on the gas. Ahead, not far, she could see the Toyota. She was positive it was the same vehicle that had been behind her and Altman on the way to the Old Fort Hotel. Pimped-out, with tinted windows. "I think that's my suspect," she said as the Toyota swung dangerously fast through a lane of traffic and onto the highway.

As she followed, she realized it was leading her the way she'd come, back to West Des Moines. The Toyota slowed slightly as it turned off the highway, into a maze of residential streets near the Walnut Woods State Park. Riley slowed too, keeping her distance.

Another turn, onto a neat street lined with cookie-cutter houses that backed onto fields, bone white under the gleam of a moon. Festive decorations sparkled on every house. Every house except one, which stood alone, dark and brooding. In the shadows of the garage, Riley saw a black Tahoe.

Noah followed her gaze. "Hey. Isn't that Peter's BuRide?" His brow was furrowed in the dashboard lights. "Riley, what's going on?"

The Toyota had come to a stop a short distance down the street. The driver was parking. She turned into a driveway and killed the lights. She watched someone climb out of the vehicle and jog down the street. As the figure passed beneath a streetlight, she glimpsed swirls of black ink etched on his shaved scalp. Scott Sawyer had something in his hand. She saw him stuff it down the waistband of his jeans as he hastened up the drive to the house. She realized now that there was some light in there, faint behind the closed curtains.

"Riley?" Noah pressed.

The man was at the door. She saw it open. She caught a brief glimpse of Altman's face, eyes widening in shock, before Sawyer barged inside. The door slammed shut behind them.

"I think Altman's in trouble."

Noah's frown deepened. "What sort of trouble?"

"The sort of trouble I don't want to say unless I'm certain." Riley pressed on before the young agent could object. "Keep watch out front, OK? I'll shout if I need backup."

Not waiting for an answer, she climbed out.

Outside, in the biting air, she smelled the smoke from the cabin on her clothes, trailing her like an acrid perfume. She looked down the street to where the Toyota was parked, its hood bladed with light from a streetlamp. As far as she could see, the vehicle was empty, although with the tinted windows it was hard to be certain. Keeping to the shadows, she drew her Glock and made her way up Altman's driveway, sticking close to the neighbor's lawn to avoid being seen from the house.

Something burst into bright life beside her. The air filled with singing.

"Silent night, holy night."

Riley swung around, pointing her gun at a trio of illuminated snowmen. The carol streamed out as they rotated on a base.

"Fuck," she breathed, her heart galloping.

The snowmen rumbled around, the song still playing. She'd tripped a motion sensor. Riley looked back at Altman's house. The door hadn't opened. The curtains hadn't twitched.

Drawing a breath, she continued. Behind her, the snowmen finished their verse and stuttered into silence, the lights winking out.

The night settled and stilled.

Reaching the garage where Altman's Tahoe was parked, she moved down the side of the house, into a garden. Beyond, fields stretched into the darkness of the woods. There was a deck built out at the back of the house. She climbed the steps cautiously. A door led into a shadowy kitchen. Light seeped from somewhere deeper in. She tried the handle. The door opened.

Inside, down a hallway, she could hear men's voices. She couldn't make out what they were saying.

She moved through a modern kitchen, past a dining table covered in papers. She recognized the list of names Altman had taken from the Old Fort Hotel records. There were other files from their investigation, a pair of reading glasses discarded beside them along with a bottle of red wine, half empty, and a glass, half full. So, he had been working then, at some point. On the kitchen counter, she saw his bureau-issued Smith & Wesson, lying in its holster.

She left the kitchen and entered the hallway, where the voices became clearer. Ahead, to her left, was a door. It was ajar, light spilling out. Outside it was a small table with mail piled up. Altman's cell phone lay on top of the heap. Farther down was another door, by the front entrance. To her right, stairs led up. Thankful for the carpeted floor, she approached the partially open door. By pressing herself against the wall, she could just see through the gap.

She saw Altman sitting on a chair, hunched forward, elbows on his knees. His face was tense, eyes tracking movement in the room. Riley saw a shadow. Heard the creak of a floorboard.

"It didn't have to go down like this. You know what I want. Why've you gone soft on me?"

Riley guessed the voice—half swagger, half grit—belonged to Scott Sawyer.

"We had a deal," Altman said. "Now, you're following me to my work? My house? Who the fuck gave you my address?" Altman's jaw tightened. "It was Travis, wasn't it? Do you know how much time you could get in federal for this?"

Sawyer laughed. It was the laugh of a man who wasn't afraid. Riley's grip tightened on her Glock. It was warm in the house and her palms were starting to sweat.

"You really gonna go there? We'd be sharing the same cell." Sawyer paused as Altman hung his head. "I'm the only one who can help you hunt her down. We both know it."

Riley's skin prickled. *Hunt her down?*

"It's a simple transaction, Altman. That's all. No need to over-think it."

Riley stiffened as Sawyer came into view, his back to her. There was a Colt 1911 in his hand. The man was clearly not fool enough to get any closer to Altman, but stood a few yards back, keeping the gun trained on him.

"Tell you what, you give me what I want and it'll be the last you see of me. Cross my heart."

Altman looked up and Riley saw the defeat in his eyes: the realization this promise meant nothing. He started to nod when a loud chiming filled the hallway. Altman's cell phone, lying on the table with the mail, lit up as it rang. A name flashed on the screen. *Connie Meadows.*

Riley flinched back from the sound, knocking her elbow against the wall. Altman's eyes flicked up. They widened as he caught sight of her, visible through the gap in the door. Sawyer jerked around, following Altman's gaze. He veered, the Colt's barrel swinging toward Riley.

The world seemed to slow. Memory punched into her mind. A figure silhouetted against a burning barn, gun coming up. The flash and the bang. The explosion of pain in her shoulder.

Then, everything speeded up, as Altman launched himself out of the chair and barreled into the man. They disappeared out of sight, crashing through something that shattered. Riley was up and lunging for the door when a gunshot cracked the air. There was a bellow of pain.

She kicked the door wide, Glock before her. Sawyer had scrabbled off Altman, now lying on the floor in the wreckage of a glass coffee table. She yelled as the man charged across the room. *"Freeze!"*

Sawyer shot at her in answer. He was midrun and well off the mark, the bullet punching through the wall in a white puff of plaster, but as Riley ducked, it gave him the chance to dive out through a second door. It was the one by the front entrance, she realized as he disappeared. She was moving after him when Altman groaned.

The agent was on his back, among shards of glass and splintered wood, one hand clutched to his side. She could see the blood oozing dark between his fingers. She crossed quickly to him, hearing the front door bang open. She took out her phone as she grabbed a blanket from the couch and knelt by Altman, wedging it against his side. He groaned again.

"Need immediate assistance. Officer down!" She rattled off the address to dispatch as Altman squeezed his eyes shut.

Hearing shouting, Riley twisted around. Out in the street, gunshots erupted.

Noah.

Altman clutched at her wrist. "Go!" he urged, through gritted teeth. *"Go!"*

As she raced down the hall, toward the open front door, her mind filled with awful images of what she would find. Noah Case lying there, bleeding out in the snow.

But the scene that confronted her as she plunged into the raw night air was entirely different.

There was a body in the snow, but it wasn't Noah—who was shielded behind the open door of her Chevy, his gun extended. The body, sprawled on the lawn of Altman's neighbor, was Sawyer.

Noah's gun cocked up as Riley emerged from the house, then he checked himself. "I think he's alive," he shouted in warning.

Riley made her way carefully toward the body. Sawyer's fall had tripped the motion sensor on the snowmen, revolving as they sang, throwing light across his prone form. Blood from a gunshot wound in his thigh was turning the snow into a grisly red slushy.

"Silent night, holy night."

People all along the street were coming out of their front doors, calling in worry and confusion. One man had his phone up and was videoing it all. Sirens were screaming in the distance.

"All is calm, all is bright."

In the glow from the singing snowmen, Riley spotted the Colt, a few yards from Sawyer's hand. She went over, keeping her gun trained on him, and kicked the weapon away. Noah converged on her position. The man moaned and turned his head, his outstretched hand feeling blindly for his gun. He went still when he saw Riley, eyes slitting in resignation. He lay there, compliant, as Noah cuffed his hands behind his back.

Now the immediate danger had passed, Riley realized the sirens sounded strange. She could hear the whine of them, coming closer, but there was another high-pitched sound mingled among their rise and fall. She searched for its source. There, down the street, in the window of the white Toyota, was a boy. His palms were pressed against the tinted glass. He was screaming.

She turned, hearing a grunt of pain, to see Altman staggering from his front door, one hand clutched to his bloodied side. His eyes went from the body to the boy. "Bring the kid inside, Riley." His voice cracked with the effort of speaking. "He shouldn't be out here."

Riley glanced at Noah, crouched beside the handcuffed man. The young agent looked pale. His trench coat was soaking up snow, his Tom Ford glasses were crooked on his nose, and she noticed his hands shook a little. She guessed he'd most likely never fired his weapon on duty before. "You OK?"

Noah inhaled and nodded.

Ignoring the people clustered on the sidewalk, Riley holstered her Glock and went to the Toyota. When she opened the door, the boy tumbled out and tried to run to the fallen man, but she took his arm and steered him, firmly but gently, up the path to Altman's house.

"*Dad!*" screamed the kid, twisting to look over his shoulder.

"It's all right," she told him. "He's going to be OK."

Inside, Altman had groped his way back down the hall, leaving bloody handprints on the walls. Riley followed, leading the shivering boy into the warmth of the living room. The agent was sagged in a chair, his face waxy and gray. "The paramedics aren't far," she assured, eyes on the wound in his side, his T-shirt slick with blood.

Altman gestured weakly to a chest, beyond the shattered remains of the coffee table. "There're some things in there. Toys and stuff." His eyes were on the boy.

Riley realized the kid had stopped trying to fight her and was just standing there, hand limp in hers. His face was white, his teeth chattering. Cold, or shock. She led him to the couch and sat him down. Inside the chest, she found a jumble of toys, games, and puzzles. On the top was a stuffed bear—the one she'd seen weeks ago, lying on the back seat of Altman's ride. Picking it up, she took it over to the kid. The boy accepted the bear in silence, small fingers pressing into the tufted fur, already well-loved by another child's hands.

She returned to Altman, who'd slumped lower. He needed urgent medical attention, but she needed answers. The words she'd heard Sawyer say earlier rattled a warning in her mind.

Hunt her down.

"What is all this?"

"My daughter." Altman licked his dry lips. "They're my daughter's."

Riley realized he was looking at the toy chest, thinking her question had been about that.

"I need you to find her," he continued, his eyes fixing on her. His breathing was shallow. "If I don't make it."

"You'll make it." Picking up the blanket he'd discarded, she pressed it to his side again, ignoring his hiss of pain.

Sirens wailed, filling the night with their urgent song. Blue and red lights pulsed, strobing the walls.

"I need you to promise me." Altman grabbed her arm. His hand was sticky with blood.

"I promise, OK."

Altman swallowed thickly and nodded. "Her name's Paige. She's three years old. Her mom's named Leah Darby. We got together four years ago when I was undercover."

Riley thought of what Roach had told her. "The drug bust?"

"Leah was my informant."

"You slept with her?"

"It's not what you think." He drew a shaky breath. "I mean, we fell in love. I got her off that shit. Helped her get clean."

Riley thought of Noah chuckling at the idea of Altman having a wife or kids. Clearly, he'd hidden all of this from his colleagues, but there wasn't time to probe the morals of his actions, sleeping with an informant—a vulnerable addict at that.

Outside, the sirens had stopped. She heard the bang of doors. The clatter of a gurney. Noah calling to the paramedics.

"Six months ago, Leah fell back in."

Six months? Right around the time Karl Madden was planning his attack on Jess Cook in protest against the lockdown. Right around the time Altman missed that vital call and started messing up on the investigation with Roach.

"I got her into rehab. Thought she was OK. But two months ago, she vanished. Took Paige. Her parents, her friends—no one's heard from her. I've searched everywhere. Run down every contact I have. Cops. Social workers." Altman paused, seeing her working out the depths of his desperation. "Yeah, and dealers. I *know* these people, Riley. The thought of my daughter . . ." He trailed off. His gaze went to the window, then to the boy perched on the couch. "Sawyer was part of the gang I busted. He slipped under the radar when the others went down. Picked up where they left off. He knows all the dealers, the dens. I knew if anyone could find her, he could."

"What did he want in return?"

Altman looked up at her. "Intel. Details of areas and persons of interest the FBI and DEA are concentrating their efforts on in the city. Information to help him evade them."

"Christ," she murmured.

"It was for Paige," he said in a flash of defiance, then winced. "Sawyer gave me the address of a den where Leah had been spotted. I kept watch. Saw her." His frustration was plain. "But I lost her."

Riley imagined him sitting alone in the dark of his car, waiting and watching, the stuffed bear ready on the back seat in case he found his daughter. It was hard not to pity him, despite her anger. "That's why you wanted to stay in the city?"

He hung his head in answer.

"Why didn't you go to Meadows? Tell her what was going on?"

Altman's face tightened. "You've been here weeks. Ask me that in a few years."

Riley heard an echo of Roach's bitterness in his tone.

The front door banged, footsteps hastening down the hall.

Riley stepped back as the paramedics entered, hauling medical bags and a stretcher. Altman grunted as one went to him and carefully lifted his T-shirt to inspect the wound.

Riley spoke quickly to the other about the kid. The paramedic crouched by the boy, speaking in calm tones. "I'll check on Noah," she told Altman.

Altman's head twisted to her. "Wait! The lab. They called."

"Quantico?"

"The key ring. They compared it with the results from the state lab. It was burned with a different accelerant."

She shook her head, not understanding.

"The key ring wasn't in the car when it was set alight. It was burned elsewhere. Looks like someone planted it after the fire." Altman gasped as the paramedics helped him onto the stretcher. "I think someone wanted us to find it."

"We need to get him to the hospital," the paramedic told Riley. "Now."

Outside, West Des Moines PD had arrived. Some of the officers were coaxing people back inside their houses; others were taking statements. Another team of paramedics was tending to Sawyer, who was uttering enough expletives to tell Riley he would be just fine. The snowmen were still singing. Altman's neighbor had come out of his house and was talking to Noah, shaking his head in bewilderment at the scene on his lawn.

Riley's head swarmed with questions, but she felt weirdly focused. Adrenaline made her feel as sharp and clear as the night air. The lights of the ambulances and squad cars flashed across the neighbor's curtains as she made her way toward Noah. With every revolution of the lights, the curtains were stained blue, then red.

Red drapes over windows. Red curtains hanging over a stage.

All at once, she knew why the ballroom of the Old Fort Hotel was familiar—why she felt she'd been there before. It wasn't a childhood memory or déjà vu. She had seen it in another photograph, framed on a wall.

45

It was dawn by the time Riley returned to her apartment. After she and Noah had dealt with the aftermath of the shootings, she'd been called back to the agency to brief Meadows. She had wanted Altman to be the one to tell their boss the truth, but with him in surgery it had been left to her to explain his deal with Sawyer, his hope of finding his missing daughter.

The few stony words Meadows had uttered told Riley she was more worried about the reaction of her superiors in Washington. Internal Affairs had been notified and a team would be on its way to investigate. Altman—whose condition was critical but stable—could be looking at criminal charges. Riley sensed Meadows calculating how she would come out of all this.

What she'd initially thought was the older woman's brisk professionalism had morphed into something colder, harder. She realized, now, that many of her own doubts about her capability in this role had come from Meadows and the hostile environment she'd created down in the basement. She was furious at Altman for putting their investigation at risk, but she was angry at Meadows, too, for not noticing one of her own agents had been drowning, even if in a pool of his own making. She thought of Meadows's contempt for Roach and the sense she'd gotten from the ex-agent of a culture of intimidation and competition. She recalled something her grandfather used to say about bad police departments.

The fish always rots from the head down.

Riley's fears about the job had shifted. She was no longer worried about whether she could succeed here, but whether she wanted to.

She thought about her promise to Altman that she would find his daughter. Yet again playing mom to a kid who wasn't hers. It felt like so much of what she had run from when she'd packed up her life and left Cedar Falls. Messy lives and failed relationships, addiction and bad parenting. She'd hoped for a clean getaway, a fresh start. Not a deep dive into someone else's shit.

She hauled herself out of the Chevy. She'd left the Dodge at the agency, would pick it up later. A cat turned and stared at her, eyes gleaming in the spectral glow of a streetlight, before slinking away. Fogg had said he would be here shortly. If she was quick, she would just have time to change, and knock back as much caffeine as she physically could. She was running on fumes.

Riley locked the car and turned. She froze. There was a light on in her bedroom, shining through the curtains. It had been morning when she'd left here to meet Patty. All the lights had been off.

Inside the block, she headed upstairs, keeping her footsteps as light as she could. The building was silent, its inhabitants still asleep. She paused outside her apartment and listened. Nothing. A faint yellow glow spilled beneath the door.

She eased her key in the lock until it clicked. She stood against the frame and pushed the door open slowly with her free hand, her gun in the other. The hall and the kitchen beyond were in shadow, but there was enough light from the bedroom to show her they were empty. She walked through, eyes alert for movement. The apartment smelled of old microwave meals and fresh-sawn timber, where the repairman had fixed the window. The bedroom door was ajar. Heart hammering, she approached.

She pressed herself against the frame. As she swung in, gun raised, the door banged loudly against the wall. There was movement from the bed. A figure rising, blankets falling.

"Hands up!"

A terrified yelp. "Riley! Riley, it's me!"

Riley pulled her gun up, her heart in her mouth, as she saw Maddie, sitting up wide-eyed in the bed. Her niece was dressed in her old college sweatshirt. Her hair was stuck up on one side of her head where she'd been lying asleep.

"Maddie? Jesus Christ!"

"I'm sorry!" Maddie still had her hands up. Her face had drained of color. "I'm sorry!"

Riley stuffed the Glock in its holster. Her whole body was trembling at the release of adrenaline. She thought she might throw up. She hastened to the kitchen, leaned over the basin and cupped cold, metal-tasting water into her mouth. She hung there for a moment. Over the sound of the water, she heard Maddie padding into the room behind her. She turned off the faucet and looked around. "What the hell, Maddie?"

"I'm so sorry." Maddie's voice was a whisper. "Didn't you get my message? I left it last night."

Riley shook her head. "I've been busy." She almost laughed at the absurdity of the understatement. Instead, she flipped on the kitchen light. She saw a backpack hanging on one of the chairs. A winter jacket on another. A pair of snow boots on the floor. The remains of a microwave meal had hardened in its tray on the table. There was a root beer open beside it. Maddie had made herself at home. *Like goddamn Goldilocks.*

Riley took off her coat.

Maddie's eyes widened farther. "Oh my God. Is that—*blood*?"

Riley glanced down at her sweater. It was dark brown in places. Altman's. "It's not mine." She crossed to the bedroom, pulled off the stained sweater and took a clean one from a drawer. "Maddie, how did you get in?"

"The man who lives next door. With all the tattoos? He found me sitting outside. When I told him who I was, he called the landlord, got him to let me in."

"When did you get here?"

Maddie hung her head, hair slipping in front of her face. "Yesterday afternoon. I took a bus from Waterloo."

Riley closed her eyes, thought of the missed calls from Ethan. "Does your father know where you are?"

"I told him I was with you." Maddie flushed, averted her eyes. "That you'd said it was OK."

"God, Maddie."

"Please don't hate me."

Riley looked at her niece standing there, pale-faced, one arm crossed tight over her body. The girl's socks, which were covered in snowmen, were bunched unevenly around her ankles. Her shock and anger ebbed away. "Of course I don't hate you." She went to Maddie and folded her into her arms. She kissed the top of her head, then drew back, gripping her niece's shoulders. "But this isn't OK. You know that, right? I'm going to have to call your dad, tell him to come get you."

"But . . ." Seeing Riley's expression, Maddie let her protest trail off. She nodded mutely.

As Riley was taking her cell out to call Ethan, it rang. *Fogg.*

"I'm outside."

Riley flipped up the kitchen blinds with her fingers. She could see Fogg's Buick, down in the street. The sky was just starting to lighten. "Damn it."

"Something wrong?"

"Just some personal stuff." Riley paused, looking around at Maddie. "I don't suppose either of your daughters would want to pocket some dollars for a couple of hours? I've got a bit of a problem here."

Fifteen minutes later, Riley headed out of the apartment block. She had left Maddie on the couch with the heat up and the TV on. She'd given the girl strict instructions to remain inside the apartment and answer the door only to Sherri Verne, who would be over within the hour. She'd left a voice mail for Ethan, telling him what had happened and asking him to come pick up his daughter. She'd had no time to change. No time for coffee. But the shock of finding her niece in her bed had been like a cold shower, leaving her awake and wired.

"Thank you," she told Fogg, sliding into the passenger seat. "Tell Sherri I'll pay her as soon as I'm home."

"It's no trouble." Fogg looked at her. "You sure you're up to this?"

"Yes."

"You heard about the protest?" he asked, pulling away from the sidewalk.

"I caught some of it."

It had been on the morning news when she'd turned the TV on for Maddie. What had begun as a vigil yesterday evening outside Des Moines PD had turned, overnight, into a major protest. While she'd stuffed a spare clip of ammo in her belt, she'd watched a shot of the crowds—arrayed in front of hastily erected barricades—holding up placards plastered with the faces of the Sin Eater's victims.

How many more? they asked.

As Fogg drove through the city, Riley glimpsed a police helicopter hovering over the department. She looked out over the unsettled waters as they crossed the Des Moines River. In the distance, the Iowa Women of Achievement Bridge arched like a white rainbow against the sky, not far from the underpass where Hayley had been attacked.

She sat in silence as Fogg steered the Buick through the early morning traffic to Beaver Avenue, where they'd gone, all those weeks earlier, to the house with yellow shutters. The house Riley had remembered last night, in the red wash of the cop car lights.

As they made their way up the drive, she noticed the Pontiac Firebird wasn't in the garage. Mrs. Jessip opened the door, her face falling when she saw them. When Fogg told her they needed to speak with her husband again, she directed them into his study.

As they entered, Riley noted a large carryall in the corner of the study by the leather couch. Her full attention was reserved for the wall of photographs, but before she had time to scan them properly, Mustang John appeared. He looked different—paler and less composed than the last time they'd questioned him. His eyes were bloodshot, his greased-back hair mussed.

"So," he said stiffly, closing the door behind him. "How can I help you folks?"

"Going somewhere?" Riley asked, nodding to the bag.

It took Mustang John a beat to answer. "Staying a few days with family." He went to sit behind his desk, eyes flicking between Riley and Fogg as if expecting them to take the couch.

Fogg remained standing while Riley crossed to the wall. Her gaze moved over the framed article talking about the body shop, and came to rest on the photograph of him seated at a round table with a group of men. Behind them was a ballroom with gold-shimmering wallpaper and a stage, red curtains hanging. On the stage was a podium with a banner above it. In the photograph she'd found at the cabin only the bottom part of the writing was visible. Here, she could read it all.

Release the Beast!

The stage was empty, waiting for a young man with gray eyes.

Last night, at Altman's, Riley had replayed it all: Bret Childs's bravado at their questioning, his smirk, then the look of fear on his face when she'd caught him on his phone in the workshop.

Riley turned from the photograph to Mustang John, whose face was a bloodless white. "Bret called you that day, didn't he? Before we arrived here?"

"No." His voice was husky. He cleared his throat. "Of course not."

"He called and asked you to provide him with an alibi for the afternoon Hayley Abbot was attacked."

Mustang John was starting to sweat. It beaded on his forehead and glistened on his upper lip. He shook his head. "Like I told you, he was working on the car of a client."

Riley switched tactics. "When were you at the Old Fort Hotel?" she asked, pointing to the photograph.

"I don't see what—"

"Funny thing is, the place keeps cropping up in our investigation. This photograph. A cabin in Winneshiek County." Riley saw his eyes dart to the carryall. She wondered, suddenly, if Mustang John had been one of the men in the woods, their faces obscured by hoods as they hauled those sleds of gasoline through the snow. "We found a key ring from the same hotel in a car that was used to deliver a threat to Governor Cook and her family."

Now, Mustang John's eyes met hers. Riley saw his brow furrow. She couldn't be sure, but this particular piece of information seemed like a surprise to him.

He was breathing harder, sweat starting to roll down his cheeks. He raised an arm, wiped it away with the back of his hand. As he did so, his shirt sleeve rode up and Riley saw it.

The red whip of a serpent's tail.

She drew her gun. "Put your hands up, Mr. Jessip."

Fogg started forward, surprised, then saw what she had seen. He, too, drew his weapon. For a moment, the three of them were frozen there. Then, the door opened, and Mrs. Jessip entered, clutching a mug with Steve McQueen's face on it.

She gasped at the tableau: two guns pointed at her husband. Riley and Fogg glanced her way. There was a heavy thump as Mustang John slid out of his chair and collapsed on the floor. His wife dropped the mug, which shattered.

Riley went around the desk, keeping her gun trained on the man, who was lying on his back, clutching his chest. His face was gray, his shirt soaked through with sweat. He was gasping like a fish out of water. "Shit, he's having a heart attack." She holstered her gun and crouched, tugging open his shirt collar while Fogg moved in, keeping his weapon on the suspect. "Ma'am, I need you to call 911." Riley looked around when the woman didn't move. "Ma'am!"

Mustang John's wife hesitated a moment longer, her eyes a battleground of emotion. Fear, confusion, and something else. *Relief.*

Then the woman was gone, rushing for the phone.

The paramedics were on scene in less than ten minutes. Enough time for Riley to get a good look at the tattoo on Mustang John's arm: a red snake with a sword plunging through its body.

State Patrol arrived, summoned by Fogg, to follow their suspect to the hospital and stay on guard until he could be stabilized and questioned.

As Fogg met the troopers outside, Riley stayed behind in the study, donning a pair of protective gloves. She opened the carryall first, unsurprised by the smell of gasoline that greeted her from the clothes inside, still wet from snow. Next, she took down the photograph of Mustang John and the other men in the ballroom of the Old Fort Hotel.

Her mom had always written the dates and names of people on the backs of family snapshots—in the days when people still had photographs printed, put them in albums or hung them on walls, wanting the reminder of where they were and when. Mustang John was of the same mind.

Billy Ames, Release the Beast Tour
The Old Fort Hotel, 2004

Riley let out a breath.

"I've asked Jenna to go through state records," said Fogg, appearing in the doorway. "See if Mustang John changed his name more than once." He pushed a hand through his hair. "God, if he's our suspect . . . ?"

Riley looked around. "I don't think he is. I mean, I don't think he's the Sin Eater."

"But the tattoo? Him covering for Bret? Hayley? They could have been working together. Two suspects, like you said?"

Riley showed him the framed photograph of Mustang John and the other men in the ballroom. "There's a William Ames on the list of clients the hotel manager gave us. I think the picture I found at the cabin is of him. On this stage." She turned the photograph over. "Billy Ames."

Fogg stared at it, his brow furrowing.

"Mustang John. Bret Childs. Raymond Adamson. The men at the cabin." Riley pointed to the photograph. "Billy Ames." She heard Dr. Hale's voice in her mind, emerging from the static on the old tape. "Remember what Hale said? That Raymond spoke to him of building a church? I don't think we're looking at just two suspects."

Fogg met her gaze. "Jesus. A whole goddamn congregation?"

46

Kody could still taste blood at the back of his throat. The pain he'd felt when Harlan punched him had dulled to an incessant throb. It incited him, spurring him forward at each red light, foot slamming on the gas. He had scraped through driver's ed, barely, and his mom's old car was a manual, with a stick shift that stuck. He'd stalled several times, cursing as drivers behind him leaned on their horns.

At an intersection, he pulled out without looking, narrowly avoiding a stream of cop cars hurtling west, sirens blaring. He lurched to a stop, a sick plunge in his stomach. It was several moments before his shaking hands could work the gears.

He turned with relief into the industrial park, threading his way past warehouses and factories. The river, winding beside him, was iron gray. The plows had cleared the main routes, but as he approached the buckled gate, Kody realized there was no way his mom's car would make it down the potholed road. The trucks and Jeeps that had driven through last night had carved deep grooves through the snow. They were now scabbed over with a treacherous crust of ice. Kody parked in the empty lot of a warehouse, then slipped through the gate, sneakers sinking in pockets of slush.

The blistering cold made his nose throb even more. His eyes were streaming by the time he saw the sagging roof of the abandoned site office between the trees. He quickened his pace, thinking through what he would say.

Billy didn't strike him as someone who would look kindly on weakness, so he doubted the sight of his swollen face would raise any sympathy. No. He needed to focus on Harlan's error—leaving that bloodstained hood for him to find. From what he'd witnessed last night, any mistake now, at what was clearly a crucial moment, would surely be frowned upon.

Kody faltered. Maybe Harlan had been sloppy, but would Billy go so far as to expel the man from the group? He thought of the sword being etched on Harlan's arm, his eighteen-wheeler loaded with weapons. Suddenly, his whole plan felt stupid. He cringed, imagining how he would look, standing there with his bloody nose, telling Billy—a terrifying latter-day Jesus who slept with a pump-action shotgun by his bed and held sway over a host of violent disciples—that Harlan had stolen his reward and smashed up his console. The bullies at school had always been eager to see if he'd tell on them, ready to make his life even more miserable.

But Billy had invited him to be part of all this. Billy—his gray eyes glinting, asking if he wanted to play a game. His hand on his shoulder, encouraging him to share his feelings about Reagan.

Be the maggot in the apple that chokes her.

Billy handing over the money, telling him he was one of them.

A Son of Adam.

There was a clear hierarchy in the group. Orders and rules to the game. Perhaps Billy would dislike someone going over his head—doling out punishment without his permission? At the very least, Harlan might be dissuaded from taking his winnings again. He remembered Dirch backing down immediately at Billy's soft-spoken threat.

Kody emerged from the trees that bordered the road to see the trailer home across the lot, the ashen morning light showing up the years of dirt. Tire marks, footprints, and cigarette butts were the only signs of last night's activity. Harlan's eighteen-wheeler, loaded with guns and gear, had gone.

For a moment, Kody thought there was no one there, then he saw a single vehicle parked there. It was a cherry red pickup, brand-new. He'd not seen it before. He stiffened as a figure stepped out of the trailer, carrying a box. It was a woman.

She was slight of build and wore a white quilted jacket, skintight black jeans, and fur-trimmed boots. A sparkly pom-pom hat covered her head, from beneath which flame-colored hair hung long and loose. With her mirrored shades she looked like the sort of woman who belonged in a skiing brochure, not an abandoned lot.

As she crossed to the pickup, her back to him, Kody slipped into the dark of the ruined site office. He was wondering whether to call Harlan, have the man warn Billy someone was here, when another figure emerged from the trailer, carrying bags.

Billy.

He hauled the bags onto the pickup's cargo bed, alongside the box the woman had placed there.

She watched him, hands on her hips. "I still don't get why you want all this stuff." Her voice carried to Kody on the brittle air. Her nose wrinkled. "I can't believe you've been sleeping here. I had no idea how gross it was."

"It was good enough for my mom," Billy told the woman, following her gaze to the trailer.

"She's long gone, honey. We've got so much else to pack. This is all just junk."

"I want to take something with me. Something of her. Something of me." Billy looked at the woman. "When we leave, we can never come back." He pushed a stray strand of red hair from her face. "You know that."

As Billy turned toward the trailer, the woman grabbed his arm. "Why don't we go now? We've got enough. More than."

Billy cupped her chin. "This one last assignment, then I'm done." He made his way through the snow. "Help me with the rest of it."

"If he finds out, he'll kill you!" the woman called at his back. "You told me what he's capable of."

Billy turned, his face implacable. "Darlene."

At his tone, the woman relented and followed him back into the trailer.

Kody stood trembling in the shadows.

Darlene?

Billy's ex-wife. The woman he'd railed against in front of the Sons of Adam. The woman they all hated with a vengeance.

Billy's own Eve.

Kody stumbled his way back down the road. The freezing air had squeezed his lungs into knots. He felt like he'd been punched in the gut. Each breath was a challenge.

Once inside his mom's car, teeth chattering, he tried to think—to come up with some explanation for what he'd just seen and heard. But his eyes and ears kept bringing him back to the same conclusions.

The woman's fancy clothes, the brand-new pickup, her nose wrinkling at the trailer. The way Billy looked at her as he touched her face. The same way Kody had seen Troy look at Reagan. Like there was no one else in the room.

It was a lie. All of it.

All this time he'd thought Billy must be even poorer than him. From the trailer and the way Billy lived, he'd guessed the money the man collected from the group must have been going elsewhere—their mysterious founder, he'd assumed. But his apparent poverty had only made Kody admire him more. If Billy, who had so little, could rise to be so powerful, it meant that maybe he could too. Maybe he could be something bigger than his scrawny body. Something more valuable than the boy whose father hadn't bothered to stick around. More than a shadow in the schoolyard—a punching bag or an afterthought.

But it seemed Billy—who'd beckoned him with soft words and glittering promises—was nothing more than a mirage. The man he'd been walking toward had vanished.

Kody's vision filled with red as the pickup came trundling down the potholed road, its bed loaded with stuff from the trailer. Billy was driving. Darlene close at his side.

Kody sank down in the seat. He waited until they passed. Then, put his foot on the gas and followed.

47

Riley moved through the trailer, past a grimy kitchen area, the walls spattered with grease. A trash can had been knocked over, spilling takeout cartons. A technician from the state lab was picking through it with gloved fingers. Another was photographing a table by a couch, littered with fortune cookie wrappers and empty beer bottles.

"We've got a helluva lot of tire tracks and footprints out there."

Riley turned at Fogg's voice.

He stepped into the trailer. "Looks like an eighteen-wheeler was parked here. The tracks are fresh. Techs reckon it was moved sometime in the last day or so."

Always one step ahead.

"What's the word from Mustang John's?" Riley asked.

"State Patrol is at the body shop now. No sign of Bret Childs. They're checking his home address and—" Fogg dug into his pocket as his cell rang. "Yes? Speaking." He headed back outside.

Riley looked around, imagining the place in its former years. An internet search had pulled up pictures of rows of trailer homes that had once stood on this plot, families in lawn chairs, kids playing, wash hanging in the sun. Over the years, people had left as the factories of the industrial park sprang up, polluting the river. The state records that led them here had revealed that the last remaining trailer belonged to a Mrs. Ames, who'd died five years ago, leaving one son.

Billy.

On the way here, Riley had watched a grainy video on YouTube, from one of Billy's Release the Beast seminars, years ago. The video had jigged across the heads of the audience, all men, the camcorder struggling to track Billy as he strode back and forth across the stage of the Old Fort Hotel.

His audience had been rapt, hanging on his every word. He spoke to them of loneliness and disillusionment, of a world where they no longer had power. A world where they found themselves usurped, in the boardroom and in the bedroom.

He beckoned some of them up onstage. At first these men had grinned, embarrassed. But the more Billy spoke, delving into their lives and their frustrations, the more serious they became. Some wept, talking of divorces and custody battles, dysfunction and disempowerment.

He broke them down, then built them up. Taught them how to take back control—command respect from their wives and girlfriends, mothers and colleagues. He quoted the Bible and men of history, his words strengthened by others' authority. He was magnetic. From the way the men rose to cheer him, she saw how he compelled them. A preacher. A pied piper, who called to their deepest fears and darkest fantasies. Urging them to release the beast within.

The trailer steps creaked as Fogg returned. "That was the Iowa State Penitentiary. They had a William Ames who served three years for credit card fraud back in two thousand." He sounded excited. "Guess who his cellmate for two of those years was?"

"Raymond Adamson," said Riley, heart skipping.

"Yup. In for burglary, as your waitress said."

Riley frowned, trying to put the pieces together. "OK, so they meet in prison. Raymond tells Billy about his past. His attacks in the nineties as the Sin Eater."

"I'm guessing so. They would have clearly found affinity over their views on women."

Riley thought back to the video. "Billy gets out of jail, starts running his seminars at the Old Fort Hotel and is given the loyalty package. He pulls in a lot of angry men. Plays on their worst instincts. Dr. Hale spoke of Raymond building a church. Patty told me Raymond was getting money from one of his brothers—that he was using it to create something." She closed her eyes, recalling the woman's words. "Something that would change the way the world looked at him." She opened her eyes. "What if Billy was recruiting men for Raymond's church in his seminars? We know Mustang John attended one. What if Billy has been inciting them to go after women, using Raymond's attacks as a sort of template?"

Fogg pushed a hand through his hair. "The hoods put on victims and the mask the attacker wears—both could be intended to disguise the fact our suspects aren't the same man. And the photographs? That's something the Sin Eater never did before. Are they being used as proof to show Raymond they've done the job?"

Riley couldn't answer. She felt sick at the thought of it. The injuries on the women. The brutality. The hatred. It was awful enough thinking of one man doing those things. That there might be a whole group, all feeding off one another, was truly terrifying.

"The key ring, though?" murmured Fogg, deep in thought.

"Maybe Raymond had Billy target the governor? Maybe it was Billy who left the message for her?"

"But you said the lab results show the key ring was burned elsewhere, then put in the car after the fire. Why would Billy plant it when it's led us to him?"

Riley nodded slowly. "OK, then could Raymond be using Billy as a scapegoat? Trying to pin the recent attacks, or at least the threat to Governor Cook, on him? Maybe Billy left the loyalty package at the cabin. If they were friends, it's possible he spent time there. Raymond could have planted the key ring to set Billy up."

Before Fogg could answer, there was a shout outside. "Detective Verne!"

A state trooper appeared in the doorway. He was out of breath and holding up his radio. "The panic button at Ella Cook's school—it was just activated."

48

They tore through the city, Fogg's foot barely off the gas. The lights of cruisers flashed ahead, cars swerving to mount sidewalks as the convoy screamed past, ignoring every red light. The police helicopter, hovering like a hornet over the protest outside Des Moines PD, veered off in their direction as the call went out—the governor's daughter was in danger.

Riley's mind was a maelstrom, memories flashing. Ella Cook dancing with her father. Sitting cross-legged on the floor at the mansion, her face pinched with worry as she looked to her mom.

Is it me?

The effigy hanging from the tree, turning slowly on the noose, its mouth a wide red scream.

The promise she'd made at the gala.

I'll do everything in my power to catch him. You have my word.

Jess Cook's hand reaching across the table, warm on hers.

State Patrol was already at the school by the time they reached it, vehicles parked haphazardly in the yard. There were troopers on the steps by the open front doors, weapons drawn. The windows of the school were crowded with kids' festive drawings of Santas and reindeer. Riley recognized the building from the photograph left with the threat, Ella in the foreground in her pumpkin costume, snapped unawares.

THIS IS YOUR CURSE
THE PRICE YOU MUST PAY
OR THEY WILL PAY IT FOR YOU

Riley hopped out of the Buick and ran across the yard, following Fogg toward the troopers. The wail of sirens and the throb of helicopter blades assaulted her ears. Halfway across, she slipped on a patch of ice. She went down, ripping open the knee of her cargo pants and the skin beneath. Fighting back pain, she pushed herself to her feet and chased up the steps in Fogg's wake.

"We've got officers inside," one of the troopers was telling Fogg. "Unclear what's happening in there. No sign yet of an intruder. But it was the alarm in Ella Cook's classroom that was activated. We're holding the perimeter."

Fogg and Riley entered, unholstering their weapons. They moved together down the corridor, past a row of lockers with stickers of animals on them, heading toward the crackle of radios and calls of troopers inside the building. Through the glass doors of classrooms, Riley glimpsed upturned chairs and empty desks, littered with books and pens. The kids and teachers, well trained in active shooter drills, would be hiding out of sight.

They rounded a corner and saw three state troopers with a woman outside a classroom. One was speaking into his radio; the other two were talking to the woman.

One turned as Fogg and Riley approached. "Detective Verne. Looks like a false alarm."

"What?"

The trooper gestured to the woman. "The principal says someone activated the panic button, but she doesn't know who. The kids were all out on break at the time. They think it could have been some sort of prank."

"Who other than the teachers would know where it was?" Riley asked, looking from the trooper to Fogg. Neither had an answer. "Where's Ella Cook?"

As she voiced the question, shouts echoed in the corridor. A man came running, several troopers hastening behind him. It was Mark Cook, the First Gentleman.

"What's happening? Where's my daughter?"

The principal answered. "She's fine, Mr. Cook." She opened the classroom door and beckoned.

A young woman emerged, holding the hand of a girl. Ella Cook had a smudge of paint on her face and appeared a little bewildered, glancing between the troopers, her teachers, and her harried father. But she was safe and unharmed.

Riley felt a wash of relief. She watched as Mark lifted his daughter into his arms, brushing curls from her face. The state troopers backed away, sharing thankful looks. Guns were holstered, reinforcements radioed to stand down.

There came the sound of hurrying footsteps. A man appeared from an adjoining corridor, escorting a boy around Ella's age. "Mrs. Sanderson!" he called, raising a hand to the principal, who was talking to Mark Cook. "Leon here told me he saw a man leaving this room while the class was on break." He pointed to the room Ella had emerged from. "The man ran off when he saw him."

"Spread out," snapped one of the troopers, gesturing to the others. "Check every room. The grounds too."

Riley felt her relief flow away. Another tide was rushing in. A rearing wave of cold. She turned to the trooper who was giving orders. "Where's the governor?"

The man paused midshout, frowning at the interruption. "What?"

"Where is she? Right now?"

"She's visiting a women's shelter this morning. She has a full security team with her," the trooper added. "I spoke to the chief officer just now. They're bringing the governor back to the capitol."

Riley saw, by the horror dawning on Fogg's face, that he'd guessed the same.

"It's a diversion."

What's happening?" Jess Cook demanded as the state troopers hustled her out of the building.

Rebecca Page followed, offering the manager of the women's shelter a swift apology for the abrupt exit.

"Governor, please," said Officer Teal, head of her security team, ushering her across the lot toward the vehicles—three Iowa State Patrol cars and an SUV. There was a handful of reporters and photographers loitering there, hopeful for a comment on her visit.

"I need to know my daughter's safe," Jess said, turning to Teal. "I want you to take me to her school. Now."

"Our team is securing the area. It's an active situation. I'm told your husband is on his way to the school with the mansion detail. Ma'am, I need to you to get into the vehicle." Teal's tone left no room for argument.

The gaggle of reporters swarmed forward as Jess approached the SUV. A few called out, asking if she could give any details of her morning at the shelter.

Another piped up, wanting to know if she supported the protestors at Des Moines PD. "What do you think of Mrs. Abbot's accusation the police are protecting the Sin Eater? That he could be one of them?"

One man elbowed through the scrum, thrusting out his phone. It was the reporter from the *Des Moines Register* who'd first alerted her to the lack of votes for her bill. "You've got the final reading in the senate next week, Governor. How do you think it will go? Will you close the pay gap, as you've promised the women of this state?"

Rebecca stepped out in front. "I'm afraid Governor Cook has no comments today. She has a meeting at the capitol."

The air was filling with the sound of phones. Reporters were turning away, glancing at their screens. Some were checking in with one another, eyes widening in surprise.

They know, thought Jess as Teal opened the door of the SUV. She got in, Rebecca hopping up behind her.

The driver set off at a fast pace, running the gauntlet of snapping cameras. Two patrol cars raced ahead; one swung in behind. The shelter was on the southeastern edge of the city, but at this speed it wouldn't take long to reach the capitol. Jess clutched the door handle, her knuckles white.

"It's going to be OK," Rebecca said. "Ella's going to be fine."

But her chief of staff's voice was too sharp to be convincing.

Jess couldn't answer. She stared, without seeing, at fields of snow flashing past through the trees. This was her fault. If she hadn't been so determined to be a politician—*desperately ambitious* as one newspaper put it—her daughter wouldn't be in danger. She closed her eyes, thinking of Mark's words outside the mansion, when he'd asked her to step back. The fear and frustration in his face.

You're not the only one he's threatened.

Teal was in the front passenger seat, talking urgently to someone.

Jess barely heard him. Since she'd decided to run for office, her family had been behind her all the way. Mark especially. Through all her moments of self-doubt and worry, he'd been at her side, cheering her on. Had made her feel better when the moms at Ella's school had thrown disapproving glances her way on a rare occasion she'd made an appearance there. The expectation, even from other women, that you must be able to do everything, and do it perfectly. The chest-tightening guilt she'd felt, home late from some meeting or dinner having promised to read Ella a story, only to find her daughter already asleep, the book still closed, waiting beside her.

I don't want to let Ella down. Or you.

But she had, hadn't she? She'd known they were in danger the moment she opened that envelope lying on her desk and saw the photograph of her little girl. Why hadn't she stepped back as Mark had suggested, at least until the suspect was caught? Why did she always have to fight?

The cabinet of dolls removed from the capitol; Ted Pierce's lips pursed in disapproval. Bill Hamilton's allies muttering about her connection to terrorists. His downfall. Her rise. The implication that she wouldn't have been able to get to this position without foul play—no matter that Hamilton was a proven criminal. This goddamn bill she'd fought tooth and nail for, even as the votes started slipping. She'd been so preoccupied with the battle these past few months, she'd barely spent any time at all with her daughter.

But, then, she wanted Ella to grow up in a world where she was valued for more than her sex—where she wasn't held back, or diminished by it. Where the same doors of opportunity that opened for men would open for her.

"Governor?"

Jess opened her eyes. Officer Teal had turned in his seat and was looking at her. He was smiling. *Why the hell was he smiling?*

"Ella's fine. I just got word. Your husband is with her. They're not sure what happened. False alarm."

Jess let out a little gulp. She felt Rebecca take her hand. Her chief of staff was smiling too, eyes bright.

Teal was back to talking to whoever was in his earpiece. "Say that again?"

The two patrol cars slowed, forcing the SUV to follow suit. Through the windshield, Jess saw an eighteen-wheeler. It was blocking the road ahead. Breakdown, or an accident?

The state trooper at the wheel cursed. He put a hand on the back of Teal's seat, craning his head to see as he started to reverse. The patrol car at their rear had halted and was doing the same. There was a roar of engines from somewhere behind. A squeal of brakes. Two Jeeps careened to a stop at the back of the patrol car, barring its path.

Jess had time to hear Teal shout at the driver. "Get us the fuck out of here! Go! *Go!*"

Then, the back of the eighteen-wheeler opened and a host of figures jumped out.

They were dressed in an odd assortment of camouflage and flak jackets, helmets and balaclavas. She saw the black blocky menace of raised guns. Heard shouts as the patrol car doors opened, state troopers unholstering their weapons, yelling at the incoming men to stand down.

Jess had time to suck in a breath, feel the tightening of Rebecca's hand around hers, before the world outside exploded in gunfire.

49

"I t's not your fault, Riley."

Riley came back to herself at Fogg's voice. Had he read her mind, or had she murmured what she'd been thinking out loud?

Wasn't it her fault?

She had been tasked with keeping the governor safe. She had failed.

As Fogg brought the Buick to a stop, she realized they were at her apartment already. She couldn't even remember the drive here from the school. Her mind kept replaying it. Over and over. The sounds coming through the state trooper's radio, echoing obscenely in that corridor lined with children's drawings.

The shouts. The gunshots. The screams.

Mark Cook's face turning to ash. Fogg catching the man's arm as he stumbled. Ella barely comprehending what was happening, but instinctively wailing for her mother.

Riley thought of Hayley in the underpass, the baseball bat swinging in. Again. Again. Cracking her eye, her jaw, her skull. The brute force behind each blow. She was certain, now, Bret Childs had been the one whose hands had gripped that bat.

Because Hayley said no. Because she rejected him. Because he felt he was entitled to more. Because Billy Ames had taught him that.

There had been no sign of Bret at the body shop, or his home, where his parents were being questioned. But based on initial reports from surviving troopers at the abduction site, it was conceivable he had been among the large armed group that had ambushed the governor's motorcade and taken Jess Cook at gunpoint, leaving three officers dead.

Riley thought of the women pinned on the boards in the incident room and all those who might be unknown, undiscovered, their voices unheard. Ghosts in the margins of police reports, dismissed and forgotten. Stories told only to the pages of secret diaries or in the private hush of therapists' rooms. Shallow graves in a forest glade. She thought of that trunk of trophies in Raymond's cabin and the unexpected flash of relief in the eyes of Mustang John's wife when she'd seen her husband lying on the floor, struggling for breath. *How many more?* the protestor's placards had asked.

How many indeed.

Then she thought of the men—ordinary men—in that ballroom, cheering as Billy Ames strode across that stage, enraging them, inciting them. How all their frustrations and disappointments had been dragged up and turned outward, away from themselves. No accountability. A hundred eyes seeking someone else to blame. And who better than woman? Daughter of Eve.

The original sinner.

Dear God, what will they do to her?

Riley felt a rush of nausea. She pushed open the door of the Buick and stumbled out, sucking in gulps of air. She hung there, palm splayed on the hood.

Fogg came around the car to join her. He put a hand on her shoulder. "We'll find her. They got the plates of the truck. Every officer and deputy in the state is on this. The moment Mustang John is out of surgery we'll go to the hospital. See what the son of a bitch knows. They won't get far."

Riley wanted to agree. She knew the state troopers were moving into action, had heard the calls and orders going out. Roads out of the city were being blockaded. The airport was being shut down. She'd spoken to Meadows. An FBI SWAT team had been mobilized and would arrive within hours.

"See to that," Fogg said. "Then we'll head to base."

Riley followed his gaze to her knee. The torn material of her cargo pants was flapping in the breeze. Beneath she could see blood still oozing from the wound, peppered with grit from the schoolyard. It was throbbing. She remembered now—Fogg saying they could stop at her apartment on the way to DCI headquarters. Once they had any word of the governor's possible location, things would proceed at breakneck pace and there would be no time for anything else.

As she turned toward the building, Riley's gaze snagged on the fire escape. She thought of the footprints she'd seen there. For days now, her mind had been focused on Altman. But it seemed clear the agent's transgressions were entirely personal—nothing to do with the governor or their investigation. But the cabin? Those men arriving while she was there? The panic button activated at Ella's school? The tape from Dr. Hale sent to the wrong lab?

She turned back to Fogg.

He knew where she lived. They had all shared their personal information when they'd created the task force, in case of emergencies. He knew about the cabin and the panic button.

Covering for one of their own.

"Why did you take so long to get back to me? After my meeting with Patty?"

Fogg frowned. "I told you. I was trying to track down Hale's tape."

"Pretty coincidental it was misplaced? Our only real piece of evidence in that moment?"

"What are you saying?"

"Those men out at the cabin. As if they knew?"

"I didn't think you'd be foolish enough to go out there on your own. I told you to wait. Christ, Riley. You really think I had anything to do with this?" Fogg looked hurt. And pissed.

"I—" She faltered. Did she think that? She wasn't sure of anything anymore.

Fogg looked as if he was about to say something further when his cell rang. He answered, his voice curt. "Marcia, I'm sorry, I can't speak right—" The creases in his brow deepened. "What? When?" He turned away. "No. I'll be there. I'm coming." He looked at Riley as he opened the car door. "Keira. My daughter. She's been attacked at our home."

"What?"

"They've taken her to MercyOne. Marcia and Sherri are there now. I've got to go."

"Of course. I've got this."

Fogg hesitated, then nodded and climbed in.

Riley watched him speed away. As she turned toward her apartment, the realization hit her. If Sherri had gone to the hospital, that meant Maddie was up there alone. Another thought slammed in on its heels. Was the attack on Keira random? Or were they being targeted?

Inside the building, Riley raced upstairs to her apartment. She cursed as the key stuck in the lock, then pushed the door open. "Maddie?" She went into the kitchen. "Maddie? Are you here?" Maddie's backpack was gone. So, too, were her boots and jacket. The TV in the living room was off.

Riley breathed out. Maybe Sherri had taken Maddie with her to the hospital? She nodded to herself, her heart rate ticking down. She called Maddie. It went to voice mail.

Walking into the bedroom, she tried Fogg. The curtains were still closed, the light now off. Her niece had made the bed. Riley caught sight of her reflection in the mirror. She hardly recognized herself. Face smudged with dirt, hair dragged from its knot, eyes red from lack of sleep.

Fogg's voice came curt on the line. "Riley?"

"Fogg, I'm sorry. I just need to know if Maddie's with Sherri, at MercyOne?"

"No. Sherri went alone." Fogg raised his voice over the wail of an ambulance. "I'm heading in now. I'll call you back in a minute, OK?"

As the line went dead, Riley heard a noise behind her. She turned to the window.

There—silhouetted against the curtain—was a shadow. The size and shape of a man. Her breath caught, goose bumps breaking out across her skin. She heard the window jiggle in its frame as the shadow tried to pry it open. The window, fixed and locked, didn't budge. But the shadow tried again.

As if it knew it should open.

Putting the phone in her pocket, Riley drew her gun. She backed out of the room, then checked the peephole in her apartment door. The hallway fish-eyed beyond, empty. She opened the door and made her way down, keeping close to the wall to avoid being spotted from the stairwell. She had flashes of memory from Hogan's Alley—the fake town in Quantico where she'd been confronted in doorways, ambushed in alleys, shot at from moving vehicles.

At the front door, she paused. She could hear the low rumble of freight on the railroad. The street was empty. She stepped out, boots sinking in snow, her breath coming in white bursts. As she slipped to the side of the building and pressed herself against the wall, she heard the sound of feet coming down the metal treads of the fire escape.

She swung around the corner, gun raised.

50

Harlan Judd crouched on the bedroom floor, stuffing the last of his belongings into his carryall. He checked his pocket one more time, feeling the reassuring wedge of the fake passport he'd procured with help from the twins, then grabbed his work ID from Shelley's vanity.

His job as a trucker was finished. There would be no more long nights behind the wheel. No more bad roadside diners, squatting in cornfields when there were no restrooms. The troopers who'd survived the shoot-out on the road would have gotten his plates. The transport company would be swarming with cops by now. No going back. Harlan tossed the ID in the bag, his mind on Billy's promise, made in return for his sacrifice.

He had been bored that first day—the first day he'd heard of Billy Ames—stuck in a jam on the interstate, scrolling listlessly through a truckers' chat room he sometimes frequented, mostly to vent about the state of the country, or share private pictures of wives and girlfriends, when he'd seen a link to a seminar at the Old Fort Hotel. Men only. Some guy on the thread claimed it had changed his life. Harlan had gone along out of idle curiosity. The entrance fee had been steep, but it was payday and he hadn't anything better to do. It had changed his life too, just not that first night.

He had never seen himself like the other Sons of Adam: Cuddy, whose days hadn't been this good since summers at the water park, leering at girls in bikinis, or Dirch, product of an ugly divorce that stripped him down to his shirt and who had only the group to give his life meaning. Or the twins, with their unfathomable hatred of women that seemed to go right down to their souls. Yeah, Harlan would smack a bitch up if she got out of line, but he wasn't the same as those sad, lonely fucks trailing Billy like he was the Second Coming, hanging on his every word and holding up their hands for the crumbs he flung to them when they followed his orders. Soldiers in his holy war.

Before, in the early days, it had been different. There had been beer and banter, hunting trips and drag car racing with Mustang John and his pals. Billy would always be there, doling out advice, teaching some men how to win women's affections, others how to hide assets so their wives wouldn't have access. A cross between a bachelor party and a self-help group, although Harlan didn't brook that shit. Sure, there had been all the stuff about their founder, Raymond Adamson, who observed them from the shadows, praising them—via Billy—for their commitment to his cause and promising them a share in a fortune when his church was finally established. But, for Harlan, it had mostly been a bit of fun. Something to whet the dull edge of his days.

At first, the orders were little more than role-playing. Billy would hand out assignments—get the men to punish willful wives or coax an unwilling girl into bed—and there would be a ceremony where he'd give prizes. *You're advancing up the tiers of manhood*, Billy would tell them. *Raymond is proud of you.* And the men would return and pay him whatever they could afford for more advice and guidance. Over the past few months, however, things had begun to change. Raymond seemed to have a fire under his ass, because his orders had grown ever more extreme.

But where the stakes were higher, so too was the promise of wealth, and that's what had kept Harlan's interest and obedience. For years, with the church still a pipe dream, Raymond had dangled that fortune in front of them, just out of reach, but Harlan had seen how much cash

Billy had been splashing around at their gatherings recently and sensed it was closer than ever. That was why he'd offered up his truck for the mission. And, with it, his old life.

Today was payday. Today, the crumbs from Billy's table would become a feast. The Last Supper. Harlan grinned as he pulled on his bomber jacket over his red plaid shirt. The new addition to his tattoo stung beneath the sleeve—a small price to pay to show he was worthy of a lion's share of the jackpot. Just one tier below Billy himself. Soon he'd be in Mexico. Margaritas and señoritas.

In the hall, Harlan dumped the set of keys Shelley had given him. The door to Kody's room was open. There was no sign of him. Probably off licking his wounds somewhere. No loss. He felt the bulge in the pocket of his jeans from the six hundred he'd taken. A little bonus for having to put up with the kid these past weeks, after that stupid mistake with the hood.

Hefting his carryall on his shoulder, Harlan left the house and went to his pickup, which he would drive for the last time. He threw the bag in the back and climbed in. He paused, one hand on the wheel, as the gravity of what he—what all of them—were about to do struck him. The shrink had been easy, really. He had no idea why Megan Thomas had been targeted, but once he was into it, he'd enjoyed it: the power he'd felt in the face of her terror. But this? His bowels shifted uneasily.

Steeling himself, Harlan leaned forward and opened the glove compartment. He stared into the blank space.

His gun was gone.

51

The man on the fire escape flinched back as Riley swung around the corner. His hands went up as he saw the Glock. He was young, early twenties. He licked his lips, his eyes seeking means of escape. Had he come here before? Had he left those footprints?

"Who are you? Why are you trying to break into my place?"

He shook his head in denial, but guilt colored his cheeks.

Riley's voice hardened. "Who sent you? Where's my niece?"

The man's eyes fixed on something over her shoulder. They widened in anticipation.

Riley heard the rapid crunch of boots. She whipped around, too late. Someone barreled into her, throwing her off her feet. The gun jumped from her grip and skidded across the hard-packed snow. She panicked, grasping for the vanished weapon. A vicious punch to her side slammed the world into sharp focus. The sickening rush of pain incited her. Using the icy ground to her advantage, she twisted out from under the man, kicking at his face as he grabbed for her. The heel of her boot connected with a satisfying thud. The man's head jerked back. He let out a yelp. Riley pushed herself to her feet, but the man was up too. He lunged at her, teeth bared and bloody. She knew him.

Bret Childs.

Her first emotion was fear. She knew what he was capable of. The

second was rage. She saw it in bursts. The dank underpass. The bruises
on Hayley's face. Her dull blue eye.

The images eclipsed Riley's fear, propelling her forward. She ducked
Bret's first strike and launched her fist into his face. She'd learned hand-
to-hand combat at the academy and although she'd had only months
of training, she knew enough to pivot her full weight into the punch,
striking his nose side-on. Adrenaline numbed the bruising connection.
Fist to flesh. She felt his nose crack beneath her knuckles. His shout of
pain sang a wild song through her.

Bret reeled back, more blood bursting from the pale moon of his
face. He roared, spitting red into the snow, and came at her again. He
aimed a brute kick at her stomach, but it was a clumsy move. She side-
stepped and elbowed him in the kidney. He buckled. She was back on
the mat at Quantico, lungs burning, smells of sweat and gym shoes.
Her instructor yelling at her from the sidelines.

Now make him pay!

A front jab to blind and disorient him, then a hook to the stomach
to double him over. While he was down, she grabbed a fistful of his hair
and kneed him in the face. Bret staggered, hands still trying to grab
for her. With him disoriented, she yanked her cuffs from her belt and
flipped one around his wrist. He fought back, snarling now. She took a
blow to the cheek from his free hand. Ignoring the pain, she shouldered
him toward the fire escape.

Bret lost his footing on a patch of ice and went down. Riley, still
gripping the other end of the cuffs, fell on top of him, her knee landing
in his stomach. The air came out of him in a long wheeze. Panting now,
she wrestled his arm toward the fire escape. A couple of frantic twists
and she latched the free cuff onto the metal railing. As she rolled away
from him, Bret lunged. He was brought up short by the cuff. Seeing
she'd caught him, he let out an enraged bellow.

It was only when she pushed herself to her feet, out of his reach, her
cheek smarting from his blow, that she realized the other man was no
longer on the fire escape.

Behind her came a voice.

"Let him go!"

She turned. Bret's accomplice was a short distance away, feet planted in the snow. He had seized her fallen Glock and was pointing it at her.

Bret, sagged on the bottom step of the fire escape, let out a hiss of satisfaction.

Riley raised her palms, keeping her eyes on the young man with her gun. He still looked nervous, but there was something defiant there too. "I'm a federal agent," she told him.

"We know who you are." The young man's hands shook a little. "*Bitch*," he added, to compensate.

Had they come to keep her out of the way while Jess Cook's abduction went down? Had others gone to Fogg's house to do the same— found Keira?

"Put the gun down." Her voice was calm, but her heart was hammering. Sweat trickled down her cheeks, cool in the glacial air. She kept her eyes on his.

The man hesitated.

"Shoot her, you fucking pussy!" yelled Bret.

Riley saw the man's face harden, his body tightening in readiness for the recoil. She sucked in a last gasp of frozen air as images flashed through her mind, plucked from the years. Maddie asleep in the old porch chair, feet tucked under her. Scrounger curled in the shade beneath, sun slanting through the sycamores. Ethan on the steps outside their house, arms folded, meeting her eyes in the rearview as he stood there watching her go. Logan, cheeks stained with light from the candle, leaning across the table toward her. Her mom in the kitchen, hands white with flour, turning to smile.

Hey, sweetheart.

There was a rush of movement from around the side of the apartment block. A great mass of a man barreled into the assailant in a quarterback tackle, flinging him sideways like he was made of rags. The man-mountain was her neighbor, barefoot, in tank top and joggers.

Riley dashed across the snow, seeing her assailant had dropped her gun. She snatched it up, then turned to help her neighbor. She saw, at once, he didn't need it. He was twice the size of the young man and had him pinned, one arm wrenched high up his back. The man was gasping in pain.

Her eyes were drawn to the tattoos spidering around her neighbor's arms. She'd only glimpsed them in the gloom of the hallway as he'd disappeared behind his door with a rattle and snap of bolts. Now, in daylight, she saw a pair of wings on the muscle of his upper arm. In the center was a skull, crowned with a red beret. Written on a scroll beneath—AIRBORNE.

Riley turned her gun on Bret. "OK, you son of a bitch, where's my niece?"

"Ma'am?"

She glanced back at her neighbor. "I'm a federal agent, sir. Just hold on. I'll call for assistance."

Her neighbor nodded down the street. "I think the young lady in question is over there."

Riley followed his gaze to see Maddie. Her niece was running down the street toward her, backpack bouncing on her back. She was clutching a grocery store bag. Her eyes, on the scene outside the apartment, were wide with fear and confusion.

Riley was flooded with relief at the sight of her, but she shouted for Maddie to stay back. Maddie came to a halt on the sidewalk, gaze darting between her aunt and the three men.

Holstering her gun, Riley called for backup.

Bret spat blood into the snow. "You think we're the only ones? You have no fucking clue!"

Riley's neighbor looked placidly over at him. "You want me to come and wash that mouth out for you, son?"

Bret went quiet, glaring at him.

After she'd called dispatch, Riley was about to contact Fogg when her gaze alighted on a car parked across the street. A black Pontiac Firebird.

She crossed to it, pausing to check on Maddie. "Are you all right?"

Maddie nodded. "Sherri had to leave. She said it was an emergency. I told her it was OK." She hugged the grocery bag tighter. "I went to the store. I just wanted to make you dinner."

Riley ignored the spike of emotion she felt at Maddie's plaintive expression. "It's OK. Wait here, sweetheart." She went to the vehicle, ignoring a volley of threats from Bret. Curtains twitched in the overlooking apartments, people staring out. She sent up a prayer of thanks that her neighbor had been roused by the commotion.

There was no one in the Pontiac and the trunk was unlocked. Inside was a large bag, similar to the one she'd seen at Mustang John's. Riley opened it. There was camouflage clothing, plastic ties, two black masks with snakes on them, and a white hood. Nestled among them was a long, tapered object. A baseball bat.

Riley imagined coming home, turning the key in the lock. Bret and his accomplice crouched in the darkness of her apartment. The bat striking her before she could go for her gun.

The sound of sirens pulled her from the image. She returned to Bret and his comrade, looked between them. "First one of you to tell me where the governor's been taken gets a deal."

52

It hadn't snowed in days, but the last fall remained on side-walks and rooftops, gardens and trees, pitted by human activity. White had turned to gray. Soft powder to icy scab.

In the abandoned water park, water dripped from the rusted slides. Stagnant puddles were black mirrors, reflecting a yellow rind of moon. The only real light came from the fires in oil drums, dancing across the walls of the wave pool. Sparks crackled. Shadows shifted. At the deep end stood the black tree, tied to the rusty ladders. Billy Ames paced in front of it, his voice echoing in the night. Dirch and the twins flanked him. Around them, the Sons of Adam had gathered in a crescent.

A few of their number were missing. Two had been wounded in the shoot-out on the highway, some were on other assignments, and several simply hadn't shown. Scared, no doubt; unworthy of this sacred moment. Unlike them—those who stood here dressed for war, excitement humming through them like a storm charge.

It was a war they had fought in secret, in homes and offices, schools and alleys. A slap celebrated. A put-down rewarded. All this time they had been feeding off the legacy of Raymond Adamson. Greedily gulping down nuggets of wisdom his conduit, Billy, fed to them. It was a feast that had made them feel strong. Nourishment for the emptiness of their lives. Now, here they were, at the moment all those days had been leading to. Vast and awe-inspiring. Eyes glittered over black masks, all focused on the tree.

Tied to the tree was a woman. A white hood daubed with a red apple hid her face. Her head twitched, following Billy's voice. She had struggled and shouted, threatened then pleaded. Now, she was silent. As were they. This was a holy moment, after all.

Cuddy trailed Billy, a phone in his hands, recording the proceedings. In Billy's fist was a sword, its naked blade shining in the firelight. Tonight, it would plunge through the heart of the serpent. Tonight, Raymond Adamson's vision would be known across the world.

Riley waited in the dark of the overgrown parking lot. The Kevlar vest was a tight band around her chest. She wore her FBI windbreaker over the top. Strapped to her calf was the switchblade Logan had given her. Her hair was pulled back, her Glock sat snug in its holster and, under layers of thermals, the gold star pressed against her neck, warmed by the pulse of her blood.

All around men, and a scattering of women, moved into position. The FBI SWAT team, helicoptered in from the field office in Omaha, had taken command, their number bolstered by a huge presence of state troopers and officers from Des Moines PD. The SWAT commander and officers in charge were consulting a map of the water park, quietly issuing orders. Glocks and Remington pump-action shotguns were racked and readied.

Riley glanced at Fogg, waiting beside her, his tall form made bulky by his vest. The silver in his hair glinted like frost in the moonlight. She could feel the tension bristling off him. His face was taut, the creases deepened by shadows.

Keira was still at MercyOne. She had been attacked while putting out the trash in the driveway of their home by a man in a mask. Marcia had run to their daughter's aid and the assailant fled, but Keira had fallen in the fight, sustaining a head wound. Fogg had said she would be

OK, that she was just being kept in for observation, but Riley had seen how much it had scared him.

She got the sense he blamed himself. That his work had followed him home. That if only he'd solved this case sooner none of this would have happened. His daughter. Hayley. Megan. Jess Cook. Riley wanted to assure him that it wasn't his fault, but things had been strained between them since she'd leveled those accusations against him.

Back at her apartment, Bret's accomplice had tripped over himself to confess, desperate to cut himself a deal. From what she'd learned, Billy Ames had sent the two men to her apartment—under orders from Raymond himself. But her assailant claimed to have no idea how Billy or Raymond knew where she lived. That question lingered, unsettling. But there had been no time to answer it, events rolling like an avalanche since the young man told them where the governor had been taken. An avalanche that had swept them here to this forsaken place, beneath the long curve of the overpass.

Headlights flared, now and then, but all the streetlights in the area had guttered out an hour ago. The power had been so intermittent since the storms, the cops had banked on the men in the park not noticing the new depths of the darkness.

All at once it was time to go. The SWAT team went first, fanning out along the trails that led into the park. Helmets and night-vision goggles turned faces alien. Riley and Fogg moved out in the second wave, with the troopers and officers, passing the hulk of an eighteen-wheeler abandoned in the lot, doors open, yawning empty. There were other vehicles beyond, parked haphazardly. Jeeps and pickups.

As they walked, guns ready, Riley felt a tug in her gut. A feeling that hovered between thrill and terror—two edges of the same blade. Her senses sharpened. The night seemed clearer, the trees spiking black against the sky. Her eyes had become accustomed to the darkness. Branches crackled underfoot. She could hear the breaths of those around her and, fainter, a man's voice, echoing from somewhere. A smell of frozen mud filled her nostrils. In the distance, through the trees, firelight bloomed.

Bret's accomplice had said there would be scouts and, sure enough, as they reached a ruined building, beside a set of broken turnstiles, agents were standing over the bodies of two men dressed in camouflage. The men lay facedown, hands tied behind their backs. It was hard to tell if they were dead or unconscious.

Riley moved on with the others, following in the wake of the SWAT team. The man's voice was closer now. She passed beneath the rusted loops of slides and plastic sculptures of smiling turtles. Wooden shacks, long shuttered, were covered in rusted signs advertising snow cones and Popsicles.

Ahead, fires guttered from oil drums in the depths of a wave pool. Down there, a crowd was gathered. Taking up position with Fogg behind a block of restrooms, Riley counted at least forty figures. A man stood in front of them, addressing them. In the flame-light, she saw his black mask was different from the others. Not a red serpent, but yellow lines. Although his voice was muffled by the fabric, she recognized it from the video she'd seen. The man was Billy Ames. In his hand, he held a sword.

Rising behind him was a black tree. For a moment, Riley thought it had somehow grown up out of the pool, then she realized it wasn't real, but stuck together with wire and tape, tied to the ladders at the deep end. Bound to its trunk was a figure, a hood over their head. By the slim-fitting pantsuit, it was clear she was a woman. Riley felt her nerves tighten.

"Cook," murmured Fogg.

There was a large man prowling in front of the governor, his phone held up, recording.

Riley caught movement in her peripheral vision. Agents were taking up defensive positions behind shacks and crawling across the rooftop of a café. No one in the pool noticed. They were all fixated on Billy.

"Each woman is an Eve, Tertullian told us." Billy's voice rang across his rapt audience, echoing off the walls of the pool. "A temple built over a sewer. The gate to hell itself. And until that gate is closed, those to Eden will never be open."

"Amen," came the calls.

"Tonight, we close that gate." Billy gestured to the governor, his finger pointing like an accusation. "Tonight, we strike down the serpent's ally. The one who cursed us. The one who would have us in chains, beneath her and her whole wretched sex. The one who must be shown her place."

Billy turned toward Jess Cook. She struggled against her bonds, sensing the danger. He raised the sword. Its blade shimmered with fire.

A shout built in Riley's throat, but before she could unleash it, the air cracked with a single gunshot from one of the snipers on the café rooftop.

Billy jerked backward, the sword slipping from his hand. The crowd around him began shouting, turning. Weapons were tugged from waistbands and holsters. The night exploded in the flash and smoke of gunfire.

The men in the pool were sitting ducks. Several of them went down in the first few seconds. Others began firing wildly into the darkness, blinded by firelight. Bullets peppered the air, exploding off concrete and tree trunks. The sound was concussive. Deafening. One shot clipped a nearby state trooper, who collapsed. The masked men were rushing up out of the pool, a swarm of rats seeking safety. More were picked off, sent spinning into the walls or slumping over rocks.

Beyond them, the governor, still bound to the tree, had sunk to her knees. Riley couldn't tell if she'd managed to duck down, or if she'd been hit. The man who'd been videoing her was sprawled nearby, a great bloody lump in the snow. Billy Ames had vanished.

"I'm going in," Riley shouted, eyes on the governor.

The agents and troopers were focused on the men firing at them. Most of those still standing had emerged from the death trap of the pool and were engaging from more defensive positions. Another officer went down, a bullet punching through his neck. An agent from the SWAT team dragged him behind a fountain.

"I'll cover you," Fogg told her, nodding to a wooden shack between them and the pool. "Go!"

Riley gripped her Glock and went. Bullets streaked past. One punched into the side of the restroom behind her in a billow of dust. She heard a harsh cry as someone got hit. She made it to the shack, pressed herself against it, and risked a look back. She felt a rush of relief as she saw Fogg crouched down, gun extended. There was a man sprawled on the ground a short distance away.

Seeing her chance, Riley took it, ducking across the open ground between the shack and the shallow end of the pool. She passed several bodies, blood fanning out in the snow around them. The walls of the pool were spattered with it. She skidded down the slope into the deep end, where more bodies were strewn. She heard groans and pleas coming from some of the wounded. Others lay still. Riley fixed on the tree between the fires, the hooded figure of Jess Cook kneeling at its foot. Riley was halfway across the pool when a body lunged to life and grabbed her ankle.

Riley fell into the dank stew of frozen leaves and garbage that lined the bottom of the pool. She twisted around, kicking away the clutching hand and bringing up her gun. In the firelight she saw a man with dark eyes. His mask had come loose and hung around his neck. He wore a bomber jacket and a red plaid shirt. Part of his face was missing, blown out by a shotgun round. He looked like he was trying to form words, but nothing came. The man's fingers stopped clawing the air and he sank back, blood pulsing into the snow.

Riley heard a warning shout between volleys of gunfire. Fogg was halfway down the pool's slope, clutching a ladder for purchase. His gaze was fixed on something behind her. Riley turned to see a tall man rising up. His head was shaved and he was dressed in camo gear. In his hand he held the fallen sword. Jess Cook knelt before him, blinded by the hood, fighting against her bonds.

Riley rose. Her eyes narrowed into the sights of her Glock. One shot. There was a burst of red mist from the man's skull. He went down on his knees then toppled sideways, sword beside him.

Riley ran the last few yards.

Jess Cook cried out as the hood was tugged off, flinching instinctively away. It took her a moment to recognize Riley. She let out a shuddering breath. Her hair was sticking to her cheeks, wet with sweat and tears.

"It's OK," Riley told her. "You're OK." As Fogg came panting up behind, followed by a group of state troopers, Riley holstered her gun and pulled her switchblade from its sheath. Crouching, she cut the ropes around the governor's wrists. Her hands were shaking.

Gunshots still peppered the night around them, but fewer now and farther away, the men trying to escape being picked off one by one.

"My daughter," croaked Jess.

"Ella's safe. She's at the mansion with your husband."

Jess nodded, fighting tears. "Rebecca? I think she was hit. In the car."

Riley had been told the governor's chief of staff was in the hospital, but her condition was said to be stable. "She's OK."

"Ma'am."

All at once, the state troopers were there, helping the governor up. Jess turned, looking over her shoulder at Riley, as they surrounded her and escorted her away to where the paramedics were waiting. Other officers were moving in, spreading out around the pool, kicking weapons away from limp hands and checking the dead and wounded.

Riley straightened. She felt breathless, the bulletproof vest squeezing her chest like a vise. She sensed points of pain springing up around her body. God, she would hurt tomorrow. But her attention, for now, was on the weird tree. Its branches were strung with things. A blue ribbon and a silver charm bracelet, a pair of panties and a horseshoe pendant. Her eyes fixed on a pink beanie hat. She remembered Hayley saying she wore one for running. That her attacker had taken it.

"My God."

She turned. Fogg, too, was staring at it. She saw the same knowledge in his eyes: that each trinket represented a crime.

A tree of sorrows.

Riley looked down as something caught her eye. Lying in the bloody snow was a black mask with yellow lines, like bars on a gate.

There was a patch of blood beside it.

53

Billy Ames pulled into the driveway, steering one-handed. The front wheel of the Jeep knocked over one of Darlene's lawn ornaments. He heard it break. He sat there, sucking in breaths. His cheeks rolled with sweat, and nausea jittered through him. The pain was the worst he'd ever felt: a red-hot lance through his shoulder where the sniper's bullet had entered, a sick, pulsing mass at the back where it had exited. Nerves fizzed, sending desperate signals through his body. As he leaned over, scrabbling to open the Jeep's door with his good arm, he could feel where the blood had stuck his clothes to the wound. More trickled down his sleeve, dripping onto the seat.

His thoughts jumped, past to present and future. He needed medical attention, but they had to get out of the city. The men missing from the ceremony skittered through his mind. Mustang John. Bret Childs. Others. Any of them could have been betrayed him—told the FBI where they were.

He'd known this had all gotten too big a while back. Conspiracies were dangerous. The longer the chain got, the more likely a weak link. But the glittering prize on the horizon had kept his attention, more than the worry of what could go wrong. He had orchestrated this for so long now, he'd thought himself invincible.

Billy swallowed thickly and let go of the door handle, forcing himself to think. The house looming before him—three stories of suburban perfection that, with its grandiose columns, hinted at the wealth of ancient empires—was a rental in Darlene's name. None of the Sons of Adam knew about it. None of them knew he'd never left his wife. But the cops could track him here in time.

The U-Haul was in the garage, beside their cherry red pickup. A single light burned, illuminating the last piles of boxes still stacked up. Frustration prickled through his pain. Darlene had promised to finish packing by the time he returned. No matter. They would have to leave with what they had. All he really needed was the passport he'd paid for and the recovery phrase for his crypto account, which he would access when they'd crossed the border. Darlene had been keeping it safe. The key to a fortune—sixteen years in the making.

It had started as a small but steady trickle of cash: the fees for his seminars and the trips he'd organized for his growing army of fans. Sweaty wads siphoned from alimony and child support, pressed into his palm in exchange for his advice. Thick bundles won at the track or creamed off a paycheck and slipped into his pocket along with a fervent handshake. And, of course, the blocks of dollars that would arrive through the mail to a PO box he'd set up, after he'd convinced Raymond Adamson—one airless night in their shared cell—that he was the man who could help him change the world.

All of it had been squirreled away over the years, into savings and investments. When a member of the Sons of Adam turned out to be an early advocate of cryptocurrency, Billy had seen the potential and started switching into the asset. The pandemic had sent it soaring. Fear, panic, and mistrust—music to a con man's ears.

Yes, he had failed in his final assignment. Governor Cook was still alive and most of the Sons of Adam would be dead or arrested. But, at the end of the day, the two million Raymond promised him for tonight was pocket change against the current value of his assets.

There was a rap on the passenger window. Billy flinched, his whole body going rigid. It was his neighbor, Karen. She waved as he saw her. Perfect teeth and hair, gleaming in the lights from her grand house, tastefully garlanded for Christmas. Billy forced a smile and wound the window down, hoping, in the dark of the interior, she wouldn't see the blood soaking black through his clothes.

"New car?" Karen inquired in her chirpy tone.

"Borrowed it from a friend. Ours has a flat." Billy smoothed his voice into the well-spoken cadence of the neighborhood. No trailer park twang here.

"Oh, what a pain. You guys nearly set? I was hoping to say goodbye to Darlene, but she wasn't in when I stopped by earlier."

"She's been running errands. Last-minute stuff. You know how it is."

"I can imagine. Moving before Christmas? You must both be run ragged."

"We were idiots," Billy agreed. He tried to grin sheepishly, but it felt strained and his mouth twitched involuntarily.

Karen faltered. "Gee, Billy. You look terrible. I hope you're not getting sick?"

"Yeah, it would be just my luck to catch the virus now."

"Oh goodness," Karen said, straightening and stepping back from the open window. "Well, I'll leave you to get on with it."

He waited, one hand clutching the door handle, gritted against the rolling waves of pain, watching her head up the driveway to her double front door. She glanced back, then entered.

Billy stumbled from the Jeep. He clung to the door for a moment, feeling like he might pass out, then staggered up the driveway. Had Karen noticed the blood? Would she speak to her husband? Would they call the cops? He thought not. This was a neighborhood of manners and polite discretion. He had known exactly the sort of man he needed to be the moment they moved here, Darlene clutching his arm, giddy at the sight of the palatial houses.

He had always been a chameleon. Settling into whatever shape people expected, whether that was onstage under the hot lights and greedy gaze of two hundred men, in the trailer with his downtrodden disciples, or here at a poolside grill with the great and the good. It was human nature. People were comforted when you presented them with a version of themselves. A mirror held up for them to see what they wanted. Not what you were.

He had always been good at it—making people believe. His first con had been as a kid on the trailer park lot, charming money from the old folk who lived there. He bought junk from Goodwill, pulled it from scrapyards and bins, sold it to them at inflated prices. *Sell a man something he thinks he needs, and he'll thank you for it.*

Billy knew how to gild things. How to make them seem more valuable than they were. Including himself. Leaving school early, he'd worked as a salesman, door-to-door, then telephone. He was talented but easily bored, and he'd never liked taking orders. By the time he got caught for credit card fraud and sent to the Iowa State Penitentiary, he knew exactly how to mold and manipulate others. His cellmate, Raymond Adamson, had seen that talent.

Raymond had been unreadable to Billy at first. A puzzle with a void at the center. A maze without end. The man had intrigued—and scared—him, reminding him of another, from a time before. Slowly, carefully, he'd unwrapped the riddle, until one night in the sweltering dark, whispering between the footsteps of the guards, Raymond confessed that his conviction for burglary was a mere hiccup in the face of his true crimes. His real crimes were legendary, burned into the soul of the state. A terror that stalked. A nightmare made real.

The Sin Eater, they had called him.

In truth, Billy could have left this city months ago. Darlene had been right, back at the trailer. He had enough—more than enough. He had played the long con, seeking out the weak and the bored, the angry and vulnerable, using the power of Raymond's vision to give them meaning and direction. All those lost boys.

He had no real need to follow Raymond's orders—jumping, encrypted, into his inbox with more frequency these past months—the man's demands growing riskier and more extreme. No need to wait for that final payout. But it wasn't the money that had made him stay the distance.

As he slumped against his oversize front door, yanking his keys from his pocket, Billy saw it in his mind, where it had lived, rent-free, all these years—the trailer on the far edge of the lot, away from his mother's and all the rest, in the shadows of the trees. The roof had been mottled with bird droppings in summer, leaves in fall, snow in winter.

He saw the door creaking open. A man stood framed in the doorway, cigarette smoldering between yellowed fingers. A smile cracking his dry lips as he saw curious little Billy Ames approaching. That smooth voice like a broken record reverberating always in his head.

Wanna play a game?

Billy twisted the key in the lock and pushed open the door. He hadn't left yet because he'd wanted to win. Wanted to see this through and come out on top. There would be no church built, as he'd promised Raymond all these years. He would take the money the man had given him to invest in that insane dream and run, laughing, all the way to the border. Maybe then, he could leave that trailer and the shadows of those trees. Because Raymond wasn't the first monster Billy Ames had met.

And Billy had wanted to con the devil.

The house was dark. It smelled of furniture polish from their cleaner, and Darlene's Chanel perfume. There were more boxes and bags stacked up here.

"Darlene?" he rasped into the hush.

Billy limped into the expansive living area, clutching his arm, blood dripping a trail across the white carpet. Here, he stopped. There was Darlene. She was tied to a chair at the head of the long, polished table. Packing tape was plastered across her mouth, her eyes big and wet in the gloom. Behind her stood a skinny kid.

A gun quivered in the kid's hand.

54

It was early morning by the time Riley arrived at DCI headquarters. Jenna let her into the office, eyes widening at the sight of Riley's filthy skin and clothes. The young woman's expression was pinched, her face washed out from lack of sleep. She'd been here all night, on standby for anything Fogg needed while they were out at the scene.

"How is he?" Jenna asked, showing Riley into the incident room.

"Fogg's fine. He'll be in shortly. He stopped at the hospital to check on Keira."

"Of course. Let me get you some coffee."

Riley stood alone in the room, among desks littered with files and papers. Fogg's team had been working all hours, combing through state records, speaking to witnesses, and following leads. The trash can was brimming with takeout cartons and energy drinks.

The first rays of sun were slanting in to gild the photographs on the wall. In the far corner, untouched by light, the composite of Raymond Adamson glared out, all black lines and hard angles. The puzzle of his features seemed to mock her.

Not one face, but many.

The survivors from the water park had been arrested and taken for questioning, the wounded carted off by paramedics, the dead photographed and bagged. After Jess Cook was bundled to safety, Riley and Fogg joined the troopers and agents scouring the park. They found four men hiding in changing rooms. SWAT had stormed the building, the men were neutralized, and a search revealed a locker room filled with old lifeguard uniforms, rat droppings, and moldy white laundry bags. Some of the bags had been cut up, tied into makeshift hoods.

Riley took her eyes from the Sin Eater, let them travel instead over the faces of the women. Young and old. Then and now. She followed the lines of colored thread that connected each of them to the place where their lives had altered or stopped. Those lines were neat and ordered. Nothing like what the investigation had turned out to be. She imagined the coming days, all the threads spooling out.

Warrants had been issued and interrogation rooms were being set up. The hunt for Billy Ames and others who'd escaped in the chaos of the gunfight was gathering pace, BOLOs going out across all agencies. Connie Meadows and Fogg's boss at the DCI had been coordinating the task force's response, but it was clear the prosecution of this case would quickly expand beyond their jurisdiction. A state governor had been the target of a hate group. Washington was now involved, and a Joint Terrorism Task Force was being mobilized. Within hours this would be world news.

Riley sank into a chair, facing the window. It felt like a mistake: there was so much to do. But she just needed to close her eyes for a minute, let the sun warm her chapped cheeks.

She woke with a jolt, her cell vibrating in her pocket. On the desk in front of her was a coffee, steam curling. She hadn't even heard Jenna come in.

It was Fogg.

"Are you at DCI?"

"Yes." Riley stifled a yawn. "How's Keira?"

"She'll be home later today." Relief thickened his voice.

"That's great, Fogg. Please thank Marcia for letting Maddie stay last night. I've spoken to her father. He's on his way."

"It's no trouble." Fogg sounded out of breath. She heard the beep of a car being unlocked. "Listen, I just spoke to the medical examiner in Winneshiek County. That gravesite you found near the cabin? There was a body."

Riley saw it in her mind—the mound of earth blanketed in snow. The trunk of trophies in the cobwebbed gloom of the shed. She sighed. "Another victim?"

"No. Riley, it's Raymond Adamson."

She sat up as Fogg continued, suddenly wide-awake.

"Raymond had dental work done when he was at the Iowa State Penitentiary. The ME compared X-rays with those on record at the prison. They're a match. It's him."

"How did he die? When?"

"The forensic team has only done preliminary tests. No indication yet of cause of death. But early estimates suggest he's been in the ground for at least a year, maybe longer."

Riley's eyes went to the second cluster of photographs. Hayley and Megan and the others. "Raymond had nothing to do with the recent attacks?"

"No. If he's been in the ground much longer than a year, it's entirely possible Sydney Williams was his last known victim."

"But the man at my apartment? Bret's accomplice? He said Billy sent him—that Raymond had ordered it."

"I know. We need to find Billy Ames. See who's really been pulling his strings. Because it sure as hell isn't Raymond Adamson." Fogg paused. "Hang on, I've got another call coming through. I'll be there shortly."

After the line went dead, Riley picked up the coffee Jenna had left. It was weak and watery. She stared at the composite sketch as she drank. All this time, they had been chasing a ghost. She needed to clear her head. Needed to think. Needed more caffeine.

Finishing the cup with a grimace, she headed out into the reception area. Jenna was gone from her desk. Riley could hear a photocopier humming in one of the nearby offices and the trill of a phone. There was a coffeepot behind Jenna's desk. She crossed to it and refilled her cup. As she drank, her gaze glanced across Jenna's neat work trays, stacked files, and pots of marker pens. Her eyes caught on a pencil, candy-striped in blue and pink and green. The colors were familiar. A blast from the past.

Riley pulled it from the pot as she sipped at her coffee. There was writing along the pencil's length. BUCKIE'S DREAM.

"Do you need something?"

Riley turned to see Jenna, frowning in question. "Sorry, I was looking for a refill." She held up the pencil. "Senator Davenport's company?"

Jenna's cheeks bloomed pink. "Is it?" Her hand reached up, fingers picking at the high neck of her sweater. "Oh—yes, I think I was given that at a fundraising event."

Riley watched the stain on Jenna's cheeks darken. *The tape. The cabin.* Her heart began to thump, but she offered the young woman a friendly smile. "We used to eat it back home. Reminds me of old times."

"Right." Jenna's face relaxed a little. "Good memories?"

"A few."

Jenna gave a knowing laugh that made her sound older than her years. "That's family for you. Gotta take the bitter with the sweet, right?"

The words chimed a clear cold note through Riley.

"I'll make a fresh pot for you," Jenna said.

As the young woman walked away, Riley's mind tilted, swinging her back to that night at the gala. She pulled out her phone, her finger sliding over the cracked screen. The woman in the red dress emerging from the shadows of the skywalk, slamming into her. Her phone falling from her fingers. The woman's high, false laugh. The streaks of mascara and the tell of an old bruise.

Gotta take the bitter with the sweet.

An old-fashioned saying from an old-fashioned world. The kind of thing her grandmother would have murmured. Take the bad with the good. Rough with the smooth. Like it and lump it.

She searched quickly. The *Des Moines Register* had done a feature on the gala. There was Jess Cook smiling for the camera, Mark at her side, Ella grinning between them. There was the senate minority leader, Ted Pierce, arm snaked around the waist of a younger woman. At the bottom of the article were more pictures. Riley swiped through them.

And there she was—the woman in red—standing in front of a step and repeat, earlier in the evening. No streaks of makeup. No tears. Just a poised smile and a fixed stare. A perfect mannequin beside a handsome young man with a boyish crease in his cheek. On his finger was a wedding ring.

Senator Nate Davenport and wife, Alice.

Fingers clumsy in haste, her mouth dry, Riley did a search for Buckie's Dream. The company website had a page dedicated to its history. She skimmed the highlights.

Founded in 1920, it was already a prominent Iowa company by 1960, when Buckie Davenport took over from his father. There was a black-and-white image of a stiff, unsmiling man outside the gates of a factory. Buckie himself. Riley had seen those gates before, in one of the photographs at the cabin. On the website, there was mention of only two sons, who'd inherited the family business. But in that photograph there had been three boys. One of them she'd recognized as Raymond. Patty had said that on Raymond's release from Clermont, he discovered his brothers had taken over and he'd been disowned. She'd also said Raymond had reconnected with one of his brothers.

The final photograph on the website confirmed it.

A young man in an expensive suit stood outside those gates—the gates of his grandfather's factory—now a sprawling industrial complex for a major brand, which he had inherited.

She thought of the boy in the pictures at the cabin, standing proudly over a dead deer. Those envelopes with their childish scrawl.

Nate Davenport was Raymond Adamson's nephew.

55

"Why?"

Riley glanced at Fogg, sitting beside her. It was the same question he'd been asking for two days straight, eyes on the silent young woman sitting before them.

She understood why he wanted that answer more than any other. Jenna's betrayal had cut him to the core. It wasn't just her treachery—or the fact she'd put them all in grave danger and Fogg's daughter in the hospital—it was that he hadn't seen it. Seen her. The snake in the grass. The knife poised at his back. Riley knew Fogg blamed himself and there had been nothing she could say to change that.

Jenna pressed her lips together and stared at the surface of the interview room table. Her lawyer, a soft-spoken older man, glanced her way, but said nothing.

"We searched your place," Fogg said, sitting back. "We found the tape."

Riley had been the one to come across the tape from Dr. Hale, squirreled in a drawer in Jenna's apartment. From what they'd been able to piece together, Jenna—knowing Riley was in possession of the tape and assuming she would send it to Quantico—had alerted Nate Davenport. Nate had instructed the Sons of Adam to retrieve it while luring Riley from her apartment with his claim to have information on the threat to the governor. The busted window, a stroke of luck for the would-be thieves, allowed them entry, but they'd been unsuccessful. Then, the following morning when Riley, ordered by Meadows, had signed the tape over to the DCI, it had fallen straight into Jenna's hands.

It was now at the state lab, being checked. Riley guessed Nate's fear was that there could be more clues to Raymond's true identity in the meditations of his psychiatrist. Raymond—who they now knew had changed his name years ago, when his family disowned him, from Davenport to Adamson.

I am the son of Adam.

Officers in Winnebago County had spoken to Henry Whyte, the manager at Clermont Manor. The man confessed he'd been paid by the Davenport family over the years to keep the secret of their disturbed and damaged son. The monster they had helped to create, then erased from their legacy.

"You must have thought we would start to suspect something?" Fogg continued, his eyes on Jenna. "When the lab you said you'd sent the tape to claimed to know nothing of it. What were you hoping? That Davenport would come for you before then? That you'd escape into the sunset together?"

Jenna's cheeks reddened.

Fogg shook his head. "You must know he was using you? He had no interest in you beyond your value to his plans." He tapped the file in front of him with the end of his pen. "We found your diary."

Jenna's eyes flicked up. Big, blue, and frightened.

"We know you've been having an affair with him. We know Davenport used his connections at the senate to help you secure the job here five months ago, so he could keep tabs on my investigation. He doesn't care about you, Jenna. He hasn't mentioned you once."

That was true, although Nate Davenport hadn't mentioned much of anything at all. They had brought the senator in for questioning two days ago, but it was his legal team—high-level, hotshot, well-paid—who had done most of the talking. No charges had been brought against him as yet, and Fogg's boss had been clear they would need a watertight case before they leveled any.

For now, it was all circumstantial. They knew Davenport was Raymond's nephew, but that was not a crime. They knew he had a connection to Jenna, although the suggestion of an affair had been breezily explained away by his lawyers as a young woman's fantasy, alive only in the pages of her diary. Other than that, they had nothing. Only guesswork.

Riley and Fogg suspected Davenport had known all about his uncle's dark past and his connection to Billy Ames and the Sons of Adam. Riley guessed the letters and photographs at the cabin would have shown evidence of this, which was why they'd been burned. Preliminary tests on the remains in the grave didn't indicate a violent death and it was possible Raymond simply died of natural causes and Davenport had found and buried him there.

Jenna knew Riley was going to the cabin that day. She knew where the panic button had been installed at Ella's school. Knew where they lived. She had been Nate Davenport's eyes and ears, allowing him to stay one step ahead of their investigation.

But what is Davenport's motive? Their superiors had wanted to know.

Riley and Fogg had pulled up reports that showed Buckie's Dream had been in trouble ever since Jess Cook had taken office. First, her environmental initiatives to crack down on large-scale polluters had eroded their profits. This downturn had worsened during the pandemic, when production at the factory had ground to a halt during her restrictions. But, more damaging still, over two-thirds of factory workers at Buckie's Dream were women. Jess Cook's bill to tackle the gender pay gap, if passed, would seriously affect the business.

The motive was there. But without evidence to back it up all they had was speculation. The Davenport family had been interviewed and search warrants obtained for the factory and Nate Davenport's home. But, everywhere, the walls of wealth and privilege had gone up, penning them in with stony silence and implacable authority.

They had been keeping close tabs on any alerts for Billy Ames, but there had been no sign of the man since he'd vanished from the water park. The Joint Terrorism Task Force mobilized by the bureau—made up of specialist investigators and analysts—had begun interviewing the Sons of Adam, but all those who had divulged anything claimed Raymond Adamson had been the one guiding them and that he and Billy had been working together since their time in jail.

One man, named Dirch, admitted to stealing the car and leaving the message for Governor Cook, but he claimed Billy had told him what to do. He knew nothing of any hotel key ring. And none of them knew anything about Nate Davenport. Riley and Fogg thought it likely that Davenport, who would have known the parking lot surveillance would pick up the messenger, had planted the key ring after the fire. A breadcrumb for them to follow to Billy—a perfect scapegoat in the wake of Jess Cook's execution. Leaving Davenport with his problem solved and his hands clean.

But, despite all this, Jenna was their only real link to him. And Nate had clamped her shut.

Fogg changed tactics, opening the file on the table and sliding out photographs, one by one. Hayley Abbot bruised and broken. Megan Thomas slumped in a hospital bed after surgery. "You really want to protect him, Jenna? A man who could do something like this to these women?"

"He didn't." Jenna flushed again as the words jumped out of her.

"Perhaps he didn't hold the bat or wield the knife. But he followed in his uncle's footsteps. Inspired those men. Goaded them to do these terrible things. All for his own gain. All for profit."

Jenna opened her mouth, then shook her head.

Riley saw it then—the blindness in the young woman's eyes. The sense that if she didn't turn to acknowledge the darkness, she could never be swept into it herself. But she had. She was part of it. Had aided and abetted it.

There was a knock at the door. One of Fogg's team poked his head in and raised a meaningful eyebrow.

"All right," said Fogg, wearily. "Let's take a break."

Leaving the photographs of the women arrayed in front of Jenna, he suspended the interview.

Riley followed him out, rubbing her neck, sore from all the hours bent over a desk. She was running on bad coffee and a few snatched hours of sleep.

"There's a woman here to see you," the man said. "Says it's important. Will only speak to you."

Riley and Fogg went to the room indicated. Inside, standing at the window, looking out at the gold dome of the capitol, was a slim figure in an expensive coat. As she turned, Riley recognized her. No red dress today. No makeup. No tear tracks either.

Alice Davenport drew a breath. "I want to talk about my husband."

56

Riley sat in the Chevy, watching as the agents from the Joint Terrorism Task Force filed out of the grand house. Some carried boxes; others held sealed bags filled with evidence. The broad, tree-lined street had been closed off and a crowd was gathered at the barricades. Satellite vans were parked on the sidewalk. Reporters and camera crews craned their necks, hoping to catch an image or two for prime time.

Two FBI agents emerged, holding a man between them. Nate Davenport's hands were behind his back, but the agents had covered the cuffs with a windbreaker. An act of dignity for a man who didn't deserve it. But that's how it worked with wealth and privilege.

Raymond, sick with his own darkness and cast out from society, had been the boogeyman. The monster. The Sin Eater. But Nate, senator and husband, heir to a profitable family business, member of the country club—he had welcomed that same darkness in, used it for his own ends. His was a different type of sickness, all the more insidious and disturbing because it was a sickness that flowed unnoticed through all those institutions, like blood beneath the skin.

Riley glanced around as a car pulled up across the street from her. It had the DCI logo on the side. She turned back to see Nate Davenport looking in her direction. As his eyes met hers, a knowing half smile lifted the corner of his mouth. She felt anger rise in her. Then, Nate's attention flicked away, caught by something else. That smile slipped. His eyes narrowed. She followed his gaze to the DCI car. A woman had climbed out and was standing on the sidewalk. Alice Davenport.

As Nate was ushered into the waiting car by the two agents, one placing a protective hand on his head, Riley got out and headed over to the woman. Alice looked drained from the many hours she'd spent in interview rooms.

From her testimony they'd been able to piece together a picture of her husband's life, of his relationship with Raymond, and of the time the two had spent at the cabin over the years. Looking at the abuse doled out to Raymond by Buckie Davenport, it was clear that fortune and power were not the only things inherited by the sons of this family. From his own father, Nate learned that charm, manipulation, and violence were easy ways to get what he wanted, particularly from women. Alice had suffered in silence, behind closed doors, for years. In recent months, she'd been seeing a therapist and was planning to leave him. That therapist was Megan Thomas. When Nate discovered leaflets on domestic abuse in Alice's possession, he had set the Sons of Adam on Megan.

When it was put to Alice that Nate had been pulling the strings of these men, using them to get whatever he wanted, she had told them it was the kind of thing he would have taken pleasure in.

Alice nodded to Riley, then returned her gaze to the car Nate had been placed in.

"Are you OK?" Riley asked her.

"No." Alice watched as the car headed toward the barricades, a host of cameras and phones rising eagerly. "But I will be."

The road unfurled before him as he drove south, both hands on the wheel, thumbs drumming to the music coming through the speakers. Kody wished Troy could see him now. His ride was the sickest he'd ever seen. A jacked-up, gleaming beast. The man at the dealership had been reluctant to even let him sit in it. He'd sure swallowed back that reserve when Kody had paid for the truck in cash. The man had even given him a branded pen and umbrella. Called him sir.

Part of Kody had wanted to stay in the city. That night—gunpowder on his fingers, flecks of Billy's and Darlene's blood on his clothes, sirens screaming in the distance—he'd lingered in the dark outside his home, shivering in cold and fear, watching his mom preparing dinner in the empty kitchen, setting out the table just the way Harlan liked it. Kody had thought about going to Troy's, confiding in his friend. Troy would ditch Reagan and they would drive around Des Moines in his new ride. Kody would buy a mansion, like Billy's, where they could play games all day.

But he'd known that dream was impossible. He had to leave and never come back. The only comfort was the password in his wallet. Key to a fortune beyond his imagining. Kody had had to reread all those zeroes ten times before he could accept what the screen in the late-night internet café was telling him.

At first, after buying the truck, he'd driven aimlessly on icy back roads, passing snow-covered fields and lone farms, drifting out of Iowa, unsure where to head. He had stayed in hotels on the highway, ordered the most expensive room service, until he'd caught one woman looking suspiciously at him and knew he needed to be more careful.

He knew, too, that he was different from the kid he'd been. The taking of two lives had altered him. He could feel the change, deep down inside. Something—someone—waiting to be born.

He thought often of Billy. Saw him sometimes in the unfamiliar darkness of motel rooms, sitting across from him, those eyes like glass in the shadows. A big part of him missed the man, far more than he missed his mom or Troy. With Billy, Kody had taken a bite of something new, and the strange sweetness of that still lingered.

In the end, he'd picked a destination from one of his favorite games. Now, here he was, warm ocean breeze drifting through the truck's open window, a new city rising before him, white towers and glass. He didn't know, exactly, what he would do here. What he would become. But it didn't matter right now. A man could do anything—be anyone—with millions of dollars.

Smiling, Kody turned onto the freeway, burrowing through traffic, heading for the city's heart.

57

It was Christmas Eve and miserable, sleet needling the windows. A raw wind whipped along the streets of West Des Moines, sending last-minute shoppers at the Christmas market scurrying for shelter.

Down in the basement of the resident agency, Riley closed the file on her desk and headed out of her office. As she passed Audrey's station, she noticed a new crystal animal had joined the menagerie. A little cat with ruby eyes.

The secretary was pulling on her coat. "Agent Fisher." Audrey took something from her drawer. "Noah left this for you."

It was a small, gift-wrapped box. Riley felt bad that she hadn't gotten anything for the agent, who'd left yesterday for the holiday. Noah had been helping her and Fogg with the investigation, and his youthful enthusiasm had brought some much-needed energy to the grinding hours.

Audrey nodded to her. "Merry Christmas, Riley."

Clutching the gift, Riley walked down the corridor. She knocked on the door at the end.

"Enter," came the brisk voice.

Riley opened the door, then halted. Connie Meadows was at her desk, packing up a box. The drawers to the filing cabinet were open. Empty. "Ma'am?"

Meadows looked up briefly. "Transfer."

"Where to?" Riley asked, surprised.

"Omaha. Field office."

The bite in Meadows's voice told Riley this wasn't a reward, but a punishment. She guessed Internal Affairs had not been pleased with what they'd uncovered here.

Peter Altman was still at the hospital, recovering from surgery. He'd been suspended while inquiries into his dealings with Scott Sawyer continued. His ex, Leah, had been found during a raid on a meth den. She was back in rehab. Their daughter, Paige, had been taken to live with Altman's parents in Florida until a more permanent arrangement could be worked out.

Riley had visited him in the hospital. Lying there, hooked up to tubes and machines, the agent was the most at peace she had seen him. It left her with an uneasy sense of the way the job had stripped him down to the bones of himself. What it had turned him into.

"What about the case?" she asked Meadows, watching the woman pack.

"Washington will send my replacement after the holidays. The team is more than capable of handling things until then."

Riley nodded. She and Fogg were still involved in the investigation, but since the arrest of Nate Davenport things had taken on a life of their own. The team, bolstered by specialists from the bureau's task force, was now several dozen strong.

There were still many gaps in their knowledge, not least the mystery of Billy Ames. Their prime suspect had been found dead in a stately suburb the night of Jess Cook's rescue. A neighbor had reported hearing gunshots—seen a kid running from the house. Billy, in possession of a fake passport, had been falsely identified at the time, alongside a dead woman. It was only two days ago that the bodies had been ID'd as Billy and his wife, Darlene. They'd been shot, point-blank.

There was no sign of the kid seen fleeing the scene, but it left Riley thinking of the sneaker print in the snow outside the governor's mansion and the skinny youth she'd seen trailing the men to the cabin.

Meadows cast a final look around her office. The space was already empty, her few personal items rattling in the box.

"I'm sorry," Riley said.

Meadows's eyes narrowed at the pity in her tone. "That's the way it goes in this job. Don't get too attached to anything, Fisher. You never know where they'll send you next." The older woman hefted the box and moved past her. "You'll see that soon enough."

Riley lingered for a moment after Meadows had gone, then flicked off the light and closed the door.

Back in her office, she unwrapped the gift from Noah. She smiled as she saw the mug. She set it on the desk, realizing that, other than the stacks of files, she had nothing of herself here. She made a mental note to bring some things from her apartment after the holidays. Photographs of Maddie, Rose, and Lori and Ben. A plant or two. She would make it messy. Personal. Not a blank white space on which the pressures of the job would slowly etch themselves.

Law enforcement wasn't about hard targets. Or, at least, not the sort of law enforcement her grandfather had taught her. It was human beings and emotions, complex lives and flawed relationships. Troubled pasts and uncertain futures. For the first time since she'd graduated from the academy, Riley felt suited to the role.

She took the elevator up from the basement, said goodbye to the security guard, and headed into the deserted lot. She flipped up the collar of her mom's wool coat against the rain.

In her BuRide, she turned on the heat and moved the copy of the *Des Moines Register* from the dashboard. The headlines were still dominated by Nate Davenport's arrest and the conspiracy to murder the governor. Shares in Buckie's Dream had plummeted.

The second half of the page had a photograph of Jess Cook in front of the Christmas tree at the mansion with Mark and Ella. Last week, the senate voted to pass her bill into legislation. Jess had praised the work of her colleagues and said it would help open new pathways to women in the workforce, but she had sounded a note of caution too, saying they still had a long way to go.

Riley could only agree. The investigation into the Sons of Adam had shown not so much a gap, but a schism. The Sons of Adam weren't monsters, but ordinary men capable of monstrous deeds. Husbands and fathers, retired doctors, football coaches, and veterans. Yes, they had been groomed and used, first by Raymond and Billy, then Nate from the shadows. But it had been all too easy to direct their blame for the disillusionment with their own lives onto women.

Adam versus Eve. The most ancient of grudges.

The Sin Eater had been a terror who stalked the city, but there was something more terrifying in the way his shadow had spread so easily. Every stone they overturned in the investigation revealed more stories of abuse behind closed doors and seemingly random acts of violence that now formed patterns. But they also found wives and mothers who were adamant their husbands and sons were innocent, had either been led astray or forced to take action.

She was asking for it. Men can't control themselves.

There was a clear sense in these households that the worst thing for a man to be was vulnerable.

Boys don't cry. Man up.

Hayley Abbot had spoken about this in an interview, sitting alongside Megan Thomas and Sydney Williams. After the protests, some of the victims of the Sons of Adam had formed a support group and were speaking out about their experiences. There was a determined sense of them wanting to try to change the narrative. That men and women needed to work together.

"We have the conversations with our daughters," Megan had said. "We tell them to be careful. To not walk home alone. We need to start having conversations with our sons."

Riley, watching the interview alone in her apartment, had found her eyes blurring with tears. Those words had seized at a deep, hurting part of her, making her imagine, if Hunter had been taught something different, how things might have turned out. She had seen it, for a moment—sitting in the warm summer grass with her friends in the flush of fair lights, taking the bottle as it was passed to her. Waking the next morning with nothing more than a headache.

As it should have been.

Riley put the newspaper on the passenger seat, on top of the gifts she hadn't had time to wrap. A sweater for Ethan and ice skates for Maddie. A bottle of bourbon for Fogg.

The streets were slick with rain as she headed west to a quiet neighborhood on her route out of the city. The weather had turned unexpectedly mild. Just a few dirty clumps of snow remained on sidewalks and lawns.

As Riley pulled up outside the house, she saw Christmas lights in the windows. She headed up the driveway and knocked on the door. A young woman answered. Riley saw she still had a scar on her forehead, but the bruising had faded and her smile was bright.

"Hi, Keira. Is your father in?"

"Sure. I'll get him."

A few moments later, Fogg appeared wearing an apron dusted with flour. He looked different out of his suit. Relaxed and rested. "Riley. Everything OK?"

"All good. Just wanted to tell you I'm heading home. And give you this." She handed him the bourbon. "I'm sorry, I wasn't sure what you like."

"Thank you," said Fogg, studying it appreciatively. "This is great." He gestured down the hallway, which was perfumed with pine needles and baking smells. "Why don't you come in? Marcia's making eggnog."

"I should hit the road. Holiday traffic. But I'll see you back at the office in a few days."

"Hang on." Fogg disappeared, then returned holding a small box. "I meant to give this to you yesterday."

Riley opened the box. Inside was an old pocket compass in a gold case. "It's beautiful."

"Found it in an antique store in the East Village." Fogg stuck his hands in the pockets of his apron. "Marcia and I have been talking about me taking early retirement when this case is finished. Maybe heading out of the city."

Riley caught the note of pain in his voice. She knew he'd been finding it hard at the DCI. She'd seen how often his gaze was snared by Jenna's empty desk.

Fogg nodded to the compass. "I guess I was thinking about that when I bought it. About passing the baton on. About you finding your own way."

He held out his hand. Riley shook it.

She headed down the drive, leaving Fogg to close the door and return to his wife and daughters, and the warmth of their home.

Back in her car, Riley opened the glove compartment to stow the gift. The slip of paper she'd left in there all those weeks ago fell out, Roach's writing scrawled across it.

Tomorrow never comes.

"Unless you make it," she murmured, putting her foot on the gas.

As she drove out of the city, Riley thought of her old house with its cracks and its ghosts, of Maddie and Ethan, and all the mess and complication of their family. All the bitter and the sweet. And she thought of Logan Wood with a feeling that jittered and jumped in her chest.

Turning onto the highway, she took the exit to Cedar Falls, heading north toward home.

Acknowledgments

This novel was my lockdown baby—and a tough one to write. Thankfully, I have an amazing team who cheered me on.

I want to start by thanking my agents, Antony Topping and Dan Conaway, who keep my feet on the ground. Antony, thank you so much for all your thoughtful and invaluable suggestions that helped me shape this novel at every step, and for always managing to make me laugh. And Dan, thank you for your eye for detail, and for your kind yet incisive guidance. (I'd be a lot more nuts without you both!)

My thanks to everyone at Greene & Heaton and Writers House, with a special thank-you to Kate Rizzo, and to my agent, Sylvie Rabineau at WME, for championing Riley Fisher from the earliest days.

A huge thank-you to the awesome team at Flatiron. It's been a pleasure working with you all, and I'm enormously grateful for the work you've put in behind the scenes, from the brilliant designers and compositors to the hardworking sales reps, keen-eyed copy editors, and proofreaders.

An extra special shout-out to Maxine Charles, Christopher Smith, Erin Kibby, Marlena Bittner, and Nancy Trypuc. And last, but certainly not least, to my fantastic editor, Zack Wagman—thank you for taking such a deep dive into this novel with me. Your insightful thoughts and comments always illuminated the way.

My gratitude goes to the brilliant team at Hodder & Stoughton in the UK for being champions of all my novels for the past eighteen years. I've known many people there in that time, and every one of them has been a joy to work with. An extra big thank-you to Vero Norton and Alice Morley.

And to my editor, Nick Sayers (who's more like family to me)—thank you so much for everything, from your ever-perceptive and wise suggestions to your support and friendship over the years. And laughter—lots of laughter. And wine!

Thank you to all the fantastic teams of agents, editors, designers, publicists, those in sales and marketing, and of course the translators—in the Netherlands, Italy, Germany, Taiwan, and France—who've helped bring Riley to life in other languages.

Thank you to all the readers, reviewers, bloggers, and booksellers who helped put *The Fields* on the map and paved the way for this novel, with a special thank-you to Goldsboro Books.

My thanks to the crime and thriller community, who welcomed me so warmly into their dark fold. With massive hugs to all my fellow authors, and dear friends and family, whose support means the world to me.

Lastly, my heartfelt gratitude goes to Rupert Heath, to whom this book is dedicated and without whom it probably wouldn't exist.

And my love to Lee, who always sits beside me on the rollercoaster, holds my hand on the downs, and laughs with me on the ups.

About the Author

ERIN YOUNG is the author of *The Fields*, which introduced Riley Fisher. *The Fields* was a finalist for the International Thriller Writers' hardcover of the year, a *Glamour* Book of the Year, and a *Times* Thriller of the Month. Erin was also named in *Oprah Daily* as one of the best emerging female thriller writers. *The Fields* is currently in development for TV by the producers of *Big Little Lies* and *City on a Hill*.